D0505364

## WE'LL MEET AGAIN: PART II
The End of an Era

The LWT series WE'LL MEET AGAIN was so popular
that the *Daily Mail* commissioned a special sequel from
David Butler. Now the author has turned this successful
serialization into a book to delight his thousands of fans.

## Also available

**WE'LL MEET AGAIN**

David Butler

# We'll Meet Again:
## Part II The End of an Era

Futura

A *Futura* Book

First published in Great Britain in 1983 by
Futura Publications
Reprinted 1983
This edition published by Futura Publications 1995

ISBN 0 7088 2288 6

Printed in England by Clays Ltd, St Ives plc

Futura Publications
A Division of
Macdonald & Co (Publishers)
Brettenham House
Lancaster Place
London WC2E 7EN

I would like to express my special
indebtedness to the *Daily Mail*,
to Sir David English without whom
'Ginger Rogers' would never have flown
again, and to Nick Gordon for his
patience, enthusiasm and creative
support.

D.B.

# ONE

Helen Dereham heard the children's voices as soon as she entered the cottage hospital. '... No crib for a bed, the little Lord Jesus lay down his sweet head.' The carol came from the surgical ward along the corridor past her office and she joined the group of nurses listening at the open swing doors.

The patients in the ward were US airmen from the 525th Bomb Group stationed just outside the small town of Market Wetherby in East Anglia. All the beds were occupied, the men in them too badly wounded to be transferred yet to their own Combat Wing Hospital. Ten months before, when the Group's squadrons had arrived back battered from their first mission over Nazi-occupied Europe, the cottage hospital had been turned temporarily into an Emergency Medical Service where injured aircrew could be given immediate attention. The fearful casualties suffered by the Eighth Air Force in carrying out Allied Command's orders for an intensified campaign of daylight strategic bombing meant that the arrangement had become permanent.

A choir of seven- to ten-year-olds from Market Wetherby school stood in the central aisle of the ward and beyond them with the medical superintendent were several USAAF officers, led by the 525th's commander, Colonel Krasnowici. Of the others with him, two were chaplains. The third man, a tall major, had his back to the door and Helen caught her breath. She nearly stepped forward, then he looked round and she saw that it was not Jim.

The children sang sweetly, not at all frightened although most of the patients were heavily bandaged, many in traction. It was very touching. The superintendent spotted

7

Helen and waved, but she moved away, going into her own office. She needed to be alone.

Helen Dereham was at a dangerous age. Born in the first decade of the century, a child of Edwardian confidence and security, she was now, like the country itself, undergoing changes so fast that she was aware that she was losing her bearings. Those bearings, until a year or so ago, had been the classical and seemingly unchangeable standards of British middle-class respectability.

She had married young to an attractive and moderately wealthy young landowner. The wedding had been reported in the *Tatler*. Marriage had not interrupted her university career. And the birth of her daughter, Pat, when she was twenty-one, did not stop her fulfilling her ambition and going to medical school. Ronnie Dereham had been able to provide housemaids, a first class nanny and, even more importantly, firm support for Helen's desire to be a doctor. Indeed, for the time, the mid 1920s, he had been progressively keen that his wife should work and have a meaningful career, an attitude rare enough to be frowned upon by his family and friends.

But his support had helped to solidify their marriage into a classically comfortable pre-war relationship. It was founded on politeness, respect and affection and secured by duty and routine, giving a pattern for existence which seemed as orderly as nature itself. It was not a passionate relationship, but then Helen had not been brought up to expect passion in her marriage, nor in herself.

She was a modern squire's wife, with a special position in the community because she was a doctor. She combined her medicine with the social patterns of the times and she tried to be a modern and sympathetic mother to Pat.

She knew she was attractive, but her dress was conventionally restrained to suit her position, as was her behaviour. She had never slept with any other man than her husband and never expected to.

Then came the war. There was rationing. The men, including Ronnie, went to the regiments. Yet all that was expected. So, too, was the extra work that fell on Helen and the other women. But gradually she began to recognize real changes, not yet fully perceived. Changes which would affect her and all women, changes triggered by the tension and disturbance of war, which would speed up even more dramatically after the war, leading to a sweeping cultural revision of western society.

Helen Dereham became aware of her sexuality. At first, her clinical mind put it down to Ronnie's absence. She understood the psychological pressures of having an orderly routine of life disturbed. And she was aware also of her age – she had just passed her fortieth birthday. On the surface she maintained her calm, tranquil, almost porcelain appearance. Underneath, a different woman was coming into being.

And it was that woman who took over when she first met Major Jim Kiley, the very first day the American Army Air Force had come to Market Wetherby.

The chemistry exploded into a chain reaction. Helen Dereham fell in love at first sight. At the beginning she did not recognize it for what it was. She was merely conscious of feeling unsettled. When the truth finally came to her, all kinds of emotions swept through her mind. First, she realized that she had never been in love before. Not even with Ronnie. Not like this. Secondly, she felt fear.

All the force of her English middle-class respectability was marshalled to give her strength to fight something which she knew could only bring hidden guilt and open scandal. So she had shown overt hostility to Jim Kiley, almost willing him to stay out of her life. But she knew, and he knew, that the hostility was only one way of channelling the deep emotions that their meeting unleashed in her. And so it had begun. The ultra respectable wife of an English officer and gentleman became the mistress, the passionate mistress, of an American flyer.

Their need for each other was whetted by the tensions and sharpened perceptions of wartime. Helen Dereham found amazing heights of happiness and very deep wells of guilt and fear. When her husband came home, paralysed, after the tank battles in Tunisia, her guilt increased. She discovered, however, that she had unthought-of skills of deception. Raised not to show her emotions in public, she remained on the surface, to her husband and friends, exactly as she always had been.

The affair progressed. She surrendered to Jim Kiley sexually and emotionally because she loved him and feared for him. She was very aware that death was the constant wingman to bomber crews and one half of her was determined not to waste a second of her happiness, which could end at any minute.

The other half, the half of duty and self-respect and rational thought, made her fight him. That half was always trying to break away. And two months before, that half had won.

Since that dramatic night when having to deliver Letty Mundy's premature baby had stopped her from going off with Jim, he had kept his promise not to contact her. It was the sensible, the right thing to do and, after the first ache had faded, she was grateful to him. Life had returned more or less to normal with her husband. She had absorbed herself in her work at the hospital and thought she had got Jim out of her system. Her reaction to seeing the major in the ward and the wild hope that had coursed through her had shaken her. Her pulse was racing. 'You're behaving like a schoolgirl,' she scolded herself. But she could not deny the bitter disappointment that it had not been him and she was dangerously near to tears.

There was a knock at the door and she barely had time to compose herself before Rufus Krasnowici came in.

A blunt, forceful man in his early fifties, he was one of the veterans of the US Army Air Force. Rufus was expected to follow his brothers into their father's trucking business in Oregon after Engineering School, but instead, fired by a heady mixture of idealism and thirst for adventure, he had volunteered in 1916 for Britain's Royal Flying Corps. It was as an experienced pilot that he had transferred to his own country's Air Service, when America entered the First World War. Since then he had seen action in the Philippines and the Far East. An advocate of preparedness, his uncompromising views had retarded his promotion in the isolationist years before this present war. The fact that he had now been vindicated gave him little satisfaction.

Thousands of young men had had to be drafted to meet the needs of US Bomber Command, committed to its policy of massive daylight strategic bombing. After basic training they were rushed to bases in England, arriving full of confidence having been taught to drop a bomb in a pickle barrel from 30,000 feet. What they had learnt in the clear skies of Wyoming, however, was very different from the reality of the ETO – the European Theatre of Operations – where muddy skies, rain and fog, and thick cloud masking the target were the norm; where instruments iced up and feet and fingers froze in spite of electrically-heated flying suits; where bombing runs had to be made through a hail of deadly accurate anti-aircraft fire and the attacks of German fighters.

He cursed the short time he was allowed to turn his eager greenhorns into combat crews. Only a small percentage of them would survive the twenty-five missions that made up an aircrew member's tour of duty. Maybe one in four. It sickened him, but he had a job to do.

Yet being Commanding Officer had its compensations, like being able to pause for an occasional chat with Helen Dereham. A shrewd judge of character, he had developed an appreciation for this cool, capable Englishwoman. There was something about her, something in the clear eyes and firm chin that reminded him of his own wife, Allie, back home in Portland. He smiled and saluted. 'I just wanted to thank you, Dr Dereham, for setting up the little carol concert. Those kids are wonderful.'

'I didn't have much to do with it, Colonel,' Helen told him.

'I hear different. And I want you to know on behalf of

my boys, I appreciate it. By the way, how is your husband these days?'

'Well, thank you. As well as can be expected.'

'No improvement?'

'Ronnie is permanently disabled, Colonel. That is something we have to accept.'

Rufus nodded. 'I – uh – used to get occasional progress reports on him from Jim Kiley.'

He could understand the attraction she had for his Air Executive Officer and although he would be the last to suspect any shenanigans between them, it was undeniable that they got on very well together. Shared interests, he guessed. Jim fitted into the kind of cultivated, middle-class milieu of the Derehams. Yet something had happened to interrupt the friendship.

Rufus hoped it wasn't that things had got out of hand and the husband had objected. That would be out of keeping with Jim's usually meticulous behaviour, but whatever it was, he had become as jumpy as a moose with a beehive stuck to its antlers.

'But I believe Jim hasn't seen either of you for a while,' he said carefully.

'No, we haven't run across each other,' Helen answered levelly. She could not resist asking, 'How is Major Kiley?'

'As far as the Air Force is concerned, a tower of strength. But I'm a bit bothered about him.' Helen waited. 'He doesn't seem able to relax and I don't want him to crack up. There was a time when he thought very highly of you, I know. But . . . I gather he doesn't have that safety valve any more.'

Helen was not sure how much Krasnowici knew. Much more, she suspected, than his blunt features revealed. She replied just as guardedly, 'We have both been very busy. Naturally, my husband and I would be pleased to see him.'

'Naturally, naturally,' Rufus nodded. 'Now I realize you're very busy, but there is one more thing.'

'I have Out Patients in five minutes, Colonel.' Thinking of her clinic, Helen remembered that the first appointment was for Vi Ericson and frowned. Vi had been disappointed before.

Rufus misinterpreted her frown. 'This is kind of important – something my boys cooked up.' He smiled. 'So if you'd let me have that five minutes?'

Jim Kiley rubbed the bristles on his chin with distaste. He would have to shave again. The last time had been at three-thirty in the morning, when he had got up to study the details of the briefing he would give aircrews for that day's mission to the Messerschmitt factory at Gotha. Everything had gone like clockwork. For once the skies had been relatively clear and the Flying Fortresses had roared off on schedule. Then the RAF meteorologists had reported heavy cloud over the target and thick fog in the English Channel and the Group had to be recalled, the sixth aborted mission out of the last nine. No mission, but on 'Sonova B' one of the Tokyo gas tanks added to the wingtips to give extra range had gone on fire and the fort had exploded with the loss of all its crew. Ten good men lost for nothing.

Ten men ... just the number of the crew he had captained when his ocean-going yacht had been runner-up in the Bermuda Race. His new yacht, with which he had planned to challenge for the America's Cup, was tied up in Nantucket for the duration. How long had his family been trying to win that damned race? Ever since the days of his grandfather, old Marcus Kiley, founder of the Kiley steel and railroad empire.

Old Marcus's battles had been in the boardroom and he had won every one of them – except against Andrew Carnegie. Mention Carnegie to old Marcus and it would be like putting in a good word for Hitler to Winston Churchill. Helen would have liked him ... He must be tired. His mind was wandering.

The squadron commanders and operations officers were watching him. 'Thank you, gentlemen, that's all. I needn't remind you we'll be on standby for tomorrow.'

As they trooped out, Captain Red Burwash, acting commander of 888 Squadron, paused by the door. 'If anyone had told me in 'forty-one that two years later I'd spend Christmas trying to bomb the hell out of places I'd never heard of,' he drawled, 'I wouldn't have believed it.' He saluted casually and went out.

Lester Carson, the adjutant, had remained behind. A mild-mannered, diplomatic man, he saw Jim's involuntary anger at Burwash's nonchalance and tried to defuse it. 'Lousy weather,' he remarked. 'As the guy said, why do the British bother to defend this island? Why not just cut the barrage balloons free and let it sink?'

Jim smiled briefly at the old joke. But it was rapidly becoming unfunny. 'Have you seen the MP reports, Lester?'

'One or two guys getting out of line. Nothing much. Maybe we should give them a little more time off.'

'Just the opposite,' Jim said. 'There's been too much sitting around on their butts. From tomorrow reveille will be at six a.m.'

Lester blinked. 'What for?'

'Physical training. And exercises in perimeter defence. If the weather's clear locally and there's no mission, aircrews will go on practice bombing runs.'

'Where to?'

'Whatever target's clear – Liverpool, Hull, Manchester.'

'English cities? You'll scare the hell out of them!'

'High level practice, Lester. They won't even know we've been there. I'll clear it with Rufe and you can post the orders tonight.'

Lester sighed. There was no arguing with the Air Exec when he was in this mood.

When the adjutant had gone, Jim turned to the window. Lousy weather. In a way he envied Red Burwash. The younger man had the perfect attitude for a bomber pilot, total concentration on the mission, forget about it when you're off.

How many years were there between them? Fourteen, if

Burwash was twenty-five. Jim would be . . . thirty-nine on his next birthday.

It had taken him a long time to find himself. He had been born into a privileged background. Fifth Avenue mansion, summer estate at Newport, stables and yachts, limousines and private railcars. The ethnic background was Irish and Scots with Scandinavian way back. The family was already second generation American before grandfather Marcus had begun his climb from railroad clerk to President of the Board. Jim was third generation money, which meant there was no pressure on him to enter the family business, more than ably continued by his father.

After gaining a good degree in Modern History at Princeton, he had discovered a fascination for architecture. It was the one thing he really cared about and yet he had never become a practising architect. It is not easy to persist, to struggle to have one's vision realized, when there is no need for success, no financial necessity. He was not proud of it.

The social commitments of his family took up so much time, there was little left to consider where he was really going. He became a polo star and a ranking yachtsman. He enjoyed motor racing, but not with the same passion that absorbed many of his friends. Then one night at dinner he met Howard Hughes and, hearing him talk, developed an interest in airplanes. In the air he found the release and exhilaration that Hughes had spoken of and for a year or two thought only of flying. He had an unresolved ambition to enter for the Schneider Trophy, but had to admit to himself that there were other men more driven, more dedicated than himself, who would always win. Winning, after all, he told himself, was not important.

He had become one of the Four Hundred's most eligible bachelors. Women were attracted to him and he enjoyed their company, quickly learning to spot the ones whose main interest was his future inheritance. Only once was he completely deceived, and it was to recover from that affair, with a minor Broadway singing-star, that he spent most of 1937 in Europe. He joined in the London season, sailed at Cowes and shot in the Highlands near Balmoral. After taking in opera at Venice and Milan, he skied in Austria and, early the following year, made what he thought of as a pilgrimage to Nuremberg to study the drawings of Dürer.

It was Hitler's birthday and, hearing that there was to be a parade, he joined the people waiting in the streets. The excitement was infectious, but the sight of the thousands of SS in their black uniforms, steel helmets and jackboots, with their swastikas and deaths-head insignia, disturbed him. He went along with the crowds to the stadium and after the immensely theatrical ceremonies heard Streicher, the Jew-hater, speak; then Hess and Goebbels, and finally Hitler himself.

A spellbinding orator, slow and stilted at first, his harsh voice rising in volume and his gestures becoming more abruptly dramatic as his huge audience began to respond, his appeal was mesmeric. Jim was shaken by the effect on the people around him, a carefree holiday crowd who were transformed, uplifted, swept away by that voice, until they turned into mere extensions of the single figure on the podium, roaring their responses, living only to serve and obey.

Jim heard someone laughing and recognized a Dutch tourist who was staying at the same hotel. Nothing was said or done, but later that night his body, beaten to bloody unconsciousness, was found in an alleyway behind the hotel.

Jim returned to the States. Until now he had been aware of what was happening in the world only in the most general way, wrapped up in his sports and social obligations, shielded from reality. Now he began to read and to question and soon was convinced that a second world war was inevitable. He suspected that America would again try not to be involved, yet would eventually have no choice. He could not see why so few people seemed to realize it. At the same time, the argument that any future war would be decided in the air by the use of strategic bombing made sense to him and, to the astonishment of everyone who knew him, he joined the Army Air Corps, as it was then known.

In the Air Corps, Jim found what he had always been searching for, discipline and a sense of purpose. He led one of the first B-17 squadrons to fly to Britain in 1942 and won his campaign medals the hard way, taking part in the earliest and most traumatic missions, when the heavy American bombers and their inexperienced crews were shot out of the sky all round him by battle-trained German fighters.

After his first tour of twenty-five missions, he served for a time as an Operations Officer, then was posted, with the rank of Major, to be Air Executive Officer of the newly formed 525th Group, taking over and extending the small RAF station at Market Wetherby in East Anglia.

The CO, Rufus Krasnowici, had used him to beat his greenhorn aircrews into shape. Most of them were cocky and know-all, convinced they had nothing more to learn and itching to get at the Krauts. They grumbled when Jim threw them into a non-stop programme of retraining, leading them himself on an exhausting series of practice formation take-offs, and landings, air assembly and formation flying. He gained himself a reputation for being hard and unfeeling, but he had given many of them a chance of survival by drilling into them the lessons he himself had learned.

He had nursed them through the shock of their first disastrous mission, given them back their confidence and helped to turn them into one of the most highly rated Groups in the entire Eighth Air Force.

On the non-operation side, he had done much to defuse the tension between the local townspeople and the men of the Base, among whom were many whose brash inexperience led them to boast they had come to win the war for England and to assume that any local girl was theirs for the asking. Of course, many girls were immediately dazzled by them and behaved foolishly, which led in turn to clashes with British Servicemen who saw themselves cut out by rivals who spoke like Hollywood film stars, were considerably better paid and wore uniforms that made them all look like officers.

It was through Krasnowici's insistence on establishing better relations with the local community that he had been thrown into the company of Helen Dereham, head of the Anglo-American Goodwill Committee.

Their first meeting was accidental and he had thought her cold and haughty. Gradually he had come to see through the façade. She was poised, not haughty, reserved, not cold. Her care for his wounded men won his admiration, but when he attempted to establish their relationship on a more friendly footing, she froze him off.

He caught himself thinking about her frequently, looking forward to seeing her. There was an element of challenge, although he would not specify it to himself. A ludicrous interlude when her nineteen-year-old, but immature, daughter developed a teenager's crush on him brought them closer.

He had only once met her husband, Ronald Dereham, before Ronnie was posted to North Africa to command a Tank Unit. She was alone and Jim would have despised himself for attempting to seduce the wife of a man on active service. Yet he continued to contrive meetings with her.

He was relieved when she finally confessed that she enjoyed his company and they agreed that, as they were both adult and responsible, there could be no harm in their spending an hour or two together from time to time. It was purely social. They liked each other. They discovered common interests, a compatible sense of humour. In case their friendship was misinterpreted, they were very discreet.

The return of Ronnie Dereham, crippled after a direct hit on his tank, made Helen feel guilty at having enjoyed the company of another man. She had also to admit to herself that being with Jim had become important to her. It was by way of atonement to Ronnie that she decided that they must meet much less frequently.

The inevitable happened. Not seeing each other, though they both wanted to, brought their feelings into the open. It was against every tenet of the creed by which they had lived and both fought against it. Yet nothing could prevent them from becoming lovers. Jim had almost hoped that by giving in to their passion they would quench it. It only made them want each other more.

It was an impossible situation. If Ronnie had not been crippled, it might have been otherwise, but Jim knew that Helen, by her very nature, could not desert her husband, of whom she was still fond. She hated having to lie to him, yet she could not bring herself to give Jim up. At the same time, Jim's position meant he could not afford to become involved in a divorce. They had tried meeting only occasionally, in secret, and it had not worked.

Jim had to decide for both of them. There would be less hurt, especially for Ronnie, if they did not meet at all, except in passing. He promised to make no attempt to see her, not even to telephone her.

This morning he had been sorely tempted. Rufus had practically ordered him to come to the hospital with the chaplains and Ground Exec, but he had pleaded pressure of work. Yet he regretted it. It would have been an excuse. Staying away had been the hardest thing he had ever done. But he had promised her, denying his own feelings, to save her the pain of having to live a lie.

Lousy weather . . . Albert Mundy thought. He was peering out of his shop window at the rainswept square of Market Wetherby. There was sleet in the rain and he'd had no more than five customers all day. Christmas rush . . . That was a joke. He'd got tired of telling people there were no currants or raisins, no dried fruit for cakes and puddings, even if they had the points.

Something was irritating him. He had tried to put it out

of his mind, but it was no use. He looked at his wife, Vera, doing her accounts behind the window of the post office section of their grocery shop. 'That baby's still crying.'

'Poor little mite,' Vera said, not looking up.

'Well, go and do something about it!' Mundy rapped. 'Or tell Letty to. I can't hear myself think!'

'I will in a minute, Albert. But I can't leave these.'

Mundy glowered at her. When he could stand the squalling no longer, he marched through into the back parlour himself, fuming.

The baby was lying in its crib. There was no sign of his daughter. 'Letty!' he shouted. 'Letty, get down here!' No answer. As if it wasn't enough for her to bring shame on them with an illegitimate child. His fault, Vera had said. For being too strict. Obviously, he hadn't been strict enough or she wouldn't have thrown herself at the first fancy Romeo in Yankee uniform who – 'Oh, shut up!' he said to the crib. 'Enough of that now!'

The only effect was to make the baby cry louder. He moved closer, trying another tack. 'Give over,' he said more quietly. 'There's a good baby.' He leaned down nearer, and smiled. The baby's face was red and distorted, its limbs flailing. Mundy was alarmed. What on earth was the matter with it? He picked it up and, too late, realized his mistake. Its nightie and nappy were wringing wet. 'Oh, Gaw . . .' he muttered disgustedly. There was nothing else for it. The morning paper was on the table. He opened it out and laid the baby on it. At least he knew it wouldn't roll off.

Where the devil was Letty? She neglected her baby girl, hadn't even given it a proper name yet. Without thinking, he had wiped his hands on his beige overall, and grimaced. Oh, well, in for a penny . . . He stripped off the baby's nightie and sopping nappy and tossed them into the sink. He could not see anything else, so dried her with his handkerchief, then threw it on the fire. He found a dry nappy on the clothes-horse and a handful of pins. He slid it under the baby's bottom and drew an edge up between her legs. Bunching it together in front, he managed to fasten it together like an envelope with five pins. It didn't look exactly right, but it would do.

He realized something. Miraculously, the baby had stopped crying. 'Feeling better, eh?' he asked and poked at her chest. Her left hand closed round his finger. When he tried to draw it away, the little hand held on tighter.

Albert Mundy gazed down at his grand-daughter for a long moment. He was aware of the most extraordinary protective feeling. 'Poor little bugger,' he muttered. 'No name, eh? We'll see about that.'

# TWO

Jack Blair looked up from polishing the bar counter in The Plough when his daughter Vi came in. 'No work this afternoon?'

'Got off early,' Vi smiled, 'so I thought I'd give you a hand.'

Jack was grateful. Since his younger daughter Rosie had started at the parachute factory, he had had to manage both bars by himself during the day. Vi had a hard slog as a landgirl up at the Dereham place, but seemed to thrive on it. She was humming to herself as she started to help him clear up and he was glad to see her so happy.

When her husband of a day, Master Sergeant Chuck Ericson had been shot down over Belgium, she had been very withdrawn. His return out of the blue two months ago had brought her back to life. Even then it hadn't been plain sailing. Having escaped from enemy-occupied territory, Chuck was automatically repatriated to the United States. Even though he had made his way home on his own, he was not allowed to fly and risk capture, until Intelligence was certain he would not endanger any of their Resistance networks. Vi could not get a permit to accompany him, so had to wait more months for his return. At least she knew he was safe.

'Mrs Dereham give you the news?' Jack wondered.

Vi was startled. She had told no one about her visit to the hospital. Although she was certain within herself this time, Dr Dereham had said it was too soon for the tests to be positive. 'What news, Dad?'

'About the party. Christmas party.'

Sally Bilton was gazing at Master Sergeant Joe McGraw.

'All of them?' she asked.

'Not so loud, Sal,' Mac warned. 'Don't want to spoil the surprise.' He glanced at her small daughter Betty, who was busy painting a 'secret' Christmas card for him.

He had virtually moved into the Biltons' cottage, taking the place of her husband, killed in action. Many locals were scandalized by it. Sally paid them no heed. 'But all the children in town?' she said.

'Can't be more'n fifty or sixty,' Mac shrugged. 'And if maybe there's a few more, what the heck, we can manage.'

Sally smiled. Her Mac looked craggy and tough as boot leather, but when it came to kids he was as soft as butter.

'A splendid idea,' Ronnie Dereham decided. 'And most generous. I'd offer them the house, but I suppose they want to hold it at their Base.'

'That's the suggestion,' Helen told him.

'Well, don't look so worried,' Ronnie smiled. 'Of course, you've got a lot on your plate already, but it's an honour to be asked to help organize it. And Pat'll be back from Cambridge by then. She'll pitch in.' He swivelled his wheelchair back round to the wallmap he had been studying. It showed the European Theatre of Operations, with tiny flags marking the Allied advance up from the heel of Italy. 'Some of my old Division will be there at Cassino,' he muttered, 'bound to be.' He seemed shrunken, somehow.

Helen sat watching him. It was hard to remember how vital and dynamic he had been. She felt a surge of resentment and was ashamed of herself. He couldn't help how he was now. Yet he might have realized that what was troubling her was not the organization of the children's party, but the inevitability through it of her meeting Jim again.

There were two surprises at the Base that Christmas Eve. The first was not planned.

The day's raid had been on the marshalling yards at Cologne and first reports were good. Colonel Krasnowici had led the formation himself and, as soon as he reached the coast, he radioed in that the strike had been good to excellent and there was damage to the Group, but no losses. When Rufus landed, he joined Jim Kiley at the control tower to count the rest of the Group in. It was still light in the late afternoon, but the cloud ceiling was low and drifting fog patches created a false twilight.

'Back home, Allie'll just be about getting up now,' Rufus said, half to himself. 'Wonder if she got my card? I told her to stick it up where it could see the Christmas tree. I must be going soft in the head.'

A red flare dropped from the cloud to signal that the ship coming in had wounded on board and Jim checked automatically that the ambulances and fire trucks were in position by the main runway. The first B-17 Flying Fortress came into sight, obviously the one that had dropped the flare. 'It's "Near as Dammit",' McGraw, the Line Chief, shouted up from below. Her engines were labouring. There was a rip in her fuselage under her belly and up her starboard flank and one of her tail-stabilizers had been blown off. She began to shudder as she sank towards the field.

'Make it!' Jim urged silently. 'Come on, girl – make it!'

She touched down as sweetly as on a training flight, but she was still travelling at speed and the moment her pilot began to apply the brakes, her landing-gear buckled. Screeching along on her belly, she tilted crazily from side to side, the tips of her huge wings throwing up smoke and sparks even from the wet macadam of the runway. With great presence of mind, just as her power gave out, her pilot managed to swing her round so that she skidded to the left off the track and on to the wide grass verge, where she came to a jolting stop, bogged down in the thick clinging mud. Within seconds the fire trucks and ambulances had surrounded her, the injured and the shaken crewmen were helped out and hoses blanketed her in case of fire.

'God rest ye merry, gentlemen,' Rufus grunted. 'That was as near as dammit, right enough.'

The next three ships landed without incident. Their wounded were taken off and they taxied to their hard-stands, where the crew chiefs were waiting to see what damage would have to be repaired by morning. Another B-17 was making her final approach and Jim was relieved to see she was untouched. It was 'Ginger Rogers II', Burwash's ship.

As he began to ease her down, Red Burwash became aware of the navigation lights of another ship emerging from the clouds right behind him. 'You're too damned close!' he yelled into his R/T. 'Get off my tail!' Instinctively, he pushed 'Ginger's' nose down and, at almost the same moment, tracer bullets lanced past where it had been a second before. As Red plunged to port in evasion, his attacker swept past him, a German ME 410 Hornet, immediately followed by a JU 88.

Reaching the field, they split apart, the Junkers making for the control tower. Jim had gripped the rail in front of him. His mouth half open to shout, he saw the Hornet streak at a slant across the runway, all guns firing. A bomb arced down from it and the damaged ship on the grass verge bounced once before bursting apart in a spout of smoke and flames.

At the same instant, Jim and Rufus flung themselves flat on the platform, seeing the black-painted Junkers tear towards them, spitting bullets which pockmarked the wall of the control tower and shattered the windows above them. It roared over them to strafe the headquarters complex, crews' quarters and stores.

The Hornet flew parallel to the runway, shooting up the groundcrews and the ships already on their hardstands, dropping two more bombs. The last of them hit a stack of bomb crates at the far end of the field beyond dispersal.

The action lasted only seconds and, by the time the Base defences had opened up, both enemy aircraft had vanished. They had made use of the fog and cloud to infiltrate the returning Group, but, by good luck, had launched their attack too soon. Twenty minutes later, with most of the B-17s landed and moving to their hardstands, the destruction could have been appalling. As it was, despite bullet damage, only poor 'Near as Dammit' had been destroyed. Other bombs had demolished the headquarters jeep, two parachute stores and the RC chapel. Four men were injured, only one seriously.

The stack of bomb crates on the edge of the field were empties, built into a rough shelter by some of the crew chiefs for protection against the sleet and the rain.

All in all, the result could have been much worse and Rufus decided, after consulting with his staff officers, that the treat planned for the local children should go ahead. His decision was strengthened by the report that the ME 410 had been observed heading across Channel for home and the Junkers 88 had been shot down by RAF Mosquitoes. Perimeter defences were kept on the alert, but as soon as the airfield had been cleared the children who had been waiting in the village hall were led into trucks and driven to the Base, where almost the entire personnel turned out to welcome them.

The Mess Hall was like an Aladdin's cave with bunting and streamers, cakes and sweets and jellies. The Quartermaster Company had even managed to make icecream, which many of the younger children had never tasted. Helen refused to make a speech since the British helpers had done so little and she left Rufus to welcome the guests on behalf of their honorary uncles in the 525th.

Undoubtedly, the highspot was the arrival and landing of the Group's Judas aircraft, an old B-17 painted in garish red, yellow and green stripes to assist in formation assembly. From it stepped Line Chief McGraw dressed in a scarlet Santa Claus costume, flying boots and cottonwool whiskers, from which protruded the stub of a black cigar. His Crew Chiefs followed him, dressed as gnomes and each carrying a sack filled with toys made by the men on the base. Each child was given one, along with a hug from Santa.

The only momentary upset came when little Billy Bilton recognized McGraw and squealed, 'Uncle Joe! It's Uncle Joe!' McGraw chuckled and passed him on to Sally who was helping, but she was anxious, seeing how puzzled Betty was, watching McGraw and trying to believe like the others that he was really Santa.

In spite of the party's great success, it was distressing for Helen. She had been nerving herself up to meet Jim and, when it happened, he merely shook her hand and thanked her formally for her assistance. He made no attempt to speak to her later. Even Pat noticed his apparent indifference and resented it on her mother's behalf, so that when he said hello, she did not even reply.

At the end of the party, Jim watched Helen leave without a glance at him. Maybe he had played it wrong, he thought. He felt empty and would have gone after her, but became aware of Rufus standing beside him. He made himself relax. 'Well, looks like the men enjoyed it almost as much as the kids.'

'Maybe even more,' Rufus agreed quietly. 'After all, their own kids are anything from three to six thousand miles away.'

That evening there were parties all over Market Wetherby as many people opened their doors to men from the Base. Many new friendships were made, and old ones reaffirmed. The watch night service at the church was crowded. There was an impromptu dance at the village hall.

The Plough was packed to the doors and Rosie Blair was surprised to see Peter Mundy pushing through towards the bar. He was on forty-eight hours' leave, in uniform, looking older and more self-assured.

His confidence had grown ever since he had walked into his father's shop that morning. Albert Mundy was presiding over chaos. His mother was at the WI. The shop was full of customers and the baby, Letty's baby, was crying.

27

Peter had never seen his father so ill at ease. Albert was trying to comfort her.

'Where the devil's Letty?' he snapped, by way of welcome.

'Search me,' Peter said, pushing his forage cap through his epaulette.

Mundy's eyes narrowed. Was that a proper manner to speak to one's father? Some damned Yankee expression. He saw how Peter held himself, shoulders back. The boy had filled out a little and he was looking straight at him, not blinking and glancing away as he had always done before he joined up. An improvement there, a definite improvement. 'Well, son,' he said, 'they're making a man of you.'

Albert looked from the baby in his arms to the young man in the uniform he himself had once worn. Yes, he thought, the Suffolk Regiment was doing Peter proud.

'Hello, stranger,' Rosie smiled. Before Peter could reply, a group of US lieutenants called to her and she swayed seductively along to serve them.

Sergeants Elmer Jones and Hymie Stutz were seated at the bar, waiting as always to find out which of them would be allowed to take Rosie to the dance, if either.

Hymie and Elmer were inseparable, but if it had not been for the war it was unlikely they would ever have met, far less have become friends.

Fair, plump and slow-moving, Elmer Jones was of Anglo-Saxon stock, his family having emigrated from the West Country to the New York area four generations ago. They had not found the streets paved with gold. His father was a milk delivery man, as his grandfather had been. The only real success in the Jones clan was his uncle, who owned a small cigar store in Yonkers.

Hymie Stutz, on the other hand, was from Milwaukee. His grandparents had emigrated to the United States in the 1880s, when work was hard to find in their native Bavaria. Since then, most of them had been employed in Wisconsin's huge canning factories. Short and dark, with a fiery temper, Hymie wore a narrow Ronald Colman moustache which partially disguised his long upper lip, but did not, as he mistakenly believed, give him the film star's allure. Meeting him for the first time, other US Servicemen, in innocence or with small town prejudice, would sometimes say, 'Stutz? That's a Jewish name, ain't it?' Hymie would draw himself up, smoothing his pencil moustache with a flick of his index finger, and reply, 'Nah, it's American. But I had a Jewish grandmother. So that makes me kinda Jew-*ish*, I guess. Wanna make something out of it?'

Any questioner who decided to take up the challenge would find himself facing not only the aggressive Hymie, but also Elmer, his normally sociable expression replaced by indignation and determination. And backing him was the rest of the crew of 'Ginger Rogers II'.

'Hiya, Pete,' Elmer said.

'Yeah, how's tricks?' Hymie added. 'Gettin' any?'

'No more than either of you by the looks of it,' Peter said, and glanced towards Rosie. She was wearing her minx's smile, pretending not to react to the compliments which the lieutenants were paying her, but lapping them up.

Hymie drew himself up indignantly to his full five foot five, but Elmer grinned. 'He's got a point there, Stutzie. We oughta form a club – for the all-time losers.'

Entering headquarters at six o'clock the next morning, Jim returned the seasonal greetings of the duty sergeant. 'Merry Christmas,' he repeated to himself as he went into his bleak office and shut the door. He had had a restless, unsettled night after a drink too many at the Officers' Club. It hadn't even fuddled him, only made him more conscious of his need.

He thought of Helen not a mile away. He had forced himself not to speak to her the day before and now the urge to see her, even just to hear her voice, was almost overwhelming, but she would not be at the hospital and he could not telephone her at her home. Tomorrow he would call her at her office, he promised himself. Or perhaps New Year's Day. That's it. Nothing would seem more natural, and nothing else could make the year ahead seem bearable.

At Bridge Cottage, Betty Bilton woke to discover by her bed a large and beautiful doll which McGraw had managed to have smuggled in from the States. Sally heard her cry of delight and hurried in. Betty was sitting up, holding the doll. 'You don't mind,' Sally asked cautiously, 'about Santa being Uncle Joe?'

Betty had been thinking. 'No,' she said. 'Because that's just what Santa should be like – Uncle Joe with whiskers.'

Sally laughed and hugged her. 'Happy Christmas, darling,' she said.

# THREE

Jim Kiley sat hunched over his desk, studying the graphs prepared for him by Group Intelligence. Of the six missions flown by the 525th in January, only one had had to be aborted. One had to go for the secondary target. The other four had been textbook – for the loss of ten ships. He grunted, noting that two of these had been apparently caused by fire in their long range Tokyo tanks.

He was trying to concentrate, but try as he might he could not stop himself looking at the telephone. He had thought often of the children's Christmas party where he had deliberately avoided Helen, to make it easier for both of them. Now it bothered him. Especially since Rufus had said afterwards it had looked as if Jim was going out of his way to ignore her and she seemed upset. Maybe I played it badly, Jim thought, maybe I should've acted more natural, friendly.

He gave up, reached for the telephone and had himself put through to the cottage hospital. 'Might I speak with Dr Dereham, please? This is Major Kiley.' He waited several minutes to be told that Helen was not available, no one could estimate how long she would be. 'Kindly tell her I called,' he said. When he turned back to the graphs, the pencil he had picked up snapped between his hands and he threw it down irritably.

The door was opening. 'I said I wasn't to be disturbed!' he growled.

'Did you now?' the CO, Rufus Krasnowici, murmured.

'Oh – sorry, sir.' Jim began to rise. Sometimes the Colonel was a stickler for the formalities.

Rufus waved him down and nodded at the graphs. 'I had a look at these. What do they say to you?'

'Well – that we're on the beam again.'

'That we are,' Rufus agreed. 'And with the new P-51 Mustangs for long range fighter cover and the B-17s' extra fuel tanks, we can now strike deeper into Germany than ever before. The Krauts must be starting to think.'

'There's a problem, though,' Jim told him. 'Those wingtip fuel tanks are dangerously explosive.'

'They seem to be. Though no one can say for sure whether that's due to enemy action, malfunction or simple, damn bad luck. One thing for sure, however,' Rufus went on, 'we're gearing up.'

He was right. The Eighth Air Force had been taken over by the dynamic Lieutenant General James Doolittle, with General Carl Spaatz in command of US Strategic Air Forces. At the same time, Eisenhower had been made Commander-in-Chief, to prepare for the Allied invasion of Europe. 'Ike's the man to do it,' Jim said.

'You betcha,' Rufus agreed. 'And while we're at it, I'd like to see a few less long faces around here. It's time our guys realized just how well they've done. Last October and on through the fall, the German Air Force had the Eighth licked. They'd fought us to a standstill. I hate to admit it, but it's a fact. Since then, however, our boys, through retraining and determination, and sheer guts, have pulled themselves up again. Another six months and we'll have blasted Goering's Luftwaffe right out of the sky.'

In their Nissen hut half a mile away, the crew of 'Ginger Rogers II' huddled round the stove trying to keep warm. What a depressing bunch, Ben Kulik thought. A sergeant radio operator, he was the newest member of the crew and could not get used to its moods, alternately high spirited and jokey, then sunk in gloom. 'Flak happy' was what the ground crews called it.

Elmer Jones was lying on his bunk playing his mouth organ. When he began the same plaintive blues for the third time, Kulik complained, 'Knock it off, can't you, Elmer?'

'Yeah, I've told you before where you can stuff that tin toothpick,' Hymie Stutz muttered.

Elmer was about to retort, but stopped himself. He knew what was bugging Hymie, only too well. Apart from Red Burwash and the co-pilot, they were the only ones left of the original 'Ginger Rogers II' crew. He wouldn't even let himself think about the first 'Ginger'. The last mission which had been aborted would have been the twenty first for both Hymie and himself, leaving only four more to complete their tour of twenty five, after which they'd be shipped home. But the formation had only reached midway across the Channel before recall and the rule was, if you didn't touch enemy territory, it didn't count. So they still had five to go. And the odds against them making it were growing longer.

Elmer raised his mouth organ to his lips, remembered and laid it on his chest, closing his eyes.

Albert Mundy came in from the shop. Vera was sitting trying to coax the baby to take more milk from its bottle.

'Feeding any better?' he asked.

'She took a little more this time,' Vera said.

Mundy grunted. His wife weighed their grand-daughter regularly on the scales in the shop and had discovered a steady weight loss. It worried them. Not that Letty showed the slightest interest. It was over three months now since the birth and she still pleaded tiredness. That was her excuse, too, for not helping with the customers. And she was excused warwork, having a child to look after. That was a laugh. Vera did it all. While Letty slopped around doing nothing – sneaking out too in the evenings, as soon as his back was turned.

'Try her again,' he suggested, and Vera put the bottle to the baby's mouth. Little Vicky . . . Vera Victoria Mundy. He had made the arrangements for the christening with the vicar himself, including some discreet bribery with a few tins of spam and such. And he'd chosen the names, Victoria after the old Queen. Also, although he would never admit it to anyone, not even his wife, because of Victoria . . . and Albert.

Mundy was Market Wetherby born and bred. He prided himself on that. As he did on many things. He had a position in the community. His father had founded this shop in Victoria's reign and he had expanded it, brought it up to date. By now it might have been half the size again, if it hadn't been for the war.

The war . . . not like the war he knew. The real war, over there at Ypres and the Somme. When he had won his DSM. He didn't need to close his eyes to remember the numbing thunder of the guns, the scream of the whizz-bangs, the crump as the big shells landed. Jack Johnsons, they'd called them.

He would like to see how those Yanks stood up to even ten minutes of how it was then. Stinking mud to your waist in the trench, lice and the constant terror of gas attacks. He'd watched his best friend cough his lungs out in green froth. It took discipline to stand it. That was one thing he had learnt – the most important thing is discipline.

He had tried to instil it in his children. He had worked hard all his life to make a decent home for them. You'd think they'd have the common decency to do as he wanted, what was best for them, without always having to be shouted at.

Peter, he was going to be all right, though. Sensitive, his mother had called him. He had just been a damned shirker. Never helping out in the shop, always ready to sneak off and play that blessed piano. All he thought about. That and his talk about how brave the conchies were, suffering for their convictions rather than fight. Mundy had been terrified that his son would become one of them, refuse his call-up. But breeding had told, and now he was in Mundy's old regiment, the Suffolks. It was making a man of him, you could see that.

Odd how things turn out. His daughter, Letty, she'd been the apple of his eye, dutiful, pretty, helpful about the

34

house. Everything she could be. He'd always thought of her as making up for Peter. Until the Yanks came.

He could hear her coming down now and glanced up from the baby, as Letty slouched in, hair uncombed, still in her dressing gown, looking for a filmstar magazine she had left downstairs. 'You haven't asked if Vicky's putting on any weight yet,' he said.

Letty shrugged. 'Has she?'

'Nearly an ounce, love,' Vera smiled. 'So you mustn't worry.'

Letty was already going back out. Her father headed after her and called up the stairs, incensed, 'And where were you last night, when I was out at Civil Defence? I've told you about that! You're not too old for me to take my belt to you, my girl!' There was no reply.

'Shh, Albert,' Vera warned. 'You'll upset the baby.'

Mundy moved quietly back into the shop, but once inside he slammed the door in sudden anger. 'What's this place comin' to?' he fumed. 'When am I to be master again in my own house?'


'Are you sure?' Sally Bilton asked. Vi smiled and nodded. 'I mean, you remember last time—'

'Oh, that was just a false alarm,' Vi said. 'Wishful thinking. But this time it's definite. I'm pregnant. I'm going to have Chuck's baby.'

'Is that what you want?' Sally asked, carefully.

'Of course!' Vi laughed. 'It's what I want most in the world.'

'It's only that Joe says—'

'I know. We ought to wait till after the war. But don't you see, Sally? Whatever happens, now I'll always have a part of him. Something that's us – forever.'

Sally smiled and touched her friend's hand. 'Your father'll be pleased.'

'Oh, I haven't told him.' Vi saw Sally's surprise. 'Dad's worried enough for me with Chuck being away in America, even though it's daft. Anyway, I thought it best he didn't

35

know, not just yet. It won't show for another couple of months and, by then, Chuck may be back. And everything will be . . . marvellous.'

Sally could not prevent a slight feeling of envy at Vi's happiness. It was silly, really, she thought. There was no reason for envy. With Joe and the kids, Sally had everything she could want.

Still, as she put the kettle on for tea, she had to confess to herself that she did not have quite everything. She couldn't love her own children more, Betty and Billy, and she couldn't be more content than with Joe, yet there was something missing.

Her husband, Stan, had been a good man, a good husband and father. Quite ordinary, really, a car mechanic. She had hopes that after the war she might help him to make something of himself. She was grateful to Joe McGraw, the Line Chief. He had arranged for her to get some laundry work for the Base. She could just about manage on her allowance from Stan's army pay, but the work helped her to make sure the kids did not go without and to put something by.

Then the news had arrived that Stan had been killed. By that time, Joe had become a friend. Nothing more. He was fond of the children and her cottage was somewhere he could relax with a family. His presence comforted her.

The news of Stan's death changed everything. Quite soon after, Joe and she had both realized that they felt more than just friendship for each other. She had been reluctant to admit even to herself that he was everything Stan was not, more positive, more capable, stronger, more fun to be with. He was big and craggy, like one of those blocks at Stonehenge, yet he could be so gentle. She herself was nothing much to look at, she knew, with no great charm or education. Just a sensible, homely woman. She could not think what he saw in her. Yet the explosion of desire and love between them had been overpowering. She had never felt so contented, nor so safe, as in his arms.

What had followed she could still scarcely believe. Stan's

death had been misreported and he walked in one night, on leave, finding her with Joe. There had been a fight, a terrible row. She had been sorry for Stan, deeply sorry, but he was already part of her past. When he left again to rejoin his unit in Italy, she could only feel relief. Even when the news of his death came, his real death this time, even while she mourned, it was for someone already remote, someone she had half forgotten.

Before Stan's return her involvement with Joe had been suspected only by a few. Afterwards, everyone seemed to know. Of course, it had caused a scandal. Some people who had been friends for years crossed the street rather than talk to her. Worst of all was Stan's mother, old Ruby, who had lived with her for a while. She had even tried to steal the children.

There were many who called Sally a scarlet woman and sympathized with Ruby. It was hard to take at times, never being sure who understood or who condemned, as it was so easy to do without knowing the facts. If it had not been for a few friends like Vi, she would have been lonely. As Line Chief, responsible for the repair and maintenance of all the aircraft on the Base, Joe was sometimes only able to snatch an hour or two with her in a week. And she could not merely close the door when they were together and say nothing else mattered. She was sure he loved her and needed her, that she and the kids gave him a feeling of belonging. That was the trouble. Part of him accepted that gladly, but another part rebelled against it. He had been in the Air Force since he was a boy and had never had a home life. His one attempt before to settle down, a marriage to a showgirl from a club in Hawaii, had been a disaster and had left emotional scars which had still not fully healed.

He was not a man who was afraid of much, if anything. But the one thing that worried him was commitment. He was afraid to commit himself, in case the dream ended again, the bubble burst. He had tried to leave her because of it and his need for her, his concern for the children, had brought him back. Even then, he would make no promises. 'Not till the war's over, Sal,' he always said. 'Not till we see how things turn out.'

She could bear anything, all the sidelong looks, the sneers of the old women, as long as he was with her. As long as he was, she told herself that she had everything. But it was not true. She could not say it, but she wanted to belong to him, to have his name. And seeing Vi sit smiling, lost in her thoughts of the future, Sally knew that she wanted another child herself, hers and Joe's, to make the family complete.

Jim Kiley felt self conscious as soon as he entered the cottage hospital. He was well known and several people recognized him on the way to Helen's office, but when he got there, he found it empty. He had no idea where she might be. He stopped a sister in the corridor, who told him that Dr Dereham was assisting in the operating theatre. She could be out any moment, but on the other hand it could be hours.

Jim waited outside the office for ten minutes, then as long again inside. Just being here reminded him so acutely of Helen, of holding her in his arms, that it was almost unbearable. He was also aware that hanging around like this would expose both of them, especially her, to gossip. It was crazy to come on spec, but he had felt an overpowering need to see her. After another couple of minutes, he tore a page from her small notepad and wrote, 'Tried to see you. Need to. J.' He folded it and placed it in the centre of her desk.

When he opened the door, the draught slid his note to the edge of the desk. When the door closed, it dropped to the floor beside the wastepaper basket. Half an hour later, the volunteer cleaner put it in the basket from which she thought it had fallen and carried it out with the rest of the rubbish.

*

Rosie Blair's normally pretty face was set and sulky. 'She shouldn't be here,' she muttered.

'Can't keep her out,' her father said quietly. He glanced over at where Letty Mundy sat with a good looking young GI, smiling and listening to him while her eyes searched the lounge bar for better prospects. 'Anyway, she's your friend.'

'Friend . . .' Rosie repeated, darkly. She had another reason for sulking, besides Letty attracting the attention of all the servicemen in the bar. Hymie and Elmer and the others had promised to come tonight, but had been put on standby for tomorrow. The only US airmen here were ground personnel. 'She's welcome to them,' Rosie sniffed.

One of those watching Letty was a dark, narrow-faced sergeant. He saw how she sat with her coat thrown open to show her figure, which she had regained after the birth, her dress short, revealing her good legs. Wearing nylons, too. No guessing where she'd got those. Nor how. He moved over and smiled. 'Hi.' Letty looked up at him. 'Maybe you don't remember me. We met before. I was a pal of Mario's. Mario Bottone?'

At the mention of Mario, Letty's smile faltered. But she recovered. Mario, after all, was dead. 'Yes, I remember you.'

'Patsy. Patsy Petrillo.' He seated himself beside her without waiting to be asked. On her other side, the GI realized the sergeant from the PX store had effectively cut him out. 'I ain't seen you around much.'

His dark looks and cocky self-assurance reminded her of Mario. 'Maybe you haven't been looking,' she answered, with a touch of her new pertness.

'I'll do the lookin', Lady,' Patsy said, 'if you'll put on the show.'

Letty laughed. He was *so* like Mario.

Helen and Ronnie Dereham had had their first row in months. It was over something trivial. She had sent off to the wastepaper collection a pile of newspapers he had been

39

keeping to fill in Allied progress on the Italian campaign map which had become his obsession. Afterwards, Ronnie had apologized and wheeled himself off to the downstairs room he used as his bedroom. She thought of following him to make sure he was not brooding, but she had had to do that so often lately.

She sat in the drawing room and, instead, thought of Jim Kiley. She had been told about the curt phone call that morning. Perhaps he felt badly about how he had snubbed her at the party. If so, he would call again. Yet he had not done so. She knew nothing of his visit, nor of the note he had left. She wanted so much to believe the best of him, that he had not merely used her and dropped her, as Pat had said so cruelly. Wanting and hoping and waiting proved too much for her and tears came, which she could not hold back. She sat alone, crying silently.

The thirty-five-ton B-17s roared off into the dawn sky at thirty second intervals. The collapse of the designated mission commander had left Colonel Krasnowici with no choice and he had had to give in to his Air Exec's long-standing request. In command of the lead squadron, Jim Kiley was in his element again. On the climb to formation altitude, there was only one tricky moment, when Bur-wash's 'Ginger Rogers', leading 888 Squadron, was caught in the downstream of the spiralling Forts above and nearly flipped over, scattering the ships below him. It had taken time to reassemble.

After that, everything had gone like a practice flight, a milk run all the way to Kiel and back. Coming in sight of the English coast again, Jim gave permission for one of the B-17s with stabilization problems to land at the nearest airfield. He had brought them all home.

They were only two minutes from their own field when he heard his co-pilot, Lieutenant Paget, gasp. 'Look there, sir!' Wisps of smoke were streaming back from the Tokyo tank at the end of the starboard wing. Jim cursed under his breath. They hadn't been hit. It could only be spontaneous combustion in the gases left in the tank. He called the radio operator and told him to warn the base to have fire wagons and ambulances ready. The chief danger was from fire spreading down the wing to the main, jelly rubber fuel tanks. On the theory that fire flows upwards, Jim tilted the ship as much as he dared. 'Pilot to crew – pilot to crew! Get ready to jump!'

It came in the next minute, with devastating suddenness. A massive explosion blew the end off the starboard wing and flames spouted out from it. The ship bucked and shuddered as though she would shake herself to pieces. Banking and wrestling with the wheel, Jim somehow managed to level off, to force the controls to obey him. He could never remember the moments of bringing her down and taxi-ing to a halt. All he could remember was getting out of the cockpit after Paget so fast that he nearly landed on top of him. To his amazement he saw the rest of the crew piling out. It said much for their trust in him that they had remained on board.

Within seconds the ship was surrounded by fire wagons and drenched in foam from their hoses. Line Chief McGraw screeched up in his jeep and sat gazing at the six or seven feet blown off the wing. He was followed immediately by Rufus, who marched up to Jim and clapped him on both shoulders. 'You brought that big ass bird in on a wing and a prayer, Jim. By Golliver, I've never seen anything like it!'

'By Golliver, Colonel, sir, neither have I,' McGraw agreed.

That evening Jim went to the Officers' Club for the first time in many weeks. He tended to avoid it, finding his presence made the junior officers awkward. He had a purpose, as well as a need for relaxation. He had had a stupid argument with Red Burwash at debriefing, due entirely to tension. Red could in no way be blamed for the hold-up at assembly.

As he came into the club and looked around, he saw a WAAC lieutenant coming towards him. She was attractive, unmistakably American, her hair a dark red, her figure slim and graceful even in uniform. She paused and smiled, 'Good evening, Major. I believe you are Major Kiley, the Air Executive officer?'

'Yes, I am. And you are—'

'Lieutenant Somers, sir. Lorna Jane Somers.' Her accent was educated Eastern, with Culpeper County overtones.

'A pleasure to meet you, Lieutenant,' Jim said. 'But I don't recall you being here when I left this morning.'

'I wasn't,' she smiled. 'Six of us were attached for duty here. We only arrived today. At the moment, I appear to be acting as hostess. May I get you a drink?'

'Thank you. A scotch . . . on the rocks.'

Wonders will never cease, he thought, watching her return to the bar. She even looked good from the rear. Aware that there were many eyes on him, he headed for Red Burwash who was standing alone by the fire, drinking morosely. Now was the time to make his peace with him.

At the bar, Lorna Jane turned and looked across at the Air Exec. She liked what she saw. She liked it very much.

# FOUR

Nanny had brought cups of tea for Ronnie Dereham and
Vi, who had come to run over with him the work done by
the landgirls on his estate, of whom she was in charge. He
was more than satisfied. She had started the spring barley
drilling and begun to undersow some of the lower fields
with clover and ryegrass to be made later into hay. He was
so pleased with her that it was with a sense of shock that
he heard her explain that she would be able to carry on for
only a few weeks more herself, as she would then be nearly
five months pregnant. 'I'm hoping that by then Chuck will
be back from America,' she told him. 'He's applied to
rejoin the Bomb Group.'

'You could at least keep on with the paperwork for a
while longer,' Ronnie suggested.

'Well, if you'd like me to, Major,' Vi said. 'If it would be
a help.'

When she had gone, Ronnie sat motionless. A help? She
was the only one he had thought he could totally depend
on. Helen, of course, but she had her medical work. They
could no longer be man and wife, in the full sense, since he
was crippled. Pat was at Cambridge, wrapped up in her
own interests. And Nanny was so old, half the time she
seemed to live in a world of her own. There was no one
now – not even Vi. Vi had been like another daughter, a
right arm to him. How could she—?

He drew himself up in his wheelchair. He was grateful
there was no such thing as telepathy. The idea of anyone
eavesdropping on his self pity was sickening. He had
become a useless creature. No, that was more of it. He was
appalled to realize how sorry for himself he had become.
He could not even rejoice with Vi at her news. He must of
late have been dreadful company for Helen. It was

43

something he would have to watch or he would drive her away. Something which even her passing infatuation with the American major had not done.

How could he even consider such things rationally, he wondered. That his wife could be drawn to another man would have been unthinkable only a year ago. That he would accept it, even give an appearance of condoning it, impossible. Everything in his background and upbringing revolted at the idea.

There had been Derehams at Market Wetherby since one ancestor had followed Henry Tudor into exile and returned to fight in his bodyguard at Bosworth Field. After the victory, Ranulf Dereham was granted the manor of Wetherby and built the original house, much of which could still be seen in the hall and west wing. Derehams had served sovereign and country faithfully ever after, some as obscure country gentlemen and magistrates, some as Members of Parliament, some as lawyers and churchmen and many as soldiers.

The early 'twenties had been the happiest time for him, serving as a junior officer in a crack cavalry regiment, meeting Helen, the beautiful, capable daughter of a good academic family. She was a medical student then, dedicated, and had only agreed to marry him on condition that she was allowed to complete her degree and to practise for a few years. That had not been easy and caused some raised eyebrows in the Mess, but it had all worked out very well and few of his friends, meeting Helen, could help but feel envious. Pat's unexpected arrival had interrupted her career for a year or two, but she had taken it up again. Even when his brother Edward died and he had resigned reluctantly from the army to manage Dereham House and the estate which he had inherited, Helen continued to work part time at the local cottage hospital. He welcomed it, as knitting them more closely to the community. Neither of them would have been content merely to be squire and lady of the manor without contributing anything. On the declaration of war, he had rejoined his regiment, now transferred to tanks, and Helen had taken a full-time post to release one of the registrars for the Services.

The war had changed everything, as it had done for so many others. Their life had been cosy, its course placid and predictable, but the bustle, the coping with shortages and discomfort, the extraordinary energy and feeling of determination which seemed to uplift the whole country, rejuvenated them. It was particularly noticeable in Helen. She was tireless, as vividly alive as she had been when he first met her. He had to admit that their private life had become a little stagnant, that physical intimacy between them had grown infrequent, had lost its urgency. He loved her deeply, as he believed she loved him. As she still loved him. Yet it had become a relationship based on understanding, mutual affection, shared friendships and memories. After Dunkirk, on the occasions when he was home on leave, their marriage had been revitalized and they had responded to each other with an eagerness they both realized had been missing for several years.

It had been a wrench when he was posted to North Africa and, all through that campaign, with the Seventh Armoured Brigade drawing nearer to Tunis, he had thought of her more and more, of how lucky he was to have her and how close they had come to drifting into premature middle age. At times he was almost grateful to the war. The direct hit on his tank which wiped out his crew had left him paralysed from the waist down. He still suffered from bouts of pain, but the deepest hurt was the knowledge that that new lease of life had been snatched away from them.

He had been an active man. To be crippled was hard enough to take on its own. After his return home, he had been so wrapped up in himself, in his own suffering and sense of loss, that at first he had not noticed the change in Helen. She had been as loving and as caring as he had known she would be, yet there was a reserve in her, hesitancies, occasional distraction, unexplained absences. She was, of course, very hard worked at the hospital, with

45

long and erratic hours. That explained it. It was their daughter Pat who had first made him aware of Helen's involvement with the American major, Kiley.

If he had been able to bring it out into the open, if they had been one of those couples who could talk about such things freely, it might have been better, but the restraints and social conventions of their time and upbringing prevented it.

Afterwards, when he felt stronger and more able to face it, it was too late. He had sensed how much Helen herself was suffering. He knew that whatever it was that had drawn her to Kiley was no simple infatuation. It was totally against her nature to have a casual affair. He had met and liked Jim Kiley, an honourable, decent man, who might have become a friend. It was a difficult situation for all of them. Ronnie had schooled himself to say nothing. He would not reprove or tax Helen with it. Certainly, he would not plead with her.

She had to work it out on her own, in her own time. Perhaps it was cowardly, yet he knew instinctively that if he tried to force her to a decision he would lose her. Left to herself, she would never desert her duty and her obligations.

As weeks went by, however, he had become increasingly conscious of the strain in her and almost longed for her to talk about it. He wished there was some way he could comfort her, but his own need for her was too great, and his pride held him back. Then one night, Pat went to the Base, without even understanding the situation fully, to beg Kiley to stop seeing her mother. When she broke down, Kiley had brought her home and the two men came face to face at last.

To his own surprise, Ronnie had heard himself say that he would give Helen her freedom, if that was what she wanted, that he would not stand between them. All that was important to him was her happiness. What happened next, he could never forget. Kiley had looked at him in silence for a long moment, then said quietly, 'Okay, you win.' He loved Helen, but he would stop meeting her. On condition that Ronnie never told her of this conversation.

When Jim Kiley left, Ronnie did not feel elated, but more wretched than ever. Unconsciously, he had exploited his injury, his defencelessness, and the younger man had taken pity on him. Since then, Kiley had kept his word and only seen Helen in passing, on official business. What reason he had given her, pressure of work, guilt at the relationship, Ronnie did not know, but he had been aware of Helen's hurt and her unhappiness at the abrupt ending. Only time could heal it. Only time could tell what would happen. He longed for the war to be over. And the Americans to go home.

Since her arrival on the Base, Lorna Jane Somers had had no lack of proposals. To be more exact, propositions. It was something she had become used to in the past six months. She was more than pretty, with the kind of lithe figure that looked sensational in a close-fitting uniform. To be one of only six females on a Base containing nearly two thousand men was something for which many of her girlfriends back home would give their proverbial right arm. Or anything else that might reasonably be asked of them.

Each day as she sidestepped advances and, at night, as she got into her cot bed in the female officers' quarters, the approach to them strictly guarded by white-helmeted MPs, she asked herself why she was dumb enough to be interested in only one man out of the two thousand. And him the most inaccessible. There just seemed to be no practical means of bringing herself to the attention of the Air Exec. She might as well be merely another piece of equipment for all the notice he took of her. Except that he probably thought any piece of equipment of more value to his precious Group than a female junior lieutenant.

It had taken her several evenings at the Club, many hours of listening to interminable flying talk, dirty stories and pre-war life histories, a couple of dozen requests for dates, from the shy and hesitant to the direct how's about it, arms draped nonchalantly around her shoulders and fingers surreptitiously tweaking her butt, to learn that Jim Kiley was not one to socialize. That first evening when he had come to the Officers' Club had been the exception. He seemed to take most of his meals in his office. If he had a drink, it was in his own quarters. 'He's a machine,' she was told. 'Never stops working. He lives, breathes, eats and dreams B-17s. Under that flying suit, there is no heart. There's a tachometer.'

She saw him at briefings, on the platform, dynamic and incisive. She saw him on inspections with the Colonel. He was polite and considerate, always asked her how she was fitting in. Then he was gone just after she'd said fine. She saw him counting in the returning planes, or deep in conversation with McGraw and the crew chiefs. She saw him on parade at the CO's shoulder. She never saw him alone, unless it was to salute as he shot past her in his jeep, heading for the hardstands or the technical site.

She was with her boss one day, the captain in charge of the administrative side of Operations. A dumpy, bespectacled man, a lawyer in civilian life, he looked up from the telephone and called for his corporal clerk, but the man was not at his desk. 'What am I gonna do?' he complained. 'The Air Exec wants these reports right away.'

Lorna Jane thought swiftly. 'I'll run them over,' she volunteered.

'Thanks for the offer,' the captain said. 'But it's okay. I'll get one of the orderlies.' He was jiggling the telephone receiver.

'No trouble,' Lorna Jane told him. 'I could do with the exercise.' She rose and took the reports.

'Well, if you're sure.' She put on her cap, smiled to him and left before he could change his mind. What did I do? he wondered. She looked as happy as if I'd just given her a box of chocolates.

Lorna Jane came out of the operations block and slipped the folder with the reports into the basket above the rear wheel of her bicycle. Bicycles almost had to be nailed down on the Base to prevent them being stolen, but not hers. Because of the distances most personnel had to cover they were in great demand, and in short supply, yet all the WAAC officers had been provided with them immediately. Lorna Jane thought it was a charming gesture, until she realized they were not ladies' bicycles. The bar between seat and handlebars meant that tight skirts had to be hitched well up to mount. It took considerable practice to manage it with any degree of modesty and fast pedalling tended to disclose a fair amount of nylon-clad knee. She sometimes wondered if it came under the heading of conduct prejudicial to good order and discipline. It was probably good for morale.

Reaching headquarters, she hurried along the corridor, pausing to straighten her tunic and cap before going into the outer office. The orderly sergeant offered to take the reports in for her, but she told him she must hand them to the Air Exec personally.

Jim had not been unaware of Lorna Jane. He noticed her and her fellow WAACs as he moved about the Base. They certainly brightened the place up, apart from providing endless speculation as to their availability or otherwise. Lorna Jane was the pick of the bunch.

He watched her as she brought the folder to his desk. She was undeniably attractive, with a cool presence, a hint of challenge. He could imagine some of the younger men falling hard for her.

'You wanted the Mission Strike Reports, sir,' she said.

'Ah, yes. Thank you, Lieutenant.'

She hesitated, as she turned away. He was looking at her, frowning slightly. 'Was there something else, sir?'

'Matter of fact, yes. There was something I wanted to ask you.' He paused. 'What's a nice girl like you doing in a joint like this?'

She was thrown only for a second. 'Just got lucky, I guess,' she said, with a hint of a smile. Jim laughed, surprising himself. It was the first time he had laughed so easily in months.

Vera was delighted that Albert had decided to come with her. He had never walked the baby with her before. Although he looked self-conscious and refused to push their grand-daughter's pram, at least he was here. It reminded her of years before when they used to stroll out with the twins, Letty and Peter, each with a separate pram. How proud she had been.

The weather was brighter, though still cold, as they walked slowly round the pond. Mundy cleared his throat. 'I wanted to get out of the house, Vera, because we can't talk there. Customers are always dropping in, and Letty might overhear us.'

'Why shouldn't she?'

'Because it's her we have to talk about, woman!' Mundy had raised his voice and, after glancing round, lowered it again to a more confidential level. 'What are we going to do about her? She's turning into a proper little tart.'

Vera stopped, shocked. 'Albert!'

'Well, what else would you call her?'

'She flirts a bit—'

'Flirts? She flirts? I wish I was sure that's all it was.' An elderly couple, occasional customers, were passing and Mundy raised his hat to them, ingratiatingly.

'How can you even think such a thing?' Vera whispered.

'That's a really intelligent question, and you pushin' that pram!'

'Albert . . . that was the lesson she had to learn, a hard one. That and the boy she loved bein' killed. She'll be much more careful now.' He snorted. 'I'm certain of it. She's your daughter.'

'What's that supposed to mean?' Mundy demanded. 'We all know which side of the family she gets – well, be that as it may. I've tried everything with her – advice, threats, sympathy. I thought the baby, at least, might settle her down.'

50

'She's its mother,' Vera said, inconsequentially.

'You tell her that! Keep reminding her. Most of the time she acts like she's trying to pretend it isn't there!'

'That's nonsense. She's just taking a little while to adjust to it. We'll have to trust her.'

'I suppose so,' Mundy conceded reluctantly. 'It's either that or lock her in her room. She doesn't listen to a word I say any more.'

At that moment Letty Mundy was in the back of a saloon car parked off the Ipswich road. She had been making love to Sergeant Patsy Petrillo and panted as he eased away from her. Patsy was useful to know. Through the Quartermaster company he had access to all sorts of things that were almost unobtainable, lipsticks, silk stockings, perfume. Already Letty was checking through what he had brought her. 'You sure that ain't all you're interested in, doll?' he asked.

Letty pecked his cheek. 'You know I like you, Patsy.' His hand moved on her stocking top. She flicked it away and wriggled her tight dress down. 'My Dad'll kill me, if I'm out this afternoon and again tonight.'

'I can't think how you stand the old lunk,' Patsy said.

'It's not so bad,' Letty smiled. 'Not now I know his bark's worse than 'is bite.'

They moved round into the front seats. He switched on the ignition and paused. 'We had a date for tonight. Well, I'm sorry, doll, but I can't make it. I got some important business. The point is, there's this pal of mine, Moe Rosen – you met him. Well, he's kinda keen to stand in for me.'

Letty thought about it. Moe was a good bit older than Patsy, going bald, but he played drums in the Base jazz combo, one of its stars. And he was good fun. 'Why not?' she shrugged.

'Right.' Patsy let in the clutch. 'I'll tell him. And he's a generous guy, too. Know what I mean?'

Jim had fallen into the habit of having an occasional drink

with Lorna Jane in the Officers' Club. She was now permanently attached to Administration S-3. He found himself wishing she had been attached to Headquarters, instead. Daughter of a country judge, she had been to the best schools. She was bright and civilized and amusing, the kind of girl he used to meet at weekend parties before the war in Newport or in summer on Nantucket. She spoke his language. Sometimes they ate together in the mess. It was pleasant and harmless and he was amused to see how skilfully she fended off the frequent attempts by junior officers to strike up more personal relationships.

He was not surprised that Rufus sometimes joined them for a drink. The Colonel had nothing against pretty knees. Yet Jim had been disturbed at one of the flying officers' parties, when Rufus had watched her dance past with Harry Paget and remarked, 'That's what I call a fine girl, Jim. I'm glad you're getting on so well together. Same social background and all, just the ticket. Take care you don't let one of these young bucks cut you out.' He hoped that Rufus hadn't mistaken his liking for Lorna for something else. Even more, he hoped that she hadn't.

Because he was with her at the end of the party, he offered to drive her back to her quarters. The drive was silent. He was preoccupied with the ceaseless problem of where to find replacement ships and crews for the coming major offensives. When he saw her to her door, she said, 'You've been very quiet.'

'Things on my mind,' he smiled.

She misunderstood. 'It might just work. I'm not an artificial flower. I don't break when I'm squeezed.'

It would have been both boorish and insulting not to kiss her. She was warm, and softer than he had imagined, the kiss more intense than he had meant. 'I'm sorry,' he said.

Her hands were still on his shoulders. 'Don't you give me all that stuff about you being so much older and me being only a lieutenant, Major. That's a lot of crud.'

'Where did you pick up language like that?'

'In the Air Force.' Her smile matched his and they kissed again, more lingeringly.

They did not progress beyond a kiss now and then, but an intimacy had been set up between them and Jim could not deny that he always looked forward to being with her.

Vi was helping out her father in the pub, since Rosie had the evening off. 'Is she often here?' she asked him.

Jack knew she meant Letty, who was sitting in the far corner with a balding sergeant. 'More often than I'd like,' Jack said, troubled. 'But as long as she behaves herself.'

Letty was laughing, pulling up the sergeant's hands from under the table and setting them down on top of it. It was obvious what was going on and Vi hoped her father did not notice.

There was laughter from the opposite corner, too, where Rosie sat with Elmer and Hymie. For once she had brought another girl along, Jilly Binns, her friend from the parachute factory, a short, round girl with frizzy, fair hair. The best thing about her was her smile. The girls were enjoying themselves, but Elmer and Hymie resented having a third party upset the balance of their longstanding threesome. Jack had just received a small consignment of gin and both men offered to fetch refills.

As they crossed to the bar, Hymie said, 'Why don't you take Jilly off somewhere?'

'Why don't you?' Elmer countered.

'Not my type. As a broad, she's a little too broad. More your size.'

'Watch it,' Elmer warned. They ordered four pink gins and looked back at their table. Elmer let his annoyance show. 'Why'd we have to get stuck with a cluck like that?'

'Oh, I dunno,' Hymie decided. 'She's got a nice smile.' When they rejoined the girls, in a sudden outburst of gallantry he concentrated on Jilly for ten minutes. To his surprised delight, he discovered that she understood when he was joking, which not everyone did, and laughed at the right time. Rosie was piqued at losing his attention and worked to get it back, which she did without too much trouble. At the same time, she let Elmer hold her hand, although she did not return his meaningful pressures. He was left puzzled, but hopeful.

It was two days later that Jim Kiley went to the cottage hospital. He could not put off visiting wounded aircrew any longer, but he left it until almost the close of the official visiting hours, when he was pretty certain Helen would have gone home. In the event, he ran straight into her the moment he came out of the last ward. She was leaving her office, pulling on her coat, and stopped dead, seeing him.

She felt a momentary rush of panic. 'I wasn't told you were here,' she said.

'I didn't—' he began. 'I mean, I assumed you'd be at home by now.'

'No, I was writing up my reports.'

Jim nodded. It was difficult for them to talk. The last visitors were leaving, nurses passing. 'I rang you,' he said.

'Yes.'

'And that day I dropped by, I was sorry I missed you.'

'When was that?'

'Couple of weeks ago. I left you a note.' He could tell that she did not know what he was talking about. 'Didn't you get it? I wanted to – that party, I was afraid maybe you didn't understand why I stayed away from you. Not because I wanted to. I thought it best for both of us.'

Helen's mind was spinning. She had got used to the thought that he was out of her life, that he had chosen to be. She had resigned herself, come to terms with it. She would devote herself to her work, to Ronnie, to ensure that the rest of his life was as normal and as meaningful as his condition would allow. Her own feelings did not come into it, the decision easier to take with the thought, however hurtful, that Jim was making a deliberate attempt to forget her. But if that wasn't so – a note, he'd said. She had received nothing from him. She was confused, and she could see the consultant physician making for her. Jim was looking at her, concerned. Sending men off to die day after day, he had schooled his expression to give nothing away, but she had learned to read behind the surface. Realizing that he was troubled, anxious to heal the breach between them, all her need for him swept back. Yet she felt hideously vulnerable. Knowing how *he* really felt would make it easier to go on. But she had to be certain. 'We should meet,' she said.

'I guess so,' Jim agreed quickly. His mouth twisted. 'Only I don't know when. We've a big campaign coming up, the biggest so far. It could be weeks before I had more than a few minutes free – and that wouldn't be enough.'

Dr Heywood reached them, a pleasant, slightly stooping man. 'Good evening, Major. You're quite a stranger.'

Jim glanced at Helen. 'Yes, I've been kind of busy.'

Heywood chuckled. 'I imagine so.' He turned to Helen. 'If you can spare the time, I'd like to run over the notes on that suspected renal failure with you.'

'Yes, of course,' Helen said, calmly. Like Jim, she had schooled herself.

Jim touched his hand to his cap. 'Well, if you'll excuse me, Dr Dereham, I'll have to be running along. Perhaps one day we can have a longer chat.'

'That would be nice, Major Kiley,' Helen said. She made herself smile politely and watched him walk down the corridor and go out through the swing doors, shoulders square, one hand in the pocket of his trench coat. As always, she looked cool and poised, but she did not hear one word of what Heywood was saying to her.

# FIVE

The noise in De-briefing was nearly deafening. The long, low hut was filled with small tables, one for each of the B-17s in the Group, an officer at each table taking down the crew members' reports on the mission they had just completed. More aircrews were still arriving, still in flying gear, shouting, waving to their friends. Some were exhausted, some had minor wounds covered by dressings, but all had to make their reports while the details were still clear in their minds.

'An ME 109 – I got him! I know I got him!' Elmer Jones was laughing, while Hymie clapped him on the back.

'It'll have to be confirmed,' the de-briefing officer said. Hymie Stutz stuck up two fingers, which the officer ignored.

Jim Kiley walked round slowly from table to table with Colonel Krasnowici. Behind them was the Group Medical Officer. Pausing every now and then to ask a question, Jim and the CO came to a table where there were only four men. The young pilot sat holding himself in tightly to stop himself shaking. His head was bandaged. He had lost six of his crew.

'What happened, son?' Rufus Krasnowici asked gently.

'We were hit on the way out, sir. It slowed us up some, but we managed to reach the IP and drop our bombs. Then on the way back, we just couldn't keep up. We-we lost contact with the Group and that's-that's when four German fighters found us. They kept coming at us, playing with us – like it was target practice.' Rufus grunted. 'They kept shooting bits out of us – picking off my guys . . . If we hadn't run into cloud . . .' He was shivering.

Rufus glanced at the MO, who nodded. 'All right, son,' Rufus said and touched the young pilot's shoulder. 'Get along to the sick bay. We'll hear the full report when you've had that head seen to.'

The crew of 'Ginger Rogers II' straggled into their quarters. Hymie flopped out on his bed. Elmer plumped down on the end of his and began to unfasten the RAF flying boots he wore in preference to the shorter US issue. He paused. 'Hey, Hymie, I just remembered. We promised to take Rosie to the movies tonight.'

'Movies?' Hymie muttered, his eyes closed. 'Yeah, I could do with some excitement for a change . . .'

Elmer finished taking off his boots. 'Well, we promised. I mean, if you don't wanna go – if you're too bushed – I mean, I don't mind goin' on my own. What do you say, Hymie? Hymie?' Hymie was fast asleep and Elmer felt the stirring of a crazy elation. For once, he could have Rosie all to himself.

Vi helped Sally Bilton put Betty and William to bed, then read them a story. When she came back down the narrow cottage stairs, Sally was ironing the pile of fatigues she laundered every few days for McGraw's engineering groundcrews. 'Thanks, Vi,' Sally said.

Vi smiled. 'I have to get used to it.' At five and a half months, her pregnancy was noticeable. 'Can I give you a hand with these?'

'No, I'll just finish this one, then I'll put a kettle on.' Sally watched Vi settle into a chair by the fire. Approaching motherhood had brought a new softness to the girl, a gentler prettiness. 'You given up work altogether now?'

'More or less,' Vi said. 'Oh, I help Major Dereham with the paperwork at the farm, stock lists, things like that, but no heavy work. I'm not sorry to miss the hoeing.'

'Not in this weather,' Sally agreed. 'How is the Major?'

'Fine,' Vi said. She thought about it. 'Well, not really. He's changed. He used to be such a – such a splendid man.'

'Being paralysed like that must be terrible.'

57

'Specially for someone like him. He broods a lot. His wife, Mrs Dereham, she's wonderful with him – patient, understanding. If it wasn't for her, I don't know what he'd – Damn the war!'

To change the subject Sally asked, 'How's your father taken to the idea of the baby?'

'Oh, he's over the moon about it,' Vi smiled. 'I'm not sure about Rosie, though. In one way, she's excited about it. But she's not so sure that she'll like being called "Aunt Rosie".'

'Aunt Rosie . . .' Sally laughed.

Rosie was sitting next to Elmer at the back of the Roxie cinema. The film was Hope and Crosby in *Road to Morocco* and she let him put his arm round her, after he whispered that she looked exactly like Dorothy Lamour. She even let him kiss her, while Bing sang 'Moonlight Becomes You.' He had almost forgotten how sweet she could be. She snuggled against him when he told her he loved her. And when he said afterwards, 'I know I'm not much and I can't expect you to commit yourself, but just as long as I can hope, Rosie,' she smiled. He had never felt so close to her.

Letty Mundy woke before dawn. It was a habit she couldn't break herself of, lying listening to the planes to take off. Always the first thing she thought of was Harvey, handsome and smiling. How different everything would be, if he hadn't been killed . . . She had known him only for such a short time. She had known many men in the last two or three months. Some of them, she couldn't even remember their names. But she could never forget him.

As she lit one of the American cigarettes she kept under her pillow, she heard Vicky cry out from her cot in Peter's old room. She froze in case her father called to her to get up and see to her, as he sometimes did. If he smelt the cigarette smoke, it would only mean another shouting match, but there was silence. The cry wasn't repeated.

58

She hated this house. She almost resented Peter for being in the army. At least he had got away, away from Dad's rages and his 'you behave yourself, my girl', and his cruddy little shop. Away from the baby . . . You were supposed to love them, but she wasn't going to give up the rest of her life for it. It was a dead weight round her neck.

She listened. It would be any minute now.

The engines of the B-17s were warming up, the sound of the Wright Cyclones earsplitting. The flare signalled take-off and the first of the Flying Fortresses, made sluggish by its bombload, went rumbling down the taxiway.

Circling 'Ginger Rogers II' up to the assembly point, Red Burwash marvelled for the hundredth time at how ungainly the B-17 was on the deck, and how graceful and manoeuvrable she was in the air. And nothing that had ever been designed to fly was so dependable. It was crazy to talk about them as if they were women. He wondered briefly if Elmer and Hymie were still not speaking to each other. How could two friends fall out so often over the same dame?

From his radio compartment, Kulik peered round the bulkhead and grinned, watching Elmer Jones check out his fifty-calibre waist gun. Near Elmer, Hymie Stutz pointedly ignored him as he cranked his ball turret round until the door in the floor of the airplane could be opened. Two nights ago, when Elmer had returned from his solo date with Rosie, Hymie had leapt at him, shouting 'Rat fink! Rat fink!' They had fallen to the floor, kneeing and punching, until they had been pulled apart. Since then they had not spoken to each other.

Hymie replaced the crank handle in its clip, hooked on his oxygen mask and climbed down into his turret, a partly glass bowl suspended under the Fort's belly. Here he was in a world of his own, just him and two Point Fifty machine guns. There was only room for him to squat, his back against the metal door, his feet on two rests, one on either side of the glass panel through which he could see the rest

59

of the Group climbing up to join them. As he plugged in his electrically-heated suit and waited for Red to give him the order to test his guns, he thought about Elmer. It wasn't so much that he minded his being alone with Rosie, it was the sneaky way it was done. Threesomes weren't too much fun, anyway. He wondered, if he'd been there, if Rosie would have brought her friend Jilly along. He didn't mind Jilly. In fact, he kinda liked her.

Jim Kiley was envious of Rufus leading the mission. He sat in his office, studying the operational details. By now the 525th would be over the Channel, joining up with the other Groups and the whole formation setting course for the target, the factories at Schweinfurt. How many times had they tried to knock them out? The first attempt had been a disaster, one entire Group wiped out, 166 bombers lost in only six missions. How would it go today?

There was a knock and the door opened. Lorna came in and saluted. 'Lieutenant Somers reporting, sir.'

'For what, Lieutenant?'

She smiled, 'Whatever you have in mind.'

Jim considered her. 'How about a cup of coffee?'

A pot was stewing on the stove. She filled two mugs, brought him his and perched on a corner of the desk. 'I'll get up if anyone comes in.'

'You'd better.' He smiled. 'You're looking very well today.'

'Thank you, Major. I have reason. I've just been told I can have a six day pass.'

'Hey, that's good!' Jim said. 'They're like gold. What are you going to do?'

'Some sightseeing, I guess. London or wherever. I was wondering, just wondering,' she said carefully, 'if maybe you could fix a pass, too, Jim. I'll need someone to show me around.' He was silent, surprised. 'Cat got your tongue?'

Jim couldn't think what to say. He could not simply brush it aside. It was a serious proposition, and one it must have cost her an effort to make. While he thought, the telephone rang. He picked it up and everything else was pushed into second place. 'They're over the enemy coast. Weather conditions are favourable. No recall.'

The anti-aircraft batteries had opened up the minute they reached the coastal defences. Red felt the ship rock as bursts came close. There was an occasional spatter of shrapnel fragments along the fuselage. After a few minutes he thought they had won clear, then there was an almighty crash and 'Ginger Rogers' heaved as a flak shell exploded just below her. She was dancing like her namesake and Red had to fight to bring her under control. A small fire broke out amidships, but it was doused immediately. Red touched his throat mike. 'Pilot to ball turret – you okay, Hymie?'

Hymie's voice was hoarse. 'Okay, Skip.'

'What's the damage down there?'

Gyrating his glass globe, Hymie checked. 'Coupla holes through the left elevator – maybe a dozen round the bomb bay doors and the landing-gear.' He breathed out. And one helluva lucky ball gunner. Hanging down here in his goldfish bowl, he felt naked when flak came.

The bomb bay doors were tested. There was no loss of speed and the Fortress flew on.

Red had been to Schweinfurt before and knew what to expect. It was one of the most heavily defended areas in Germany, ringed like a porcupine with gun batteries. His memory did not let him down. Two hours later as they began their bomb run, the skies erupted around them, black with flak, so thick – as Mario used to say – you could get out and walk on it.

Four ships of the ninety plane formation were down already. Another plunged past them in flames. In the cockpit of 'Ginger Rogers', Red concentrated on holding steady on course, watching the bombardier ahead of him in the nose. The moment the lead B-17 released her bombs, the bombardier pulled his toggle switch and 'Ginger' lifted with the sudden lightness as her own bombs fell away. On the ground below there was devastation. The strike had been good to excellent and the formation swung for home, leaving the flak behind.

Red had lost one of his squadron and 'Ginger Rogers' had sustained more damage, a jagged rent torn in her right stabilizer and more holes through the hull, some big enough to stick your head through. The second waist gunner had had three fingers severed and the navigator's cheek had been sliced open.

'Pilot to crew – keep your eyes peeled.' There had been no sign of German fighters on the way out. They were becoming more cautious, fewer in number, but Red knew they were around somewhere. He was grateful for their escort of Mustangs.

The attack came as they crossed the Belgian coast. A wave of FW 190s dived at the formation head on, where its firepower was least, streaking through the protective screen of Mustangs. Slugs tore apart the top turret on 'Ginger Rogers', killing the flight engineer outright. Another two ships went down. Links from the ammunition belts showered round Hymie's feet as his guns blazed. Above him, Elmer's gun chattered in unison as he followed the Focke-Wulfs.

The attack was over in seconds, but after a few minutes the raiders came again. This time, however, the US fighters were ready for them and few of the FWs got through. The formation ploughed on towards the English coast. The hardest thing in the world was to sit tight and maintain position in the Group with enemy fighters diving straight for you. But it was the only way for a bomber formation to survive. Red was glad it was over.

For about the millionth time Red wondered if he would not be happier flying fighters, with Zemke's Wolf Pack or the Fourth Group at Debden, say. These were the crack units with tallies of hundreds of enemy aircraft shot down. He had been on the point of resigning his brand new commission in the Air Corps and crossing over into Canada to volunteer for the Eagle Squadron, the US pilots who flew Spitfires with the RAF, when the Japs had struck Pearl Harbor. Suddenly the war was no longer an abstract affair of Fascism v. Democracy, but a fight for survival. After Pearl, there was no room for individual preference. The first priority was to build up American air capacity, to fight a war on two fronts, against Japan in the Pacific and Germany in Europe, where reinforcements were urgently needed by Great Britain, which had fought alone for two years.

Experienced pilots were rushed into the newly created Bomb Groups and flew their own ships over to England, while thousands of young men were being trained at every available US base to follow them. As he took off from Arizona, Red had joined in the Air Corps' song with his crew, 'Off we go into the wide blue yonder . . .' He had sung louder than any, for there had been a real possibility that he might be posted as an instructor. And more than anything, Red had wanted to get to Europe, to fly his ship in the same skies his father had flown through in 1917 as wingman to Eddie Rickenbacker.

He was glad he had been put on B-17s. The Flying Fortress was a hell of a plane. He could have struck out and been on B-24s, Liberators. Their jockeys swore by them, but to all Fortress crews Liberators were nothing but banana boats. They had the edge on the Fort for speed, but at anything above 20,000 feet they were tricky to handle, real bitches. The extra 5,000 feet of altitude you got in a Fort was a genuine comfort, when the Krauts were throwing heavy flak up at you.

Bombers were sitting ducks. It was one big lottery, whether the flak hit you or not, whether it whistled past or tore a slice out of the fuselage or blew you to kingdom come. Sometimes in the night he woke up, sweating, hearing the crump of it burst all round him, holding on to the bed as if it rocked and jolted. He had been once to a Flak House for a week's rest and recuperation, but all the guys round him had been so jumpy it was like a nut house.

63

He signed out on the Wednesday and spent the next three days dead drunk. Where he had been or what he had done, he still couldn't remember. He had woken up in some dame's bed in a back street in Norwich. Not bad looking, but a total stranger. She complained he had never even touched her. She had touched him, all right. Not a penny left in his pants pocket. He had to hitch a ride back to Market Wetherby. At least he didn't have a souvenir like so many guys brought back with them, a nice little dose of the clap.

It was time for him to take over from his co-pilot again. On missions they flew fifteen minute stretches.

On a visit to Seventy-Eighth Fighter Group at Duxford, he had been allowed a trial flight in a T-bolt, the P-47 Thunderbolt. What a gas that was . . . He'd felt like a king with all that speed and mobility at his command. There was never a time when bandits hit the formation, seeing Focke-Wulfs or Messerschmitts dive past him, that he did not long to take off after them in a T-bolt, or one of the new Mustangs which were even faster, six ·50 calibre machine guns at his fingertips. Just him, one to one against Hitler's flyboys. No responsibilities to anyone but himself, gambling solely on his own skill and reflexes. He'd like that.

Not that he'd trade 'Ginger Rogers' for anything else ever designed to fly. There was no other Fort to compare with her, and that meant she was the cream of the cream. Just as his crew was the best in the Group. Great guys, every one of them. He tried not to think about Deke, the flight engineer, whose riddled body was propping open the door of the radio compartment. He'd been Chuck's replacement and they couldn't have asked for better, a quiet, cheerful guy, with a little wife waiting for him back in Detroit. Red would have to write to her. As skipper and squadron commander. Of all the jobs that fell to him, these letters were the worst. He only hoped they did some good. Each one tore a part out of him. He would think about it when they were safely on the deck, get it over with. Then have a drink for Deke. And forget about him. For now, he had to get this baby home.

He frowned. He was so sensitive to 'Ginger's' controls, she was almost an extension of him. And there was something wrong. Something about the way she handled. He had used up more gas than he'd thought. Most likely the main tank had been punctured. That last fighter attack hadn't done her any good. Not at all.

'Pilot to all sections, give me a visual check,' he said on the intercom. His sixth sense was jangling like a fire alarm.

When she had been hit, No. 2 engine had been knocked out and Red could see oil spreading over the wing. Another section of the right stabilizer had broken away. All at once, without warning, she went into a steep dive, her wings vibrating with the speed.

In his ball turret, Hymie's mouth opened in a silent scream. The water had seemed so far away and now he was hurtling towards it. 'Pull her up, Skip! Pull her up!' he was praying. Like a miracle, at less than a thousand feet she began to level out. It was a near run thing. She skimmed the surface and the ball turret actually bounced on one of the waves, before Red could start to coax her up again.

There was a fuel leak and he was running out of flying time. Above him the Groups were peeling off to head for their own fields. He contacted the 525th's lead plane and got permission from the colonel to put down wherever he could.

The shock came when he discovered his landing-gear was jammed, probably by the first flak barrage. He would have to bring her down on her belly and he had a swift vision of the ball turret. 'Better get outa there, Hymie,' he suggested.

'On my way, Skip,' Hymie called back, gratefully. He swivelled his turret into alignment with the hatch and unclipped his safety belt. When he tried to operate the hatch, however, he found it had jammed – just like the landing-gear. Fighting down panic, Hymie reported it.

The hatch would have to be cranked open from above. The flight engineer was dead, but Elmer had seen Hymie do it often enough.

The full danger of Hymie's position became clear when it was realized that the crank handle and other tools which might have substituted had been blown out through the fuselage. The ball turret could not be released, could not even be jettisoned into the sea. Hymie was trapped.

Hymie sat hunched in his glass prison. He knew Red had no choice. To save the ship and the rest of the crew, he had to land as soon as possible. He could see the English coast approaching, and shivered. It had always been a moment to watch out for, the white cliffs ahead. To feel he was nearly home and dry. But not this time. He had been ready to die in combat, but to be squashed like a bug in a bottle . . .

Red was shocked out of his habitual nonchalance. His co-pilot and navigator were silent, watching him, waiting for him to perform a miracle. Like the rest of the crew all over the ship were waiting. He was the skipper. The choices ahead of him were few, and he liked none of them. In less than ten minutes, he would have to set her down. It would be like murder.

In the event, the decision was taken out of his hands. He had left his R/T switched on and Rufus had heard everything. He wasted no time and Red looked up to see the lead plane circling back to find him. Rufus was depending on Red's flying skill to hold his course and speed steady. Matching his speed exactly, Rufus stationed himself directly above him, easing forward until their cockpits overlapped. A crank handle was lowered on a cord and angled until the bombardier could catch it from the hole where 'Ginger Rogers'' top turret had been. He untied it and took it straight to Elmer.

The ball turret hung from a gimbal fixed by a wide tube to the aircraft's ceiling. Elmer was sweating. He wiped his hands and turned the elevation clutches to hand operation and slotted the crank into the manual shaft. Although time was running out, he forced himself to work carefully. With the bombardier releasing the brake, he rotated the turret until it was in position for the escape door to be unfastened.

Hymie was trying to keep calm, listening to Red's quite voice telling him what was being done. He controlled the trembling of his hands and took off his Mae West. If the escape hatch could be opened, he did not want to get stuck. He could see the Colonel's ship off to the side and the crewmen in it, watching. He had a crazy impulse to wave to them. Instead, he had to stop himself from screaming at Elmer when the turret at last began to inch round. Then he heard Red's voice again. 'Okay, try the escape door now.' Mercifully, it was not jammed as he had feared. His knees were like jelly when he was hauled out and Elmer and the bombardier had to support him while they hugged him.

His relief was short-lived. Hearing the shouts to brace themselves, Elmer dragged him forward to crouch with their backs against the radio compartment's bulkhead. In the few minutes left, they took off their flak jackets and sat on them to have a little more protection between them and the approaching ground.

'Ginger Rogers' was coming in low over the coast, making for the nearest airfield, RAF Keating. Two of her remaining engines were feathering and a third cut out just as Red caught sight of the field. It had been cleared and he had a glimpse of fire trucks and meat wagons lined up along the runway. Then they were down, skimming the tarmac. The runway looked much shorter suddenly and he let her belly touch the ground. There was a sickening crunch and jolt as she made contact and he thought he had blown it.

She skittered and swivelled along at 120 miles an hour, but he held her steady until the last moment when she swerved abruptly on to the grass verge, across the emergency runway, through a hedge and shuddered to a halt in the marshy field beyond. She had stopped just short of a wide irrigation ditch which would have broken her back.

His co-pilot was knocked unconscious. No one else was injured.

As Red climbed out, he saw that the tip of one of 'Ginger's' wings was buckled, and the tips of her rudders. He did not hear the whoops of relief and excitement as the rest of the crew leaped out on to the marshy ground. He was saying a short prayer of thanks to their ship. She had brought them back and, although she looked battered and bruised, she could be patched up. In a couple of days she would be flying again.

As they relaxed afterwards in the RAF Sergeants' Mess, Elmer and Hymie made it up. Elmer kept punching Hymie on the chest, as if to make sure he was really there, and Hymie kept beaming. 'Elmer,' he said, 'you're beautiful. I could kiss you.'

'That'd be the quickest way to get a busted nose,' Elmer warned him. Hymie laughed. 'Tell you what,' Elmer said. 'Soon as we get back, we'll take Rosie out, the both of us.'

'That's what we'll do,' Hymie agreed. He thought for a moment. 'And we'll ask that friend of Rosie's to join us.'

Elmer was puzzled. Rosie's friend? 'The kind of plump girl with frizzy hair? Jilly Binns?'

'That's the one. Jelly Beans,' Hymie grinned. 'Hey, that's a good name for her. She's just like a bag of jelly beans.' He remembered her warm laugh and big, happy smile. 'I don't mind if she joins us.'

An hour ago, he had been wondering what they would put on his grave marker. Now he found he was really looking forward to tonight.

# SIX

Sally saw Joe McGraw stir in the chair and his eyes flickered open. 'Sorry, Sal,' he muttered. 'Must've dropped off.'

'I'm not surprised,' she said. He and his men worked right round the clock sometimes to keep as many planes as possible in the air. He was fumbling at his collar to fasten it. 'What are you doing?'

'I have to get back.'

'Stay here,' she said. As soon as he arrived that evening, she could tell he was exhausted. They had just sat and chatted, until he fell asleep.

'Have to . . . make sure the work's been done,' he said groggily. He was trying to rise.

'You're in no condition to go anywhere,' Sally told him. 'Tomorrow or the day after, you'll collapse if you don't have some rest now. Come on, you can sleep here.' He did not have the strength to argue, and let her help him up the stairs to the bedroom. As she took off his boots, he made her promise to wake him at four o'clock. Before he had heard her answer, his head fell back on the pillow.

She slipped off her dress and lay down beside him, watching him. It felt so right to be with him now, natural. She knew there were some who still pointed a finger at her, taking up with 'one of *them*' while her husband was off fighting, and dying, for his country. She didn't care what they said. Even though she didn't know how their relationship would end, or when. He was determined that neither of them should make any promises, or take any decisions, while the war was still on. He wouldn't be like Chuck or a dozen other GIs at the Base who had married English girls. Some of them were widows now, some already separated. All right, she had agreed, no strings. It was enough to be with him, to have him for now, even if that was all there was to be. But there could never be anyone else, not for her.

He looked so vulnerable, when he was sleeping. She pulled the coverlet up and tucked it round him, very gently.

The Base was on stand-down, the day's mission cancelled just before it got airborne. Aircrews felt it most. The sudden release of tension after hours of preparation played hell with their nerves. There were some who were elated, but the anticlimax left most feeling empty.

In the crew quarters, Kulik, the new radio operator on 'Ginger Rogers', sat gazing at the blank wall. Only a month before, he had considered the twenty-five missions that lay ahead, until he had completed his tour, as a piece of cake. Now he kept asking himself, how could anyone's sanity survive that many?

The senior crew members were more specific. They knew the odds were against them. They had less than a thirty-five per cent chance of surviving. 'Way I look at it,' Hymie explained, 'I think of each mission as the last. I mean, I tell myself I'm not gonna get through it. Then if I do—' He shrugged. 'It's one less.'

Elmer nodded. It was a subject that was usually avoided, but for all crew members nearing the end of their tour it had become obsessional. Hymie and he had only two missions left to fly, but the odds were heavily against them surviving in one piece. He'd seen guys go crazy with the strain. They all had talismen, lucky charms. Hymie kept touching a star-shaped fragment of shrapnel that had ripped open his flying jacket and lodged in his flak vest. Elmer used to count off the crew members every time they returned, a ritual. 'Ten little Indians – nine little Indians . . .' As the numbers shrank, he had given up. He kept hearing in his mind the words, 'And then there were none.'

Hymie was putting on his cap. 'I'm takin' a walk. You

70

wanna come?' Elmer shook his head. All aircrew had been confined to Base for the day. He planned to spend most of it sleeping. Maybe he'd write to his uncle in Yonkers.

Hymie set out to walk round the perimeter. At first he marched on doggedly, his hands in his pockets in spite of the risk of being spotted by MPs, but he gradually slowed. He was angry at the cancellation of the mission, especially when they were all ready, all nerved up, sitting waiting for take-off. They knew it was a big one – the aircraft factories at Hannover. Germany was desperate to keep its Luftwaffe in the air and they had been warned to expect Ack-Ack defences that would make even Schweinfurt seem like a pushover. There were fewer German fighters, but now they were equipped with eight-inch rockets and bigger cannons. It used to take about twenty hits to bring down a B-17. Now one rocket could turn it into a ball of fire.

The mission was cancelled, but they had been told that, weather permitting, they would be given another crack at the target tomorrow. Big deal ... That gave Hymie another whole day and night to think about it.

He was fingering the sharp edge of the piece of shrapnel in his pocket, and it pricked him. He looked up. It was crazy to have started this walk. All the way round the perimeter track was miles. It was a bleak day with occasional blustery showers. He had not even brought his coat. He headed towards the hardstands, making for 'Ginger Rogers'. Closer to, he could see the fresh patches covering her latest scars.

McGraw had been checking out her circuits and dropped down from the nose hatch. 'Hi, Hymie. Anythin' I can do for you?'

Hymie shook his head. He was looking at the Fort's belly where his ball turret hung and remembering the crash landing that so nearly had turned him into strawberry jam. He shivered.

'Yeah, it's a raw day,' Mac said. 'But things are hotting up. More planes, replacement crews. Getting ready for the invasion, I guess.' Hymie nodded. 'Hey, you heard the

71

rumour?' Mac went on. 'They say that tours for aircrew are to be extended from twenty-five to thirty.'

Hymie's throat was dry. 'No. I – I hadn't heard that.'

'Be announced any day now, they say. Rough on guys like you, who were so nearly out of it.'

Hymie went straight to the Sergeants' Club. Only one or two had heard the rumour, but most of them believed it. It figured. The Brass would need every available man, not least experienced aircrew, for the coming invasion of Europe. Hymie had a couple of drinks, then another couple. He needed to take his mind off it, but everywhere he looked there were guys just like him, and outside were only planes. He saw a group in a corner, whispering and laughing round Patsy Petrillo, and drifted over.

Patsy grinned at him. 'Lookin' for some action?'

Since it was Patsy, it could hardly be legal, but Hymie nodded. 'Sure.'

He went out with the others and, while one kept watch, they climbed the fence by the woods. After a little, Hymie could make it out, a large truck parked among the trees, Patsy's 'Passion Wagon'. Through contacts in London, Petrillo had brought down some girls. There were guys already waiting by the truck. When the canvas back opened and one came out, Hymie saw one of the women. She was blowsy and raddled, wearing only a slip. He turned away in disgust.

A sharp-faced Englishman, wearing a double-breasted suit and snapbrim hat, was watching. 'Not to yer fancy, mate?' he asked.

'Not in my class,' Hymie muttered.

The Englishman tapped his arm. 'Over there, then. Somethin' special. But it'll cost you.'

Hymie looked and saw Patsy's saloon car parked further down the path. It was a mystery where he had got it and how he found the gas to run it. Intrigued, Hymie moved to the saloon and looked in.

Sitting in the back was Letty Mundy.

*

It was late afternoon before Hymie was missed and evening before Elmer became anxious. He looked everywhere, but there was no sign of the little ball gunner. No one knew where he was. Finally, Elmer rang Red Burwash, their skipper, and asked him to come to the crew's quarters.

The whole crew of 'Ginger Rogers' was waiting for Red and he quickly established that Hymie was in none of the usual places. Kulik remembered him drinking in the Club earlier. 'The trouble is, Skip,' Elmer said, 'Hymie's been acting kinda strange lately. I mean, we're all nervy – but it seemed to be really getting to him.'

'You mean, you think he's gone AWOL?' Red asked. Elmer was reluctant to admit it, yet finally nodded. There was no hiding how serious it was for a crew member to be absent without leave, especially on standby for a mission. He could not escape a court martial, probably for desertion. If he was caught, nothing could stop it. 'Right,' Red decided. 'We have to find him before anyone else does, before they start looking for him. Elm, you lie down in the back of my jeep and I'll get you into town. The rest of you, search the base.'

Concealing attempted desertion was serious and Kulik hesitated. 'Jeese, Skip, he could be anywhere.'

'If you don't wanna help, that's up to you,' Red said. 'And tomorrow you can find yourself another crew.'

Letty had been startled, when she recognized Hymie. She recovered quickly, however, and smiled. She was heavily made up, the eyeshadow and bright lipstick turning her prettiness to allure. She was wearing a coat with very little under it. When she began to open it, Hymie backed away. She had on only a brassiere and lace panties. He remembered her at the dances a year ago, virginal and shy, clinging to the arm of Harvey Wallis.

He was raging at what had become of her. Damn this lousy stinking world! Damn the whole lousy, stinking war and what it's done to us! he was shouting inside. He walked blindly down the path until he came to the road.

Then he started to run. He did not even choose a direction. When he saw Market Wetherby steeple ahead, he made for it.

An MP sergeant spotted him, when he came to the bridge, and recognized him as aircrew. 'Hey, buddy!' he called. Hymie had slowed to a walk. In spite of the white-helmeted military policeman he kept on going. The sergeant crossed the road to block his way, pulling out his nightstick. 'Hold it right there,' he warned. Hymie was short, but tough and a fighter. He was hunched. He straightened quickly and his fist slammed into the sergeant's jaw, knocking him out cold. Hymie walked on, though he did not know where he was going.

When Red dropped him in the town, Elmer went at once to The Plough. There was no sign of Hymie. Neither Jack Blair nor Rosie had seen him. They were worried when Elmer explained and Rosie hurried to fetch her coat to help him search. They looked in the other public house and the Empire Cafe, without result. The Roxy Cinema was closed, but it gave Elmer an idea and, on the offchance, they tried the Mundys.

Vera came to the door, carrying the baby. 'I remember the boy,' she said. 'But he hasn't come here. Why would he?' Elmer thanked her embarrassedly. As they turned to leave, she asked, 'By the way, have you seen Letty tonight?'

'She's not been in the pub, Mrs Mundy,' Rosie said.

Vera watched them go. She was anxious. Letty had gone out in the early afternoon without saying anything, and had not returned. Albert was furious and threatening that, this time, he would take a stick to her. He might just do it.

Elmer and Rosie could think of nowhere else to look. They had been walking aimlessly in the streets and it was pointless. It was a miracle the MPs had not picked Elmer up, himself. 'He must be *somewhere*!' Elmer muttered. He could tell that Rosie was just as worried as he was. Guiltily, he wondered if she would care as much, if it was him.

Rosie had been thinking. 'There is one place,' she said reluctantly. 'He did take Jilly home the other night.'

Jilly had a room in one of the old houses near the parachute factory where she and Rosie worked. When she opened the door and saw them, she gasped, 'Oh, thank God . . .'

'Is he here?' Elmer asked.

'For about three hours! He just walked in. He was talking wild – I couldn't understand him. Then he sat on the sofa and – and passed out.'

Rosie was relieved to see Hymie stretched out as Jilly had said, relieved they had found him. Yet she could not hide that she was less than pleased. Why had Hymie come here, instead of to her at The Plough? For a year he had been swearing there never could be anyone else but her. So what had been going on here? The look she gave her friend left Jilly in no doubt how she felt. 'I wasn't expecting him or anything,' Jilly whispered.

Elmer was slapping Hymie on the cheeks to rouse him. When his eyes opened and he saw they had come for him, he started to struggle. Elmer held him down and signed to Rosie. Her father had given them a half bottle of scotch when they left The Plough, in case it was needed. With Elmer and Jilly holding him, Rosie fed most of the bottle into Hymie's mouth. In his state of grogginess, the whisky made him almost insensible.

McGraw knew the MP sergeant Hymie had knocked out. He found him lying unconscious by the bridge and carried him into Sally's cottage. He took some time to recover and was still unsteady, when Red arrived. The sergeant, Lou Gruner, was angry and eager to report the assault. Red made him listen. 'Gee, Captain,' Gruner said, uncomfortably, 'I didn't know he was the guy in the ball turret. But what am I supposed to do? He assaulted me!'

'One punch, Lou,' McGraw said, soothingly. 'He was just blowing off steam. Probably didn't even think what he was doing.'

'I dunno, Mac,' Gruner said. 'Okay, I'm sorry for the

75

guy. But if he's AWOL . . .' Sally had made tea and gave him a cup.

'Why don't you drink that?' Red suggested. 'Wait just a little. Give him a break.'

Elmer had arranged to rendezvous with his skipper at Bridge Cottage. Red heard him arrive and helped him carry Hymie in. Sergeant Gruner rose to his feet, bulky and menacing, while Hymie smiled happily at Mac and Sally. He peered at Gruner. 'Hey,' he slurred, 'don't I know you?'

At two o'clock in the morning, Albert Mundy woke Sergeant Lewis at the local police station. Lewis listened to what he had to say and scratched his ear. 'Well, if you've tried the hospital, Albert, I can't think what else to suggest.'

'It's your duty!' Mundy fumed. 'Get out and find her! She's missing – and she's only eighteen!'

Lewis coughed. 'Perhaps I shouldn't say it, Albert, but – it might be better not to start anything. There have been . . . stories about Letty. She's been seen with some fairly unsavoury characters.'

Mundy stared at him. 'I'll thank you to keep a civil tongue in your head!' he snapped. 'You're talking about a respectable family. It's the likes of me who pay your wages – and don't you forget it, when you go saying things about my daughter!' He stormed out.

At the shop, Vera sat waiting. There was something she hadn't thought of doing. She was almost afraid of it, yet she made herself go up to Letty's room and look in the wardrobe. All her clothes were gone, and her suitcase. The dressing-table was cleared. On the bed lay the threadbare teddy bear she had slept with since she was four. Letty had left home.

Hymie knew he was the luckiest guy on the base, probably in the entire Eighth Air Force. Red had smuggled him back in and taken turns with the rest of the crew to watch him, in case he pulled any other damnfool stunt. His head was splitting and he let Elmer help him up as their briefing in the gunners' briefing room ended. Lucky, lucky. He had got away with it, and it could've been curtains. He felt Elmer stiffen beside him.

MP Sergeant Gruner had come in and signed to them. 'Colonel wants to see you. On the double!'

Colonel Krasnowici was standing with Jim Kiley by the control tower, wearing his flying gear. Red waited a few steps away with Hymie and Elmer. Krasnowici turned. 'I've been hearing some might funny things, Burwash. What's been going on?'

'Going on, sir?' Red asked, innocently.

The Colonel looked at Hymie. 'More specifically, about you, Stutz. Anything to tell me?'

Hymie hesitated. 'I'd better confess, Colonel. Last night I got drunk – pretty drunk. And I went into town . . . to see my girl.'

Krasnowici's face was set.

'He didn't know what he was doing, Colonel – sir,' Elmer stammered. 'So I went into town after him and – and brought him back.'

'You mean to tell me that two of my sergeants break orders and go into town, the night before a mission – and one of them gets drunk?' Krasnowici growled. His eyes went to Hymie. 'What am I to do with you?'

'Fine me a day's pay, sir?' Hymie suggested, hopefully.

'I'll fine you a week's pay – and both of you are restricted to Base for a month!' Krasnowici roared. 'Now get the hell outa here!' Hymie and Elmer saluted smartly and left. Red waited to be dismissed. 'What do we do with him, Jim?'

'He'd better go with them. Their ship can't take off without him,' Jim Kiley said.

'That it cannot,' the Colonel agreed. He smiled to Red. 'And mind you get it back safe.'

# SEVEN

Vi heard the shot as she walked towards Dereham House. She saw birds fly up from its eaves at the report and walked on, taking it easy, since she was nearly eight months into her pregnancy. As she reached the front of the house, she heard a second shot. It came from the rear and she went round to the Georgian terrace, going through the kitchen garden.

Ronnie Dereham was satisfied as he loaded his ·22 rifle. At least he could still shoot. He had felt the need to do something, so had strung up some empty tin cans on the pergola at the lower end of the lawn. They made an impressive clang when they were struck.

He had been at a loss. The fall of Rome to the Allies ten days ago had been the climax of the campaign he had been following so intently. Yet the news had been swept off the headlines the following day by the invasion of Normandy. The papers were all full of attacks and advances in France. It was odd. He had been so wrapped up in the Italian campaign, where his old tanks were in action, that he felt disoriented. He could take no real, personal interest in Normandy. It was almost as if it was no longer his war.

He was very pleased to see Vi, although concerned that she had walked so far. 'The exercise is good for me, Major,' she told him. 'Dad and Rosie won't let me do anything in the house. I've been sitting around too much.' She was fascinated by his rifle and he shot for her, a good hit; the tin rang and spun on its string.

'I want to be ready for the shooting season,' he explained. 'Every scrap is useful for the pot, these days. No reason why I can't shoot just as well from a wheelchair as standing.' He propelled himself over to the bench by the wall. It was in the sun, flanked by white roses. 'Here, you come and sit down.'

As Vi sat, she could no longer hold back her news. Her husband, Chuck, was arriving in two or three days.

'Oh, my dear, that's splendid!' Ronnie said, sincerely. He had got over his obsessive interest in her, when she had seemed to be the only one on whom he could rely, but he was still very fond of her. 'You've been waiting so long.'

'I can't believe it – that he'll be here,' she said.

Helen had seen her from the house and came to join them. She kissed Vi, when she heard. 'He couldn't have chosen a better time,' she said, 'just when you need him. He must be so happy.'

Vi smiled. 'Yes, he is. Except he's annoyed at missing D-Day.' They laughed. 'He wanted to be with his old Group for that. He's joining them again.'

'Will he be flying?' Helen asked.

'No, thank heavens. He's to be an instructor.' Vi's relief showed. 'I used to get so nervous when I knew he was flying. Now I can sleep easy.' It was like a miracle. When her husband had reappeared, months after being posted missing, she had only had him for a few days before he was sent back to the States. At long last, they would be together and he would be here for the birth of their child.

Helen laughed. It was impossible to be with Vi and not be touched by her happiness.

Sally Bilton took her ration book back and picked up the two pounds of flour Vera had saved for her. Her little boy William was rattling the handle of the shop door and she saw Albert Mundy glowering at him. 'Stop that, now, Billy,' she called. Mundy tucked his head down over the boiled ham he was slicing very thinly. Sally lowered her voice. 'I wanted to ask, Mrs Mundy – have you had any word of Letty?'

Vera glanced at Albert. Since their daughter had run away, he would not allow her name to be spoken in public.

Her eyes showed the strain she was under. 'We haven't heard anything, Mrs Bilton. She's just disappeared.'

Jim Kiley was finishing coffee in the Officers' Club with Lorna Jane. He was aware of the envious looks thrown at him by most of the younger men and realized it was only his position as Air Exec that stopped them trying to cut him out. Lorna Jane knocked the rest of the WAACs into a cocked hat. There were days, like today, when she was so alive and attractive, she seemed to have her very own spotlight trained on her. He had moved towards the S-3 Captain, thinking Lorna might like to join some of her colleagues in Intelligence, but she had firmly steered him to a table at the side, where they could be alone.

God knows, we have little enough opportunity, she thought. She had once debated whether her hometown or the rather good girls' school she attended had been the more smallminded and gossipy. Neither of them could hold a candle to an all male Bomb Base. Everywhere she went, every move she made, she was watched. Her friend, Louise, another lieutenant, was exhilarated by it. 'I've never had so much attention in my life,' she laughed. 'The only place I don't feel eyes on me is in the shower – and even then I'm not so sure.' Lorna Jane hated it. It meant she could seldom have more than a moment or two alone with Jim.

She accepted that he had to be careful as Number Two in the Group. What was the male equivalent of Caesar's wife? That was him. And he showed no possessiveness, made no move that might compromise her reputation. Even so, he was more scrupulous and gentlemanly than was called for. She was reasonably proud of her looks and her figure. She had never spent any time with a man without him making a pass at her. Until she had met Jim.

The few times he had kissed her, she had melted, not leaving him in any doubt that she liked it and wanted more. She had felt his response. He could have taken whatever he wanted from her, but always he kept himself in check. He couldn't have misread the signals she had given him. And it couldn't be that he was afraid of her, afraid of sex. He was too much a man for that. There had to be something else that stopped him. Maybe he had been hurt in the past. Maybe he was reluctant to commit himself, because of the war and the nature of his duties. She felt sick every time he took off on a mission and cried inside with relief when she saw him return. Fortunately, the Colonel made sure that he did not go on sorties too often. Jim complained about it, but when the planes took off and he was not with them, she said a prayer of thankfulness.

She could hardly credit his effect on her, how she felt about him. She was used to men making the running and had developed excellent evasion tactics. Yet here she was virtually throwing herself at him, leaving him in no doubt that she was his for the asking. And he treated her not like a lover but as a friend, a buddy. She would not give up. She was determined that one day she would break through that barrier, heal that hurt or whatever it was, overcome that inexplicable reluctance to become involved. There was one thing she had to make clear.

'Louise was telling me about a friend of hers who wanted some advice,' she said. 'We disagreed, but I'm sure I was right.'

'About what?' Jim asked.

Lorna Jane shrugged. 'It's the old wartime romance. Only, Louise's friend is certain it's more than that. So's her guy. They're made for each other, apparently. Anyway, he's in . . . motor torpedo boats. A pretty risky outfit, so she never knows from one day to the next whether he's going to come back. She works at the base where he's stationed.'

'Must be rough on her,' Jim said.

'I guess she'd rather be there than a hundred miles away, wondering all the time what was happening to him.' Lorna Jane looked down at her cup. 'Anyway, what's

81

worrying her is the old question. They're in love, but not married. She's never had an affair with anyone.'

'And her guy wants her to sleep with him.'

'I wouldn't put it so crudely,' Lorna Jane said, and smiled. 'But I suppose that's what it adds up to. Since they love each other, he doesn't see why they should wait. When any day might be the last.'

'That's the motive for a lot of affairs in wartime,' Jim said. 'It seems so urgent.'

'Louise doesn't agree. She thinks her friend should hold back, that it would be less painful for her, suppose something happens to him, if they hadn't been lovers.'

Jim was looking at her very seriously. 'And what do you think?'

Lorna Jane hesitated. 'Just the opposite. If he was killed, I don't believe she'd ever forgive herself. Since they love each other, and want each other, at least she would have the memory of that. She would never regret it.'

'Sometimes it takes a lot more courage,' Jim said slowly, 'it can be a lot harder to hold back, to put love into a box marked, Not to be opened till after the war. It's harder, but in the long run maybe it causes less pain.' Lorna Jane was puzzled, not understanding him. 'I can't generalize about it,' Jim went on. 'It depends on the circumstances, on the couple. They're the only ones who can know if what they feel is real or not. If it would go on existing, even though they denied themselves. If they really need each other, if it gets too strong for them, nothing'll stop it.'

She was still puzzled. She wanted to ask, But how does that apply to us? There was something in his voice she could not make out. Had he not realized what she was telling him?

Before she could think of another way to put it, he pushed his cup aside and smiled. 'I'm not much good at moralizing. Once I thought right and wrong were clearcut. Not any more. The war's turned everything upside down. Louise's friend will just have to work it out for herself.'

A minute or two later, when they came out of the Club, she saw how he looked automatically at the sky.

Jim's head was lifted, as if he was sniffing the wind. The horizon was still clear, only a light haze. Even though an operation was in progress, a good number of B-17s were still on their hardstands. Many replacements had flown in over the past month and now, although Colonel Krasnowici had taken off with a full Group that morning to raid Flying Bomb sites in Northern France, there were still as many ships left as had once been their full complement. Changed days, as the Colonel so often had predicted. The beginning of the end.

Lorna watched him. She had become used to his silences. She had learnt that it was not moodiness. His mind was racing through problems of logistics, armament, training, forward planning, weather conditions. He was so handsome, the planes of his face firm, as though carved out of granite. Like one of those heads on Mt Rushmore. The idea amused her and she smiled.

'Sorry,' he said. 'I was in a dream.'

'No,' she corrected. 'You were in a B-17.'

His sudden smile lit his features, making him seem younger. He did not smile often enough and, when he did, she always wanted to kiss him before it went away. 'So now you're off duty,' he said.

'As of now. Six blissful days.' She had put it off as long as possible, hoping he would be able to join her. 'I still wish you were coming with me, Jim.'

He smiled again. 'I can hardly remember when I was last on leave.' The idea was tempting, though. A little of her was good for him. A lot – it might be disastrous, but it could be very interesting. A quiet little hotel somewhere, just the two of them. Even as he thought it, he felt guilty. Because he enjoyed her company, they had drifted into a relationship that had clearly become important to her. It was a weakness in him that he could not explain to her that his heart, if he had one, had been lost long ago. How do you tell a beautiful girl, with charm and intelligence, with everything to make her the perfect companion, that she is just too late?

'Oh, Major, your devotion to duty does you credit,' she sighed, 'but sometimes I wonder if it's the war that makes you so serious, or if it comes natural.'

He thought about it. 'I guess part of if comes natural.' She laughed. 'You're off to London?'

'By the afternoon train. I still haven't finished packing.'

'I'd better let you go, then.' He could see she wanted him to kiss her. It was impossible, in broad daylight with half the Air Force undoubtedly watching. Probably just as well. A break away from each other would do them both good.

A jeep swung round them and stopped with a squeal of brakes. Red Burwash was driving. 'Is it right you're going to London?' he asked Lorna. 'So am I. I'll take you to the station.'

'I haven't done packing,' she told him. 'I have to go back to my quarters.'

'I'll wait,' Red said. 'Hop in. The sooner you're ready, the sooner you'll be out of Stalag Luft Market Wetherby.'

She smiled and turned to Jim. 'Goodbye, Major.' She saluted.

He returned the salute. 'Goodbye, Lieutenant. Have a good trip.' She climbed into the jeep and looked straight ahead. He nodded to Red. 'See you in a month.'

Red grinned and took off fast, tyres protesting as he spun the jeep round the corner. For all Red's unorthodox attitudes, Jim admired him. Red's thirty mission tour was over. He had survived and could return to the States with a chestful of campaign medals. They had given a party for him in the Combat Crew Mess. Immediately after it, he had volunteered for a second tour. The Air Force was only too happy to accept and had granted him thirty days leave. A day for every time he had risked his life.

As Jim headed for his own jeep, a young lieutenant drew himself up and saluted. Fairhaired, freshfaced, he was obviously one of the newest arrivals, yet he had two medal ribbons. 'I know you from somewhere,' Jim said.

'Coogan, sir,' the lieutenant answered. 'Danny Coogan.'

Of course . . . Coogan was the young sergeant gunner who had been badly wounded on the 525th's very first mission, but not before shooting down two ME 109s. 'Welcome back,' Jim said, and they shook hands. He heard how, after repatriation to the States and convalescence, Coogan had persisted until he was permitted to begin pilot training. He had passed out near the top of his course. 'I look forward to flying with you,' Jim told him.

Yes, he remembered Coogan. It was seeing her concern for the boy that had given him his first glimpse behind the coolness and professional detachment of Helen Dereham.

Helen was grateful for the cup of tea that Sister Dickson had brought her. She was bone tired. The whole hospital had been rushed off its feet.

Two weeks ago, every road in England had seemed crammed with vehicles, truckloads of troops, columns of tanks and armoured cars, all moving south in preparation for the invasion. As soon as it was launched, the countryside seemed empty. But the bomber campaign had intensified, pounding German defences and rail communications and gun emplacements. The Market Wetherby Group had been part of it and had taken many casualties. Yet for once there seemed a real point to it.

She could not understand Ronnie's indifference. This was the most significant step towards breaking Hitler's grip, to ending the war. It was possible to imagine an end to it now, so that everything could return to normal, all the men go home.

She set down her cup at the thought. One day in the not too distant future, all those thousands of soldiers and airmen, all those officers and GIs would be going home to America. And Jim would be going with them.

*

'We hit them, Jim. We hit them good,' Rufus was saying as Jim followed him into the CO's office after de-briefing. 'God, I hate those dooblebugs! A bomb that flies itself and strikes at random – that's inhuman.' As he spoke, he took a bottle of bourbon from a drawer of his desk. Jim had never seen him drink in the office before and Rufus noticed his surprise. 'Highly irregular, but this is a little private celebration. I haven't said anything, but today's was my last mission – anyway, with the 525th.'

Jim was shaken. 'You're kidding!'

'Wish I was. No, the fact is, I'm leaving here.'

It would not sink in. The Group without Rufe was unthinkable. 'But why?'

'Someone up there thinks I'm getting too stiff in the joints for bomb runs, but sufficiently long in the tooth to be of use to operational planning at Command. I'll be gone in a couple of days.'

Jim accepted his glass, his mind blank. 'What's going to happen?'

'You'll be Temporary Commanding Officer, of course – until a new one is appointed. I wish it could be you, Jim, but it's not policy. Meanwhile, if there's a mission tomorrow, you'll lead it.'

'Be happy to.'

Rufus chuckled. 'I thought so.' They toasted each other. 'I don't want any ceremony when I leave. But I have arranged a little get-together of my own, to say thank you to the Staff Officers and so on. Tomorrow evening early – but you'll make it.' Jim nodded. He was sorry Lorna Jane would miss it. 'By the way,' Rufus went on, 'I've invited a few locals to whom I owe favours – the Maylies. And Mr and Mrs Dereham.'

As soon as he landed and had reported, Chuck Ericson went to the Aircrew Mess and rang The Plough. There was no reply. He tried three more times at ten minute intervals, but still no one answered. When the chance of an earlier flight to England had come up, he had grabbed it. He had meant to give his wife, Vi, a surprise. Now he wished he had sent a cable. She could be anywhere.

The people in the Mess were all strangers, except for the barman, who told him that Elmer and Hymie were on a mission with the Air Exec, hunting doodlebug sites in France. He got tired of kicking his heels and managed to hitch a ride into Market Wetherby, where he found The Plough locked up. He was becoming anxious. He couldn't wait to see Vi, to find out how she really was. There was only a month to go now, until the baby was due. Suppose something had gone wrong that he didn't know about? He knocked at the door next to the pub and the woman who opened it recognized him. She told him that nothing was wrong that she'd heard. Rosie was at work and Vi and her father had both gone out somewhere, that was all.

Vi had written that she spent much of her spare time with Sally Bilton. He set off for Sally's cottage down by the bridge. It was a walk full of memories. The first time he kissed Vi had been in the shadow of the trees by the bridge. He had thought of that night often, both when he had made his way down through Occupied France and across Spain to Portugal and when he had been sent back to the States. He could remember the rustle of the leaves mixed with the sounds of the river, Vi's face in the moonlight, her expression serious and uncertain, her awkwardness when he put his arms around her, and then how right it had seemed and how soft she became, when he kissed her. From that night they had both known there could never be anyone else.

It had not been easy. Her father wanted them to wait. He had been warned by everyone, over and again by Red, his skipper. Even the Air Exec, Major Kiley, had called him in for the standard lecture on wartime marriages. 'Where are you from, Ericson?' Nebraska, sir. 'Well, how do you think she'll fit in when you get her over there? How will she make out with your parents?' I don't have any parents left, sir. She'll be my family, and she'll fit in just fine.

They had been married just one day before he was shot down. And they'd been allowed only a handful of days before he had to leave her again. They had warned him it could be tough. The toughest part was the fight to get back to her, back to England and his old Group. She must've been afraid he wouldn't make it in time, that he wouldn't be here for the birth of their child. Her letters were brave and she said it was his that had kept her going. He had written how he felt, but he could never really put down in words just how much he had missed her.

Sally's cottage was empty. It was not locked, but there was nobody home. He lit a cigarette, while he decided what to do. It was half shut day in town. Even the Empire Cafe was closed. 'Shee-it!' he said aloud and flicked his cigarette over the parapet of the bridge into the water.

Returning to the Base, he was happy when he ran into McGraw. At last he had met a friendly face. 'You're here,' Mac said. 'Vi wasn't expecting you till tomorrow or the day after.'

'Any idea where she is?' Chuck asked.

'She's gone into Ipswich with Sally,' Mac told him. 'Shopping. They won't be back till later.'

'How much later?'

'Eight or nine. Depending on which bus they catch.' Mac chuckled. 'Wait will she sees you. You'll still give her a big surprise.'

The Group returned in late afternoon. When Elmer and Hymie had finished with de-briefing and dumped their flying gear, they started back for their own quarters. A tall, rangy Master Sergeant was leaning against the outside wall of the hut, his hands behind his head. Seeing his slow, slightly quizzical grin, they stopped. Hymie pretended to rub his eyes and they ran at Chuck, whooping. While Elmer hugged him, Hymie jumped on his back, laughing and pummelling. Hymie pulled Chuck's ear. 'Who's gonna be a big daddy, then?'

Jim was pleased with the day's results. They had knocked

out two German-run component factories north of Evreux, but he had to force himself to concentrate on the way home and the de-briefing process had seemed interminable. He had just time to shower and change into his pinks before going to Rufus's party in the Officers' Club. He felt undeniably nervous. It was not merely the prospect of meeting Helen, but that her husband would be with her. He had always got on well with Ronnie Dereham, yet they had never been at ease together. It was scarcely to be expected.

As he looked round, however, he could not see Ronnie. He spoke briefly to Sir Arthur and Lady Maylie and excused himself. Helen was with Rufus, Lester Carson and one of the chaplains. He crossed to them and Rufus clapped him on the shoulder. 'You made it, Jim! Good!'

Jim bowed slightly. 'Good evening, Mrs Dereham.'

'. . . Major.' Helen smiled, acknowledging him. She was as poised and as beautiful as ever. Rufus was telling her about some hunting prints he had bought. He planned to hang them in his den in his home in Oregon, as a permanent memento. Jim watched Helen, but she did not so much as glance at him. They were given no opportunity to be alone and when he at last managed to have a few words with her, they were both ill at ease and made no special contact.

'When can I talk to you properly?' he asked.

'That's what you asked me over a month ago,' she said, levelly.

He could not credit it had been so long. He tried to smile, to show her that he really meant everything he had said to her, but it came out as a grimace. 'I'd hoped we could have . . . got together before now.'

'I hoped so, too,' Helen said. Rufus came to them and took her arm, leading her over to meet the new Medical Officer.

The bus from Ipswich was only half full. Vi and Sally sat near the centre, their packages on their laps. 'The days are getting longer,' Sally said. 'We'll be back before black-out, anyway.'

'I feel quite tired,' Vi said.

'Well, you've been on your feet a lot today. At least, you got what you wanted.'

Vi smiled. The afternoon had not started off too well. She had been saving up her clothing coupons, but she had seen nothing she liked and had resigned herself to windowshopping, while Sally bought things for Betty and Billy. Then after tea she had spotted the very dress she had in mind, a soft artificial silk in very pale blue. She wanted to look nice for Chuck coming.

'And you can take it in easily,' Sally said. 'When you get your figure back.'

'If I ever do,' Vi sighed, and they laughed.

Sally thought the extra weight suited her. Approaching motherhood had brought a glow to her. She had certainly never looked prettier.

The bus driver was stubbing out his cigarette, when he saw something heading towards them, a small aeroplane. Something was wrong with it. It was wobbling a bit. Funny kind of thing, long and pointed, with stubby wings. It was curving down towards the road. When all at once he realized what it was, he stepped hard on the brakes.

Vi and Sally had heard the putter of the doodlbug's engine. Then it cut out. They were thrown forward, when the bus stopped sharply, their packages spilling. A woman down the front screamed. 'What's wrong?' Sally called.

The flying bomb hit the road about twenty yards ahead of them and exploded with gouts of flame and debris. All the windows in the bus shattered and the driver's face turned into a bloody pulp. The bus slewed round violently, tilted and crashed over on its side in the ditch.

When Chuck reached the hospital, he found Jack Blair and Rosie waiting outside the recovery room. Rosie was huddled on a bench, sobbing. Jack looked grey and, suddenly, much older. 'Thank God you've come, son,' he said.

Chuck went cold. He was unable to ask.

'No, they're both all right,' Jack told him gently. 'Sally was sent home. Vi's in there. The doctor says we can't see her just yet, but all she needs is rest. She's going to be fine.' He paused. 'But . . . I'm afraid she lost the baby.'

Chuck swayed as if he had been struck. Jack put out his hand to touch him, but he pushed it away. Stumbling, he turned and went quickly down the corridor. He came out of the door and swung round the pillar at the side, pressing against the wall. He was glad of the darkness. He did not want anyone to see him cry.

# EIGHT

The tap at the door was hesitant and Jack Blair paused in his sweeping, wondering if he had misheard. When the tap was repeated, he propped the brush against the bar and went through to The Plough's rear parlour.

Vera Mundy was hovering, nervous of being seen by the neighbours. He stepped aside. 'Come in, Vera.' He closed the door and waited for her to speak, very aware that it was the first time in many years they had been alone together. 'You're looking well,' he said. She smiled quickly, but it did not hide the signs of strain. When she still did not speak, he chuckled. 'You've caught me, I'm afraid. I was just doing some cleaning up.' He was wearing a woman's apron and untied it. 'One of Vi's.'

'How is she?' Vera asked.

'Oh, not too bad at all. She'll be home at the weekend.' He gestured. 'Won't you sit down?'

'No, thanks. I – I can't stop,' Vera said. 'I wanted to ask you, if you knew anything – if you'd heard anything?'

Jack understood. 'About Letty? No, sorry, love, I don't have any idea where she might be.'

'I just thought – since she used to come here.'

'Quite often,' Jack nodded. 'But not with anyone in particular. Lots of different chaps. What does Albert think about it?'

'He won't talk about her, won't even let her name be mentioned.'

Jack's voice was gentle. 'I shouldn't worry, Vera. She'll be back – because of her child.'

'Vicky doesn't mean anything to her,' Vera said, distressed. 'She never wanted her, could hardly bring herself to take care of her.'

How unjust life was, Jack thought. His daughter, who

92

had been desperate to have a baby, had lost hers. While Vera's daughter . . . 'Hang on,' he said. 'There was one chap she saw quite a bit of for a while. One of their sergeants.'

'When was that?' Vera asked, hopefully.

'Oh, it was months ago. Petrillo – Patsy Petrillo. I thought you might know him. He was a friend of your brother Sid.'


Very cute pins, the Orderly Room Sergeant thought, watching Lorna Jane Somers as she waited outside the door of the CO's office. The pins went right up to a trim little ass. Very cute everything. Yessir, ma'am, that was one officer he would follow anywhere.

Lorna was reading and rereading the nameplate on the door. 'Commanding Officer: Lt Col James A Kiley'. Jim's promotion and his assumption of command had happened while she was on leave. It made her so proud of him.


'What does your wife think about this?' Jim asked.

M/Sgt Chuck Ericson was standing in front of his desk. 'Vi's still in hospital, sir,' he said. 'No call to bother her.'

'In other words, you haven't talked it over with her.'

'Wouldn't make any difference, sir,' Chuck said determinedly. 'I know what I want, and that's not to be grounded. I'm aircrew, sir.'

Jim considered him. 'Well, I'll tell you what I'll do. You're too valuable as an instructor for me to recommend a transfer. But if any pilot needs a stand-in flight engineer for any particular mission, you'll be the first to be given the opportunity to volunteer.'

'Thank you, sir.' Chuck saluted, turned smartly and left.

Jim made a note on his pad. He could understand Ericson's motives. It was natural for a man to want to fight the enemy who had killed his unborn child.

He had not heard Lorna come in. She was holding herself rigidly at attention. 'Permission to ask if we are lunching together, Colonel?'

'If the lieutenant would settle for a sandwich and a cup of coffee.'

'She would.' Lorna smiled and relaxed. 'I've hardly had a chance to tell you about my leave.'

Jim passed her a cigarette. 'Sorry. I had little enough spare time as Air Exec. Now I've got none.'

She leaned in closer for him to light her cigarette, her voice a fair imitation of Mae West's. 'So whaddya do for relaxation, huh?'

'I eat insubordinate lieutenants and spit the pips out.'

She laughed and straightened. 'You make a lovely Commanding Officer, Jim.' She paused. 'I can't see why it's only to be temporary.'

He was serious. 'I wish it didn't have to be. I'm damned proud of commanding the 525th. But the theory is that, if changes and improvements have to be made, a new broom is the best one to make them.'

Rosie Blair came from the parachute factory with her friend Jilly, turning up the collar of her overall against the light drizzle. Her thick hair was done up in a snood and Jilly wore a turban over her curlers. 'Beetroot and boiled haddock,' Rosie was saying, disgustedly. 'Every day this week in the canteen. When I asked if I couldn't have something else, that fat one, you know, she said, "Course, luv. How about boiled haddock and beetroot?" '

'It's not so bad with spam,' Jilly said. 'But with fish . . .'

They stopped and chatted for a minute outside Jilly's house, neither of them aware that they had been followed all the way from the factory gate.

When Rosie walked on, a hand gripped her arm. She gasped and looked round. Right into the face of Albert Mundy. He released her arm, but he seemed so strange, his eyes so intent, that Rosie backed away. 'I didn't mean to startle you,' he said. 'I just want to talk to you.'

'What about, Mr Mundy?' Rosie asked, nervously.

For three weeks Mundy had been putting on a brave face, but he was nearly frantic with worry. 'You were

Letty's friend,' he said. 'Her only one. She must've talked to you.'

'I – I haven't seen much of her – last few months,' Rosie stammered. She had always been scared of Letty's father.

'Did she tell you she was leaving?'

'No, Mr Mundy.'

'Was there anybody . . . she might have gone away with?' Rosie shook her head. 'She must've said something!' Mundy insisted. 'Think, girl! I've seen you often enough, whispering and giggling. What were you talking about?'

'. . . Boys and stuff.' She bit her lip as he grabbed her arm again.

'What stuff? What else?'

Rosie thought. 'Well . . . she did talk a lot about London.'

Hymie Stutz listened in silence, as Rosie told Elmer and him about the meeting later that night. 'You should see my arm,' she whispered, 'where he was holding me. I was really frightened. He was . . . real scary.'

'He must've been worried,' Elmer said. 'Poor old guy.'

'No call to feel sorry for him,' Rosie said. 'If I'd been Letty, with a dad like him, I'd have left home ages ago.' A Home Guard corporal with an empty glass signalled to her from farther along the bar. She ignored him.

'You don't think—' Elmer began. 'I mean, she's just disappeared, right? She'd been fooling around. You don't think, maybe . . . she's been bumped off?' Rosie's eyes opened wide. 'What do you think, Hymie?'

Hymie had told no one about the last time he had seen Letty Mundy, half naked and available in the back of Patsy's car. If folks around here, especially her family, didn't know what she was up to, probably it was better that way. He had his own ideas about where she had gone. 'I guess she's just taken off somewheres,' he said. 'Maybe got sick of her old man bawling her out.'

Jack Blair was passing with a tray and said quietly, 'We've other customers, young lady.'

The Home Guard corporal was still waiting. He raised his glass hopefully as Rosie came towards him. Just then, the door opened and the crew of 'Hot Flush' trooped in. Fresh from the States, it was their first time off Base after three weeks of training flights. Noisy and raring to go, they crowded up to the far end of the bar. Danny Coogan, at twenty, was their skipper and the oldest member of the crew. Rosie headed straight for them, not even noticing the corporal.

There was a chorus of whistles as Rosie smiled to them. Coogan beat a tattoo on the bartop with two halfcrowns. 'We'll take ten beers, ma'am,' he grinned. 'And anything else that's going.'

Rosie lowered her violet eyes. She raised them again, slowly, with a hint of a teasing smile. 'Whatever do you mean, Lieutenant?'

Coogan was transfixed.

'Works every time,' Hymie muttered, disgustedly, watching.

'Yeah,' Elmer echoed. 'Every time we start to think one of us is getting somewhere with Rosie, new competition turns up. When are we gonna learn?'

'We're a coupla jerks,' Hymie said. 'Our kind never learn.'

High cirrus cloud had totally obscured the target and Jim had to lead the formation to the secondary target, the oil refineries at Harburg. In spite of heavy AA defences, the 525th left towering columns of black smoke from the burning refineries behind it. The cost had been within the limits of acceptability, three ships lost out of forty-five, the largest formation the Group had ever assembled. As if the loss of at least thirty men can ever be 'acceptable', Jim thought.

He was careful on the trip home to avoid as many of the known Anti-Aircraft concentrations as possible, but enemy radar kept picking them up and there were some close calls. German flak fire was increasing and becoming more accurate all the time. Rufus's prediction that the Luftwaffe would cease to exist by midsummer had not come true, although, because of Allied attacks on their production centres, GAF fighters were far less numerous. Their pilots were experienced, however, and determined. It paid to keep your eyes peeled.

They were at 25,000 feet and the Group Navigator had just given a course correction to take them out over the coast at Dunkirk, when the top turret drew Jim's attention to something. 'Ten o'clock high, sir. Little Friends.' Jim squinted up. Three US Mustangs were closing from behind. A welcome sight, since direct escort had been discontinued. All at once, he froze. They were painted like Mustangs, but they were modified JU 87s! Even as he shouted a warning, he saw sticks of phosphorus bombs drop from them, streaming down towards the closely packed formation.

The next few minutes were hideous confusion as the three tiers of the formation split apart, its pilots trying to dodge the bombs and also to avoid collision. Two B-17s were hit by the bombs, one exploding at once and scattering debris through the air. The second plummeted downwards, spinning, and creating further chaos in the scattered squadron below. Jim saw another two Fortresses collide and fall out of the sky, locked together. 'Reform!' he was shouting on his R/T. 'Get back into formation! Close up!' With its all round firepower, a Fortress formation was almost impregnable. Spread out as they were, the individual ships were vulnerable.

It was too late. A flight of the new, faster ME 109s was waiting and, with great daring, dived down through the gaps between the milling B-17s, cannons spitting. They were followed by the disguised Junkers. At a diving speed of hundreds of miles per hour, it was over in seconds, but three more Forts were destroyed, with no loss to the attackers, although one ME was seen to curve away with smoke streaming back from its cowling.

Damaged ships had to be left to fend for themselves. Ice

cool, terse, Jim whipped the stricken Group back into formation, while the bandits circled just out of range, preparing for a second attack. It never materialized. An RAF Spitfire squadron came streaking out of the west and the Messerschmitts turned tail.

As he dressed for the evening, Jim thought about the report he had just sent to Wing, twelve ships lost in all, another three badly damaged and probably irreparable. It was not pretty to read. Nor to write.

Lorna's phone call had been mysterious. They had been invited to dine, she said, by English friends of hers. He almost turned it down, but the events of the day had left him needing to relax. He had not had a break off Base in a month. When he picked her up in his jeep, he said, 'What *is* all this? Where are we going?'

'To parents of a friend of mine,' she smiled. 'I met her when I was on leave, at a concert in Trinity College. She comes from round here and – well, I told her a little about you. And this morning she rang to invite us both.'

She had put a paper bag on the seat between them, containing a tin of powdered eggs, two cakes of soap and some chocolate bars. Odd gifts to be taking to a dinner party, yet he had no doubt they would be welcome. 'We shouldn't be eating civilians' rations. Things are scarce.'

'It's not so bad for them. Her people have a farm.'

'But who is she?' Jim said. 'I have to know. I can't go off Base without leaving word where I'll be.'

'Her name's Pat,' Lorna told him. 'Pat Dereham.' Jim nearly stalled his jeep. Lorna was laughing. 'She said it would be a surprise.' He slowed down. 'Did you have a bit of a fling with her or something?'

'No. She was far too young.' What the hell was Helen's daughter playing at?

'Her parents sound nice. Her mother's a doctor at the EMS.'

'Yes, I know them quite well,' Jim said. He looked at her. Obviously, she had heard nothing about what had happened. It was some stupid game of Pat's. He should have explained the situation to Lorna weeks ago. This was not the time to do it. And if the Derehams were expecting them, he could not refuse to go at the last minute without embarrassing everyone.

Helen and Ronnie had only learned the identity of their male guest after the invitation had been sent. Helen had not seen or mentioned Jim Kiley for months and Ronnie thought the issue dead and buried. It was unforgivable of their daughter to revive it so casually. He said nothing, but spent the afternoon alone in his study.

Helen asked her why she had done it? 'I never thought he would accept!' Pat laughed. 'I only wanted to let him know he'd been found out. I mean, I met this perfectly sweet American girl – and it turns out she's his latest flame! So much for imagining him pining away in secret. It only goes to show how silly we both were.' Experience had made her daughter cynical, Helen saw. She thought she was being so adult. 'Well, after all,' Pat said, 'isn't it best to clear the air once and for all?'

Her smile to Jim had a hint of malice, as she led Lorna and him out on to the terrace. Jim was distantly correct and polite, Helen just as guarded. Any awkwardness in the atmosphere was accepted by Lorna Jane as natural at a first meeting and she coped with it by taking a bright interest in the old house and its gardens and the history of the Derehams.

It was Ronnie who saved the evening. He detected none of the former intimacy between his wife and Jim and was relieved. At the same time, he realized that Lorna was the only one liable to be hurt and set himself out to put her at her ease, asking her about her own family and background as the daughter of a country judge. She made them laugh. 'Yes,' she said, 'people back home tend to think that Virginians are snobbish. That's nonsense. Whenever I'm travelling in the US, I never even mention I'm from

Virginia – because I don't want to make everyone I meet feel inferior.'

The dinner was a success, its high spot some sliced peaches which had arrived in a food parcel from Nanny's niece in Australia. The tone of light banter continued, although even Lorna noticed how frequently her name was linked to Jim's by Pat, as if she was determined to make them out to be an established couple. Helen was the perfect hostess and, although Jim was quiet, he smiled and joined in just enough to keep the conversation moving. There was no sign that his involvement with this house had ever been anything more than casual.

It was still light when they finished and the evening was fine, so they decided to take coffee out on the terrace. The only jarring note was when Lorna offered to push Ronnie and he told her quite sharply that he permitted no one to help him. He softened it at once by challenging her, one day, to a game of wheelchair badminton. 'Of course, you'll have to find your own wheelchair.' He ushered Pat and her out and followed them.

Helen waited for Jim, but as they were going out, he closed the door and turned to her. 'It's months since we had even a moment to talk properly.'

'So it is,' she answered coolly. 'I haven't had a chance to congratulate you on your promotion.'

'Thank you.' Jim paused. 'Pat is quite the little matchmaker.'

'Lorna is a very nice girl,' Helen said. 'I like her.'

'I like her, too. But that's all it is.'

'That's something that only concerns the two of you,' she said. 'Perhaps we should join the others.'

She made to pass him and he stopped her. 'Helen, we have to talk.'

'I can't imagine there's anything left to say.'

'I think there is.' She looked down at where he was holding her wrist, and he let it go. 'If you knew how often I nearly called you.'

'Once upon a time, I could think of nothing else,' she

admitted. 'Day after day, I sat and waited for you to call, only to hear how you were. I couldn't ring you because you made me promise.'

'We both promised.'

'But I never thought you could keep it. To be only a mile away and never – it was too cruel, Jim. I'm not as strong as you are.'

'That's what I'm trying to say. Nothing's changed.'

'But it has!' She was almost angry. 'You can't expect to step out of my life completely – and step back in when you choose, as if time meant nothing. All those months, I've had to live. I've had to come to terms with it, the life I live here.'

'Helen—'

'No, Jim. I know what you're going to say – that we agreed not to see each other for all the right reasons. That we mustn't hurt Ronnie, that we both had our work to do, a position to maintain. Well . . . however much it hurts, they're still the right reasons. Feelings don't come into it. I have responsibilities and I can't give them up.'

'I thought you said you weren't strong,' Jim said quietly. 'But I want you to know that I meant it. I love you. I still love you and I won't give you up. Unless you can tell me now that you've changed, that you don't feel the same. Then I'll leave this house tonight and never bother you again.'

Helen was torn. His face was tense, but his eyes pleaded with her and all her instincts fought against her sense of duty, making her long to reach out and touch him. 'That's unfair,' she whispered.

'Who said any of it was fair? Every minute I'm without you is unfair,' Jim said. 'If it hadn't been for the war, nothing would have kept us apart. You think it's been hard for you, because I didn't keep calling. How could we have gone on as we were, seeing each other but unable to be together? Every hour of every day I want you and need you. And you can't tell me it's not the same for you. Well,

I give you warning. When all this is over, I'm coming back for you. And I won't take no for an answer.'

Helen was gazing at him, hearing the words she had dreamed of hearing for nearly a year.

As they moved slowly together, the door opened and Nanny came in, carrying an empty tray. She noticed nothing unusual. 'Oh, sorry,' she smiled, 'I thought you'd all gone outside. I'll just clear these things away. Don't let me disturb you.'

'We really should join the others,' Helen said. He touched her arm. Her eyes closed briefly, and they went out on to the terrace for coffee.

# NINE

The new CO was a son-of-a-bitch.

Jim returned from a messy raid on Hamburg to find Colonel Lincoln C. Brownlee already in his office. A stocky, square-shouldered man with sandy hair and clear blue eyes, he turned from studying the wallmap of the European Theatre of Operations. In Normandy, the Germans were retreating. Allied forces had invaded the south of France and, in Italy, had liberated Florence.

Jim saluted and they shook hands. He knew of Brownlee's reputation as a tough fighter and strict disciplinarian. 'I am taking command as of now,' Brownlee told him.

There was a knock at the door and the orderly sergeant came in with a copy of the Strike Report. He made to hand it to Jim and Brownlee said, 'I'll take that.' The sergeant gave him the report and turned to leave. 'It is customary to salute on entering and leaving the presence of a superior officer!' Brownlee snapped. 'And while we're about it, your blouse is unfastened. Correct it at once. And do not let me see you again improperly dressed!' Flushing, the sergeant stood to attention, buttoning his uniform blouse. He saluted, glanced at Jim and left.

Brownlee's eyes flicked to Jim and away. 'Kindly see that all personnel, including officers, are informed that in future they will be expected to be properly dressed at all times. Sloppy dress is a sign of sloppy attitudes. Flying gear, for example, will be used for flying. It will not be worn in the Mess, the Aircrew Club or any offices.'

Jim was still in his leather jacket and carrying his flying helmet. He accepted the implied rebuke in silence. He laid the helmet down and said, 'I haven't had a chance to clear out the desk. If you like, I could do it now, sir.'

Brownlee nodded. 'It would be appreciated.' Jim's

nameplate was standing on the desk. He tipped it over precisely on to its face.

Jim loaded the few personal possessions he kept here into a wire correspondence basket, his spare razor, a carton of Luckies, a copy of *The Great Gatsby*. Checking the drawers, he saw the remains of the bottle of bourbon with which Rufus had toasted his departure. There was no harm in trying to break the ice. 'Can I offer you a drink, Colonel,' he said, 'to welcome you to the 525th?'

Brownlee's voice was cold. 'I appreciate the sentiment, Colonel Kiley. But please understand that the one thing I will not tolerate in my office or the working areas of any Base under my command is alcohol.'

The second rebuke. Jim stopped himself from attempting to make an excuse. 'Yes, sir,' he answered, flatly. He placed the offending bottle in the basket.

'As you have just returned from a mission,' Brownlee went on, 'no doubt you will wish to shower and change. We have a great deal to go over, but it can wait until then. I have informed the adjutant that I shall address all Staff Officers at nineteen hundred hours. I wish to familiarize myself as quickly as possible with the capabilities and problems of this Group. Capabilities will be extended, problems answered. Nothing less than one hundred per cent effort and efficiency will be accepted.'

Jim saluted. As he reached the door, he glanced back. Correction, he told himself. Colonel Brownlee's blue eyes were not clear. They were steely.

'The guy's a monster,' Elmer complained. McGraw grunted noncommittally and shifted gears. He was driving Elmer, Hymie and Chuck into town. 'Spit and polish, parades – this is Market Wetherby, not West Point!'

'Thirty-eight missions and he still has us on training flights,' Hymie snorted.

'It's knocked nearly ten minutes off formation assembly,' Chuck said.

'So what? That's gonna win the war?'

'No,' McGraw agreed, 'but you got to remember the training's not just for you hotshots. We're putting up forty-five and sixty ship formations nowadays, not once in a while, but regular. That includes a lotta greenhorn pilots. When you take off in bad weather or you're circling for an hour through thick cloud, you better be glad they know what they're doing.'

'We were getting along fine under Colonel Kiley,' Elmer said.

'Sure. But who do you think runs the training flights? Brownlee orders them. Kiley carries them out.' McGraw drew up outside Bridge Cottage. 'You guys wanna come in?'

'No, thanks, Mac,' Hymie said. 'It's Rosie's evening off. We're gonna take her to the movies.'

McGraw and Chuck watched the two friends and rivals set off up the road. McGraw shook his head. 'Hope springs eternal,' Chuck murmured. They went inside where Vi and Sally were waiting for them.

Little Billy was in bed. Vi had Betty perched on her knee and was helping her with her first reading book. The book was forgotten when McGraw appeared. Betty ran to him and he scooped her up in one brawny arm, carrying her through to where Sally was lifting clean-boiled fatigues out of the steaming copper with a pair of wooden tongs. 'You're early,' she said, pleased. 'Nearly finished. Betty, you help Uncle Joe put a kettle on.'

Chuck crouched by Vi's chair and kissed her cheek. She had recovered physically from the loss of her baby, although it had left her subdued and drawn in on herself again. She still helped her father occasionally in The Plough, but the rest of the time showed no inclination to do anything much or take up the threads of her life again. Since Chuck's return they had not made love. He was grateful to Mac and Sally. On the evenings Vi and he spent here with them, she seemed able to relax more in the company of the sensible, down-to-earth older couple.

Vi was watching Sally lever the last of the heavy fatigues

from the boiler. 'Sally keeps so busy, she makes me feel guilty,' she said.

'Take it easy,' Chuck said. 'You've got to get your strength back.'

'I got it back ages ago,' she told him quietly. 'I've just been sitting around useless.'

'Nobody thinks that,' he said, soothingly.

'I think it. I think it's time I went back into the Land Army.'

It was a hopeful sign, yet Chuck was concerned. 'If you want to. But you're sure it's not too soon?'

'It's long overdue. Life must go on, as Mac says. Besides, the harder we all pull together, the sooner this war will be over.' Chuck took her hand and held it tight. She looked down shyly. 'Sally says we can have the spare room at weekends – if you can arrange to get off.' Chuck was gazing at her. Their honeymoon had lasted for one day. On his return from Europe, they had had only six days together before he was sent back to the States. 'It's time we started our married life,' she whispered.

McGraw was carrying Betty into the parlour. Seeing Chuck draw Vi to him and hold her, he turned back to the scullery. Sally smiled to him.


Vera Mundy had come to dread the evenings, when her husband sat silent and brooding. She could not even talk about what ailed him, since at any mention of Letty he flew into a rage. Then one night, she found him bent over the counter in the dark shop, weeping. 'Get away, woman,' he sobbed.

'There's no shame in crying, Albert,' Vera said quietly. 'Not when we both know what it's about.' She led him through into the back and sat him in his chair.

He kept his eyes covered with his hand. 'God forgive me,' he said. 'Our son's out there in France, fighting for us, for his country – but all I can think about is Letty. I failed her. Everything I did was meant for the best, but somehow I failed her, our little girl. Well I won't fail her again.' Vera did not understand. 'She's out there some-where. I'm going to find her. I'm going to find her . . . and bring her home.'

It was the old, old story for Elmer and Hymie. When they told Rosie they had come to pick her up, she shrugged. 'I only said maybe.' They watched her farther along the bar, smiling and flirting with Danny Coogan.

Coogan had grown up a lot in the last six weeks of missions. As Jim Kiley had observed, they took off as boys, and came back men. Yet it was not flak or German fighters that were on his mind. 'Her name was Ann,' he was saying. 'Ann Weston. She was the nurse that looked after me, when I was in hospital here. She was . . . nothing special to look at, I guess. There was just something about her.'

'Was she your girl?' Rosie asked.

'Sort of. I wanted her to be. We just talked and that. When I got shipped back to the States to convalesce, we said we'd write. I wrote lots of times. She only answered twice, then the letters stopped coming.'

Rosie was sympathetic. 'She'd forgotten you?'

'I don't know. Maybe so. I had a crazy idea that, when I came back here, I'd meet up with her again. But she's gone. I asked some of the nurses at the EMS. They'd never heard of her.' He pushed his glass round slowly on the counter, widening the wet ring it left.

'You need cheering up,' Rosie said. 'There's a new picture starting at the Roxy tonight – Betty Grable. It's supposed to be great.'

'I don't like goin' to the movies on my own,' Coogan said.

'Well–' Rosie began. She felt a momentary twinge of guilt over Elmer and Hymie. 'I get off in ten minutes.'

Coogan smiled, boyishly. 'You mean you'd come with me? That would be real swell of you, Rosie. Only – you don't have to.'

'I'm not just being kind,' Rosie smiled. 'I might even enjoy it.'

'That does it,' Hymie muttered. 'That's the straw that bust the camel's hump – or whatever it bust.'

'You said it,' Elmer agreed. At the same moment, it occurred to him that if Hymie dropped out of the running, he himself would be ahead of anyone else in the chase after Rosie, on points.


Jack Blair was surprised to see Vera Mundy sitting in the snug, when he went in to collect some glasses. 'Come in for a drink, Vera?'

'Not really,' she told him quietly. 'Just couldn't stand being on my own.'

'Where's Albert?'

'He's gone,' Vera said, worriedly. 'He's gone to London.' Albert and she had reached the same conclusion, that that was the most likely place for Letty to be.

'I hope not,' Jack said. 'It's no place for a young girl on her own these days. Never has been. Where's Albert thinking of looking?'

'He's going to try and find my brother, Sid,' Vera told him.

Jack frowned. The last he had heard of Sid Davis was that he had been sent to jail for draft dodging and involvement in the Black Market. Vera explained that his sentence had been commuted to a year, when he turned King's evidence on most of his associates, with the proviso that on release he joined the Forces. The irony was that, at his medical, he was discovered to have a previously undetected heart murmur. He was not accepted. 'Well, well,' Jack said. 'Letty certainly used to be impressed by all his big talk.'

'That's what makes Albert certain she's there,' Vera said. 'He's convinced that if he can find Sid, Letty won't be far away.'


Rosie was disappointed when Danny brought her home from the pictures, thanked her politely, saluted and left. He had not even tried to kiss her. That was almost unique, even on a first date. She decided he must be very shy and liked him even more.

Helen had been working late at the hospital. Administration was taking more and more of her time. Every ward was crowded, among the wounded many from the savage fighting in France. There was even a ward of German prisoners, numbed, pathetically grateful men, almost unable to accept that they were being given the same conscientious care as their enemies.

As she came from her office, Helen saw the young lieutenant talking to Sister Dickson and smiled, remembering him. 'Danny Coogan, isn't it?'

Coogan saluted. 'Yes, ma'am.' On his walk back to the Base, he had called in at the EMS. He was disappointed when Sister Dickson confirmed what the other nurses had told him. Ann Weston had only been training here. She had been posted over a year ago and could be anywhere by now. It's the old snafu, he thought. Maybe she didn't even get my letters. Maybe they were redirected several times and just got lost. She might still wonder now and then why she hadn't heard from me.

He smiled and pretended it did not matter, but Helen was sorry for him, seeing him leave. Like him, she had once thought that life was simple. His generation had found out quicker than its elders, in a world run mad, that few things could be taken for granted. The old order changeth . . . When she looked at the future, she saw only uncertainty. Much of the world she had known, which changed only imperceptibly, had gone for ever. Even these boys with their gum and jitterbug, their jeeps and brashness and democratic disrespect for tradition, had helped to accelerate the change. Through them, many people, especially the young, had glimpsed a new and exciting style of life. After the war, they would never settle for the old, slow ways. But somehow, one still had to hold on to some of the old values or it would have solved nothing. What England stood for would be lost. After the war . . .

Jim had said he would come for her. But her duties and responsibilities would not have changed. What answer could she give him?

Albert Mundy had been searching the streets of London for three days. The first night he had slept in Liverpool Street station, the others on Underground platforms, still crowded although the second Blitz campaign had ended. The danger now was from increasing numbers of flying bombs. The violent explosion when they landed reminded Mundy of the crack of heavy artillery shells on the Somme, but the Londoners amazed him. They paid no attention to a missile puttering overhead. Only when its engine cut out and it began its abrupt descent did they step back into doorways or freeze, listening. After its thunderous detonation, perhaps only a street away, they carried on as if nothing had happened, picking up conversations again, getting on with their jobs. Those who could went to see if they could assist the firemen or ambulances.

The police were sympathetic and took down Letty's name and description. They did not hold out much hope of locating her, however. Neither did the Welfare Services. Too many had been bombed out, they explained, there was too much movement of population. Identity cards had ceased to have any practical meaning. It was easy for anyone who wanted to vanish completely. The only address he had for Sid turned out to be a blackened, burnt-out shell.

On the fourth day he was trudging from Piccadilly to Leicester Square when he spotted someone in one of the two queues at the separate entrances of Lyons Corner House. In his flashy, pinstripe suit, snapbrim hat and handpainted tie, it was Sid Davis. Sid had one glimpse of Mundy heading for him, left his bodyguards and slid past the startled doorman into the restaurant. When Mundy tried to follow him, the doorman stopped him. 'But there's a man just gone in,' Mundy protested. 'I have to see him!'

'Sorry, sir, you'll have to wait in the queue,' the doorman insisted. To a chorus of laughter and comments, Mundy fell back to the end of the long line. He was just in time to see Sid slip out of the other door and dodge across the street, making for Piccadilly Tube.

Mundy ran after him and caught him up at the foot of the stairs. 'Hold on!' he shouted. 'I want to talk to you!'

Sid stopped and turned. As Mundy reached him, two heavily-built men came clattering down the steps and fell in on either side of him. One had his fist swung back to strike. 'It's all right, boys,' Sid said easily, 'this upright citizen is a friend of mine, my brother-in-law.' The men relaxed, though their eyes were wary. Mundy breathed out again. Sid was eyeing his unshaven face, crumpled suit and the small case he carried. 'Well now, Albert,' he said, 'you look like you could do with a wash an' brush up.' He took Mundy's arm, led him into the Gentlemen's, nodded to the attendant and perched himself on one of the sinks. He grinned. 'Fancy meetin' you.'

'What did you – what did you run away like that for?' Mundy panted.

'Ah well, now, Albert,' Sid winked. 'There's certain parties it's as well for me to avoid. I see someone comin' for me, I don't 'ang about, old son – spite of my two assistants. So what brings you up the Smoke? Come for a dirty weekend?' He listened in silence as Mundy explained. 'Letty? She's done a bunk, has she? Well, well. The young these days, Albert.' He sucked his teeth.

'I thought – Vera and I thought you might have seen her.'

'Me?' Sid chuckled. 'She wouldn't come to me, Albert. Stands to reason. I'm 'er uncle. She knows I'd ship her straight back home.' He smoothed his lapels. 'How is my dear sister, by the way?'

'Vera's fine,' Mundy said. 'Worried about Letty.'

'Only natural,' Sid conceded. 'Poor old Vera. Come on, Albert – little pub I know, round the corner. We'll 'ave a quiet chat.'

Followed by the two bodyguards, Sid took Mundy to a public house off Gerrard Street, where he was greeted with much respect. Mundy was impressed. 'Yeah, I'm doin' all right, you might say,' Sid told him. 'Same line of business as before, only on a bigger scale, if you follow me.'

'And how are you keeping, yourself? I mean – your heart?' Mundy asked.

Sid chuckled. 'Only thing wrong with my ticker is the certificate that says it's dicky. Fifty quid to a poor, overworked doctor works wonders.' Mundy's mouth opened, and closed again. Sid tapped his knee. 'Now what's all this about Letty?'

He lit a Chesterfield and listened attentively, while Mundy poured out all that had happened, all his fears, his daughter's neglect of her baby.

'She don't go for her own kid? Your grand-daughter, Albert. That's so unwomanly.' Sid sucked his teeth again. Two US soldiers had handed an overnight bag full of cartons of cigarettes to the barman, who put them quickly under the counter. They made for Sid and he waved them away. 'Later, boys.' He turned back to Mundy. 'Seems to me you're wastin' your time, old son. Even if she's here – which ain't a cert – you could spend a hundred years and not run across 'er. Not a chance.' Mundy's head lowered in despair. 'But I tell you what I'll do,' Sid went on. 'The Law can't help you, but maybe I can. I've a good set-up, lot of people workin' for me. I'll put the word out, 'ave them keep an eye open for her. If she's anywhere within ten miles of Piccadilly Circus, they'll find her.'

'I – I don't how to thank you,' Mundy said.

'Think nothin' of it,' Sid told him. 'We're family. You go 'ome and look after Vera an' your nice shop. If little Letty turns up, I'll see 'er feet don't touch the ground till she's back in Market Wetherby.'

In the taxi to the station which Sid had insisted on paying for, Albert Mundy felt more at ease in himself than he had done for weeks. If anyone could find Letty, it would be Sid. The box of lipsticks and packets of nylons which he had been given as presents for Vera lay on his lap. They were visible proof that Sid was still in the Black Market, more deeply involved than ever, but what was important was his helpful attitude. As he had said, he was family. For the first time, Albert Mundy admitted to himself that he might have misjudged his brother-in-law.

Just as Mundy's taxi pulled into Liverpool Street, another taxi stopped by an apartment block in a cul de sac off Maida Vale and Sid Davis climbed out. His two bodyguards waited in the hall, while he went up to a flat on the third floor. The middle-aged maid who answered the door looked at him in surprise. 'Lucky for you Benny's not 'ere,' she said.

He pinched her cheek. 'Would I have come if 'e was, my duck?' Brushing her aside, he went into the lounge.

Letty was lying on the divan, buffing her nails. 'See who the cat dragged in,' she said. His eyes were on her silk-stockinged legs and she twitched her housecoat together over them.

'Don't mind me, love,' he smiled. 'Doesn't bother me.' He had to hand it to his niece. Introduced to his chief business rival as a peace offering and softener, she had lasted much longer than the one night intended. In fact, Benny was besotted with her and had set her up in this very tasty little apartment. Exclusive. No trade, or callers by order. If she played her cards right, she had it made. And she seemed shrewd enough to do just that.

Letty saw him glance at the Chinese lacquer drinks cabinet. 'Help yourself,' she told him. He crossed to pour himself a brandy. 'So to what do I owe the honour?' When he explained, she sat up quickly. 'Did you tell him where I was?'

'What d'you take me for, my love?' Sid grinned. 'Your old Dad's one of nature's losers, a punter, that's all. Less they know, the better. But I said I'd pass the message on – and I have.' He added a splash of soda to his brandy.

'He wanted me to give this up and go back home – to look after that kid and be an usherette at the Roxy?' Letty laughed. 'That's a real giggle.'

Sid smiled and toasted her. He couldn't agree more.

# TEN

Rosie could not understand Danny Coogan. He was young, really quite handsome in his way. Some of the others spoke about him as if he was a kind of hero, one of the best pilots in the Group. But he was certainly backward with girls. She knew he liked her. He took her out, was polite and attentive – yet he never tried anything. Even when she closed her eyes and waited, when they said goodnight, he never went beyond one routine kiss. Other girls envied her with her young lieutenant. She didn't dare tell them.

She sat next to him in the cinema, puzzling about it. She leaned against him and he shifted aside to give her more room. She whispered to him to get him to look at her, but the people in front shushed her. For the first time in her life Rosie was driven to take the initiative. She lifted his arm and put it round her shoulders. He smiled to her and went on watching the screen.

Elmer had had a row with Hymie when Hymie insisted on sticking to his resolution not to come to The Plough. 'You're the one who's dumb,' Hymie had said. 'Eatin' your heart out, that's dumb. I got smart.' He could not explain to Hymie that it was not only Rosie. It was The Plough, itself. It had become like a second home. He liked to be asked to play a game of darts with the English guys from the Ack-Ack battery. He liked to listen to the old folk talk about the weather and the crops. He even liked the English beer. He fitted in, and it worried him. He worried how he would fit in when he was sent home at last.

How would things be in the States? Had it changed? And what would he do? He had worked for a few months as a sodajerk and for another couple of months in his uncle's cigar store in Yonkers. He would like to try something else, but he could imagine the interview. 'Well, now, we certainly need up and coming young men like you. Have you been to college?' No, sir. 'Have you had any professional training?' No, sir. 'Well, Mr Jones, what can you do?' I know how to fire a fifty-calibre machine gun.

It was a quiet night in the bar. The harsh weather of the winter of 'forty-four had kept most people indoors. Jack Blair had been watching Elmer for some time. He pulled a half pint and set it down in front of him.

'I didn't order, Mr Blair,' Elmer said.

'It's on the house,' Jack told him. 'There's so few customers, I have to keep my hand in practice.'

Elmer smiled. 'Thanks, Mr Blair.'

'You're always alone, these days,' Jack said. 'Oh, I've heard Hymie won't come here because of Rosie, but you must have other friends.' He could remember the days when Elmer and the rest of the 'Ginger Rogers' crew came piling into the bar, laughing and boasting. It had taken some of the locals a while to realize they were only young lads, keeping their spirits up, glad to have survived another mission. Elmer shook his head. 'A friendly chap like you, you must have.'

Elmer drank some of his beer. 'I'm on my third crew, Mr Blair,' he said quietly. 'Of the first one, there's only Chuck and our skipper, Red, left. Of the second, there's only Red and Hymie. I don't – I don't get too close to anyone any more.'

Jack understood. Elmer could not stand the thought of losing yet another group of close friends.

Hymie had followed Elmer into town. He had walked past The Plough four times, but could not bring himself to go in. He went to the other pub, The Weavers' Arms, near the station, but it was a cold barn and he felt out of place. He had one beer and left.

He hated the thought of trudging all the way back to

Base, but it would be another two hours till the Liberty Wagon went back. He turned his coat collar up against the icy wind and tucked his head down.

At the first corner he nearly bumped into someone, a young woman. It was Rosie's dumpy friend from the parachute factory, the one with the frizzy hair, Jilly. He had hardly seen her since the night he had passed out in her room. 'Hi, there,' he said.

Jilly was a little nervous of him. She had been frightened the night he had turned up out of nowhere, not knowing why he had come, and for days after she had had to put up with her friend's suspicious silences. 'Where's Rosie?' she asked.

Hymie shrugged. 'Otherwise engaged. Where you goin'?'

Jilly shivered in her thin coat. 'Just home.'

'Feel like a drink?'

'No, thank you, Hymie,' Jilly said. 'I don't like pubs.'

'How about a cup of coffee?' The way he felt at the moment, he did not care whether she accepted or not.

She thought about it. 'That would be nice,' she said, and smiled.

He had forgotten how warm her smile was. 'Climb aboard,' he said. He offered her his arm and they went to see if the cafe was still open.


Al Jolson's rich, full voice seemed to fill No 2 Hangar. As he sang 'I Only Have Eyes For You', the packed audience was hushed. The first and greatest of the USO stars, he had broken his journey home from the Italian Front to give some troop concerts in England.

A cheap popular song, but Jim Kiley could feel the tug of the sentiment. He let his mind drift towards Helen for a moment, before pulling it back to his current problem. Colonel Lincoln C. Brownlee had achieved the super efficiency he admired, but at a cost to everyone. For all personnel, duty hours meant non-stop work. At any minute, in any section, company or department, the

Colonel might appear and heaven help anyone who was goofing off. He drove himself to the limit, and expected nothing less from everyone under his command, especially his officers. A second chance was seldom given for inefficiency or negligence. He had abruptly relegated the commander of 890th squadron to ground duties for failure to maintain bombing standards. At the same time, he had taken Lester Carson from flying a desk and put him back in the air as second in command of the 889th and confirmed Red Burwash, now a major, as commander of the crack 888th. He himself led the 890th on operations.

Arguably, his martinet methods paid dividends. Jim had only flown with him once, as second in command of their section on the Eighth's massive raid against industrial targets inside Germany, a huge, unimaginable armada of 2,300 bombers sent to knock out once and for all the major centres of production inside the Third Reich. The problems of air movement, assembly and synchronization of bomb runs were immense and Brownlee was one of the very few commanders who led his Group back to Base intact.

On stage, Al was grinning, waving his arms to a storm of applause. 'Settle down,' he was yelling, 'settle down, guys! I got maybe another hundred songs in me!' The cheer was deafening.

Jim had listened from near the back because he could not stay to the end. He slipped out and paused to light a cigarette, hating what he had to do. Lester Carson was an old friend. He had not flown operations for eighteen months and had suddenly been plunged back into the savagery of the war in the air. Reading over the file of mission reports, Jim had noticed that Lester had had to abort four times out of the last eight, due to malfunction in his B-17. It could just be bad luck. But Jim had done some checking with McGraw, the Line Chief.

He found Lester in his quarters, half asleep in a chair. 'You didn't come to the concert,' he said.

Lester smiled. 'If it had been the Andrews Sisters or Frances Langford, I'd have been in the front row.'

'Me, too, probably.' Jim paused. 'I see you've been having some trouble with your ship.'

'Yeah,' Lester said. 'The old scow's let me down quite often lately. I even had to pull out of the last raid on Berlin.'

'Through lack of power in No 1 and No 3 engines,' Jim nodded. 'The time before, it was because of lack of response in the rudder.'

'Yeah, I had to limp back to the field. It's a crazy feeling, landing with a full bomb load.'

'Trouble is,' Jim said, carefully, 'last two times, McGraw and I have checked these things out personally. In neither case did the malfunction you reported exist.'

Lester had sat up. 'What're you trying to say?'

'I'm saying that on both occasions and possibly some of the earlier ones, you turned back not because your ship was damaged, but because you lost your nerve.'

Lester was rising. 'You shut your mouth!' he rasped, his fist swinging.

Jim blocked the punch easily and slammed him back into his chair. It was only then he realized Lester had been drinking. 'Now you listen,' Jim said hard, 'and you listen good! Because if you don't, I'll have to report you to the Old Man and you know what will happen. He'll have you on a charge of cowardice before you can spit!'

Lester's face was ashen. 'What are you going to do?'

'I'm having you transferred at once to a Flak Home for three weeks' rest and recuperation,' Jim said. 'After that, you will fly every mission for the next two months. If you so much as pull half a length out of formation, I'll see you're busted!' Lester was trembling. 'Start packing.'

As Jim came out of Officers' Quarters, he stood still for a moment and breathed deeply. He had hated doing it, wanted to tell Lester that he understood the involuntary spasms that made the hands freeze on the controls, yet the danger from one rotten apple in the barrel was too great. Perhaps the sharp shock he had given him would help Lester to recover his nerve. If not . . .

Crossing towards the Ops Room, he heard his name called. Lorna Jane was coming after him and he stopped. He felt a passing disgust at himself for accusing Lester of cowardice. He had not yet brought himself to tell Lorna about Helen. It was long overdue. He smiled. 'The concert over?'

'No, I saw you leave,' Lorna told him. 'I thought I'd catch you up.' Her visits to his office had become less frequent with Brownlee only two doors away. There was a flurry of snow and they moved into the shelter of the side of the Briefing Hut. 'There's a party in the Officers' Club at Alconbury on Saturday,' she said. 'Red Burwash has offered to take me.'

'That should be fun,' Jim said.

Her eyes searched his face. 'You don't object?' Before he could speak, she shook her head. 'No, don't answer that. I'm being stupid.'

Jim knew that now he could put it off no longer. He owed it to her. 'Lorna–' he began.

'No, please, Jim,' she said quietly, 'you don't have to tell me. I've been getting the message for some time now, loud and clear. Only I wouldn't listen. I've . . . been throwing myself at you.' She made herself smile. 'Done everything except turn up in your room in my nightdress, but it's not on for us, is it? There's a chemical missing somewhere.'

'I wish I'd met you in the States,' Jim said.

'Oh, so do I, Colonel. You've been a perfect gentleman and it's been fun. Don't say we can still be friends. I don't want to settle for that.' Her smile was breaking up. 'It's a pity. We so nearly had everything going for us. I'm sad about it.' She paused. 'Most of all, I guess, I'm sad for myself.' She kissed his cheek and left quickly, before he could see her cry.

Jim did not understand how Germany could still fight on.

Brownlee had been called to a conference at Wing and Jim had to lead the 525th on its fourth raid on Berlin. The flak had been as intense as ever. They had lost two ships and another two were labouring to keep up. But through the scattered cloud he had seen only devastation below them, still smoking from the RAF Lancasters' night attack. He remembered the horror of the fire-bomb saturation raids on Hamburg, on Nuremberg, the destruction of Dresden. On the way home they flew near Cologne, which the Eighth had turned into a wasteland. Paris and Brussels had been liberated. US armoured forces were through Holland and poised to enter Germany itself, the Russians massing on the Polish border. Yet Hitler would not surrender. Surely not everyone down there was as crazy as he was? One attempt to assassinate him had failed. Surely there would be another attempt that would not fail? Get rid of him! Get the damn thing over with!

In 'Ginger Rogers', lead ship of the High Squadron, Major Red Burwash was thinking of Lorna. She had promised to have a scotch, a double, waiting for him. It was kind of a nice prospect. He thought of Jim, wondering if there had been a touch of coldness in his voice at briefing. It would hardly be surprising, since Red appeared to have taken over his girl. Red shook himself. What had come over him? Him of all people thinking about a dame!

His co-pilot had almost finished his fifteen minute flying spell. As Red took over, he thought of Kulik and hoped he was okay. Kulik, the radio operator, had just taken over from the wounded lefthand waist gunner, when a chunk of shrapnel had torn off his arm. There was blood everywhere amidships. He would be dead by the time they reached home. It was Red's decision. Kulik had just enough strength left to open his parachute. He had him pushed out of the plane and had watched him float away. If he was found in time, he might be saved.

Elmer broke in on his thoughts. 'Waist gunner to pilot – Little Friends. Ten o'clock.'

The sighting was reported to Jim at the same moment. And corrected at once. They had been paid another visit by the disguised JU 87s. He could make out a flight of six ME 109s closing from three o'clock level, and climbing. It was perfectly timed, just before the formation's rendezvous with its Mustang escort. He hoped to God the Group had learned its lesson.

The guns of the High Squadron were firing already. Even as he sent out an urgent call for the escort, he saw the phosphorus bombs falling from the JUs, but this time there was no panic in the formation below. The ships eased aside and the bombs whistled down harmlessly through the spaces between them. Already the formation was closing up again. We did it! We did it! Jim was shouting inside.

The MEs were already committed to their attack. Seeing themselves facing the massed firepower of the Fortress formation, two of them wheeled away. But the rest kept coming, followed by the JUs. It was almost suicide. Jim saw a Messerschmitt collide full on with a B-17. There was a sickening explosion and the two planes spun away, grappled together. A JU flashed past, not twelve feet from his own ship, which rocked and bucketed in the turbulence. There was little opportunity for the Forts' gunners to aim, but in the hail of steeljacketed bullets two more MEs went down. Hymie and at least six others claimed one of them.

The remaining hostiles had no time to regroup. The Mustang fighters, the Little Friends, had come at once and went tearing after them as they split off in all directions. Jim could hear his crew cheering.

Below and to his right, he could see a lone JU 87 heading away along the coastline. Some damage or other had slowed it down and it was flying low to avoid detection. All at once he saw a Fortress fall away from the High Squadron. Not another one, he prayed. He could not make out what was wrong with it. No figures leapt out. No one hit the silk. The B-17 went into a long and powerful dive. When he realized what was happening, he yelled. 'Commander to High Squadron! Who is that screwball?'

Red had been watching incredulously. 'It's "Hot Flush",

Colonel – Coogan's ship.' The R/T boomed as he let out a rebel yell.

'Hot Flush' was diving for the tail of the Junkers. With limited firepower from the front, Coogan planned to come up from below and to the side, banking on the B-17's manoeuvrability. The JU was struggling to rise, but did not have the power. Even its zigzags were sluggish as Coogan flattened out of his screaming dive and started to rise.

Chuck Ericson was stand-in Flight Engineer. He was in his position in the top turret, his hands tense on the handgrips of the two guns. He saw the Junkers swing away to circle and attack with its cannons, and rotated the turret, his eyes fixed on the optical sight. 'Come on, you bastard . . . come on . . .' he muttered. He pressed the trigger and his turret shook to the chatter of the guns. His bullets lanced out and raked right across the body of the JU. He could not see where he had hit and, for a moment, it flew on as if it was untouched. Suddenly flames and smoke erupted from it. He could see the pilot scrabbling at the canopy to open it, then the Junkers burst into a ball of white fire as its petrol tanks exploded.

Colonel Brownlee stood against the wall of Jim's office to listen to how he dealt with Coogan and Ericson. They were standing to attention, gazing straight ahead. 'What did you imagine you were doing?' Jim began quietly. 'Who did you think you were, Lieutenant – Errol Flynn? What did you think you were flying – a Spitfire, a Mustang? In all my time here, I have never seen anything so irresponsible! You were in command of a Flying Fortress bomber. Apart from endangering your ship and the lives of the men under you, you are perfectly aware that under no circumstances are you permitted to break formation under your own authority – certainly not to indulge in reckless acts of misplaced heroism!' He looked at Chuck. 'As for you – I understand this happened partly because of your incitement. You may have had provocation, but urging on this action was inexcusable in a member of aircrew of your experience. You will no longer be permitted to volunteer for missions.' He paused. 'You are both fined one hundred dollars. Reprimands will be entered in your reports. That is all.'

Coogan and Chuck saluted. As he turned away, Chuck was still smarting, but he did not care. No matter what the Air Exec threw at him, nothing could affect the elation he felt at having got one of them for himself, one of the enemy who had killed his child.

'One more thing,' Jim grated. He was conscious of Brownlee watching as the two men stopped at the door. 'I'm damned proud of you both.'

There was a silence after Chuck and Coogan had left. 'Of course, you intend to cancel the reprimands as soon as they're entered,' Brownlee said.

'Of course, sir,' Jim replied, tensely.

Brownlee scratched his chin. 'Call me Link,' he said. He nodded towards the stove. 'Any coffee left in that pot, Jim?'

Jim was so surprised he turned to the stove automatically and had part filled two mugs before he had fully taken in what Brownlee had said. He handed him one of the mugs.

'No doubt you think I'm a hard-nosed son-of-a . . . gun,' Brownlee said. 'Well, I am. But I've had to be. To match your reputation.' He smiled. 'And that's a fact. I knew I was joining one of the best Groups in the Air Force. I had to be pretty tough to make it *the* best – which now it is. And much of it thanks to you.'

'Thank you,' Jim said.

'That's just between us,' Brownlee went on. 'But I've no fear of it getting around – because you're clearing out.'

'Clearing out?'

Brownlee took out some papers and laid them on the desk. 'Your marching orders, Jim. You're too good to stay here any longer. You're being put in command of a B-17 Strike Group, based in France. Your objective will be to hunt out and destroy the remaining V-2 rocket sites. The

525th is going to miss you, Jim. So will I.' He held out his hand.

Helen had been down to the Far Field with tea for Vi and the other landgirls. When she returned, Nanny met her in the hall. 'You had a telephone call, Mrs Dereham,' she said. 'From that Major – no, Colonel Kiley. He was calling to say goodbye.'

Helen did not understand. 'Goodbye? Will he ring back?'

'He said he couldn't. His plane was waiting.'

Helen could not think. Jim leaving? 'Where was he going?'

'Somewhere overseas. He wouldn't tell me where.' Nanny thought. 'Now, what was it? Oh, yes, I was to tell you most particular to remember what he said.'

What he said? I'm coming back for you . . . 'Was that all?'

'Just to remember what he said.'

The door of Ronnie's study was open and he had heard. Jim Kiley had left. He was heartily grateful. Yet he had also heard the catch in Helen's voice as she questioned Nanny and her footsteps as she had gone hurrying upstairs. He would not mention it. Like so much else, he would not mention it, unless she did. He admired Kiley, and wished him well. He also wished profoundly that he would never come back.

Rosie Blair had a surprise that evening as well.

There was an impromptu party at The Plough and she was nearly as proud of Danny Coogan as Vi was of Chuck. Major Burwash was there and a pretty lady lieutenant. He toasted the 'Hot Flush' and her crew and the Junkers 8 they had shot down, although he warned them never to do anything like that again.

In the laughter and celebration, Danny whispered to her that he wanted to see her alone. She fetched her coat quickly and they slipped out the back. Rosie was very excited. She had never seen him so eager before. She could feel an eagerness in herself, a recklessness that she had always kept in check.

They did not go far, only a few steps from the door. She leaned back against the wall. 'Well?' she breathed. She was ready, willing for any move he made. He had waited all those weeks, waited until he had proved himself. He didn't have to prove anything to her. If he wanted her, she was his.

'I had to tell you, Rosie.' He was excited. 'I heard today that Ann might be over in the General Hospital at Norwich. I've got a pass tomorrow to go and look for her.'

'Ann? . . .' Rosie faltered.

'The girl I told you about – the nurse. Gee, I hope she's there! I knew you'd want to know. Wouldn't it be great?'

Rosie could not take it in. '. . . What about me, Danny?'

'You've been swell, Rosie,' Coogan said sincerely. 'Cheering me up and all. But I can't ask you to help me find her. It's something I have to do, myself.' He kissed Rosie on the cheek and went inside.

Rosie did not follow him. For the first time in her life, she was crying over a man.

# ELEVEN

The harsh weather had continued over Christmas and into the new year, thick ice and driving snow, the worst anyone could remember. With the Allied Air Forces virtually grounded by impossible flying conditions, Hitler had seized his chance and flung von Rundstedt's columns forward in the Ardennes in an attempt to cut the Allied Front in two. Their attack was finally driven back, but it had shown that Germany, whom many had thought virtually beaten, was still capable of mounting a dangerous offensive. 1945, which everyone had looked forward to with optimism, opened on a sombre note. The few sorties which the 525th had been able to make were strategic missions to assist the hard-pressed ground forces.

Jack Blair was polishing the top of the bar merely to keep busy. It was a quiet night. There would be no aircrew from the Base. For a week the weather had shown signs of improvement and they were on standby every day. From McGraw and occasional groundcrew who called in, he had heard of more casualties among the boys he knew, aircraft destroyed not so much by the enemy but by the weather, crashes on the icy taxiway at take-off, collisions in the blanketing fog.

As Jack looked up, he could hardly believe his eyes. Albert Mundy was coming in. A black figure in his Civil Defence uniform, he advanced to the bar and held his helmet under his arm, standing rigidly as though to attention. Twenty years before, Jack and Mundy had fallen out over Vera, whom Mundy later married. Jack had been a thorn in his flesh ever since, particularly when the Mundy twins had made friends with Rosie and later, when Peter, as a troubled teenager, had come to Jack for the advice he could not ask from his dictatorial father.

Farther along behind the bar, Rosie was reading *Picture Post*. She glanced up and blinked. The only time she had seen Mundy here before was one day when he had stormed in to pick a fight.

'What can I do for you, Albert?' Jack asked warily.

'I have come to drink a pint of beer,' Mundy announced. 'And to invite you to join me.'

Jack laid down his cloth. 'You mean, after all these years you want to bury the hatchet?'

'It is in honour of my son, Peter,' Mundy went on, ignoring the question. 'Whom you attempted to dissuade from serving his country and encouraged to become a conscientious objector.'

'Well, now, that's not true, Albert,' Jack said. 'The boy was worried. I—'

'Today we had word that our son, serving with his regiment in the British Second Army under Montgomery, has been wounded in the advance on the Ruhr.'

Rosie came towards them, anxiously. 'Peter's been wounded?'

Jack was shaken. 'Albert, that's terrible news! What happened?'

'Do I get my pint or not?'

'Oh, come on, man!' Jack insisted. 'What did they say? How did it happen?'

Mundy had entered with a prepared speech and was thrown for a moment. 'I dunno, do I? Just that he'd been wounded in an attack on enemy positions. He'll tell us when we see him.'

'He's coming home?'

'They said he'd be sent back to a hospital somewhere in England. But you admit it now, don't you? He's got the right stuff in him. He's a man, a proper soldier. The kind of son I always wanted.'

Jack was drawing a pint of beer. 'I'm not going to quarrel with you, Albert. I just hope Peter's not too badly hurt. I'm fond – we're all fond of the boy. For his sake, you're welcome here.' He set the glass down in front of Mundy. 'There'll be no charge.'

Mundy had been reaching into his pocket and was balked again. He had meant to march in, make his announcement, drink his beer, pay for it and stride out again, leaving Jack Blair thoroughly discomfited. It had not worked out exactly as he had imagined it. He could not leave now with the desired dignity. He mumbled a thank you and took a drink of his beer.

Rosie was worried about Peter, who had always been like a younger brother. There was less than a year between them, but it made her feel protective towards him.

Everything was going wrong. She had never been so upset over anyone as she had been over Danny Coogan. She had built up such an expectation in her mind, and then to discover that all he dreamed of was his little nurse . . . Predictably, he had not located her on his trip to Norwich. It had been a false alarm. He was hurt, but instead of turning to Rosie for consolation, he had immersed himself in his duties, hardly ever leaving the base.

Because of him, Rosie had lost Hymie, whom she had not seen for over two months. Elmer was becoming almost as much of a stranger. In preparation for the end of the war he had started a course in accountancy and book-keeping. He rationed himself to only one evening a week away from his studies. And the new aircrew who kept arriving, fresh from the USA, seemed so young. The same old jokes about the English weather and beer and money, the flirtatious remarks and fancy talk, she'd heard them all so often.

When the boys first arrived in their glamorous uniforms, with their free and easy ways, their high spirits, treating all the girls with a mixture of brashness and a mannerly politeness they had never met before, speaking in the accents of the silver screen, thousands of John Waynes and James Stewarts and Robert Taylors, they had seemed so exciting. Irresistible, many girls had found. Like Letty. It took a while to realize they were just as inexperienced as the English boys, only different, not so bashful or awkward. It had all been fun at first. She didn't like to think how many of them had been killed.

Behind Albert Mundy, she saw Chuck coming in. As she smiled to him, her mouth opened. Hymie was following him. Hands in his pockets of his coat, he sauntered over to the bar. Chuck nodded to Jack and went through to the back parlour, where Vi was finishing the ironing.

'Hymie!' Rosie exclaimed, delightedly. 'I haven't seen you in ages!'

'You noticed?' Hymie asked, innocently.

The rebuke was deserved and Rosie smiled apologetically. 'It was one of those things, Hymie. It's nice you've come back.'

Albert Mundy had stiffened the moment he saw the American uniforms. He had still not accepted the presence of US forces. All his troubles he dated from their arrival. One or two may be all right, he always said. But taken as a whole, they're not proper fighting men, no discipline, not one of them knows how to march in step. 'I wish my boy was here,' he muttered, loud enough to be heard, 'just to let them see what a real soldier looks like.'

Hymie winked to Rosie. 'Hi, Mr Mundy. How's Peter getting on?'

'Since you are kind enough to ask,' Mundy said, drawing himself up, 'he has a Blighty one. He's been wounded.'

'Well, whaddya know?' Hymie drew his left hand from his coat pocket. It was thickly padded and swathed in bandages. 'Snap.'

Rosie gasped.

Jack was concerned. 'How did you get it, son? In a raid?'

'Yeah, coupla days ago,' Hymie nodded. 'But it's nothin' at all.' The raid had been on U-boat bases at Kiel. As expected, flak was dense round the target, but Red, who led the formation, had learned from Jim Kiley how to avoid other concentrations on the way out and back. No ships were lost and the formation was starting to congratulate itself, when a terrible enemy appeared, something the 525th had only heard about. Three of the new jet fighters, ME 262s, dived out of cloud cover and began to circle the Group like sheepdogs. Their speed and their rate of climb were incredible, like nothing anyone had ever seen before. It was almost impossible to track them with a gunsight. In their attack, they streaked through the formation, wheeling and banking, seemingly impervious to bullets, while six B-17s were shot down and another two fell slowly away, later to be posted as Missing In Action. Only the jets' limited airtime saved the rest of the formation. Their fuel supply running out, the MEs made one last pass and sped away. Hymie had been so fascinated, he hardly felt any pain when a slug from one of them tore through his glass bowl, neatly severing the middle and third fingers of his left hand. He admitted he had been lucky. It had been so cold, the blood flow had frozen. Otherwise, he might not have made it.

'But what will it mean, Hymie?' Rosie asked, anxiously.

'No more combat. They're shipping me back to the good old US of A.'

Rosie was downcast. 'You're leaving?'

'Pretty well straight away. I looked in kind of to say goodbye. Milwaukee, here I come.'

'You had – what was it? – five missions still to fly,' Jack said. 'You won't have to do them now.'

'Know something, Mr Blair?' Hymie grinned. 'I don't object to that at all.'

Strictly speaking, Hymie was not telling the truth. He was not leaving 'straight away'. He had ten more days before being sent home, but he did not plan to spend them mooning around Rosie.

Later that evening, his feet were under the table in Jilly Binns's room near the parachute factory, while she served supper. He had wanted to take her out, but she told him it was a wasteful expense. Soon, he might need his money, back in civvy street.

It was a scratch meal made out of bits and pieces, whatever scraps she had left, but she had a talent. 'They look like hamburgers – but they ain't.' Hymie tasted one. 'Hey-hey . . . they're great! You could make a fortune with these!'

Jilly laughed. She was worried, however. 'Hymie, be serious,' she asked. 'What's Rosie going to say when she hears you've been coming here?'

'Who's gonna tell her?' Hymie replied, his mouth full. 'You?' She shook her head. 'And not me. What she don't know . . . You gotta understand one thing, Jilly. I don't pine for the times I spent with Rosie. She was terrific – but it wasn't real. Not like you're real.'

Jilly was embarrassed. She knew she could not compare in any way with her friend. She had no figure to speak of, she was not pretty, her hair was always a mess, however she tried to fix it. 'You don't mean it,' she said quietly.

He put down his fork. 'One thing about you, you always know when I'm kidding. Am I kidding?' After a moment, she shook her head. He grinned and took up his fork again.

'I could never work it out,' she said. 'Other boys finished their tours and went home. Yours must've been over, months ago.'

'Just before D-Day,' he nodded. 'But round about then, we were all needed. The Air Force wouldn't release any aircrew till the end of June. And that was when Red, our skipper, the one that's now Air Exec, he decided to volunteer for a second tour. Well, Elmer and me thought about it. Another thirty-five missions – shoot! But we kinda felt that if we didn't volunteer, too, we'd kinda be letting him down. Him and the old "Ginger Rogers".' He paused. 'Maybe if I hadn't, I'd still have ten fingers. But I don't regret it, not any of it.' He looked at her. 'Most of all, because if I hadn't stayed on, I'd never have gotten to know you.'

Jilly saw that, for once, Hymie was very, very serious. She hardly knew where to look.

*

131

It was nearly the end of January and the shooting season was almost over. Ronnie Dereham had been told there was still the occasional pheasant down by the copse. Food was becoming scarce again, as more and more had to be sent to the troops in Europe and to the starving populations liberated from the retreating Germans. The prospect of a bird or two for the pot was tempting. He took down his shotgun and filled the pockets of his hacking jacket with the last of the cartridges.

The day was cold and the sky was a clear, wintry blue. He wrapped a scarf round his neck. The ground had thawed, but the path to the copse past the orchard and across the High Field should be as hard as a metalled road. He was not mistaken and he was able to propel himself along in his wheelchair quite easily, stopping now and then to rest.

He had not told Helen about his latest medical examination. He had been sure he could detect a faint return of sensation in his lower limbs and had insisted on it. The specialist was very thorough, and called in a second opinion. Their findings were difficult to accept. Not only was there no improvement, there were indications of a rapidly increasing deterioration of his nervous system. In a few months, he would probably not even be able to sit up. Difficult to accept that one might soon be a vegetable, a conscious vegetable. That was the worst of it.

No, he thought, that was not the worst. He had tried not to pretend to himself. Yet the longing for life to return to normal, to be as it was, was too powerful. There were days when he raged at his immobility, his impotence. Helen never showed by any outward sign that the nature of their marriage had altered. She was unfailingly caring and attentive. Kind ... But it was not kindness he wanted from her, and that was one more thing he had to fight against resenting. They had once been very close. Mentally and physically, they had been perfectly suited. It was by that closeness that he judged the depth of the feeling which had drawn her to Jim Kiley. It must have been strong, indeed. And she must have struggled against it, as there were days when he felt she still struggled. He did not doubt that she had slept with Kiley. It hurt him, but he could not condemn her. How could he deny her for the rest of her life something which he could no longer give her?

A dangerous train of thought, he told himself. He could not be a complaisant husband. Understanding, he hoped, not complaisant. Helen was his wife. And damn the doctors and specialists! He wasn't finished yet. If he went down, he'd go down fighting. Helen had stood by him. He owed her that much, not to give in.

He had crossed the High Field and panted as he halted by the gate, a hundred yards or so from the copse. It was a good spot. The low wall would shelter him and give him cover from the birds, if there were any. His hands were stiff with cold as he loaded the gun, a cartridge in each barrel. He leaned the shotgun against the gate and chafed his hands to restore the circulation. Idiot . . . The ground sloped slightly and the gun toppled to the side. He could not reach it. Just then he heard the whir of wings and a cock pheasant, its plumage bright against the bare earth, plopped down to land halfway between himself and the copse.

He thought of his scarf and unwound it. Not making too much movement, he held it in a loop and hooked it round the barrels of the gun, raising it from the ground towards him.

Vi was in the Far Field, talking to Schuster, the German POW assigned to help her team of landgirls, a helpful, apologetic man. They both heard the sound of the shot. She thought it might be a poacher. She could never remember what made her go and look.

By the time Helen reached home, they had carried Ronnie back and laid him on the couch in the downstairs room where he had slept alone for over a year. They had found him lying crumpled by the gate, a hole torn out of his side. While Nanny called the hospital, Vi and Schuster had tried to make Ronnie comfortable. Schuster had been a medical attendant, but there was nothing he could do, nothing anyone could do.

All the way from the hospital, Helen's mind had been in a turmoil. Dr Heywood had accompanied her, but she heard none of his reassuring phrases. Ronnie was a first class shot, brought up to the gun. How could it have been accidental? She prayed that she was not too late.

When she saw him lying on the couch, pale and motionless, she felt such a surge of guilt that she nearly cried out for forgiveness. It must have been deliberate. If Jim and she had brought him to this, how could there be forgiveness?

Ronnie's sight was failing and he could just make out Helen's face as she knelt beside him. He was glad she had come. But what he read in her face troubled him. He could see that she blamed herself. The only good thing in this ridiculous business was that now she would be free. But she would never be free, if she blamed herself . . . He had barely strength to move his lips. He could not see her any more and could only hope that she and the others would hear him. '. . . Forgive me,' he whispered. 'Such a stupid, stupid accident. The first I've ever had. The safety catch . . . left off. Stupid. Not a mistake I'll make again.' The darkness was like a weight pressing on him, on his heart. 'I wanted – wanted to say I love . . .' His lips stopped moving.

Helen held his face in both her hands, gazing at him. He was dead.

# TWELVE

Vera Mundy did not care if she was breaking the law. She pared whatever she could from the customers' rations and saved her own, to be ready for her son's homecoming. It was longer to wait than she expected, but the tea she put on the table on his first day home was spectacular. Peter marvelled at it, jams and pastes, scones and cakes, tinned fruit and jelly and condensed milk. It was like a pre-war party.

He had not entirely recovered yet. The stiffness in his leg was easing, but his splinted right arm was still in a sling. They had had to reset the bones several times. 'I don't know how you manage it, Mum,' he smiled. Vera was very pleased.

His father would not let him change out of uniform. 'A corporal, eh? That's very good. A start, anyway.' He made Peter tell them several times of the attack on the machine gun emplacement which he and his platoon had carried out, with his company pinned down by mortar fire. He accepted as soldierly modesty Peter's statement that he really remembered very little about it, not all the details. All he could recall was running and dodging and firing, his sten gun growing hot in his hands, reloading and shouting at the others to come on. The mortar bomb that knocked him off his feet left him deafened for a few minutes and dazed. He was not even aware he had been wounded. He was lying on his side and something was sticking into his leg. None of the rest of the platoon were moving and the German machine gun was still chattering, holding up the advance. He rolled over on to his back and felt the front of his left leg where it hurt. There was a lump in the long, pouched pocket. It was a grenade he had stuffed down there and forgotten about.

His right arm was beginning to hurt even worse than his leg, but he managed to ease the grenade out. It was just as well he had to move slowly. If the enemy had seen him, he would have drawn their fire. Holding the grenade in his weak right hand, he drew out the pin with his left. He counted up to six, as long as he dared, then swivelled and hurled the metal pineapple up and over the sandbagged lip of the emplacement. He remembered the roar of its detonation and being spattered with earth and that was all, until he woke up in the Casualty Clearing Station.

'You'll get a medal, I shouldn't wonder,' Mundy said. 'The MC. I'll write to your Commanding Officer.'

'Please, Dad,' Peter protested.

'Let him be, Albert,' Vera said. 'He just wants to rest. Don't you, Peter, love?'

'Rest?' Mundy snorted. 'If I know him, he'll be raring to get back into action. The Hun's not beaten yet, not by a long chalk. Montgomery's crossed the Rhine, but if he's to get to Berlin first, before the Russians, he'll need every man.'

'I'm not going back overseas, Dad,' Peter said quietly. 'I'm going to Aldershot for training, when I've been passed fit.'

'Training?' Mundy wondered. 'Training for what?'

'They accepted my application,' Peter told him. 'When my arm's right again, I'm going to be a bandsman.'

'Bandsman? . . .' Mundy almost gaped at him. He had been certain the realities and discipline of army life would have knocked all those fanciful, effeminate ideas about music out of his son's head. 'Don't talk rubbish!'

'It's what I want to be,' Peter said. 'They seem quite keen to have me, since I can read music and so on.' His voice was quiet, but definite. He seemed more grown up and his father choked on what he had been about to say, realizing that arguing or sneering at him would no longer have any effect.

Vera was relieved when the outburst she had feared did

not come. 'That'll be nice, Peter,' she said. 'You'll like that.'

'I was waiting to be transferred, even before I was wounded,' Peter told her. 'I didn't want to bring it up before it was certain.' He glanced at his father, who was glowering at his plate. It would be as well to change the subject. He had learnt from his mother something about the situation with his sister and it had shaken him. They had to discuss it. 'When do you think you'll hear anything more about Letty?'

There was a silence. Vera glanced anxiously at her husband. 'I don't know anyone of that name,' Mundy said, deliberately. 'There is no one of that name in this family.' He rose and went through into the shop.

Peter looked at his mother and saw she was nearly in tears. 'We don't know any more than I told you,' she said. 'Your Uncle Sid promised your Dad he'd find her, but – we never heard from him. Please, love. Don't mention her again to your dad.'

Peter had not expected to be treated like a returning hero, but he had looked forward to a warmer welcome at The Plough. Jack Blair was pleased enough to see him and Rosie and Vi smiled, but somehow it was subdued.

'You're sure you're all right?' Rosie asked him. 'You're recovering?'

'Oh, yes,' Peter assured her. He moved his arm inside the sling. 'I feel like a fraud wearing this.' She did not smile. He saw her glance along at Vi's husband, who sat silently at the bar, gazing at an unlit cigarette which he turned over and over in his fingers.

Jack brought Peter a pint of best bitter. 'This is for you, son,' he said. 'It's good to have you back in one piece.'

'What's up, Mr Blair?' Peter asked. 'What's wrong?'

'Elmer's been shot down,' Rosie said dully.

Peter remembered the big, likable US sergeant. 'The one who played the mouth organ so well? Elmer Jones?'

Chuck had brought the news. 'That's the one,' he nodded. 'His own ship was held back for servicing this morning, fault in one of the stabilizers. Elmer volunteered to go with another crew. It was a raid on Salzburg. The ship he was on had a direct hit. And went down.'

Rosie caught her breath and turned away from the bar. 'Oh, no,' Peter heard her whisper.

'It doesn't necessarily mean—' he began. He looked at Chuck, urging him to say something to comfort her.

'There's no point in hoping,' Chuck said flatly. 'Some of the others baled out, but Elmer didn't make it. He was still on board when it crashed. Reconnaissance says it was completely burnt out.'

The B-17 had had it. Elmer had never been so sure of anything, but surprisingly he did not feel fear, only regret. He had come all this way, almost to the end of the war, for everyone knew it could last barely a few more days, and now he was going to buy it. In a handful of seconds, it was curtains. He swore gently to himself as he braced himself against the midships bulkhead and waited for the impact.

Time seemed to be frozen. He could hear the screaming of the ship as its angle of descent increased. The two starboard engines were on fire and he could see smoke billowing past his gunport. 'Please, let it be quick,' he begged whoever was up there. He had seen too many men burned, heard their agony, and had a horror of it.

The crew had been ordered to bale out ten minutes ago and those that were alive had jumped. Elmer had been unable to follow them. His own fault. Against regulations he had taken off his 'chute and hung it against the air frame to give himself more room to manoeuvre as he swung his sixty-five pound machine gun around.

When the ME 262 jet came in out of the sun, it had angled in so fast that even without the cumbersome parachute, Elmer had been unable to track his gun on to it. When they thought it had gone, back it came again, zigzagging through the formation at its incredible climbing rate. Cannon shells had ripped through Elmer's Fort, killing two crewmen and totally destroying, among other things, Elmer's 'chute.

It had all been over in seconds. They had learned to fear the jets, but their danger was over in one pass, at the most two, for the ME's tremendous fuel consumption meant it could not remain airborne for more. There was no member of the entire Eighth Air Force and RAF combined who was not thankful that Hitler had not allowed Albert Speer to build more of them, as the entire course of the war might have been altered. Nevertheless, despite the limited duration of the attack, his ship had been mortally damaged. The whole fuselage round his waist window had been riddled and the plexiglass shield of his gun shattered. He owed these last minutes of life to his helmet and flak vest. Two chunks of shrapnel had hit him so hard he was winded. Some of his ribs felt as though they were cracked. His vest was slashed open, the metal plates dented, and there was a bright metal gouge right across the crown of his helmet. The few brains he had could have been scooped out of his skull. He nearly puked at the thought.

His ears were ringing and he tried to unscramble his thoughts. Everything was supposed to go very clear, slow-motion, at times like these, but he couldn't think coherently. He caught himself fishing inside his flying suit for his harmonica. Well, at least it was there. It would go down with him. He found himself thinking wryly about Hymie. That son-of-a-bitch. Always the one to take the easy way out. A bullet in the mitt and he hitches a ride back to Milwaukee. Some win – some lose. I should have left a letter for Rosie, Elmer told himself. What the hell. If she doesn't know how I feel about her by now, she never will.

Elmer was glad that it wasn't 'Ginger Rogers' that was going down. She was a great lady, not like this flying coffin, 'Dumby Run'. He was the dumby, for volunteering to fly in her. It had been a scratch crew. He should've known better. As she began to lose altitude, falling away from the formation, he had wished Red was flying her. Then they'd have a chance. He just didn't know how this kid pilot would handle in a crisis.

That was unfair. The pilot had stayed with him, when Elmer had explained that he couldn't jump. All he knew about him was that his name was Johnnie and he came from Illinois, but he had seen that the only hope for Elmer was if he stayed on board and tried to crash land. The rest of the crew had hit the silk and by the time Elmer had quit arguing with him, it was too low for him to jump, anyway.

At 300 m.p.h. the shape of a mountain rushed towards them. It was odds on whether 'Dumby Run' would bury herself nose first into the rocky slopes or whether she would tear herself to a thousand pieces, furrowing through the woods in the valley.

It was journey's end, either way.

Johnnie's voice was quiet in Elmer's earphones. 'Okay, Elmer, I'm going to try to slow her down by traction, clipping the treetops. It's going to be a little rugged. If you can pray – say one for me.'

The sound cut off. Elmer closed his eyes, but could not think of any words to say, except 'Our Father . . . Our Father . . .'

He could feel the deck miraculously levelling out slightly as Johnnie fought her nose up. For a brief second there was a silence, broken only by the whoosh of her huge body through the air, as he cut her engines off. Then a violent cracking and bouncing, and a bone shattering crunch as 'Dumby Run' sank lower and hit the trees, which splintered like matchsticks as she sliced through them. Elmer's eyes had opened wide and his mouth had opened to scream, but the scream strangled in his throat. The last thing he saw before he blacked out was her starboard wing, mangled and trailing streamers of blazing oil, hurtling past his waist window.

He did not know how long he had been unconscious. Maybe hours. When he could focus his eyes, he looked at his watch. It had smashed. He grew aware of a dull throb in his wrist. The back of his head hurt and when he touched it, he felt blood.

Elmer picked himself up, amazed he was in good enough shape to stand. He was groggy and leaned against the shattered stump of a tree. He had been thrown clear of the ship. Behind him was a path of destruction, the valley for two or three hundred yards littered with chunks and shreds of the aircraft. She had lost her wings and her tail had snapped off. The battered fuselage was bent like a broken-backed whale. There was a smell of gasoline everywhere and small fires were scattered all along the track she had ploughed. He had to get away from her fast.

First, however, he stumbled round to the front of the plane. The cockpit was split open and he clambered up. The skipper, Johnnie, was still in his seat, slumped forward, and Elmer saw at once there was nothing to be done. His neck was broken. The smell of gas was becoming stronger. The hull must have been saturated with fuel. Elmer knew he should search for one of the survival kits, but there was no time. There was something else he had to do.

He wrenched at the broken cockpit until he could reach inside painfully and loosen the dogtag from round Johnnie's neck. Somewhere in Illinois there was a family. Elmer promised himself he would do his best for the man who had saved his life, and lost his own.

He fell back on to the ground and had to crawl a few yards before he could stand again. Get out, get away, come on! he told himself. His mind was working again. He was standing in what could become a deathtrap. Apart from the danger of an explosion, it would only be a matter of time before Germans came looking. He had to move. If only he could get nearer to the American positions. They were within fifty miles of Salzburg. He set out towards the setting sun, moving downhill away from the wreckage because he would be able to move faster.

He had only been walking for four or five minutes, when there was a roar behind him and a blast of heat that reached him even through the trees. 'Dumby Run' had turned into a funeral pyre for Johnnie Pilot.

If that didn't fetch the Krauts, nothing would . . .

In spite of his dizziness and the ache in his wrist and from his cracked ribs, Elmer made himself stumble on. He had only one thought, to get as far away as possible. Then he would have to hide, find food and shelter. If only he could lie low for a few days, the war would be over.

He desperately wanted to stop, to sink to his knees, but somehow he made himself keep going. He came to a stony path and began to follow it. He knew he was going crazy, for he was going up again. Then he understood. The path had curved round and was taking him back up the mountain which had so nearly been his tomb. He paused irresolutely, swaying, but could not face the thought of retracing his steps. It had used up most of his strength getting this far. He went on.

Night was falling and the woods around him became dark, shadowless. There was an almost unnatural silence. The only sound was his own hoarse breathing and the stumbling scrape of his steps. It was cold and soon he would have to stop. Something caught his eye. It became more distinct as he climbed. Ahead of him, off the path on a bare, rocky spur above the treeline, was a timbered hut.

Closer still, he could see that its windows were shuttered. There was no sign of anyone living there, no smoke from the brick chimney. He had to risk it, for he could go no farther. As he lurched towards the door, he wondered what he would do if it was locked. If it was the movies, he thought, he'd kick it down. Like in that film with Randolph Scott he'd seen with Rosie at the Roxy. He was light-headed, beginning to laugh. He stopped himself. If there were people inside, Germans, what would they do when they saw him? Somewhere he'd heard that Austrians were more decent. Was this Austria?

He reached for the door handle as if it were his own home. The door opened and he stumbled across the threshold. Inside, the hut smelt musty. There was no one.

The light was dim, but he could make out two bunk beds and a table with benches beside it. Hanging from a hook on the back of the door were a pair of thick serge trousers and a rough jacket.

He found a cupboard and looked in it for food. It was empty. He was grinning again. 'What the hell,' he said aloud. 'What'd you expect? Four Star service?' If he did not lie down soon, he would fall where he stood. He reeled over to the nearer bunk bed and climbed into the bottom bunk.

He lay there with his eyes shut, but he was too exhausted for sleep. His arm still throbbed. He could not move his left hand, but thankfully the blood from the wound on the back of his head had dried. He knew that in his condition he was helpless, and began to wonder what would happen to him if he was caught here. The end of the war was imminent, yet he had heard scary stories about what some Krauts were doing to prisoners. He had thrown away his helmet and torn flak jacket, but was still wearing his flying suit and uniform. Better get rid of them, he told himself.

He remembered the clothes on the back of the door. He pushed himself up, crying out when he put pressure on his wrist. He moved to the door and took down the jacket and trousers, which stank of wood smoke and sweat. Slowly and cumbersomely, he changed into them, then hid his own clothes behind the wide cupboard. When that was done, he felt a lot better. Stupid place to hide anything, he thought. He dragged his things out again, went out into the darkness and dumped them under a pile of brushwood and pine cones on the edge of the forest.

Far away to the west he could just catch the muted rumble of heavy artillery. Big guns were firing. There was an occasional flash of a larger explosion just on the horizon. Maybe that's us, he thought. There was nothing more he could do. He was here by a miracle, and would need another one to get any farther. He got himself back inside and lay listening to the distant gunfire, as he gave in to sleep.

It was more like unconsciousness than sleep, but something woke him again, less than an hour after dawn. The guns had fallen silent. He could not think why he had woken. Light was creeping into the room through chinks in the wooden walls. It was bitterly cold. All at once, the door crashed open. He tried to rise from the bunk, but before he could lever himself up, he found himself gazing into the muzzle of a Schmeisser.

The man who held it was about the same age as himself, his eyes tired and hard. He was shouting in German. Elmer shrugged and put up his hands. The man stared at him and he realized he had made a mistake, possibly fatal. A hand reached for his throat which was uncovered and tore off the dogtag. The man hissed, 'Amerikanische Luftwaffe . . .'

Elmer was now wide awake. The bulky coat the man wore was grey, held together by a military belt. The cap he wore had a deaths-head insignia above the visor. Sweet Jesus, Elmer thought. SS . . . 'Prisoner of war,' he said.

'Los! Los!!' the SS man shouted. He jabbed his Schmeisser at Elmer's face, its snout splitting his upper lip against his teeth.

Other SS soldiers were coming into the hut. Some overturned the cupboard and searched the other beds, while Elmer was hauled from his bunk and hustled outside. An officer standing by a truck turned to look at him and shouted words Elmer did not understand, but he knew what they meant. He had not fully thought out the consequences of changing into civilian clothes. 'American,' he said. 'Eighth Air Force. Prisoner of—'

The men holding him threw him forward and he stumbled, nearly falling. The SS officer was shouting at him again and, when Elmer stammered his name, rank and number, gestured abruptly. Elmer's hands were wrenched behind his back and secured by something like a strap. One man dragged him farther out into the open and turned him round. The rest of the soldiers came from

144

the hut and joined the others in a ragged line. It was a firing squad.

The man holding Elmer left him and ran to join the line. The officer had taken his Luger from its holster and moved to the side. Elmer gazed at them, motionless and disbelieving. They were just going to shoot him down. He was in no state to make a run for it. There was nothing he could do against six of them. There was no point even trying to explain, and no time. The officer had wheeled round to his men, who were raising their automatic rifles.

Elmer had hardly been conscious of the sound, but it was growing louder. As the officer gave the command to aim, it suddenly became a whistling scream that re-echoed from the cliffs of the valley. It was a sound that Elmer recognized. The SS men were looking up. Elmer turned his head quickly and saw a fighter plane diving towards them. It was a US Mustang.

Two of the firing squad began to shoot into the air. The others threw themselves to the ground. Elmer hit the deck at the same time and rolled over into a small dip behind him. It was like a drainage channel, only a foot deep. He pressed himself down into it as the Mustang opened up with all its machine guns. The earth exploded.

Elmer lay with his cheek against the ground, his bound hands behind his back. He could feel the impact of the steeljacketed slugs on the hard earth all round him. When the Mustang had roared past, he lifted his head cautiously. He could see it banking and hugged the deck again. At his height and speed, the fighter pilot could not spot any significant difference between his human targets. It was coming back and its slugs tore across the bare spur of land again, raking it from another angle. Elmer, huddling in his shallow ditch, felt them drum past only inches from his back.

Again it lasted only for seconds. This time, when Elmer raised his head, he saw the Mustang heading away, soaring and swooping, as its pilot hunted for other small batches of German troops. Elmer got cautiously to his knees, ready to try to make a break for it. There was no need. The SS soldiers lay contorted in death. The officer was trying to push himself up. Blood gushed from his mouth and he sprawled forward on his face.

Still wary, Elmer climbed to his feet. He was the only one left alive. The Mustang pilot thought he had wiped out seven Krauts, never knowing one of them was an American. Amazingly, Elmer's luck had held.

He felt now that he was inviolate. For some reason he was destined to survive. As soon as he got his arms free, he would find food in the truck. He could bind up his wrist, arm himself. Then it was simply a matter of hanging on until the US Army got here. And then it would be all over.

# THIRTEEN

The end came with bewildering suddenness. There was a constant stream of cities captured, armies surrendering. Berlin was surrounded and US and Russian forces linked up. Yet the Allies were robbed of the sense of approaching victory by the announcement of the death of President Roosevelt. Flags were at halfmast. German troops still fought on in Holland and northern Germany. Allied bomber formations were rammed head-on by German suicide pilots. London still reeled from a devastating attack of V-2 rockets. Then came the news that the Russians were in Berlin and that Hitler had shot himself.

'Do you think it's true, Albert?' Vera Mundy asked.

'It's in the papers, isn't it?' Mundy said.

'Yes, but – it's the Russians who say he's dead. They haven't found his body.'

'Got burnt, didn't it? Anyway, I daresay even the Russians wouldn't want to touch it, not with a bargepole. No, he's dead all right. Just the sort of thing his sort would do, blow his brains out rather than stay to face the music. No moral fibre.'

When Jack Blair heard the news, he did something he had never done before. The Plough was closed. He went downstairs to the bar and drew himself a pint of ale. And all by himself, he proposed a toast, to the King and Mr Churchill, to Generals Montgomery and Eisenhower and all the men who had fought under them. To the RAF and the Few who had saved Britain in the early air battles, to the Navy, to the Bomber Commands, both British and American. And especially to the officers and men of the 525th Bomb Group of Market Wetherby, to the boys he had known who had served their tours and gone home and the many others who had died in the skies over Europe. 'God bless you all,' he said.

Helen was sitting at the desk in her office. The letter she was reading distressed her and she laid it down. Outside, she could hear the radio from the nurses' restroom which had been placed in the corridor. Today everyone wanted to listen. The music from it was very loud and she wished they would turn it down.

She was tired. For weeks she had not slept well. Although she accepted that Ronnie's death had been an accident and nothing more, she could not suppress a nagging feeling of guilt. She had deceived him. He had forgiven her, but she found it much more difficult to forgive herself. She could not bear to think of what he must have thought and suffered. That it had been beyond her power to prevent was no excuse. At his funeral, when the vicar had spoken of her devoted care for him as an example to all, she had seen her daughter Pat's eyes fixed on her. She had not had a row with Pat, but her daughter had not been home since then and had written to say she would spend the summer vacation from university with friends.

Helen felt totally cut off from her past life. Pat could have been a comfort to her. They could have comforted each other. Pat clearly, however, had not yet come to terms with her father's death and wondered, as Helen often did, how truly accidental it had been. With Nanny, she had little communication. The old woman lived from day to day, more and more in the past, and sometimes could not understand why they were alone in the house. Alone was the cogent word. Through her work and the two years of looking after Ronnie, Helen had gradually got out of touch with her friends. His death prompted her to contact them again and it was only then that she realized how few they had been. Her life with Ronnie had been so completely self-sufficient that they had a wide circle of social acquaintances, but few real friends. She had colleagues at the hospital with whom her relations were good. They admired and respected her, yet none of them could be called close. Phyllis Lambourne had been the woman friend she had seen most often, but she had been under no illusions about that. Phyllis had been lonely, estranged from her husband, a naval commander, and had used Helen for company. She was really an unbearably selfish and snobbish creature, rapacious with men, condescending to anyone she considered her social inferior and undependable when help or solace were needed. She had divorced her commander a year ago and married a Polish colonel, who was nearly an alcoholic by all accounts. Since then Helen had not seen her. She had her work, occasional visits from Vi apart from meetings over the work on the estate, and she attended the WI, although she had resigned as local president. Sir Henry and Lady Maylie had invited her twice to dinner, but it was Ronnie they had really known well. Outside of that there was no one. At home in the evenings, at weekends when she was off duty, going for walks by herself, she learned what it meant to be alone.

All the time, she could not stop thinking of Jim Kiley. She could not understand why she had not heard from him, nothing. Not even after Ronnie died. He must have understood how she felt then. He had told her he would come for her, and had sent a message that she was to remember that. Yet now that she was alone, there had been no word. It was like a punishment.

The music in the corridor cut off abruptly and she heard the voice of the radio announcer, Alvar Lidell. 'We interrupt programmes to bring you the great news,' he said. 'All German forces have surrendered. The war is over. In ten minutes, the Prime Minister will speak to the nation.'

Helen had risen to her feet. She could hear cheering and voices shouting in the corridor. Some of the voices were of German patients. From the distance came a sound she had not heard for five years. The bells of Market Wetherby church were ringing.

Sister Dickson stuck her head in at the door. 'It's

wonderful news, isn't it, doctor? Wonderful!' She was almost weeping.

'Yes,' Helen said. 'The most wonderful.' She felt the same urge to weep or cheer. She needed to be with others, yet as she made for the door, she stopped. There was one thing she had to do, which, if she put it off, she might be unable to face. It was one more of the hideous ironies of the war.

Young Danny Coogan had completed his tour. An experienced pilot, much decorated, he had agreed to check out one of the latest crews to arrive from America. He was reluctant to leave England when there was still the faintest hope he might find the girl he was looking for. On the first training flight, something went wrong and the B-17 had been unable to take off. It had spun round at high speed on the runway and crashed, killing outright or injuring everyone on board. Danny Coogan had been brought back to the hospital he had left two years before. Then he had escaped death by a hairsbreadth. This time he was not so lucky. He had died in the early hours of this morning, VE Day.

By the first post, Helen had received a letter. It was from Ann Weston, the nurse for whom he had never stopped searching. She told Helen she had been posted to Egypt, then Malta, and had only recently returned. She wondered if the hospital might have kept a record of Sgt Coogan, as she had known him, when he was discharged. She had not heard from him since her overseas posting, and had been unable to contact him, as she had lost his address when the troopship she was on was divebombed on her way to Alexandria. She would be most grateful if there was any possibility of finding out his address in America. Helen did the kindest thing and wrote back that she knew of no means of discovering the present whereabouts, if any, of Sgt Coogan.

One of the strangest things was that the only American to celebrate VE Night in Market Wetherby was Elmer Jones.

The officer in temporary command of the Base, Major Lester Carson, rightly fearing that too much drinking and excessive high spirits would lead to inevitable clashes between his men and British servicemen and civilians, refused all passes and had the perimeter fence put under tight security. After a Base muster and parade, parties were held in all Mess halls and Clubs. The revelry reached such a height that all aircraft were placed under guard to prevent drunken joyriding. There were a few incidents when scores were settled with particularly unpopular members of the Military Police section, the Snowdrops.

It was the first time Red Burwash had been into the WAAC officers' quarters, the first time any man had been into Lorna Jane Somers' room. Out of her uniform, she was as beautifully female and desirable as the whole Base had guessed. Red knew that he was lucky, in more ways than one. Lucky to be with her, lucky to be the one she had chosen, lucky after two and a half years of flying with death as his co-pilot to have survived. When they made love it was an affirmation of life.

Elmer was given a tremendous welcome, when he walked up from the station. Charlie, the British sergeant from the Ack-Ack unit, was the first to see him and ran to him, grabbing his kitbag and pounding him on the back. The pounding hurt Elmer's ribs, which were tightly strapped, but he did not mention it. His wrist was strapped, too. He did not mention it, either. He had taken food and bandages from the German army truck and struck off into the woods. For two days he had limped and stumbled along barely discernible tracks just below the treeline on the slopes of the mountain, to put its bulk between him and the bodies of the SS men. On the third day, around noon, he walked right into another platoon of soldiers. Hearing them question him in German, he had given himself up for dead, until he realized what they were saying. He was in Switzerland. After some difficulty in identifying himself, he had been taken to a medical clinic where his wounds were treated and he was allowed to rest.

At the end of a week, he was handed over quietly to the nearest US authorities and shipped home via France. As he walked up the High Street with Charlie, he could hear the distant gunfire and see the celebration flares bursting over the Base, but he elected to remain with his English friends at The Plough.

Rosie cried out when she saw him. She was so glad, she kissed him until he was breathless. 'I've dreamed of you doing that, Rosie,' he sighed, 'and if I thought you'd ever do it again, I'd never want to leave England. But I've had a heap of time to think. I guess it's like Hymie said, one day I have to wake up and stop bein' a jerk.'

Albert Mundy was annoyed with himself for putting up the blackout curtains, as if they were still needed. He was even more annoyed when Vera laughed about it. He was reluctant to come out with Peter and her to join in the festivities. 'Lot of damn fools running about and shouting,' he snorted. 'We've licked the Jerries and the Wops – but we've still to sort out the Japs. And that'll take some doing, you mark my words.'

Peter's sick leave was nearly over, but he was grateful he was still at home for this special day. When he managed to squeeze through the crowd into The Plough, he saw Rosie with one arm round Elmer's neck and the other round the neck of an RAF Flight Sergeant. She left them and came to give him a kiss. He held her off, to her surprise. 'You can kiss me when you really mean it, Rosie,' he said. 'And not till then.' He left her feeling oddly intrigued and surprised at how much older he seemed. And she was annoyed when she saw him make no objection a moment later to kissing Jilly and a couple of other girls.

The next night was American night in Market Wetherby. There were parties all over the town as US servicemen were welcomed into the houses of their many friends and the families of their girlfriends. The crew of 'Ginger Rogers' brought Letty's little daughter, Vicky, a large white teddy bear. Albert Mundy would have refused to let her have it, knowing it was in memory of Harvey Wallis, but Vera would not let him.

One of the biggest and noisiest parties was at Bridge Cottage, where McGraw and Sally kept open house all night. During it he announced his coming retirement from the Air Force. There was a chorus of disbelief, but they finally had to accept that he was not kidding. 'I gave Sal my word. It was the wisest thing I ever did,' he said. 'And you know what? I'm going to stay right here. I guess this is what I've been looking for all my life.' Sally blushed and consented, when he asked her publicly to marry him.

There had been so many US servicemen for so long, their appearance and influence were so widespread, that it had become difficult to imagine Market Wetherby without them. It was assumed that it would take them a considerable time to organize their leaving. People had forgotten how suddenly the Base had come into existence, mushrooming from the open ground a mile away almost overnight. The same happened here as was happening all over England. Within a week, the first squadrons were despatched to airfields in the US. The Base hummed night and day with activity. Vast amounts of supplies were given away or burned or buried in huge pits to be filled in by bulldozers. Sobbing girls clustered round the gates, unable to believe their boyfriends had already gone. Albert Mundy had been correct. There was an urgent need of them. Most, after a period of rest and recuperation, would be sent for service in the Pacific.

Nevertheless, it was with a sense of shock, exactly one month after VE Day, that watchers round the unguarded perimeter saw Red Burwash take off in 'Ginger Rogers II' on the last flight out of Market Wetherby. People in the streets gazed up and waved as she made one pass over the town before heading off north-west into the open sky. Line Chief McGraw had made sure that she was specially groomed and serviced for the occasion and for her landing in the USA. Her hull was gleaming. The smiling, long-legged star of her logo perched on rows of miniature painted bombs testifying to the astonishing eighty-seven missions she had flown and two rows of swastikas below, representing the eighteen German fighters she had shot down.

She was one of the few B-17s to retain the original metallic finish. Some pilots thought it made them too conspicuous, but to Red this was more than compensated for by the extra ten to fifteen miles per hour airspeed it gave her, an edge that had saved her crew several times over. Now the sunlight turned her into a silver dart, ever dwindling towards the horizon, until with a final wink, like a lamp going out, she was gone. And the skies were silent.

# FOURTEEN

Helen Dereham was largely unaware of the vacuum left by the closure of the Base. The hospital was still crowded and she was needed there as much as ever. What had begun as temporary, a duty willingly undertaken for the duration of the war, became her salvation. She devoted herself to her work, on call at all hours, sometimes even forgetting the emptiness inside her.

Vi still ran the Dereham estate, with the other landgirls and Schuster, although neither of them knew for how much longer. Helen and she discussed it together. Chuck had left with the others. No permits or transport had yet been arranged for GI brides to follow their husbands. It would take some time, as there were some 70,000 of them. 'But I'll be among the first, Mrs Dereham,' Vi said confidently. She was happily, and healthily, pregnant again. There was only one small anxiety. 'You see, I must get there. I want my baby – Chuck's baby – to be born in America.'

Helen felt buoyed by the younger woman's happiness, as she walked home. It was a bright, clear day, the air fresh and pure. She had remarked to Vi how quiet it seemed, how oddly quiet, now that the planes were no longer constantly taking off and landing. She came in through the garden, so did not see the jeep parked out front.

Going into the drawing room, she caught her breath and stood absolutely still. The tall US Colonel rose from his chair. Jim Kiley seemed even taller because of his gauntness. There were traces of grey at his temples.

'I flew into Alconbury this morning,' he said. 'You weren't at the hospital, but I knew you'd turn up here sooner or later.'

He waited for her to speak, but she was silent, gazing at him.

'I couldn't get here before,' he said. 'I was shot down five months ago over Regensburg and put in an aircrew POW camp. Because of the work I'd been doing, hunting out the flying bomb production centres, I couldn't let German Intelligence find out who I was. So I gave a false name and my capture wasn't reported. I was liberated by the Russians a month ago. It took a while to get a transfer to an American command, then I had a week de-briefing.' She was still silent. 'I'm sorry. I didn't hear about Ronnie – Major Dereham, until half an hour ago.'

Helen could feel a tremor growing inside her. She had barely taken in what he had been saying. She was gazing at someone who was virtually a stranger.

'You must have wondered why I didn't get in touch,' he said. 'There was no way I could.' Then he smiled. In the smile, half affectionate, half uncertain, she saw again the Jim she had known. He shrugged. 'Well, I said I would come. And here I am.' He was tense, unsure of her reaction.

Helen had begun to tremble. Jim moved to her quickly and put his arms round her, holding her for the long minutes the trembling lasted. It was only when it was over that he kissed her, and with the kiss came peace at last, and healing.

# FIFTEEN

Peace had come to Market Wetherby.

The sense of elation, of being on the winning side, however, did not last long. After four or five weeks, the novelty of being able to switch on the lights without first drawing the curtains had worn off. There were no more casualty lists and organizations like Civil Defence and the WVS found it hard to keep their members. The Home Guard had been disbanded long before. Many people discovered that the end of the war left a vacuum in their lives.

Most noticeable of all for the townspeople of Market Wetherby was the silence. Eight hundred years of quiet existence had been shattered by the arrival of the first of the 525th's three squadrons of B-17s. The roar of the Wright Cyclone engines taking off, circling and landing, flying overhead, had at first seemed unbearable, then had slowly become part of the accepted sounds of the country-side, the rumbling thunder so constant as barely to be noticed. Except when one of the big-assed birds came back from a raid, half shot to pieces, engines labouring, some-times so low it scarcely seemed able to clear the treetops. Then ears pricked up and people paused, listening for the engine note to change, to surge and die away, meaning the lone ship had landed safely back at the Base. Or for the splintering crash and high plume of smoke that meant she had not made it.

Visitors were often shown the large crater two fields beyond the school where one Flying Fortress, fully loaded at the start of a mission and suddenly stricken with power failure in three engines and a malfunctioning rudder, had deliberately crashed with the loss of all on board rather than risk jettisoning her bombload over a populated area.

Every year, on the Sunday nearest the anniversary of the event, the vicar of the parish church said a prayer for the pilot and crew. It was a permanent link with the men of the 525th.

It was not only on Market Wetherby that the silence fell, but all over East Anglia. And with the silence came the gradual realization that the mighty Eighth Air Force really had gone. Gone were the boyfriends and fiances, the make-believe uncles and adopted sons. Apart from the girls, the children missed them most of all, the gladhanding GIs with their Hershey bars, chewing gum and Lifesavers. Life in the small towns after which the bases had been named returned to normal, yet had been changed irrevocably. People who had grumbled at the Americans' intrusive presence, their high spirits and impatience with delay, their lack of reserve and formality, their forwardness and self-esteem, found that they missed them. They missed the laughter and excitement, the occasional violent flare-ups and many gestures of goodwill.

After the girls and the children, the next group to feel their departure most keenly were the shopkeepers. Although most GIs sent a portion of their pay home or put it into War Bonds, they still had more to spend and were less careful with money than their more poorly paid British opposites. In the last six months of the war, many Americans seemed obsessed with the idea of buying presents to take home. Curio and gift shops sprang up everywhere. There was one in Market Wetherby High Street, selling everything from brass doorknockers to lampshades. Everything went, the most popular line being pottery mugs in the likeness of Mr Churchill, cigar in his left hand, making a V sign with his right.

Jack Blair would be the last to call himself a profiteer, yet the practicalities of the situation were brought home to him when he had to cut his monthly order for beer by nearly a half. In a way, the war and the existence of the Base had been a boom time for The Plough. It was fortunate he did not have extravagant tastes and had put by most of what he had made. It might have to tide him over for a good long while.

He discussed it one evening with Vi, who was helping him out in the bar. Rosie had gone to the Roxy to see the latest Judy Garland with her friend Jilly and, with only three customers, Vi was there mainly as company for her father. Jack was concerned about her. It was obvious that it would take longer than anyone had thought for the wives and fiancées of American servicemen to travel to the United States. It was partly a deliberate policy to cut down on the numbers by giving time for second thoughts, but for the many who changed their minds or became afraid of starting a new life in an unknown continent, there were thousands more who daily grew more determined and impatient to join their men.

Vi was luckier than many, as Chuck had not been sent to the Pacific where the war against Japan still continued. He was serving as an instructor at a training base in Wyoming. Her frustration came from knowing that she could have been with him, yet still had to go through the surprisingly slow wait for permits and permissions, the medical checks and almost insulting clearance of her moral background and the legality of their marriage. She had to accept reluctantly that her wish would not come true and that their child, after all, would be born in her country, not its father's.

Jack was concerned about more practical matters. He did not doubt that sooner or later she would be reunited with her husband. If it was soon, it might not be too bad. Yet the Japanese war could not last much longer. The Japs were retreating from island after island. In the foreseeable future, Chuck would be discharged and then what would happen? Like most of those young men who had joined the forces as little more than boys, he had no trade or profession. America was the land of opportunity, they said, but how many jobs and what kind of work would be available for the millions of returning servicemen whose only skills were no longer needed or even appreciated? He remembered the bright hopes that had followed the last war and the later disillusionment, the jobless and the hunger marches, the Depression. Of them all, Elmer Jones had seemed the only one to take it seriously, studying quite hard at his correspondence course in accounting. When Jack mentioned his concern, Vi laughed. 'Oh, you know Chuck, Dad. He can turn his hands to anything. He'll get a good job somewhere.'

'Yet it might take a while,' Jack said. 'Now, I've been thinking. I've got a tidy bit saved up and I won't need a quarter of it. I want to settle some of it on you and Chuck so that—'

'I wouldn't hear of it!' Vi protested. 'That's money you've worked hard for.'

'And what would I do with it, except make sure that my daughter and grandchild weren't in any need?' Jack asked.

Vi shook her head. 'Chuck would never agree to it. I know that. We talked it all over before he left, and he's sure we'll manage. It'd be better for you to spend some of your savings on doing the old Plough up a bit.'

'How do you mean?' Jack frowned. 'Nothing wrong with it.'

Vi looked round at the nineteenth century mahogany counter and brass rail, the panelled walls and narrow benches, the plain wooden chairs and rickety door into the little snug. 'Not as a museum piece,' she agreed. 'But if you want to keep up with the times, it could do with some better seating and a lot more light. Maybe you could open up the snug and put in a picture window or something.'

'Picture of what?' her father snorted. 'Albert Mundy's shop?' Vi laughed. 'The Plough's the way I like it and it's not going to be poshed up – not in my time, anyway. Don't think you can change the subject so easily, young lady.'

'Well, if you won't use your savings on the pub, think of Rosie,' Vi said. 'She could turn out to be more in need of help than Chuck and I will ever be.'

On this occasion she had managed to change the subject. He was genuinely worried about his younger daughter. In the last few months her whole personality and outlook seemed to have altered. Once outgoing and pert and vivacious, she had become moody and introspective. She had taken the departure of the Yanks very badly. For nearly three years she had been the toast of the Base, able to pick and choose, always with her two faithful admirers to fall back on, Elmer and Hymie. Hymie, her favourite, had given up the chase at last as hopeless, but Elmer remained doggedly loyal and hopeful to the end, even comforting her when she grieved over young Danny Coogan, killed on the last day of the war. No one realized how hard she had fallen for Danny, really hard for the first time in her life. She had been hoping that he would give up, as unrealistic, his quest for the girl he had known once for a week and then lost, but his death robbed her even of that hope. Then Elmer had left with the others and, suddenly, there was no one.

The few local boys and the returning British servicemen, who were beginning to be demobbed, tended to avoid her. None of them asked her out, or even took much notice of her. She had snubbed or paid little attention to them over the past three years and now they repaid the compliment. They had her marked down as a Yank-loving goodtime girl. Jack knew the reputation she had locally and was certain, too, that it was largely unjustified. Rosie had maybe been flirtatious and flighty, but she had not been promiscuous. Jack was not blind and he was pretty sure that, for all her experience of men and ability to attract admirers when she chose, Rosie was still a virgin. Not that he regretted it, far from it. He knew, however, how easy it would be for her lonely introspection to turn to self-dislike and bitterness, or on the other hand for acceptance of her reputation to lead her into something foolish.

The only times she went out now were with her plain, plump friend, Jilly. Changed days, indeed. He was grateful to Jilly, who expected little from life and was always cheerful, with her infectious laugh, chattering on about this and that. When they were together, Rosie seemed more like her old self, with no opportunity to mope over what might have been. Jilly took scarcely any interest in men, because they took almost none in her. It was when he saw Rosie at the bar, sulky and silent because the men she served ignored her, that Jack worried. When she was small, he had often warned her, 'Watch it now, it'll end in tears.' He was very much afraid that, once again, that could turn out to be true.

For Helen Dereham, the departure of the Bomb Group meant primarily a lessening of tension. As a doctor she had been sickened by the constant arrival of injured aircrew, some of the young men hideously wounded, many with disfiguring burns. At least she was spared that now. And as the worst cases from the last desperate fighting inside Germany were transferred to better equipped hospitals and the rest were gradually discharged, the EMS was slowly returning to its original function as a cottage hospital serving a rural area.

It was only natural that she would find her work less exacting and hardly knew how to react, when the medical superintendent had her in for a long chat one day and mentioned delicately that she had only been taken on temporarily to release a male member of the staff for the Forces. Now, with the men returning, she would naturally understand, if she were asked to step aside. There was no question of dismissing her, he assured her, as she was far too dedicated and valuable. She might, however, have to accept a demotion. 'Perhaps you might like to consider it,' he suggested, 'in military terms, as an Acting Captain or Major reverting to his substantive rank of First Lieutenant.'

Pompous ass, Helen told herself. She tried not to resent the thought that she would, one day soon, have to go back to helping at the hospital on a part time basis. Room had to be made for the returning men. They deserved it. Yet it was not easy to be gracious about it. In these past years she had fulfilled herself professionally and had worked frequently to the point of exhaustion. Would a man be asked so casually to stand down? Even as she thought it, she remembered the sacrifice of so many of the young aircrew. She could not shirk giving so much less.

As a widow, she might have had little to which she could look forward, an uneventful, imperceptibly declining existence. Ronnie had left her comfortably off, though not wealthy. Dereham House was hers until her death or remarriage, when it would pass automatically to Pat. There were no male members of the family to carry on the name, apart from some remote cousins, but the house would remain for at least one more generation in the direct line. Helen might have seen herself as a gentlewoman living in gradually straitening circumstances, working for the community and helping out at the hospital, growing older gracefully. But Jim had changed all that. It was still secret from most of the town, but she was only waiting for the war against Japan finally to end before she remarried.

His arrival after his release from POW camp had broken the mould which, by tradition, she would have followed. Seeing him again had swept all doubts about her future aside. As he had said, nothing now could stop them from being together. She had been shocked by the signs of the strain and privation he had undergone. He had five days' leave and she would not hear of him moving to a hotel. To the astonishment of Nanny, he was installed in the main guest bedroom. 'A single man, here with just the two of us, unchaperoned, Mrs Dereham,' the old lady had said. 'What will people think?'

'Nothing, if we don't tell them he is here,' Helen told her. 'But if it will make you happier, you can go and stay with your niece in Bexhill for a week.'

Mystified, and still puzzling over the logic of it, Nanny had left for Bexhill. Next day, Helen gave up all pretence and joined Jim in the guest bedroom. Both would have felt uncomfortable in the rooms she had once shared with Ronnie, yet here, in the guest wing where she had never slept before, Helen was completely relaxed. She was Jim's doctor and companion, nurse and lover, although they did not make love until the last day. The four days preceding had been like an encapsulated courtship with them learning to know, to value and appreciate each other, all over again. The last day had been like a honeymoon, the real start of their life together.

One person virtually unaffected by the finish of the European war was Albert Mundy. He was unreservedly delighted at the disappearance of the Americans from the streets of the town and the skies over it. 'Perhaps now we can get back to some decent standards,' he told anyone who would listen. 'The invasion of these islands is over. The fancy Romeos have packed up their chewing gum and French letters and gone home to their icecream parlours, nigger minstrels and gang wars.'

The circumstances of his life had not changed. There was little, if anything, extra on sale in his shop. Rationing still continued and seemed to many to be even stricter than before. The watchword of the new Labour Government under Clement Attlee was austerity. Sacrifice for some time to come, perhaps a few more years, was what was asked of the country, although it was not what had been promised. The fruits of victory seemed small and harsh to the taste. 'Serve them right for betraying old Winston,' Mundy told Vera. 'The country stabbed him in the back. Pulled us through it, he did. Then what happens? Agitators in His Majesty's Forces tell them to vote for Attlee and his lot and they'll get demobbed faster, every one of them with a cushy job, a motor car and six weeks paid holiday a year. So the mugs vote for them and get what they deserve for letting Mr Churchill down. Anyone who starts complaining in the shop, I tell them, well, who did you vote for? Write to your precious Sir Stafford Cripps, your Annoying Bevan. And while you're at it, I'll write to the King and say, I hope that when Attlee came to kiss hands, your Majesty remembered to wash them very carefully afterwards.'

Vera laughed. 'You do go on, Albert.'

'No point talking to you,' Mundy complained. 'Women are just not capable of understanding politics.'

'I understand one thing,' Vera told him, 'and that is that it's long past Vicky's bedtime. If you keep bouncing her like that, she'll be all excited and never get to sleep.'

At two, 'This is the way the Farmer rides' was Vicky's favourite game and Albert played it with her endlessly. He ruffled her curly blonde hair. 'Oh, no, she won't. She'll go straight off to dreamland, won't you, my lamb?'

'Granpa sing song,' Vicky demanded.

'I haven't had my supper,' Mundy said. 'Can't sing on an empty stomach.'

'Granpa sing song!'

He saw his grand-daughter's delicate features begin to pucker and gave in at once. 'All right, all right, just once though.'

Apart from 'God Save The King' and 'Land of Hope and Glory', the only song, by some odd chance, of which Mundy knew all the words was 'Ragtime Cowboy Joe'. It had become a ritual that she would not go to bed, until he had sung it to her at least three times. He glanced at the door to the shop involuntarily to make sure it was shut and cleared his throat. Vicky laughed and clapped her hands.

As he sang rather ponderously of the exploits of the rootin', tootin', highfalutin' sonofagun from Arizona, Vera smiled, watching them. Already he was far closer to his grand-daughter than he had ever been to his son or daughter. And far more indulgent to her than he had ever let himself be with them. Vera had always known there was a gentle, kind man hiding somewhere inside her aggressively hidebound and disciplinarian husband. A pity he had taken so long to show himself, but the waiting was almost worth it.

*

Events were not all humdrum at Market Wetherby. The lady from Ipswich who had opened the gift shop in the

High Street went bankrupt, having spent all her profits on new stock a few days before the 525th so unexpectedly departed.

The following week the parachute factory was shut. The workers who were dismissed, including Rosie Blair and Jilly Binns, were told that a new company making some industrial electrical product would possibly be taking over the premises soon, but if, in the meantime, they found a job, they should take it. There were few jobs to be had. Demobbed servicemen were given first priority, but many of them either had to, or chose to, leave the district to get what they wanted. Jilly was frantic, since she was helping to support her mother and younger brothers. Her father had been killed at Dunkirk. Since Vi was well into her seventh month, Jack Blair came to Jilly's rescue by taking her on as a relief barmaid. She was slow to learn the work, but proved popular with customers. And it cheered Rosie up to have Jilly laughing and joking beside her.

A month later, Vi gave birth to a girl three weeks prematurely at the cottage hospital. Helen delivered the baby and was relieved that there were no additional complications. 'Mother and child both doing well,' Jack telegraphed to Wyoming.

Helen was touched when Vi came to see her before leaving hospital and told her that, with Chuck's agreement, they had decided to name their first baby after her, if she had no objection. 'None at all. I'm very proud,' Helen assured her, and kissed her. She attended the christening, where Rosie and Sally and Joe McGraw were godparents.

McGraw's arrival in Market Wetherby had been a total surprise to everyone except Sally. With the help of his old Commanding Officer, Rufus Krasnowici, now a Lieutenant General, he had fixed a trip to England as part of a team checking on the operational state or otherwise of the B-17s and Liberators left behind for repair. Sally had arranged all matters with the Registry Office in Ipswich and, the previous day, with Jack and Vi as witnesses, she had become Mrs Joseph Henry McGraw. Very few had heard and there was an audible gasp in the church, when her new name was spoken aloud as godparent. She was grateful to Vi. The ceremony was like a blessing on her own marriage to Joe.

At the party afterwards at The Plough, Helen went upstairs alone with Vi to help to change her namesake, little Helen. She wanted a word with her on their own. 'To tell you the truth, Vi,' she said, 'my conscience is troubling me. Quite badly.' She paused. 'You see, I'm flying next week to the United States.'

There was a pause as Vi tried to work out what she meant. She slid the dry nappy under the baby. 'On some kind of business, Mrs Dereham?' she asked.

That was what made Helen feel guilty. Transatlantic flights were extremely expensive, with very few seats available for non-military travellers and most of these reserved for government officials and top businessmen. 'I'm afraid it took an awful lot of wangling,' she confessed. 'I can only imagine the kind of strings that were pulled. But just between us – because I wanted you to know – I am going out there to be married.' Vi gazed at her blankly. 'To marry Jim Kiley, Colonel Kiley, who used to be at the Base.'

So they were true, Vi thought, the rumours which she had disbelieved and always hotly denied. 'Colonel Kiley?' she echoed. Even as she accepted their truth, she felt an irresistible surge of jealousy, followed by anger. She had been waiting for nearly a year to join her husband with no likelihood of it happening for months yet, of them being together, of his seeing their child. But all Mrs Dereham had to do was want to join her lover and it was done . . . Oh yes, it was a different world for the likes of the Derehams and Kileys with their money and influence.

Helen was hurt, reading the fleeing expressions which Vi could not hide. 'I told you, because I know how desperately you want to be with Chuck and I didn't want you to think badly of me.'

'How could I do that, Mrs Dereham?' Vi said flatly. 'It's not my place to criticize you.'

'But you do,' Helen said gently. 'As I would, if I were you. If I could arrange it for you also, I would. Believe me, I have tried.'

'That's most kind of you, ma'am,' Vi said. She had not called Helen that in years. She pinned the nappy and pulled up the baby's frilly pants. 'I suppose we'd better get back down.' She could see why Mrs Dereham didn't want it talked about. Spoil people's idea of her altogether, it would. She turned to the door.

'No, Vi, please,' Helen said. Vi hesitated. Her former employer's voice sounded as if it was nearly breaking. 'I've never asked for privileges,' Helen went on. 'I've tried always to be fair, to do what I could for others, to take no more than my share. If I were your age, I would wait like you till it was my turn. That is absolutely true. But can't you see? I need Jim very much, and I have so much less time than you. You have Chuck's child. At least you have that. I shall never have Jim's. Or at least, it's very unlikely.' She tried to smile. 'But I want to be with him, while there's still the illusion of a chance. I owe it to him. Because . . . you see . . . hard though it may be to believe, I love him very, very deeply.'

Vi was looking at her now and could feel her eyes begin to fill with tears. 'I'm sorry,' she faltered. 'I didn't think. I was just being selfish.'

'It was me who came up here to apologize to you,' Helen said.

The two women smiled to each other. Vi blinked back her tears. She put out her hand and touched Helen's gently and they went downstairs together, carrying little Helen back to her christening party.

# SIXTEEN

The news, when it finally broke in Market Wetherby, was a bombshell. Many refused to credit it, until they had seen it for themselves in the local paper. They had all heard that Mrs Dereham had gone off to America and had speculated on the reason. Now there it was in black and white.

'Mrs Helen Dereham, widow of the late Major Ronald Dereham of Dereham House, Market Wetherby, was married on Tuesday last to Colonel James A. Kiley, USAAF, in a private ceremony at the groom's family home at Newport, Rhode Island. It is understood that the former Mrs Dereham will remain in the United States, where her new husband has recently received an appointment to the office of Chief of Air Staff.'

Tongues wagged furiously, none more busily than Albert Mundy's.

'You don't know for sure, Albert,' Vera objected.

'Don't I?' Mundy snorted. 'Plain as a pikestaff, what was going on all those years. When I think of how I sat on that Goodwill Committee with her . . . Just as well no one knew how much "goodwill" she was giving out!'

He was scandalized. That Helen, the lady of Major Dereham, from the House, could marry 'one of them' only eighteen months after the death of her heroic and model husband, was yet another betrayal. All the old values were crumbling. Soon, if they weren't careful, all the standards that had made England what she was would have vanished.

He returned obsessively to the subject when Peter came home again on leave. Having been called up late in the war, he would be one of the last to be demobbed. He had been through a bandsman's course after recovering from his wound and now served with the occupying forces in

Germany. He had written that he was toying with the idea of perhaps staying on for a further two years as a regular and Mundy was proud of him, although he would have preferred him to be in a fighting unit. Still, now the big show was over, it was sensible for the lad to do something where he received proper musical training, if that was what he wanted.

'So what do you think of it?' he demanded. 'The goings-on. Her at the House.' Peter listened in surprise, while his father told him the news, with interruptions from his mother, who was conscious that little Vicky was listening. She was a very clever child and you could never be certain what was going in and what would be repeated. 'And there you have it,' Mundy concluded. 'Disgusting, isn't it?'

'Not necessarily. Not at all, in fact, Dad,' Peter said. 'Her first husband is dead. She has every right to marry again, if she chooses.'

Mundy stared at him. 'And do you think your mother should marry again, if I popped off?'

'We're not talking about Mum.'

'I should hope not. We're talking about her up at the House, the Major's widow, that we all looked up to. A white sepulchre, that's what she is.'

'Maybe so,' Peter said patiently. 'But there's nothing disgusting about her marrying again.'

'Oh, isn't there, though?' his father muttered. 'And what about that business of Major Dereham shooting himself? He was one of the best shots in the county. Accident, the coroner said. Accident, my foot! It's as plain as plain. He found out about the carryings on under his very roof and, being a man of honour, took the only way out.'

'You can't think that, Albert,' Vera gasped.

'It's certainly not wise to go around saying it,' Peter agreed. 'I should imagine you might get into trouble, Dad. That's defamation, unless you can prove it.'

'Doesn't need no proof,' Mundy said. 'Stands to reason.'

A new development, however, drove the subject of Helen and Jim from their minds. Halfway through Peter's leave, a message arrived from Bethnal Green Hospital in London to inform them that one Sidney Davis, of no fixed address, was seriously ill. As Vera appeared to be his next of kin, she was hereby informed.

Vera at once wanted to go to him, but Albert forbade it. 'He's my brother, Albert,' she protested.

'Fine brother,' Mundy said. 'Nothing but trouble. I wouldn't be surprised if the whole thing wasn't just another trick of his to get money out of me.' The subject of Sid rankled. Earlier hopes that Vera's citywise brother might find Letty for them had not materialized. Twice Mundy had met requests for sums of money to aid the search, until it finally occurred to him on the third occasion that Sid had again fallen on hard times and was simply milking him. Peter on one of his leaves had taken the last payment to Sid with the warning that there would be no more, unless Letty was delivered. Meeting his uncle he had quickly seen that nothing positive was to be expected of him. Sid was a broken man, his rackets collapsed about his ears, barely able to scrape a living. Peter had wasted his leave, and the next, hunting the streets of London for Letty, himself. He had no desire to see or hear of his Uncle Sid again.

Neither he nor his father, however, were proof against Vera's tears and even more potent silences and, two days later, Peter found himself being led by an Irish Nursing Sister into the General Ward where his uncle lay motionless, his bed surrounded by screens.

'I think you're just in time,' she whispered. 'He doesn't have long now. Not good for them to go on their own.'

Peter could hardly recognize Sid. The once flamboyant fast talker lay breathing shallowly, his face sunken, his eyes dull. What was almost worse was the crisscross of razor slashes on each cheek, silvery weals, the mark of some gangland payment of scores. Peter remembered the distinct impression of fear he had received at their last meeting. There had been moments when the door of the pub in which they had met off Brewer Street had opened and the fear had become almost tangible, as Sid glanced round, nervous of who might be coming in. He had taken the money and, after a few empty assurances, had scuttled away.

Now he would run no farther.

'Hello,' Peter said. The man on the bed looked at him without a flicker of recognition. 'It's me, Uncle Sid – Peter. Mum asked me to drop in and see you.'

It was only when he repeated his name twice more that Sid blinked and a glimmer of understanding came into his eyes. 'Peter? Little Petie – Letty's brother?'

'It's me, Uncle Sid. I've – I've come to see how you are.'

Sid showed a ghost of his old smile. 'You nearly missed it, then, kid. Nearly missed the bus.'

'I'm sorry to find you so poorly,' Peter said.

'Poor . . .' Sid nodded. 'As a church mouse. 'Course, if I beat this one . . . get back on my pedal appendages, the old plates, I got plans.' His eyes closed. 'Who'm I kidding?' He was silent for a long moment before his eyes opened again. 'How's my dear sister, your mum – and 'er everlovin'?'

'They're both fine.'

Sid panted. 'Good for Vera. Never understood 'ow she could stick 'im. Miserable old bleeder.' Something seemed to be amusing him. 'I censored that for your delicate ears, sonny.' He chuckled audibly this time and it led to a fit of coughing that left him limp and breathless.

The sister came back inside the screens. 'I think perhaps you best leave now,' she whispered.

Sid had heard and from somewhere mustered the strength to raise his hand. Peter hesitated, and took hold of it. To his surprise, Sid gripped him tightly. 'Don't . . . don't go . . . not yet,' he croaked. 'Something to tell you.' Again Peter was surprised by the return of strength and the crooked smile.

'Now then, Mr Davis,' the sister warned.

'Gibber off and haunt some other grave,' Sid snarled and the sister took a step back involuntarily at the venom in his voice. 'You're not spoilin' this . . .' He looked at Peter, holding his hand tightly. 'I want my revered brother-in-law, that ever so upright citizen, to know how I done 'im.' He chuckled. 'The last stroke I pulled – and the best.' His voice faded. 'Letty . . .'

Peter was alert at once. 'What about her?'

'I've seen 'er.'

'When?'

Sid grinned. 'Every coupla days or so. Ever since she came to the Smoke.' His expression was gleefully malicious, enjoying Peter's astonishment. 'But old Albert . . . he'll never find 'er.' He laughed, his voice fading and cracking. 'I promise that.'

Malice filled the area between the screens. Peter could feel it. His uncle was not lying. He meant to die happy, needed to feel superior, knowing he had cheated his sister's husband whom he had always resented. Peter laid Sid's hand back on the bed. 'I don't believe you,' he said levelly. 'It's just another of your tricks. You don't know where she is.' He turned to leave.

'Oh, no?' Sid sneered. 'Just you look in the Double D.'

It had been a desperate shot, but it had hit the target. Peter turned back quickly. 'The Double D? What's that?'

Sid gazed at him, his eyes narrowing. 'You little . . .' he breathed. 'You did that deliberate. You've spoilt it all. You sneaky little bast–'

His lips stopped moving. He just seemed to freeze in mid sentence, his mouth beginning to twist in a rage of disappointment. Peter and the sister stood quietly for perhaps a minute, then she muttered a short prayer to herself, moved in and closed the dead man's eyes.

There was no Double D in the telephone book and no one Peter spoke to had ever heard of it. Was it a hotel, or a café or what? He finally learned its address from the Union Jack Club at Waterloo, but the sergeant at the desk advised him against going there. 'A real clipjoint, lad,' he said. 'And too pricey for the likes of us.'

He might never have found the club himself. Its official name was the Dwight D, after the generalissimo, Eisenhower, and it was located in one of the small side alleys off

Shepherds Market, in Mayfair. Its entrance was so discreet, you could tell at once it was expensive.

Peter followed two US naval officers in and paused diffidently in the narrow red plush hallway, while they carried on into the larger room beyond. At a tiny gilded desk in a corner of the foyer, a man in a dinner jacket was sitting. The room behind him was surprisingly spacious, containing a bar and about twenty-five tables at which men, mostly in uniform, sat with girls wearing lowcut evening dress, although it was only mid afternoon. He could make out, beyond the end of the black lacquered bar, a miniature dance floor with a pianist and bass player.

'Sure you've come to the right place, mate?' the man at the table asked. He was rising, his shoulders under the tight jacket bulging like a stevedore's.

'Yes, I think so,' Peter replied. He tried to sound confident, but he felt selfconscious in his heavy battledress with the corporal's stripes. 'This is the Double D, isn't it?'

'That's what the members call it,' the man nodded. 'Cost you twenty quid just to get in.' When Peter hesitated, he drew the curtains across the entrance to the main room. 'Why don't you be a good boy and just scarper?'

'No,' Peter said and the man frowned. Peter had been trying to look beyond him into the room. 'There's someone I have to see. One of the girls.'

'Oh? Which one?'

Peter doubted that Letty would be using her real name. 'If I could have a look inside.'

'Out,' the man said, not menacingly, just bored.

'It's really important,' Peter tried to explain. He kept his money with his pass and identity card in his breast pocket. He took it out. 'Here, it's all I have, six pounds. Just one look. There's someone I have to find.'

'I've been polite so far. You admit that,' the man said, moving forward.

As Peter flinched, stepping back, he heard footsteps in a little staircase to the upper rooms he had not noticed. A young woman was coming down, wearing a smart silk suit, grey with a turquoise scarf at the neck, very poised. 'What's the trouble, Rex?' she asked.

'No trouble,' the man in the dinner jacket said. 'Chummy was just leaving.'

'It's a free country,' she smiled. 'Well, some of it is. If he's got the money, he can stay a while.' Peter was staring at her. She was stunning. Her figure was slim, yet still hinted at voluptuousness, the four inch heels of her patent shoes giving her extra height. Make up accentuated her wide eyes and teasing mouth, her hair drawn back from her heartshaped face tinted a light reddish gold like Rita Hayworth. She looked at him fully for the first time and the surprise jolted her. 'Peter!' she gasped. It was Letty. But Letty transformed almost out of recognition. Even her voice was different, more refined and sophisticated like her appearance. 'What are you doing here?'

'I came to see you,' Peter said.

'Uncle Sid tell you?' Peter nodded, and Letty shrugged. 'Only to be expected, sooner or later.' The bouncer was watching them interestedly. 'My brother, Rex. We're twins.'

'Oh yeah?'

Letty had recovered and smiled to Peter. 'Better come up, then. Can't hardly send you away again.'

Rex stood aside and Peter followed her up the stairs to a small office, the first of a series of interconnected rooms. She led him through the office into the first of them. Not what he had been afraid of; it was a sitting room, more like a small salon. Behind the gauze curtains at the tall windows he could see iron bars. The room was very feminine and modern, the furniture and decor chosen with taste, rosewood and brocade and wall to wall Axminster carpeting. It had obviously cost a great deal of money. He had seen nothing like it outside a magazine. 'My flat,' she explained. Looking at him, she laughed. 'Peter . . . I can't believe you're here.' She made a move as though to kiss him, but stopped herself and motioned him to a low divan. 'Tell me how you found me.'

Without asking him, she opened a drinks cabinet and poured him a scotch, listening impassively while he told her about their uncle dying like a vagrant in the hospital. 'I can't pretend I'm sorry,' she said at last. 'Water or soda?' He shook his head and she gave him the glass. 'He was always coming round here, putting the bite on me for a tenner, twenty. Poor old Sid. He thought he was so sharp, and he ended up a loser after all.' She paused. 'By the way – Dad wouldn't be waiting just outside?'

'He doesn't know anything about this place,' Peter said. 'I wouldn't tell him.'

Letty laughed. 'You're still my favourite brother. I've missed you.'

'We've all missed you,' Peter told her. 'So has little Vicky.'

'You don't get me with that one,' Letty smiled. 'I bet she doesn't even remember me. How could she? And you – I bet you were surprised to see me.'

'I'd hardly have known you,' Peter admitted.

She smiled. 'I take that as a compliment.' Her shrug encompassed the room. 'It's a lot better here than that dump we used to live in. And this is all mine.' She enjoyed his puzzlement. 'I don't exactly work here. I'm not one of the hostesses. I run it, manage it for a friend of mine.' The friend was a Greek named Stavro, who had taken over both from their Uncle Sid and her former protector, Benny. He was generous, but ruthless and ferociously jealous, although he made few physical demands on her. In truth, she was more than a little afraid of him, but she was very, very careful to give him no reason to doubt or mistrust her. Rex was probably on the phone to him now.

She told Peter a bit about her life, her success as she called it. And he read the rest between the lines. She was a different person from the girl he remembered so clearly. As children, they had been inseparable, gone to school together, played together. In their teens, they had been allies against their dictatorial father, covering for each other. He had helped her sneak out of the house to meet Harvey. It was Peter she had relied on when she discovered she was pregnant and Harvey had been killed. Then she had been naïve and inexperienced. Now she could handle anything. She needed no help from him, none that he knew how to give. He felt sickened by what had become of her, but could not condemn her. He knew the steps that had led her to this club, this flat, and Stavro. Their parents had failed her. He had failed her himself, probably. And within her own terms she was a success. She certainly had no regrets.

Yet she was still not free. She had escaped from one prison to land in another. The only jarring note in the room was a large and crude painting of Kolossi Castle in Cyprus. Now he understood why it was there. It dominated the room, just as her 'friend' dominated her life.

Peter let none of his feelings show. He drank the scotch and gave her what news he had. She was disppointed when he said after only half an hour that he had to be going, and made him promise to look in again on his next leave, if he passed through London. He would not take the money she offered him to buy himself a good time. For a moment, she was nearly angry. It was the closest he had come to criticizing her. She saw him back down to the entrance hall, where she made sure to convince Stavro's watchdog, Rex, that he really was her brother before she kissed his cheek and let him go.

When he had gone, Rex said, 'Sorry, Let. I wouldn't 'ave hurt 'im. I thought he'd just come rubberneckin'. You know.'

Letty shrugged. 'Doesn't matter. Probably never see him again.' She went back upstairs. Meeting Peter had disturbed her. He had reminded her of too many things she thought she had safely forgotten. She had always been closer to him than anyone and, as she picked up his glass to put it away, she shook herself by bursting into tears.

Peter walked for three hours after he left the club, down to Piccadilly, through Green Park and on to Parliament Square and along the Embankment. He stood looking blankly at the river, trying not to think about the life she had led and was leading. He could not have taken money from her, knowing how she had earned it. Letty . . . He decided not to go home for the rest of his short leave. He would write to tell his parents that Uncle Sid was dead. He would not mention Letty.

While Peter was in London, Jack and Rosie Blair travelled with Vi and her baby to Liverpool to wave them off at last on the GI brides' liner to America.

Jack was appalled at the cattle truck conditions the thousands of women and small children would have to endure for the voyage. Vi was sharing a tiny cabin below the waterline with two other mothers and their children. The little boy of one of them had already been sick on the floor and the cabin was taking on the stink of sickness and nappies it would have for the next week. Jack tried to find someone to complain to, but there was such chaos he had to give up and Vi assured him she did not mind. Just to be going was enough. By the time Jack and Rosie went ashore, Vi and the other mothers were already working out how they could cope. At least she was with two sensible women. Some of those that Jack saw seemed hardly old enough to have left home, let alone be travelling thousands of miles to join husbands they might have difficulty recognizing out of uniform. They would all need help and understanding from the families they were joining. Many would fit in easily and be perfectly happy, but how many others would be bitterly disillusioned?

Everyone's uncertainty added to the excitement. It was an emotional leavetaking and, when the ropes were cast off and the liner pulled out into the Mersey, thousands of relations thronged the quayside, sobbing and waving until it was out of sight.

Vi was at the rail on the shelter deck with baby Helen in her arms. Some of the women had gone below already. Others were exploring the boat, looking at what remained of the sumptuous decoration of her lounges and smoke-rooms from the days before she had been turned into a troopship, chattering and laughing as though they were on holiday. But Vi and a few others remained at the rail, watching the shores of the river, the miles of docks and the houses, and the low hills beyond, drawing ever farther and farther away as the river widened to the bar and the open sea. She was thinking of her father and sister and the home she had left behind, which she might never see again.

She was as excited as the others to be leaving, to be joining her husband. She was one of the first to be sailing, one of the lucky ones, yet already she knew how much she would miss The Plough and the sights and sounds of Market Wetherby. It was the only world she had known and Chuck had warned her that, although the New World, America, seemed similar because people spoke English, it was really very different. How different? She decided not to think about it. She would learn soon enough and promised herself that, no matter how strange or awkward she felt, she would not show it. She would try to adapt, for Chuck's sake. At least, Helen and she would make the crossing in safety. There were no more U-boats. She had read so often of attacks on merchant vessels, ships which had set out from this same port not so long ago and were lost without trace.

She shivered and her baby whimpered, sensing her disquiet. Vi hugged her and made herself smile. 'It's all right. All right, my darling,' she whispered. 'We'll see Daddy soon. You'll see Daddy, and then everything will be fine.'

It was a silent journey home for Jack and Rosie. He was happy for Vi, that she would soon be reunited with Chuck, but concerned about the problems the future might hold for them. Chuck had written that he would soon be demobbed, perhaps would be by the time Vi arrived. He had not yet decided where they were going to live or what kind of work he wanted to do. He might try for a job with an aviation company. Jack wondered how many thousands of young men had the same idea. Time would tell. He liked Chuck and told himself there was no use worrying, but he could not help it. If only they weren't so far away. And Chuck had no family. His parents were both dead. There would be no one to help Vi.

Rosie was also happy for her sister, although it was tinged with an involuntary jealousy. She had never been jealous of Vi before, not while she had been playing the field, able to pick and choose. She was much prettier. Everyone said so. She had had innumerable proposals, yet had turned them all down. If she hadn't, she might now be sailing off to that great, fascinating country where everything would be new and exciting, to join some handsome man who would know how to appreciate her. Someone who loved her, as so many had sworn they would do, always. Life was so empty since they had gone. And she had not heard from anyone, not even from Hymie and Elmer. McGraw had come back. Maybe some of the others would. Maybe someone was thinking about her even now. She had cried for days, after they had all left. Nothing would ever be the same.

The Plough had been shut for two days, while they were away, but Jilly had a fire on and was waiting with Sally McGraw to welcome them back and hear all about it, the liner and how Vi and the baby were when it sailed.

When all the details had been told, the crowds and the boat and cabins described, Jilly Binns could keep her own news to herself no longer. She was nervous about telling Rosie, yet it had to be done. 'There was a letter this morning,' she said. 'From Hymie. Hymie Stutz.'

Rosie smiled excitedly. 'Where? Where is it?'

'It was for me,' Jilly said. She hesitated, aware of them all looking at her. She blushed. 'He – he's asked me to marry him.'

'Marry him?' Rosie echoed, disbelieving.

'I wrote back straight away. I said yes.'

As Sally told McGraw later, she had never actually seen anyone's mouth fall open with astonishment, like they wrote. But Rosie's did.

# SEVENTEEN

Helen liked it best when Jim and she could get away from the formal social life of Washington to their place on Nantucket. The island's climate reminded her of England and she loved the rambling wooden house, built by a nineteenth century whaling skipper. Jim taught her to sail and to fish for sea-bass and they spent long barefoot days living like beachcombers. It was very different from their elegant existence in the capital where Jim was talked of as one of the coming men. The canny old President, Harry Truman, thought highly of him and his beautiful, coolly intelligent English wife, and their diary was filled with invitations to dinners and receptions. On the island they could relax and be themselves.

There was no sign of the child that Helen had hoped for, but that was the only regret she had. She had been accepted very quickly by the Kiley family and the house on the island was often filled with half a dozen or so nephews and nieces with their friends and girlfriends, so that Jim laughingly suggested sometimes that they ought to open a hotel. Friends sought them out, too, and he knew that a large part of their popularity was due to his wife, who organized things so effortlessly, making everyone welcome and letting no one feel left out.

Helen's favourite amongst Jim's friends was the rising Democratic politician, Adlai Stevenson, considerate and witty, a former lawyer, one of the founders of the United Nations. In their conversations she received an insight into the confusing world of American politics. Through Adlai, they became friendly with the two older Kennedy brothers. Handsome and charming, Jack was already, at twenty-nine, congressman for the eleventh district of Massachusetts. Badly injured when the motor torpedo boat he commanded during the war was sunk by a Japanese destroyer, there were days when the pain in his back prevented him from joining in the swimming and sailing, and Jim and he would sit for hours chewing the fat, as they called it. They found they had surprisingly similar opinions on all sorts of social issues, national and international problems.

'Talking to Jim helps me to define what I really think myself,' he told Helen.

Most of the girls found him irresistible, but Helen preferred his younger brother, Bobby; shy, but more thoughtful and imaginative.

Their only real failure was when they invited Pat over, the summer she graduated from Cambridge. Helen was looking forward eagerly to seeing her daughter and had arranged a whole series of special trips and parties for her to meet their friends and see as much as possible of the country. She had discussed it with Jim and they had both decided that, if Pat wished, she was welcome to stay as long as she wished, to live with them if she wanted to.

Pat, however, had already made up her mind that she would not like the USA. She had no desire to see anything but the most obvious tourist spots or to meet anyone, and offended some of their friends by adopting a superior, critical attitude to every facet of American life. American culture, she insisted, did not exist. How could it in such an insensitive, money-mad society? At a party, at which Bobby Kennedy took her in to dinner, she puzzled him by calling herself the poor relation from Airstrip Number One. America's only interest in the rest of the world, she declared, the obvious reason for the millions of dollars poured into aid programmes for the poorer and developing nations, was the secret aim of the United States to control the world by economic means.

Pat's opinions came from the current man in her life, a student from the Gold Coast at the London School of Economics. When the other guests had left, she started on at Jim about racial discrimination and the suppression of minorities in America. International capitalism, she said, was a greater enemy to freedom than Hitler had ever been.

Jim stood it for as long as he could, then rounded on her. Helen had seldom seen him so angry. If the only result of four years of liberal education at Cambridge, he told Pat, was to turn her into a parrot of half-baked Marxism, then the money her parents had sacrificed to send her there was wasted. Had she ever looked at a map of post-war Europe? Did she ever read a newspaper to see what was happening in East Germany, Poland and Czechoslovakia, not to mention the Middle and Far East? What did she think lay behind Stalin's twisting and breaking the agreements made at Yalta and Potsdam? Where was Russia's equivalent of the Truman Doctrine for the reconstruction of Europe? Moscow had turned itself into the greatest imperial power of the twentieth century, helped by the very nations it absorbed, while pretending to protect them. Who kept intensifying the Cold War? The enormous sums of money wasted annually on troops and weapons, because Russia refused to agree to any of the calls by the Western Powers for disarmament, could have fulfilled every Utopian dream of social reform, funded technological and medical research and provided welfare, housing, jobs and education for the entire world.

At first, Pat tried to argue, but as his points came one after the other, incisive and uncontradictable, she was speechless. When he asked her at last what she imagined her father, Ronnie Dereham, would have thought of her present attitudes and opinions, she burst into tears and went to her room.

Jim was contrite. 'I could kick myself,' he told Helen. 'I hope I didn't go too far.'

'She deserved it,' Helen said quietly. She was concerned about Pat and sorry for her, yet oddly impressed by the forcefulness of Jim's arguments. 'Are you thinking of going into politics?' she asked.

Jim was surprised and laughed. 'I'll leave that to the Stevensons and Kennedys.'

The next morning Pat and he apologized to each other. For the rest of the visit Pat was more like her old self, although she was subdued and tended to avoid Jim. Though she was now twenty-three, she was still fairly immature and very uncertain about what to do with her life, as she acknowledged to Helen in a long talk before she left. The estate and Dereham House more or less ran themselves now and, as she could not think of living there on her own, she wanted to lease the house to someone for a year or two, while she tried something like teaching or social work. Helen was doubtful, but relieved when she heard the offer to lease the house came from a former friend of Ronnie's, Sir Arthur Maylie, whose sister and family were returning from India, now going through the throes of partition, and needed somewhere to stay until they could find somewhere permanent. 'Well, since Sir Arthur says you can keep your own rooms there for whenever you want them, that sounds like a very good arrangement,' Helen agreed.

From Pat, she heard some of the news of Market Wetherby.

The only American still seen quite regularly in the town was M/Sgt McGraw, who was part of a roving aircraft maintenance and survey team and spent his leaves with Sally. Sally had achieved her dearest wish and given birth at the beginning of the year to a son, Joseph McGraw Junior, and apparently Betty and Billy were delighted with their new baby brother. Not all the criticism of Sally had died out in the town, but now it was tinged with some envy as her husband was on his way to becoming a person of local consequence. McGraw had bought a plot of land beyond the bridge on the Ipswich Road with his savings and was building on it a large, modern garage which he would run on his retirement this year from the Air Force.

Helen was sorry to hear that things did not seem to be going too well for Chuck and Vi Ericson. After he was demobbed, they had returned to his home state of Nebraska, but he had found it difficult to get a suitable, permanent job. They had to struggle to make ends meet. Helen had suspected as much from Vi's occasional letters and had offered help, if it was needed. Vi had replied thanking her for the offer, but saying that they could manage. It was quite obvious that only pride stopped them from accepting.

And there was the curious affair of the Mundys. The few facts Pat had been able to tell her were intriguing and Helen would dearly like to have known what actually had happened.

Peter Mundy had returned home at last on his demob leave, after serving an extra two years in the army. He was now a sergeant and had a small but useful demob grant. His father suggested that he should invest it in the family grocery business, buying the defunct curio shop next door. When rationing finally ended, they could expand – Albert Mundy and Son. Albert was shocked when Peter told him he had plans of his own, to invest the money in forming a small danceband made up of ex-servicemen. 'A danceband?' Mundy said, incredulously. 'I've never heard of such a thing. It's out of the question!'

'Well, I'm sorry, Dad,' Peter told him, 'but that's what I've decided.' He was very definite and Mundy did not know how to deal with him. He had wanted his son to become a man, yet had not expected such a change. Peter was firm and quiet, just as stubborn as he was.

The first night he was home, Peter went to The Plough. Jack Blair was as pleased as ever to see him, but Peter was concerned. The publican had visibly aged. No, it wasn't his health, Jack told him. It was the constant worry about Vi. As well as the little girl, she now had a boy, and Chuck was no nearer finding a real job. Jack knew they were hard pushed and the only way he could assist them was to send small gifts of money to his grandchildren which could not be refused. 'The trouble is, son,' he said, 'lack of money is a terrible thing, even in the best of marriages. Sooner or later, it causes all sorts of stresses and strains that can be very destructive.'

Jack also worried about Rosie. His younger daughter had changed almost completely. Where once she had been animated and flirtatious, she was now given to long silences, alternating with attempts to appear bright and appealing. Where once it had been natural, it now seemed artificial and brittle. The unkindest cut had been her friend Jilly's marriage in the USA to Hymie Stutz. They had had a son, almost nine months to the day from the wedding, and Hymie was prospering in the catering trade, Jilly wrote happily. Rosie's confidence in herself was badly shaken and she found it difficult to respond to men. When she went out with someone, now a rare occurrence, she invariably discovered it was because of her reputation and he was only after one thing.

She had been having her supper in the back parlour and was surprised to see Peter when she came out. He seemed taller and broader, his voice deeper. She checked her involuntary smile, feeling again that unsettling sensation when he looked at her, his expression oddly assessing. He spoke to her briefly, finished his pint and left. Rosie was disappointed. Her only enjoyment now was talking to someone who remembered the days gone by, when Market Wetherby had been alive because of the Base. It seemed so empty and dreary ever since the boys had gone.

That night, Peter talked for long hours with his mother, hearing all the gossip of the past years. The next evening he returned to The Plough wearing his blue demob suit. Rosie was serving. The only other customer was a thin-faced commercial traveller who passed through every six months or so. Every time, he suggested to Rosie that they should go for a spin in his Austin 7 and every time she turned him down, not liking the leer that accompanied it.

He was standing next to Peter and saw him watch Rosie, whose skirt crept up to the darker bands at the tops of her stockings, as she reached up to place a bottle on the top shelf. 'Nice bit of stuff, eh?' he whispered, and winked. 'I hear you can do all right there. That is, if you're not too particular.' He chuckled, but it cut off when Peter took him firmly by the knot of his tie. 'What's the game?' he gasped.

'Get out,' Peter said quietly. 'Get out of here, before I spread your dirty nose right across your face.'

Peter released the commercial traveller's tie and the man's hand went to his glass tankard to use as a weapon. Peter caught his wrist and twisted it so that the beer in the tankard spilled over the man's sleeve and down his trousers, then very easily he removed the tankard and set it down out of his reach.

Rosie heard the man's gasp and glanced round. She saw him looking down at himself, flicking the beer from his hand. 'Something wrong?' she asked.

'No, he's just leaving,' Peter said.

The commercial traveller hesitated a moment, muttered a curse under his breath and went out.

Half an hour later, when Jack came down to the bar, Peter asked if he would mind him taking Rosie for a walk.

She fetched her coat and, as they set off, she said, 'You never even asked me if I wanted to.'

'Don't you?'

They walked on in silence. It was evening, but still light. After a few minutes they came to the tree-lined lane that led down to the river. Rosie had not been here for a long while. It brought back memories. 'This is where all the girls used to say goodnight, when the boys had to get back to Base,' she said.

'Lovers' Lane,' he nodded. ' "The Monkeys' Walk", my Dad used to call it. He threatened to skin Letty or me alive, if he ever caught us with anyone down here.'

They were reaching the bridge. Rosie smiled. 'Is that why I never saw you with anyone here?'

Peter was a moment in answering. 'There was only one person I ever wanted to be with.'

Rosie stopped. They were by the start of the parapet. The purling of the river was very soft. She turned, leaning against the rough stone. He was looking at her in a way she could not mistake. She had seen it in others many times. Was it possible he'd been carrying a torch for her all these years? The American slang came easy. 'I've known you longer than anyone,' she said, 'but you're the only boy who's never tried to kiss me.'

'I told you once before,' he said, 'I wouldn't kiss you until you wanted me to.' He paused. 'Do you?'

It was extraordinary, as if Rosie had already lived the scene over in her mind a hundred times without being aware of it. Yet it was unexpected, the last thing she had expected. Peter? '. . . Yes,' she said. 'I want you to.' He held her gently in his arms and, all at once, she never so much wanted to be held and kissed by anyone as she did now.

When Peter got home sometime later, his mother, Vera, had made a pot of tea. 'Just in time,' she said and poured him a cup.

He sat opposite her at the table. His father was by the fire, reading the daily paper. 'I've got something to tell you,' Peter announced. 'Something important.' Mundy looked up. 'I'm going to get married.'

'You're what?' Mundy grunted.

'I'm getting married,' Peter repeated. 'To Rosie Blair.'

His father gaped at him. 'Rosie Bl— that trollop? You're out of your mind! No decent man'll have anything to do with her.'

Peter set down his cup. 'It's a good thing you're my father. I'll say this just once. All those stories about Rosie are a pack of lies. Yes, she liked the men and they liked her, but that's all it was.'

'If you believe that—' Mundy began.

'I know it,' Peter said. 'I shouldn't have to say this. She's untouched.'

'Damaged goods!' Mundy snorted. 'I'm not having a son of mine married to the likes of her! You're to have no more to do with her, do you hear?'

'I'm sorry, Dad, but I told you it's decided. I'd like your

blessing, but if you won't give it, then that's too bad.' He rose, smiled briefly to his mother who was gazing at him and went up to his room.

Albert Mundy sat stunned. 'I – I don't believe it,' he spluttered. 'He's out of his mind!'

'He seems very determined, Albert,' Vera said. 'And you know, I've always thought Rosie was really a very nice girl.'

'Oh, nice enough, I'll be bound – to anyone that fancied her!' Mundy threw his paper down. 'What are we going to do about it?'

'Well, if he's really decided . . .' Vera was very quiet. 'Be careful, Albert. We've lost Letty. I don't want to lose my son as well.'

Mundy stood up. He was angry at being defied by his son, and not backed automatically by his wife. And another, more fearsome thought was nagging at him. 'But what are we going to tell him, woman?' Vera did not understand. 'Dammit, he has to be told that the girl might be his sister!'

Vera caught her breath, jerking as though he had struck her. '. . . Sister?'

'Well, it's a fact, isn't it?' Mundy muttered, uncomfortably. 'It's something we've had to live with.'

'You think – you've thought all this time that Jack Blair was maybe the father of your children?' Vera said, disbelievingly. 'Even when you married me? You're a fool, Albert.' He could not look at her. She was beginning to tremble. 'I liked Jack at one time, but – you're their father. There was never a doubt. But you married me thinking—? You're a fool, Albert. A blind fool.'

Mundy looked at her at last and saw that she was crying silently, her eyes closed. He moved towards her and touched her shoulder, awkwardly. 'Vera – give over, love,' he mumbled. 'I – all right, I'm a fool. You see, I always thought you preferred Jack to me back then. And when we had to get married, I was afraid – I was never sure about the children. But I didn't care . . . as long as it was me you chose. Oh dear God, why didn't we have this out years ago?' He was holding her now, clumsily, and both were crying. It was the closest they had ever been.

The marriage of Peter and Rosie was arranged to take place two months later. After initial awkwardness between Jack and Albert over the details, each wishing to take full responsibility for the wedding, matters were arranged satisfactorily, with Albert paying for the church and organist and Jack for the reception at The Plough. Rosie was still rather afraid of her prospective father-in-law, but responded to his attempts to be more friendly, although she would not promise to help him change Peter's mind about forming the danceband.

The wedding was intended to be quiet, but a large number of people turned up on the day out of curiosity. They all agreed that Rosie looked ravishingly pretty in her pale blue dress and matching hat with its small veil. She would have loved to be married in white, but it was a prohibitive waste of clothing coupons.

During the reception, to which Jack invited a fair number of people who had turned up unexpectedly, a large grey American Studebaker drew up outside The Plough. The woman in it got out. She was exceptionally well-dressed for Market Wetherby, in a figure-hugging silk couture suit, a silver fox cape, very high heels, a chic pillbox hat tilted forward on her red-gold hair. The man in the sedan had himself driven to the other pub to wait for her. He was Stavro Paneides, former gangster, now owner of several nightclubs with a stake in a number of show-business enterprises. The woman was Letty Mundy and he had come to check for himself once and for all that the young soldier who had called on her two or three times at the Double D was really her brother.

Letty's arrival at Peter and Rosie's wedding reception was nothing less than a sensation. She had not told Peter she was coming and her parents could only gape at her in astonishment for several minutes. It could have been an embarrassing scene, but she had developed the poise to carry it off. She had brought a magnificent present of a canteen of silver cutlery, and other presents, a gold bracelet for her mother, ties for her father. When Vera finally recovered from her shock, she hugged and kissed Letty, breaking down. Jack suggested they would be more private if they went into the back parlour.

Albert Mundy was almost inarticulate. When Letty came home, if ever, he expected her to be down and out, broken and repentant. This ravishing creature was like nothing he had imagined. She knew exactly how to play him, a little sad, a little contrite, but hinting at her great success. She had gone into the entertainment world, she said, dropping the names of several visiting filmstars with whom she was on intimate terms. She might go into films herself one day, she told them, if the right offer came along. Albert was bowled over and smiled as he hugged her. They both asked forgiveness of each other.

When Peter brought in the exquisitely pretty little four-year-old flower girl in her long white ruffled dress, Letty could barely accept that she was the baby she had left behind. 'Yes, it's Vicky, it's your daughter,' Vera whispered to her.

Vicky thought Letty was the most beautiful lady she had ever seen and came forward willingly to give her a kiss. She was surprised when the lady hugged her so hard and kissed her several times.

Letty was shaken by the sudden rush of feeling at seeing this child, her own daughter. She had not even thought to bring her a present. The others left them alone, standing awkwardly as Letty crouched by Vicky talking to her, laughing at her turns of speech, delighting in her. It hurt her, unreasonably, to learn that Vicky had no idea she had a living mother. She saw Vera shake her head, warning her not to break the news too abruptly.

Albert was fighting emotions inside himself. He was overjoyed at seeing Letty again, yet there were many questions he wanted to ask her. Now was not the time, perhaps, as Vera had warned him, yet there was a lot he wanted to have out with her before any reconciliation was final. Above all, he was afraid of losing Vicky, who had come to mean a great deal to him.

It was an hour or so before Letty thought to ask Peter the time. When he told her, she rose quickly, worried. 'Oh, no! I said I couldn't stay very long. I'm sorry. I'll have to be going.'

There was a chorus of protests. 'Are you going away?' little Vicky asked, disappointedly, her face puckering.

Letty was torn. 'I have to, pet,' she said gently. 'But I'll be back. I promise. You wait there by the door, and I'll be back in no time. You wait for me now.' She kissed Vicky and hurried out through the rear door.

She almost ran down the side street and round the corner to the Weavers' Arms. Stavro was waiting, becoming impatient. But he had established one thing. 'So it's all right. It's your brother. It was good to come.' He made for the door.

'Just a minute, darling,' Letty asked. Quickly, touchingly, she told him about Vicky. 'She's so pretty, Stavro,' she said. 'You must see her. I can't let her go. You do understand – now I've found her again.'

Stavro nodded. He had gone very still, his dark-skinned, heavy face expressionless. 'You should have told me before that you had a baby,' he said. 'You're a mother. It's natural you want to be with your child. I understand. One thing, though.' His voice became harder. 'Now get this. I only say it once. It's either her or me.' He went out without looking back.

Half an hour later, Vicky was still waiting by the rear door of The Plough. The beautiful lady had not returned.

It cast a shadow on the wedding party. Everyone was whispering, wondering why she did not return and what she had really been doing all those years. Albert Mundy waited with Vicky and kept assuring her, yes, the beautiful lady would come back. She had promised. He was still waiting when Rosie and Peter had to catch the train to go off on their honeymoon, and left Vera, Jack and the McGraws to see them off at the station.

'Where d'you reckon she's got to?' McGraw asked Jack Blair quietly.

'Probably halfway to London by now,' Jack said. 'Whatever brought her back here, it wasn't strong enough to keep her.'

'But how did she find out about the wedding?' Mac asked.

Rosie and Peter were kissing Vera goodbye out of the train corridor window. 'I suspect my new son-in-law knows more than he's telling. And I daresay he has good reasons to stay quiet about it.'

'Could be,' McGraw said. 'I'd guess the less the Mundys learn about their daughter, the better.'

'That's a fact,' Jack agreed. 'I don't suppose we've heard the last of it, her turning up like that. Well, if she wanted to cause a sensation, she certainly did. But I can't help thinking it would have been far better if she'd stayed away.' He moved forward to kiss Rosie.

They called good wishes as the train pulled out and waved until it swung round the far bend out of sight. Jack saw that Sally had taken Vera's arm, and that Vera was crying. 'Come along, old love,' he smiled. 'This is the best thing that's happened in years.'

'It's not that, Jack,' Vera said. 'They're made for each other. I always saw that. It's . . .' She shook her head, walking on with Sally, who was holding her. And Jack realized she was crying for Letty.

Peter and Rosie had a carriage to themselves. 'Bit of luck, isn't it?' she said, smiling. She expected him to kiss her and thought he must be as nervous as herself, when he did not. Then she noticed him frown as he looked out of the window. 'Is something wrong? You're not sorry we got married?' she asked.

'Of course not, love,' Peter smiled. 'It really is the happiest day of my life.' He hesitated. 'At least, it was.'

'Letty, you mean,' Rosie said. 'I couldn't believe my eyes, when I turned round and there she was. She brought us a lovely present.'

'Yes, she did.'

'Must have cost a fortune. She must be doing ever so well,' Rosie said. 'She's in showbusiness, she says. She's met ever so many famous people.'

'Yes.'

'And did you see that dress she was wearing? The New Look, that's what they call it. I can't imagine where she got the coupons.' Rosie paused, thinking. 'But she didn't really tell us what she's been doing. She's not married, or anything. It was a marvellous surprise to see her, but why did she come? And why did she hurry away like that?'

'I don't suppose we'll ever know,' Peter said, slowly. He put his arm round Rosie to distract her, drew her to him and kissed her. 'There, that's better. This is the first time we've been alone today, Mrs Mundy.'

'Mrs Mundy . . .' Rosie giggled.

They reached Bridlington in the East Riding by early evening and found their pleasant, small hotel overlooking the bay. Neither of them could eat much supper and they had only one drink, before going up to their room. They laughed when they discovered each was as shy as the other, and lost their shyness. Rosie was experienced in some ways, but was a virgin, as he had suspected. She asked him not to laugh at her because of it. In a short, frilly nightdress, she looked suddenly very young and Peter kissed her gently. 'Don't you laugh at me, either,' he said. 'And we'll get on fine.'

The next morning, they had breakfast late, wandered round the old town and had lunch in a pub. 'Not a patch on The Plough,' Rosie said, critically. In the afternoon, they strolled up to Flamborough Head. Peter stopped to kiss her every five minutes and they decided to go back to the hotel.

'We've got a whole week,' Rosie reminded him. 'We ought to work out what else we're going to do.'

'What else, Mrs Mundy?' Peter asked, and laughed when Rosie blushed. 'We'll just have a holiday. I'll have a lot of work putting the band together, when we get back.'

When they reached the hotel, the receptionist had a message for them. 'It was from your mother, Mr Mundy. I'm sorry to tell you, your father's been taken very ill. She thinks you ought to come home.'

When Albert Mundy realized that he had recovered his daughter, only to lose her again, he had had a stroke. He did not die, as they had feared, but he was severely paralysed down the left side. Dr Heywood at the hospital told Peter there was no hope of his father being able to work, or at any rate, not for some time.

Vera took it very well. She had always been at her best in a crisis and set to, making plans for how she could still run the shop and look after Vicky, and her husband when he was released from hospital. She would not listen when Rosie told her Peter and she would help her, but Rosie said, 'It's all decided.'

'That's right, Mum,' Peter said. 'Rosie and I have talked it over, and we can't let you try to manage everything on your own. You'll have enough on your hands with Dad and Vicky. We'll take over the shop. The danceband can wait a little. After all, it'll only be for a year or so, till Dad's back on his feet.'

By tacit agreement among them all, Letty was never mentioned again.

# EIGHTEEN

Jim Kiley's promotion to Brigadier-General brought an increased involvement in policy matters. He asked several times for a transfer to more active duty, but the Truman administration kept him on at Washington, while mounting world tension and frantic efforts by Russia to develop its own atomic bomb threatened the balance of power, which was still in favour of the West.

In his office in the Pentagon he had a call one day from his old friend, Lieutenant-General Krasnowici, but it was not to discuss the collapse of the Four Power conference on Germany, nor the planned withdrawal of certain USAAF units from South-East Asia. 'You'll like this, Jim,' Rufus chuckled. 'You know when some guy retires from the Service, he gets all the pay that's due to him, his papers, honourable discharge and a travel warrant to wherever he wants to go, right? Well, guess who came to see me this morning? Mac McGraw, remember him, the old Line Chief at Market Wetherby? Well, he had a beef. Seems like he was brought back to Dayton, Ohio, to be discharged and he didn't notice, but his warrant was made out to some place in Pennsylvania, his last recorded address. While he really wants to go to – guess where? Market Wetherby, where his wife and family are.' They laughed. 'I said we could help him out.'

'No problem, Rufe,' Jim confirmed. 'We've got flights leaving for England all the time. Tell him to ring this office and we'll fix it so he can hitch a ride. He'd better not throw away his uniform, though, until he's over there.'

While Jim was away on frequent trips escorting government officials and congressmen on fact-finding missions or for inter-Allied conferences, Helen retreated to the family house at Newport or, preferably, their summer place on

Nantucket. Apart from the peace, she had struck up a friendship with an old local doctor, who ran a pay-what-you-can clinic for the families of local fishermen. She was not licensed to practise her profession in America, but she helped him out whenever she could, on a strictly unofficial basis.

There were times, however, when she returned by herself to Washington for meetings of the committee looking into the problems and welfare of GI brides, of which she was a leading member. Jim had just left for the Philippines shortly after the phone call from Rufus, when a large, craggy-looking man turned up at the house wishing to see him. It was Joe McGraw. 'Beg pardon for disturbing you, ma'am,' he said. 'I only wanted to see the Colonel – eh, General, and thank him for helping me.'

'He'll be sorry to have missed you, Mr McGraw,' Helen said. 'I understand you're flying to England soon.'

'End of next week.'

'I wish I was coming with you. Just for a visit, of course.' Helen smiled. 'Mrs McGraw will be delighted to see you.'

'Oh, Sal can't believe the day's come at last. Me, I'm gonna turn myself into a real English gentleman.'

Helen laughed. 'Can I offer you a cup of tea, Mr McGraw?'

'Tea? Uh – no thank you, ma'am.'

'How about a drop of scotch?'

McGraw's eyes lit up. 'Well, now . . . if it wouldn't be an imposition.'

'Help yourself,' Helen said. She smiled, watching McGraw as he poured out a generous measure. 'I was just thinking about some people you must know very well, Vi and Chuck Ericson.'

'Vi and Chuck? Sure. They became just about our best friends for a while. Well, Vi was very close to Sally back then. They still keep in touch.'

'I thought they might,' Helen said. 'Does Sally ever say anything about them, how they're getting on?'

'Just that they seem fine,' McGraw told her. Something

197

in Helen's expression made him think. 'Nothing wrong, is there, ma'am?'

'I wish I was sure,' Helen said. 'You see, I hear occasionally from Vi, myself. She always sounds cheerful enough, but they've been going through difficult times. Chuck has not been able to find his feet after leaving the Air Force. Only the other day, I had a letter from Vi's father.'

'Old Jack Blair,' McGraw smiled. 'One of the best.'

'Yes,' Helen agreed. 'He's concerned about them, too. He's afraid that . . . well, being poor, always having to struggle, is beginning to affect their marriage.'

'You don't say!' Mac exclaimed. 'That's tough. Well, once I see how I'm fixed, maybe I could lend them something.'

'That's very kind, Mr McGraw, but it's not what I meant,' Helen said. 'There are several people who would gladly send them money, but they're both fiercely independent, especially Chuck, and they reject even the suggestion.'

McGraw frowned. 'There must be something that could be done.'

'That's just what I was wondering,' Helen said. 'You see, if help or advice comes from Vi's father or family, or from me, they resent it. So if any of us arrived to – what's the word? – recce the situation, they would know that something was up.'

McGraw understood. 'You mean – you want me to go to Nebraska, ma'am?' He thought about it. 'That's a tidy step.'

'I was thinking that, if we approached General Krasnowici together, we might be able to arrange something,' Helen said; 'like a flight to the nearest air base.'

'Sound thinking, ma'am.' McGraw beamed. 'After all, I have till the end of next week.'

Helen was relieved. 'Thank you, Mr McGraw. I leave it to your, I'm sure, very sound commonsense, what you say and do when you get there. Try to find out how best they can be helped. Of course, I'll settle any expenses you may have.'

'No can do, ma'am,' McGraw told her. 'Sorry, but I'll take care of that. My privilege.'

McGraw was ferried the next day to a Base in northern Nebraska, then took a train south to Ash Ridge county. It was one of the poorer parts of the great farming state, a maize and potato raising area, with a little mining and light industry.

Chuck and Vi had a small clapboard house on the outskirts of the hamlet of Winnington. It was not so bad in early summer, but in Nebraskan winters must have been freezing. A man in patched denim overalls was hoeing the dusty patch at the side of the house between the neat rows of vegetables. His shoulders were stooped. It was only when he looked up that Mac saw it was Chuck.

Chuck stared at him for a moment, then grinned disbelievingly. '. . . Mac!' The two friends met and gripped hands. 'Where the heck did you come from?' Chuck exclaimed, turning at the same time and calling, 'Vi! Vi, look who's here!'

Vi came out on to the stoop. She was wearing a faded dress, one McGraw remembered from Market Wetherby, carrying a baby on her hip. She was as amazed as Chuck, but believed McGraw's story that he had had an unexpected stop at Lockart Base and decided to look them up. 'You'll stay the night,' Chuck insisted.

'Couple nights, if you'll have me,' McGraw answered.

'Move in, buddy!'

'If only I'd know you were coming,' Vi said worriedly. 'I – I haven't been into town for the groceries this week yet.'

McGraw noticed Chuck glance at her sharply, silencing her. 'I passed a steakhouse on the way through,' he said. 'Why don't I take you both out?' When they protested, he would not listen. 'Hey, I park myself on you, it's the least I can do.'

McGraw spent the next two or three hours telling them

about Sally and his small son, Joe, about the strange affair of the Mundys with Letty's mysterious appearance and disappearance. Sally apparently had seen a picture of her in a newspaper, she was certain it was Letty, in the group of friends accompanying a visiting American crooner to a premiere in Leicester Square. In turn, he admired little Helen who was growing into the image of her mother. 'You wait till my boy Joe sees you,' he warned her. 'Oh, you better look out.' She squeaked and laughed, hiding behind Vi. He played with the baby, Danny, named after Danny Coogan.

The meal at the steakhouse was so-so, but it was obvious that it was a rare treat for Vi to go out. Helen ate everything in sight and the baby behaved itself, sleeping throughout in its carrycot. On the way home, McGraw bought a dozen cans of beer. After the kids were put to bed, the three adults sat on the stoop. After a while, Vi went to bed herself, leaving Chuck and Mac alone.

McGraw didn't push anything. He let it come naturally out of Chuck, who had had no close friend to talk to for years. They had been years of increasing desperation. He had started off with high hopes, applying for jobs with prospects. It was always the same story. He had no degrees, no qualifications. He had worked for a time as an agricultural mechanic, studying nights at Lincoln, but the travelling and exhausting hours had nearly worn him out. Then the motor works was closed and he had to give up studying. He had had to take a succession of temporary jobs, farmhand, truckdriver, cable laying, potato harvesting, anything to make enough for them just to live on. At least the regular money orders from his father-in-law to his grandchildren meant that the kids never really had to go without. 'I wanted to send it back, but Vi said it would insult her father. Money – it's the only thing we row about.'

'What's money?' McGraw shrugged.

'Everything, if you haven't got it.' Chuck sighed. 'She doesn't understand. I wanted her to have everything when she came to America. I promised her everything. And I failed her – failed at everything.'

'You'll make it yet,' Mac said, soothingly.

'I used to think so.' Chuck was silent for a minute. 'I keep remembering how it used to be. I never thought I'd miss the war, but I knew what I was, what I was doing then. We were alive then, Mac.'

'Yeah. And some of us stayed alive. Some of us.' McGraw opened another can and passed it to Chuck. 'No point tryin' to live in the past, Chuck.'

Chuck took a drink of his beer. 'I think about it all the time. The war, and before that when I used to go around with my old man. I ever tell you about him?' McGraw waited. 'We lived not too far from here. He'd been born in some little backwoods burg in Sweden, was brought over here when he was a boy, but he still had a kind of yumpin' yimminy accent. He travelled round shoeing horses, fixing broken ploughs, scythes.'

'I thought you told me he was a dentist.'

'Yup.' Chuck smiled briefly. 'That was his other special-ity – travelling dentist. He'd no training, but in would go the pincers and out would come the tooth, neat as a pin. People swore by him. They wouldn't go to hospital. They'd rather stand the pain till old Doc Ericson came by. I used to help him sometimes. Never know when it might come in handy, he said.'

Next morning, Mac went with Chuck in his old pickup truck to help him load and unload a pile of logs he had been paid to shift to the local doctor's house. It was hot and sweaty work and, as they rested at the end of it, Mac looked at the shingle hanging outside the doctor's door. 'Know something? The only difference between him and your father is that he has a certificate.' Chuck smiled. 'So why don't you get one?'

'Me?'

'Why not?' Mac said. 'Any kind of certificate. You could be a real dentist, if you wanted.' Chuck turned away. 'I'm serious. Three or four years of college, then you're set up for life. If your old dad was still alive, he'd be proud of you. So would Vi be.'

'Knock it off, Mac,' Chuck said tersely. 'Don't think I haven't thought of it. There's no way it's possible.'

'Apply for a GI grant to study.'

'Aw, come on. It's years since I left the Air Force.'

'No harm in applying. You might get enough to support you and Vi and the kids, while you're at college.'

'I don't accept handouts.'

'It wouldn't be no handout,' McGraw explained patiently. 'It's your right. You earned it in the sky above Germany. Getting shot down and coming back. You earned it, buddy.'

Chuck was more than usually silent for the rest of the day and that evening, so that Vi was worried he was upset about something, maybe because McGraw had paid for a huge delivery of groceries, enough to keep them for a couple of weeks. She was grateful, but she knew how touchy Chuck was. However, he said he didn't mind, not since it was Mac.

The following day when McGraw was leaving, Chuck said he would travel with him as far as Lincoln, the state capital. Vi was puzzled when he told her not to get her hopes up, but he was going to see about the possibility of some kind of grant.

As soon as McGraw reported back to Helen, she rang General Krasnowici. 'If by any chance he's not eligible, Rufus,' she said, 'is there any way I could pay for him without him knowing?'

'Don't worry, Helen,' Krasnowici said. 'When a man with a service record like Ericson's applies, they won't turn him down. Or they'll have me to deal with.'

Within six weeks, Chuck was enrolled at a leading dental college at Glendale, California, to start in the new session in October. Just before they left for the west coast to find somewhere to live, Vi wrote excitedly to Helen that it was like a miracle. 'And we owe it all to Mac McGraw,' she said, 'who put the idea into Chuck's head without even realizing it.'

# NINETEEN

Dear Mummy,

I hope this letter reaches you. All that moving about Jim and you do must be exhausting. But I have a special reason for wanting you to get this, because I have some rather exciting news.

I'm getting married. And I'm quite certain you'll approve. It's to Henry Maylie. Surprised? Sir Arthur says he and Daddy used to joke about it being inevitable, since Henry was the boy next door . . . Frankly, I'd never even thought about him until this summer. And then it was just inevitable, like they said.

We met at a party at the Danbys. We didn't even recognize each other. Afterwards, I began to run into him quite often. I thought at first it was by accident. As he's rather shy, it was quite a time before he confessed he'd planned it!

As you know, Henry was in the army. He ended up as a major and since then has finished his degree at Cambridge. He has taken the summer to decide what to do and has made up his mind to try to get into Parliament. Tory. I suppose that's another surprise, me marrying a Conservative – after all that stuff I used to spout. Well, at least, he says he's a Progressive Conservative.

He's up for one or two seats and we think he has a good chance of being elected. Honestly, everyone is so sick of Attlee. Henry's told me a lot of inside stuff which has really opened my eyes. Nationalization is a terrible failure, yet they keep on nationalizing everything in sight, the railways, gas, and electricity. You'd be horrified at the National Health Service – they're even going to close the cottage hospital! Well, it seems certain that Churchill will get back in at the election, so perhaps he'll be able to reverse things.

Wasn't that Berlin Blockade a frightening business? Anything could have happened. Honestly, I was so proud of Jim. You must have been even more so. Everyone says that supplies being airlifted in so quickly was largely due to him. He kept the city going in those first weeks. What were the Russians playing at?

We've fixed the date of the wedding for 20th October. It would be lovely if you and Jim could come over, but I know it's difficult. It's going to be a fairly large affair, I'm afraid. Lady Maylie insists. We're going to live here at the house. I've given up teaching and I shall devote myself to helping Henry in his career.

Market Wetherby thrives. Mr McGraw's new garage is really something to see. I was talking to him and Sally the other day – they're so happy and contented together – and he says he expects business to start booming once petrol rationing ends. As it must soon, surely –

At least now that clothes rationing is over I can splash out a bit on my dress for the wedding. Unless, that is, I could borrow yours? I found it a month or two ago in a box in the spare room. Could I? It would make me so happy.

I met old Mr Blair too, when I was down town. He sends his regards. He told me that Vi is loving the USA and his son-in-law is very much enjoying being at dental college. What a strange choice of a profession! (Wonder why he chose it?) I saw Rosie, too. She didn't say, but I've more than half an idea that she is p.g. More little Mundys to carry on the grocery shop. She seems very happy, though Mr

Mundy, I understand, can be a bit of a trial. His grand-daughter Vicky is the only one, seemingly, who can understand him sometimes. Seeing him pushed about the town in his wheelchair is so sad – reminds me of Daddy.

Well, I must close. I hope the news of the wedding has not been too much of a shock! Do write soon. Henry and I would dearly like your blessing. I do really and truly love him, Mummy. This time it's real.

Longing to see you some time. I still feel awful about what an ass I made of myself when I visited you. Too heady a dose of the LSE – as you guessed. He's head of their Board of Trade or something now. Ah, well . . .

I think of you both often.

Love

Pat

P.S. Isn't it awful, those stories that Moscow is testing its own atomic bomb? Jim was so right. I suppose we can expect trouble anywhere now. P.

P.P.S. Guess who called in to see me the other day? Major Carson, Lester Carson. You remember, he was adjutant here and in command of the Base for a while near the end of the war. He brought his wife with him. She's very nice, English. He met her in Cambridge. Apparently, he's doing very well, lecturing at the University of Virginia Law School. He says he owes it all to Jim – and can never thank him enough for getting him to 'straighten up and fly right'. Whatever that means. I suppose Jim knows. Please give my love to him.

Now I really must close. P. XX

# TWENTY

All the way from Nebraska over to the west coast, Chuck had kept up their spirits through the interminable miles of wheatfields and the long, featureless stretches of desert by singing or whistling 'California, here I come!' At the most inappropriate moments, just when Vi felt she could not bear the heat and the dust a moment longer, he would start up. Little Helen would join in. Even baby Danny seemed to recognize it, crowing in his carrycot, and Vi would find herself smiling, joining in the chorus. 'California! Here I . . . come!'

In the years after, whenever she heard that jaunty tune, she was reminded of those five days in their old pick-up truck. She had forgotten the tedium and discomfort, Helen's prickly heat, the frequent stops to mend punctures in the threadbare tyres and when the radiator boiled over. She remembered it as a happy time, an exciting, hope-filled adventure.

Neither she nor Chuck had any real idea what to expect when they reached the Golden State. He had his grant under the GI Bill of Rights to attend dental college in Glendale. They calculated that after his fees were paid there would be just enough to keep them, without any frills. It would be tough, but Chuck was determined to make a success of it after so many false starts and dead-end jobs. Vi prayed that it would not be another disappointment for him. No one could have tried or worked harder and she had felt the bitterness growing in him at being unable to provide properly for her and the children. Telling him that it did not matter as long as they were together had only made him more conscious of failure and his refusal of her offer to look for part time work herself to help out had brought about their first real argument. It had been nearly a week before they made up and she had had to be careful of what she said ever since. She even had to hide the occasional letters from England, enclosing money from her father, using the money very sparingly to buy essentials like milk and eggs.

She thought she had managed it perfectly. Then, on the day he had come back from Lincoln with the news that his grant had been approved, he handed her a package. Inside was a present for her of a dress. He had earned enough to pay for it by cleaning and waxing cars at the local garage, on the evenings she had thought he was watching baseball with friends. It was only a flowered cotton frock with a few pleats and a white collar round its yoke neck, but it was the first new dress she had had in three years and she was almost in tears when she tried it on.

'Just look at you,' he said. 'The prettiest girl in the Mid West.'

'No, I'm not,' she laughed. 'It's the dress.'

'Oh, that's nothing. One day I'm going to get you a whole wardrobe of them – only better,' he promised. 'And clothes for the kids. And bicycles and rollerskates, everything they want. And we'll have a decent place to live in and a car and – It'll be good, Vi. You'll see. But first, I'm going to pay your old man back what I calculate I owe him.'

Vi's eyes opened. 'You know about that?'

Chuck smiled. 'Well, I couldn't believe Jack had suddenly stopped writing to the kids. Then there was Helen's new shoes and Danny's playsuit, and the groceries seemed to go further every week. And the cigarettes in the pack in my overalls never seemed to run out.' He paused. 'You never bought anything for yourself. That's why I got you the dress.' She really was crying now and he held her, kissing her tears. 'I've got a real chance at last, Vi,' he told her. 'It's not something I ever thought of doing, going to college. But it's from the Good Lord and I'm going to take it with both hands.'

The uneasy strain there had been between them was

wiped out. Their last weeks in the little clapboard house with its vegetable patch and peeling picket fence were like a second honeymoon. It really was a new beginning. When they finally packed their things into the truck and headed west, Vi felt like one of the pioneer women setting out in their prairie wagons into the unknown across the great plains.

California, here we come . . .

She had been a little afraid of Los Angeles and could tell from the way Chuck laughed and joked about it that he, too, felt uncertain. Neither of them was used to big cities and they wondered how they would ever get used to living in one.

Glendale, in Los Angeles county, was a welcome surprise to them. It had not yet been totally swallowed up by the outward sprawl of the metropolis and still retained much of its own character. Built at the southern end of the San Fernando Valley between Pasadena and Burbank, much of it was residential. The climate was perfect and it was largely untouched by the intensifying smog problem of the main city. They were impressed by the amount of green space. The buildings were not too intimidating, either. Apart from the civic centre and the factory areas, few of the houses rose above two storeys, where they had expected skyscrapers and barrack-type apartment blocks. It was like one big pleasant suburb, Vi thought.

They stayed in a motel for the first two nights, then through his college Chuck found them an apartment in Verdugo Avenue. It was the upper half of a small bungalow, three rooms, kitchen and bathroom, and the retired couple who lived below were only too happy to let them use the small garden that surrounded it, in exchange for Vi cutting the lawn and looking after the plants. The bungalow was within walking distance of Chuck's college, so that was another saving.

He had two weeks before his course began and they used it to settle in and find their way around. The excitement continued. Vi could not get over the fact that she was just over the hill from Hollywood. When he drove her through it she could not sit still. She was convinced that Clark Gable had driven past them with a stunning blonde and he laughed, teasing her, singing, 'You Made Me Love You'. They spent days on the beach at Santa Monica and, one unforgettable day, Chuck drove them all the way up the coast to picnic at Santa Barbara Mission.

The second week they were there, he disappeared one morning and came back with a 'forty-one sedan. It was fairly beat-up, but it was a car. He had swapped the pickup truck for it in some country style horsetrading, where the owner thought he was outsmarting the country boy. As a former Flight Engineer, however, Chuck knew that the sedan's chassis was sound and the coughs and wheezes that made it seem perpetually on the point of breaking down could be fixed by half a day's work. When he had gone over it, it ran as well as new and did them for the next six years. That morning, he gave Vi her first driving lesson.

The four years that his course lasted were hard going. Money was always short, yet with the grant Vi could budget ahead. She was hard pushed at times to make ends meet, but tried never to bother Chuck. He had enough problems as a 'mature' student, adapting to another form of discipline, with the pressures of study and examinations and increasingly long periods of practical dentistry. It was far from easy for him, particularly when Danny started teething during the run-up to his first important exams. 'You'd think that with my chosen profession I'd be able to do something for him,' he said philosophically, 'but all I can do is carry him round and round the room and rub oil of cloves on his gums.'

Vi again tentatively suggested getting a temporary job, herself, mornings or afternoons. It would be an undeniable help with the bills and the old lady downstairs was willing to babysit, but Chuck again refused. He had not brought Vi to America, he said, to send her out to work. It quickly became an impossibility, in any case, when she discovered she was pregnant again. Eight months after they arrived in Glendale, she gave birth to another son, whom they named John Olav after their fathers. He was soon known as Jacky.

It was not all study and struggle. The social life of the college was varied and, as Chuck soon became popular, they were often invited to parties and celebrations, as well as attending the more official functions. Chuck, of course, was older than most of his fellow-students and felt older still, through the ageing effect of war service. In his class, however, were several other former GIs. Some were only along for the ride, doing just enough to keep their grants coming, but others were trying just as hard as Chuck and finding the going just as difficult. Two became his close friends, Matt Zimmer and Sam Hicks. Both were ex-Army. Matt was serious, a worrier, while Sam was just the opposite, always joking, happy-go-lucky. Both were married and the contrast extended to their wives. Matt's Rachel was as relaxed and amusing as he was solemn, while Bette Hicks looked as if she bore the cares of the world on her shoulders. 'You guys married the wrong wives,' Chuck told them. 'You ought to change around.' 'Disaster,' Sam said. 'If I'd married Rachel, we'd never get anything done for laughing. And if Matt and Bette had gotten together, long before now, it would've ended in a suicide pact.'

Vi took to Rachel and Bette at once and all three became as good friends as their husbands. It was Bette who went with her to the hospital, when baby Jack decided to arrive a week early, and sat up with her until Chuck could get there, and it was Rachel who brought her soup every day and oranges and vitamin pills. Bette had a small girl the same age as Helen. They lived less than five minutes from each other and, when their children started school, they took turns taking and collecting. Rachel insisted on joining in, although she had no children of her own. 'What are friends for?' she would say. 'Besides, it gives me something to do.'

Bette was the daughter of a Baptist minister in Fort Worth, who had prophesied doom when she married Sam, then a penniless buck private. 'It was his smile that made me marry him,' she explained. 'I'd never seen anyone whose smile lit up their whole face. It made me feel warm. It's a good thing, for we still can't afford a place with central heating.' She was not as careworn as she appeared, but her father had left her a legacy of guilt feelings and pessimism. Without constant vigilance, nothing would turn out right. She seemed to take a pleasure in finding newspaper references to GI brides from Britain whose marriages had cracked up. One in ten, an article claimed, wanted to go home. Vi insisted that it had no bearing on her and Chuck, yet it worried her, until Rachel said, 'My Lord, wouldn't every wife every now and then want to go home – if only she had somewhere to go to? One in ten? Compared to the present American divorce rate, that has to be a pretty good average.'

'I'm just being realistic,' Bette said. 'These things happen. And it's more difficult for Vi. She's a foreigner.'

'We're all foreigners!' Rachel laughed. 'She's English, you're Texas Baptist, I'm Detroit Jewish. In California we're all foreigners. Her son Jack's the only person I know who was actually born here.'

Of the two, Vi really preferred Rachel. She had never actually been friends with anyone Jewish before, and, at first, she was very careful in case she said anything hurtful by mistake.

That was until one day when Rachel said to her, 'Listen, Vi. Let me tell you – I'm not going to faint if you mention you had pork chops for dinner last night. You make me feel like a babushka.'

She had the kindest and most generous nature Vi had ever known. Nothing was too much trouble for her. She would give her time and attention to anyone in need, stranger or friend. Bette accused her of being an optimist. 'You make it sound like a disease,' Rachel laughed. 'The way life is, there's no harm in hoping it'll get better. Try a little hope, Bette. You could use it,'

Vi had a surprise one day. Rachel had asked her to drive her down to Long Beach to deliver a birthday present to her father-in-law. Vi had heard vaguely that Matt's father lived somewhere south of LA and that there was little communication between them. What surprised her was the house, when they stopped outside in the drive and Rachel dropped off her package. It was a large, ocean-fronted mansion with a landscaped garden, palm trees and a huge kidney-shaped swimming pool. Matt and Rachel were as strapped for cash as the rest of them, occasionally borrowing the odd five or ten dollars to tide them over from Vi, who kept a small emergency fund saved from the five pounds Jack Blair still sent every month to his grandchildren. Yet here was Matt's father living in obvious opulence and she could not understand.

They drove west out to the point overlooking the Pacific and, as they ate their sandwiches, Rachel explained. 'Matt's old man is a dental surgeon. Wouldn't you know it? He made a fortune out of inventing some kind of cosmetic tooth brace. Well, Matt was the younger son. Nothing was expected of him. Like in many Jewish families the elder boy was everything – handsome, brilliant, hardworking. He was studying to be a dentist like their father. He volunteered for the Marines, and was killed at the battle of Wake Island. Matt joined up at once to avenge him, but never even got abroad. He spent the rest of the war as a supply corporal at a camp in Indiana. His father never forgave him for not being the one who was killed.' She paused. 'The rest you can guess. After demob, Matt drifted for a while. Met me and got married. Pretty soon I could see that, unless he could come to terms with his father, he'd just go on drifting. He took the grant and came back here to college – to prove himself. It's a sweat. He's not as bright as your Chuck and he really has to slave at it. But even so, dear old Doctor Zimmer's sole concern is that he will flunk out and let down the family name. We only see him once a year, at Passover. And he only asks us because he wants a grandson. He's a real charmer.' She shrugged, and added ironically, 'As you can see, I'm devoted to my father-in-law.'

The only time Vi ever saw Rachel depressed was once when her friend had offered to bathe Jacky and put him to bed, while she cooked supper. When Vi had finished, she went through and found Rachel sitting in tears by the cot where Jacky lay sleeping. 'What is it, Rachel?' Vi asked. 'Whatever's wrong?'

'I never told you. We never told anyone,' Rachel said. 'I lost my own baby, a miscarriage, in the second year of our marriage. Never been able to have another. The one thing I could have done to help Matt, to bring his father closer to him, and I failed him.'

The two months of waiting for the final exam results to be published were nail-biting. Chuck had little to worry about for his practical work, which had been highly commended. The dental hospital in Burbank where he had served for a year as a student was very willing to keep him on. It was the written papers on periodontics, oral surgery, prosthodontics and related subjects in physiology, anaesthetics and materia medica which worried him. 'You'd never have guessed there was so much to learn, just to get a licence to yank out some sucker's teeth,' Sam said. Chuck became convinced he had made a mess of it and Vi blamed herself for letting him do too much. As well as the study and the long practical sessions, he had worked three nights a week in a local sandwich bar to pay for his books.

He could not wait for the official letter and Vi went with him the morning the results were pinned up at the college. Old Mrs Martins downstairs took care of the children. Matt and Sam were already at the noticeboard when they reached it, oblivious of the other students crowding round them. Sam was whooping and hollering, thumping Matt on the back. Matt's usually frowning expression was replaced by one of sheer delight. They had both passed. 'How did I do?' Chuck asked.

They both stopped smiling and just pointed at the noticeboard. Chuck moved in. He was silent and Vi pressed in beside him, almost afraid to look. He had First Class Honours, coming third from the top in his year, with special mentions both in periodontics and oral surgery. 'He's a star!' Sam laughed. 'Hey, Vi – how does it feel to be married to a star?'

The celebration that night was memorable. Vi was radiant. Even Bette broke a lifetime prohibition and had some wine. Two glasses were enough to melt her prim façade and she astonished them by insisting on dancing the rhumba with Matt. When they finally poured themselves out of Clancy's Chophouse and Sam was helping her to their car, she broke out into a spirited rendering of 'Dem bones, dem bones, dem dry bones!'

'I've never seen her having so much fun,' Vi laughed.

'Yeah,' Chuck agreed. 'But she won't forgive herself for the next ten years.'

With Chuck now qualified, other problems arose. Sam left almost straight away for a post in a municipal clinic at Abilene, Texas. 'Not very adventurous,' he said. 'But it's secure. And maybe it'll show my in-laws at last that I'm not just a bum.'

Matt had just scraped through and not so many options were open to him. 'He'll go anywhere, as long as we don't have to leave California,' Rachel said. 'Would you want to leave?'

Vi had to admit that she did not. She had grown used to the climate and the relaxed lifestyle. Helen was doing well at school. Danny had started now, and in a year or two little Jack would also be at school. She liked Glendale and had come to see it as their home. Maybe they could get a place of their own with a couple more rooms, nothing pretentious. That would be her ideal.

Chuck explained the possibilities. His degree results meant that Burbank would take him on permanently, or he could join any one of a number of hospitals as a junior staff member, like Sam. Without money for a surgery and equipment he could not think of opening a private practice. Neither could he buy into an established one. He would be a virtual employee of the man who owned it. Another possibility was that he might go back into the Air Force as a dental officer. The offer had been made, but it would mean he could be posted anywhere from Wyoming to Germany or South-East Asia and both of them knew the unsettling effect it could have on family life.

The answer was totally unexpected. It came in a letter from Dr Joseph Zimmer, Matt's father, asking Chuck to call and see him. For many years he had run a highly lucrative private practice in Long Beach. 'But I have a heart condition and should have retired long before this,' he said. 'I suppose my son deserves some consideration. At least, he bears my name. I am making the practice over to him. There are two surgeries. I want him to run one, you to run the other. The financial rewards are considerable. I shall take only a token percentage. The rest you will share between you, provided you keep an eye on Matt for me, so he does not disgrace me.'

Chuck did not hesitate, particularly when Matt welcomed the arrangement. 'I couldn't have hoped for anything so much,' Matt confessed, nearly weeping. 'It's from heaven.'

Within six months, Chuck moved Vi and the children to Palos Verdes, to a Spanish-style villa with a double garage, a pool and a view of the ocean out towards Santa Catalina. The interior was cool, Spanish Colonial, with lots of tiles and mosaic parquet flooring. Vi had never imagined them owning anywhere so palatial. 'Can we afford it?' she gasped.

'It's only a start,' Chuck told her. 'I promised you the best one day, and I meant it.'

# TWENTY-ONE

Jim Kiley's post in Washington and his frequent trips to many of the world's trouble spots gave him a first-hand knowledge of international problems. As a serving officer he was strictly required to stay out of politics, which lost him no sleep.

One thing troubled him, however. Before the war, American policy had been largely isolationist. Now, through the historical circumstances of victory, she was involved everywhere. The administration's postwar concentration on the development of democracy in West Germany and Japan was admirable, yet he was often surprised by the indifference of the wise men on Capitol Hill to what was happening elsewhere. They assumed that all nations aspired to the peace and freedom championed by the Allies. They had taken over the policing of much of the world from the British Empire, without the centuries of experience and diplomatic craft that had maintained Britain's influence, until her near financial collapse after five years of war. What troubled Jim was the naïvety of many of the speeches and assumptions he heard in Washington, the schoolboy belief that light must triumph over dark, good over evil, the plain, forthright man over the schemer.

He mentioned it so often that Helen called it his hobbyhorse, and he had to promise that it would be taboo as dinner conversation. Among their friends, the only ones who really shared his concern were Adlai and Jack Kennedy, although for Adlai it took second place to the problems of postwar reconstruction in the US, itself, the slump and unemployment that would inevitably follow the boom years.

Increasingly, during his many trips to Japan, Jim took

an interest in the cultures of South-East Asia. The paintings and sculptures he brought back intrigued Helen and they visited Hong Kong, Bangkok and Bali together. They made an expedition to Angkor Wat and spent a lazy month on a houseboat on the Mekong River. On the surface everything proceeded smoothly, yet he was made more and more uneasy by his government's simplistic approach to the problems of the countries in the area. Many senators, even cabinet members, assumed that gratitude for their deliverance from the Japanese and the massive amounts of aid in foodstuffs and medical supplies they had been given would ensure that these peoples would be eager for democracy and loyal to America and the American way of life. Although reports of riots and assassinations and the burning of the Stars and Stripes alarmed them, they were put down as local disturbances. It was not Jim's brief to instruct them, but he became more and more conscious that they were in the midst of a battle. He was not alone in realizing that, yet even amongst those who did, many seemed unaware of its true extent, that a former reluctant ally, grown more ambitious and more sure of his strength, had turned into the most subtle and dangerous enemy America had ever faced.

By 1949, Stalin's brilliant global strategy had left him in control of much of Europe, with strong influence in South America, Africa and Asia. Nowhere was his expanding power more obvious than in South-East Asia, where his recent recognition of the new Chinese People's Republic gave him a mighty ally with whom he could counter American influence in the area.

Western leaders were constantly taken by surprise by the later effects of his longterm planning. In the Potsdam Declaration he had supported the independence of Korea. The next day, his forces landed in northern Korea, ostensibly to further the war against Japan. They remained there, impelling US forces to remain in the south to prevent a Soviet occupation of the entire country, but also splitting it in two, North and South Korea.

The division caused endless political protests and upheavals. Yet while in the South the US administration moved haltingly towards preparing the country for independence and democratic self-government, in the North the Russians set about steadily creating a Democratic People's Republic on the Chinese model, controlled from Moscow. In the North a strong, well equipped army was formed. The South's new, freely elected government set up a police reserve, equipped with only small arms.

In June, 1949, the US occupying forces withdrew, leaving only five hundred men as advisers. In October, the USSR declared the Communist Republic in the North to be the only legal government of Korea. The following year, the North Koreans launched a massive invasion of the South.

UN condemnation of the Soviet-backed aggression was instant and an international force was ordered to resist the invasion, with General Douglas MacArthur in command. It was nearly too late. Most of South Korea including the capital, Seoul, had been taken. Landing in the south-east, the UN force, brilliantly led and made up mainly of battle-hardened US units, smashed the North Koreans, driving them back to the old border of the thirty-eighth parallel. Ordered by President Truman to prevent any possible future aggression, MacArthur advanced into North Korea, capturing its capital, Pyongyang, and not stopping until he had reached the Yalu River, the border of Manchuria.

Urged on by Stalin, the Chinese now entered the conflict, hurling over a million armed men across the Yalu and compelling the much smaller UN force to retreat in turn. It was almost a rout and by January 1951, Seoul was again lost and only the extreme south remained in UN hands.

Helen was in a complex of houses outside Kyoto in Japan, reserved for the wives of senior officers. She managed to keep her serenity, although it was difficult, knowing that Jim was over there on MacArthur's staff. She was surprised one day to see a face she recognized, which she had last seen on the terrace of Dereham House. It was Lorna Jane Somers.

Lorna Jane had been repatriated from England and discharged from the Air Force shortly after VJ Day. She had returned briefly to Virginia, then gone on to New York where she had begun a career in the expanding profession of advertising. She did well and had several proposals of marriage from young executives. She accepted none of them. They were attentive and handsome enough, yet there was something missing. She realized what, when she reached her office one day to find Red Burwash leaning by the side of the door. 'I've had a hell of a job tracking you down,' he said.

Red was still in the Air Force, now a Lt-Colonel. He was as casual and irreverent as ever, and Lorna Jane became abruptly aware that what she had missed in others was the hint of danger in Red, the daredevilry that made him such an outstanding combat pilot. They were married two weeks later.

At first Helen and Lorna Jane were cautious with each other, the memory of the younger woman's relationship with Jim standing between them. Gradually, however, their shared concern for their husbands drew them into friendship and Helen became very fond of Lorna Jane's five-year-old son, a sturdy, tough little boy with his father's flaming red hair. When the UN force began to advance again, they celebrated together. Surely this time, if the Chinese were driven back, it would mean the end of the war? Helen knew from Jim that the bitterest fighting yet was to be expected. She concealed her anxiety from Lorna Jane.

In the Advance Command Post on the south bank of the Pukhen-gang, the command tent was crowded with senior officers facing the tall figure of General MacArthur.

'Many of you, like people back home, have been asking why we don't push on. We've got the Chinese on the move at last. Here we are north of Seoul again. Why don't we go straight on up the middle of the peninsula, at least to the thirty-eighth parallel? We've nothing but demoralized North Koreans on our left and isolated pockets of Chinks in the mountains on our right. We can hold off the first and mop up the second at our leisure. Why have we stopped here? Colonel?'

The senior Intelligence Colonel stepped forward. 'The reason is, gentlemen, that we have very reliable reports that we are being led to believe there are only isolated pockets in the mountains. Whereas, in reality, there are two, shortly to be three, crack Chinese regiments concealed there.' There was a murmur from the assembled officers. 'Furthermore, the North Korean units on our left are merely a screen, backed by a further four Chinese Army Corps.'

'They are tempting us to move forward,' MacArthur said, 'then they'll catch us in a pincer, chopping off the head of our advance, while their main force falls on our flanks. That's why we're staying put for the moment.'

'Begging your pardon, sir,' one of the officers said, 'even supposing such a large number of gooks have gotten up into the mountains, there's no way they could have got heavy supplies or armour there.'

'It was considered impossible,' the Intelligence Colonel agreed, 'but we know there are tracks from the north.' He pointed to the map on the easel beside him. 'The one insuperable barrier was the Yakkon Valley.' He was pointing to a twisting, irregular ravine some eighteen miles long. 'Its sides are sheer, falling hundreds of feet. We've learnt that Chinese engineers have thrown two high-tensile suspension bridges across the ravine, strong enough to carry artillery and tanks. They are just completed and the supply of these enemy regiments has started.'

'Obviously, we don't intend to wait until it's finished,' MacArthur said. 'Our best plan, our only one, is to proceed with our advance as if we suspect nothing. The advance unit must be ready to dig in at a moment's notice and strong enough to defend itself. Our main advance will leave a gap. We must gamble that the enemy will commit themselves to the attack. Our artillery will concentrate on containing the right, the mountain regiments, while our main force concentrates on the left, sandwiching the enemy between us and the Marines who are at this moment making an amphibious landing north of Inch'on.' The murmur broke out again. 'All depends, however, on those two suspension bridges being destroyed, to prevent the mountain regiments from moving north and sweeping down on us along the valley of the Soyang-gang.' He glanced at Jim who stood on his left.

'It will be a highly tricky operation,' Jim said. 'We cannot attack them now with a large strike force. They are already strongly defended. It would be costly and would alert the enemy that we are aware of their plans.'

'Then how can they be got at, sir?' the commander of the Forward Air Control Team asked. It was Col Red Burwash.

'We'll attack with three, no more than those, Corsairs, armed with napalm tanks and 20-mm cannons They'll circle east and come in from the north to avoid early detection, then fly low along the ravine itself, under the level of the Anti-Aircraft guns. That's the trickiest part. At times the clearance is estimated to be no more than twenty-five feet more than a Corsair's wingspan.' He paused. 'I never ask any man to do what I won't do myself. I shall fly one of the ships myself. I'll need two more volunteers.'

Red scratched his neck, 'I can't ask my boys to fly a mission like that, General. I'll come with you, myself.'

'Me, too, sir,' added Red's second in command, a tall Texan named Parrish.

'Thank you, gentlemen,' Jim said, and smiled. 'I couldn't ask for anyone better.'

MacArthur's hawklike profile was more pronounced than ever, the steep visor of his cap drawn down, shading his eyes. 'Remember you will have only one crack at this target,' he rasped. 'If you fail, twelve thousand Americans, three thousand British and four thousand Australians, our entire advance unit, will be wiped out.'

The advancing UN troops came under heavy attack from both sides. They had been strung out to give the impression of greater numbers and closed up quickly, digging in for defence. Immediately, the UN artillery began the bombardment of the enemy's mountain positions, while the main force swung to the attack of the Chinese corps moving forward on the left.

It was still dark when Jim took off, followed by Red and Parrish. They flew up to ceiling, then out over the coast, circling north as dawn came up on their right. It was fully light when they turned again, hunting for the mouth of the ravine which ran back roughly north-east to south-west through the high mountains. Red located it first and waggled his wingtips in the agreed signal. No radio on this, absolute surprise was needed.

Jim streaked into the ravine first, followed by Parrish, with Red bringing up the rear. It was the most exacting flying any of them had ever done, needing cool judgement and instant reflexes as the narrow walls of the towering ravine flashed by, constantly changing direction, with projecting spurs and ledges. The sound of their engines trapped between the sides of the ravine was deafening. The enemy might not see them, but they would hear them coming.

In seconds, Jim's body was drenched with sweat. At this speed it would be any second now. He was sure his starboard wingtip brushed a lump of rock as he tore round a longer bend. A few inches closer . . . But he had no time to think of that. The ravine was straightening out and dead ahead he could see the suspension bridges.

He was too low! He swung the stick back sharply to come up to attack level. The AA guns could not be depressed sufficiently to get him, but he flew right through a barrage of tracer bullets, feeling his ship buck as slugs ripped through her wings and fuselage. Then the first bridge was only moments away and he dropped the napalm tanks, almost by instinct. The first burst on the steel mesh side of the bridge and plunged like a flare into the ravine. The second hit the ten-foot wide walkway of the bridge itself and ran along it in a river of searing heat. He was approaching the second bridge and tilted his Corsair slightly, pressing his firing buttons. The 20-mm cannon shells raked across the southern supports of the bridge and one of them lurched, breaking loose. Then he was past and screaming down the ravine.

Parrish, who was thirty seconds behind him missed the first machine gun barrier as they were following Jim. He came with cannons firing, his shells smashing into the first bridge. His napalm was for the second bridge, both bombs hitting it and exploding behind him in clouds of scorching incandescence. He risked a glance at his mirror and shouted as he saw the bridge split apart, both sides flailing like whips, then machine gun bullets severed his rudder. He slewed to left and right, fighting for control. His port wing hit the side of the ravine and the nose of the Corsair slammed round into the rock. It exploded as it fell into the lower darkness.

Red was last and saw the Corsair ahead of him go down in flames. He pressed the buttons, snarling. His instinct was to fire at the clifftops at the gooks who had brought down Parrish, but he kept his sights on the remaining bridge, aiming for the still burning track of Jim's napalm. One of his own bombs missed entirely, but the second hit in almost exactly the same spot as Jim's. The floor of the bridge gave way, although the side supports still held. Then he sliced through the hail of tracers and was out of danger as the ravine's wall curved again.

Red saw Jim's ship ahead of him and climbing, as he sped out of the wider southern end of the Yakkon Valley. He waggled his wingtips in response to Jim's and began to climb to join him. But his Corsair did not respond. He was losing altitude fast and realized that his tanks had been riddled. He was nearly out of gas. In a moment, his ship would be diving towards the ground.

He had only a split second to decide. Some distance ahead was a fairly level stretch like a meadow and he set his nose towards it, gliding down at as steep an angle as he dared. If he overshot he would smash into a higher, rocky bank. He just made it, braking as hard as he could and swerving round in a lurching skid which spun him to a halt on the ground.

He had to get out fast. There were gooks all around him in these foothills. Soon as he dropped out of his ship, he felt the zip of bullets passing him and flung himself to the deck.

Jim had circled back, seeing Red go down. He guessed that Parrish had bought it, but could not let himself think of that. He could see Chinese less than half a mile from Red's plane, running towards it. It was a savage campaign and he had no doubt what would happen to Red, if they caught him. He did not hesitate.

Red heard the roar of the Corsair coming down. He was running at an angle across the meadow for marshy ground with some cover beyond it. He stopped and tried to wave Jim away. 'You crazy bastard!' he yelled, then flung himself down as the Corsair skimmed over him. He saw it land and veer round, taxi-ing back. Jim was opening the cockpit. Some of the Chinese had stopped and were firing. Fortunately, at that range their light machine guns were not too accurate.

Red hared for the Corsair, reached it and jumped up just as Jim started taxi-ing again. 'Get yourself in here!' Jim shouted. Somehow, Red hauled himself up and fitted himself into whatever space there was in the cockpit and Jim took off, flying almost blind. They hedgehopped for ten miles and came down behind the UN lines.

The bridges were destroyed. Cut off from their supply line, the Chinese in the hills were forced to surrender, after heavy loss of life. They were driven out of South Korea and MacArthur proposed to chase them all the way back into mainland China, to teach the Communist world that aggression would not pay.

But by that time, Jim was back in Washington.

Both Red and he, after a monumental celebration from which it took them days to recover, had wanted to return to action with the Forward Air Control Teams. It was not to be. The news of their exploit had captured the popular imagination and they were kept at Headquarters for an apparently endless series of photographic sessions and newspaper and radio interviews.

'Hell, Jim,' Red complained one day, 'you'd think that mission had been laid on as one big PRO stunt. Some of the guys round here have even started asking for my autograph.'

Jim knew the media had seized on them to satisfy the needs of the public at home, tired of descriptions of reverses and heroic retreats and in need of something to cheer about. As MacArthur began his victorious push to the north, he told Red that they would quickly be forgotten. No one was allowed to forget the bridges of the Yakkon ravine, however. The incident received new coverage and even greater publicity, following the announcement that they had both been awarded the Congressional Medal of Honour, with a further, posthumous award for Major Parrish.

# TWENTY-TWO

Helen was exhausted, and relieved, when the euphoria which had accompanied Jim's award of the Congressional Medal, America's highest award for gallantry, had spent itself. But it had taken time – six months, in fact, from the day of the raid on the bridges over the Yakkon ravine, the dramatic operation which was seen to have changed the course of the Korean war.

First, there had been a reunion in Tokyo for the Kileys. Helen had been at the airbase, waiting for the transport from Seoul to touch down, and waiting with her was Lorna Jane.

As they watched the big transport ship lumber down the runway, Lorna shivered beside her. 'I had the funniest feeling,' she told Helen. 'It was like being back at Market Wetherby, watching the Fortresses return from a mission, counting them in one by one to see how many had survived.'

'I used to listen for them coming back, too,' Helen said. 'But actually to be there, on the base, must have been nerve-wracking.'

'Being there, I guess, was marginally better than just waiting to hear,' Lorna said, and smiled. 'Odd to think that, for a time, we were both waiting to see if the same person had made it.' She looked round eagerly as the Marine band struck up. The transport was rolling to a stop.

Helen watched the younger woman for a moment or two, seeing the excitement that brought a light flush to her finely moulded features, animating them and making her even more attractive. Was that how she looked, while she waited eight years ago for Jim?, Helen wondered. She had never known the full extent of the relationship Lorna Jane had had with him, although it was no secret that the red-headed former WAAC had been close to her husband back then. She had given Jim the benefit of the doubt at the time and over the years had more or less forgotten about it.

Her meeting with Lorna Jane last November in Tokyo had been completely unexpected. Until then, she had not even known she was married to Red Burwash. As wives of top brass, the two women had been thrown together and had warmed to each other, sharing outings and evenings in each other's apartments during the interminable days of waiting. While the fortunes of the war ebbed and flowed dramatically, with both their husbands often in extreme danger, she had been glad of Lorna Jane's presence and support, enough to forgive her occasional bouts of tactlessness. It could, after all, be the tactlessness of a completely untroubled conscience. Lorna Jane was interrupting a highly successful career in a Madison Avenue advertising agency to be as near her husband, Red, as she could possibly get. Maybe those passing, thoughtless remarks were also a sign of frustration.

All these thoughts were swept out of Helen's mind as the honour guard presented arms. Jim and Red were coming down the steps from the plane and the two wives moved forward with the reception committee, Lorna Jane holding her small son's hand. They stood silently, smiling, while their husbands saluted the welcoming generals and the first words were exchanged, but when Red turned to them, Lorna Jane could not restrain herself any longer and threw herself into his arms. He kissed her, then scooped up his son and held both of them tightly against him.

The meeting of Jim and Helen was more controlled, as suited his higher rank, but they too were conscious only of each other. As he kissed her and held her, she was suddenly aware of how close to death he had been and how lucky she was that he had come through, but his smile and the strength of him against her stopped her involuntary tremblings.

The heroes' welcome for Jim and Red was, in fact, merely the beginning of a crescendo of celebrations, culminating in the tickertape parade down Fifth Avenue, then the medal ceremony itself in Washington, with President Harry Truman making the most of it in front of a battery of cameras on the lawn of the White House. Then there were parties to attend in the capital, and back in New York, and others they hosted themselves in Newport and Nantucket.

Then, as abruptly as it began, it was all over.

They were staying that weekend at their summer home on the island. It was the place Helen liked best. Here she had felt completely at home from the very first day, loving the old wooden house, the rocky beach below the verandah and the long view of the cliffs rising away to the left, and the untouched countryside whose greenness reminded her of Suffolk.

There had only been Jim and herself for dinner, seemingly for the first occasion in weeks. Afterwards, they sat sipping cognac, looking out as blackness, inch by inch, began to ink out the cliffs and the sun dipped behind the swell of the island to their right. Rollers that had travelled from as far away as Cornwall thrashed the shoreline, turning into breakers and dying in constantly repeated, constantly changing patterns of white spume on the beach. A colder breeze came after sunset. Helen shivered and half rose from her chair.

'Are you going in?' Jim asked.

'Only to fetch a shawl.'

'I'll get it,' Jim said. He brought back her shawl and the bottle of brandy, with which he topped up their glasses. 'It's a blessed relief to be on our own for a change.'

'Isn't it?' Helen agreed. 'I love having a famous husband whom everyone wants to meet. If I haven't said it before . . . I'm proud of you. But I'm even happier just to have you to myself for once.' Jim smiled and sat again, pulling his chair closer to hers. He had a slight frown which she recognized. 'Something on your mind?'

'Can't hide anything from you, can I?' He saw her concern and smiled. 'Don't worry. It's not that bad. I've got something to tell you. And I suppose, in a way, it's a major announcement.'

'Or more accurately – a general's.'

Jim chuckled. 'You could say that.' He paused, taking her hand. 'This will be official shortly. Brigadier General James A. Kiley is quitting the service.' Helen did not comment. Her hand tightened on his. 'I guess it's a surprise to you. A disappointment?'

'Oh, my darling,' Helen breathed. 'I'm delighted.'

'Really?'

She leaned over and kissed him gently. 'I never wanted you to stay on till you got your fourth star. To tell the truth, I always resented the Air Force a little, because it took you away from me so much. But why have you made the decision now?'

Jim shrugged. 'I guess, fifteen years in uniform is long enough. And, well, the Korean thing is as good as over now.' He did not sound entirely convincing. Maybe others would have accepted it without question, but he knew Helen was still waiting for the real explanation. 'It's this MacArthur business,' he told her. The Truman administration was in dispute with the general over his implied criticism of presidential foreign policy. 'It's really made me take a look into the future. There's no way Washington's going to allow him to win this war outright. He's in command of hundreds of thousands of men, with the most effective weapons in his hands, and they've tied those hands behind his back.'

'But Jim, he'd use the Bomb. Everyone knows that.'

'Nonsense.' Jim shook his head. 'I know MacArthur. He'd threaten to use nukes. He needs the Bomb as a final sanction, to show the Chinese and Moscow that he means business. Make no mistake, this is no local war. It's a major confrontation between East and West and if we don't finish it once and for all, it'll happen again. And again. In lots of different places, all over the world.' He paused. 'MacArthur wants to scare the White House, and all those chicken politicians. Sooner or later they'll call for his head – and Truman will give it to them. Then we'll have no hope of winning the war conclusively, only of dragging it out in a stalemate along the thirty-eighth parallel.'

'So what will you do, Jim?' Helen asked.

'There's nothing I can do at the moment. First, I'm quitting the Air Force. Then we'll see.' He finished his brandy. Helen did the same and they sat quietly, still hand in hand. 'It's a long time since we had an early night,' he said at length.

Helen looked at him. He was smiling slightly, watching her, handsome, his hair beginning to be speckled with grey. 'So long ago, I can scarcely remember,' she said. Her faint smile matched his.

'Is that a complaint, Mrs Kiley?' he asked. 'Or a challenge?' They put down their glasses and rose. Their kiss was long, but gentle. Still hand in hand, they went inside.

It was not long after Jim resigned from the Air Force that he took the momentous step that would not only make him, in a matter of years, as well known as anyone in America, including the President, a figure respected round the world, but also sadly put their marriage in jeopardy. After a few months, he launched himself into politics.

Helen, of course, had suspected what he had in mind. Unlike many of his contemporaries in the forces, he had always been aware of the wider issues outside the perimeter of the Base. Jim had joined the airforce in the late 'thirties, having realized after his visit to Germany when he had witnessed Hitler's mesmeric hold over the masses at the Nuremberg rally that there was bound to be a war involving all Europe, a war of ideology in which America's era of isolationism would end.

His experiences as a pilot of a B-17 and a leader of men, developed during his posting to the 525th Bomb Group in

Market Wetherby, had been tempered by his months as a POW in Germany. Imprisonment behind barbed wire, living on meagre rations, with the continuous threat from the SS guards as the defeat of Hitler grew closer, had etched an indelible impression. When the POW camp was liberated by the Russians, he had experienced at first-hand the suspicious bureaucracy of Stalinism, reinforced by later visits to the regimes established by force behind the Iron Curtain. Having lost his liberty for a time, Jim had a highly developed respect for the need for human dignity and individual freedom. Of the body and the mind.

Since their marriage, Jim and Helen had built up a wide circle of mutual friends. One of the closest was still Adlai Stevenson, the cultivated lawyer turned politician whose liberal opinions had influenced a whole generation of younger Democrats. The Kileys were a powerful family. The steel and railroad empire built up by Jim's grandfather had always courted politicians and been courted in turn. Adlai was fascinated to learn, however, that Jim's interest extended further than merely wishing to contribute to election expenses.

He brought along Hubert Humphrey and Jim discussed his intentions with them and the younger Kennedys in their frequent visits to the summer place on Nantucket. Jack they saw most often and he became a fairly close friend of Jim's. In long conversations on the beach or on the Kiley yacht, they continued to discover a surprising similarity of attitude to many questions, with Jack deferring slightly to Jim because of the fourteen year age difference between them. 'But you're not like Adlai, Jim,' he said. 'He's kind of an elder statesman already, more like my father's generation.'

They stood together in support of Stevenson's presidential bid. In his adoption speech, Jim said, 'The young men win the wars and lose their lives. The old men lose the peace and win the elections.' He was cheered for several minutes. Jack and he celebrated together, when Jack was elected to the Senate and Jim to the House of Representatives, both for the State of Massachusetts and both with massive majorities. The one big disappointment was that Adlai failed in his bid for the presidency, losing out to Dwight D. Eisenhower, Ike, the former Supremo and immensely popular war hero.

The moment Peter Mundy saw the photograph, his heart lurched.

He had come into the back parlour from the shop for his mid morning break. There had been a rush on for the past two days and he was glad to sit down. It was May, 1950, and points rationing had just ended. Everyone seemed to be buying. Not sensibly. Just buying for the sake of it, sugar, jam, flour, everything they could think of. Rationing might have ended, but his deliveries of supplies had not improved and he reluctantly had to agree with his father that, if sales kept up at this rate, he would have to apply his own restrictions, so that regular customers would not be disappointed. Butter, sugar and eggs, especially, would have to go back under the counter, until deliveries from the wholesalers could be guaranteed.

The morning paper was lying by the cup of tea his mother, Vera, had poured for him. He glanced at the headlines. More of the new super-fortresses had arrived in Norfolk. The Americans had been gone from Market Wetherby for five years, but elsewhere they were returning. All part of the build-up of the Cold War, Joe McGraw said. It was inevitable with conflict looming in South Korea. There was a report that petrol rationing would finish by the end of the month. The Attlee government had just scraped in again and seemed desperate to prove that things were getting better after the years of austerity. It was anyone's guess how long the second Labour government could survive.

In the bottom right-hand corner of the paper was a photograph of a woman wearing a headscarf and dark glasses, climbing out of a taxi. Peter glanced at it and started to open the paper when something made him turn to the picture again. His mouth opened, but he bit off the exclamation of surprise and looked across at his father, Albert, who sat by the fire in the chair he now seldom left. Old Albert had never wholly recovered from his stroke. His speech was painfully slow and he often had difficulty in catching what people said. He had no trouble hearing his grand-daughter, Vicky, though. She was perched on a stool beside him, reading aloud one of the stories of Little Grey Rabbit, and Albert smiled as he listened.

Peter looked back at the newspaper photograph. The headline above it read, 'MYSTERY WOMAN IN VICE TRIAL'. In spite of the headscarf and dark glasses, he had no doubt about her identity. It was his twin sister, Letty.

That afternoon, Peter was on the train to London. Although his mother and Rosie were surprised, they did not question his decision to check that he would not be eligible for call up if war broke out over Korea. Albert would have seen through the lie straight away, but it had been agreed not to tell him in case he worried.

Peter read the newspaper story again and again on the journey. It concerned the trial of a Cyprus-born financier, Stavro Paneides, whose wealth apparently came from backing continental films and the European tours of US singing stars. According to the police, however, the real source of his money was a chain of illegal gambling dens and a number of 'escort' agencies, used as a cover for prostitution. He was also suspected of owning a controlling interest in two nightclubs, the Paphos Garden and the Double D. It was in connection with the Double D that the woman had been called to give evidence, creating a sensation by producing proof that she was the club's sole owner. No charges were laid against her and she was given the right to remain anonymous, but Peter had recognized her at once. He was profoundly grateful that neither his wife nor mother was a great newspaper reader, though it was possible that even Vera might not have recognized her daughter. He was only convinced of it, himself, because of the connection with the Double D.

233

Of the whole Mundy family, Peter was still the only one with any knowledge of Letty after she disappeared. He had kept his word not to tell anyone he had seen her, largely because learning of the life she was living would hurt their parents too much. It had been difficult to remain silent after her disastrous reappearance at his wedding, but he made himself not say anything. Rosie and he had enough problems, taking over the running of the family grocery shop, which they had never been able to give up. Each year, Peter's dream of Rosie and he breaking free of Market Wetherby, of forming his own dance orchestra, had receded further and further. His savings were used up in redecorating the shop and buying stock.

Not only that. They had become substitute parents for their niece Vicky, who had no idea that her real mother was still alive. Since the day of the wedding, Peter had not wanted to see his sister ever again. Now he was afraid for her.

The first thing he did on reaching London was to buy the *Evening Star*. The result of the Paneides trial was headlined – 'GUILTY'. He had been sentenced to seven years.

The Double D was shuttered and locked and Peter had to find a phone booth to call the private, unlisted number Letty had given him. She was a long time answering the telephone and sounded shaken to hear his voice. 'Are you all right, Let? That's all I want to know,' Peter said. He told her about spotting her photograph.

'Did Dad see it?' she asked after a pause.

'He can't read or write any more,' Peter told her. 'Only listens to the wireless.'

He followed her instructions on how to locate the rear door of the club, even more discreet than the front. As he waited, he wondered how he would greet her, how he would react to seeing her. Because of her, he had had to give up so much, take on so many unwanted responsibilities that had dictated the whole course of his life. Yet he could not help feeling concerned for her, protective. In the event, it was not Letty who opened the iron-barred door, but the club bouncer who handed him a bulky envelope.

'I want to see Letty,' Peter insisted.

'That's all there is, friend,' the bouncer said.

'Come on, you remember me,' Peter said. 'Let me in. I want to see her.'

'That's all there is,' the bouncer repeated. 'Now, beat it.'

The door clanged shut and Peter pounded on it until his knuckles hurt, but there was no reply. He tore open the envelope. Inside were five hundred pounds in assorted bills and a note: 'Love you for coming, Peter. This is for Vicky. Do something nice for her with it. Don't ever tell her about me. I'm all right. Don't come here again. Love always. L.'

# TWENTY-THREE

While Peter beat on the door, Letty was watching him through the net curtains at an upstairs window. She saw him open the envelope and how he nearly threw the money down. She held her breath until he stuffed the envelope roughly into his coat pocket and turned away. As he walked up the mews behind the club, he looked so disconsolate and defeated that she wanted to call out to him, to bring him back. She desperately needed someone she could depend on, yet she stopped herself.

She had controlled herself so far and was afraid that if she met Peter she might break down. No one here had ever seen her cry. She did not intend to start now. Any weakness at the moment could be fatal.

She was still boss of the Double D, or as much boss as she ever had been with Stavro standing in the shadows behind her. He had used her at first only as a front, but as she had proved her capability he had left the running of the club more and more to her. Once the US servicemen for whom they catered had gone, many small clubs had folded or turned into cheap clipjoints. She had preserved the Double D, making it even more exclusive, moving it up market. She chose the hostesses for their looks and a touch of class. From Stavro she had learnt about food and wine and had engaged an excellent chef. Stavro's touring stars visited the club and, through them, a fairly regular clientele of film and showbiz personalities was built up. They attracted others. Many deals were made there and although the hostesses were available after hours, they were very careful. Intensive investigation of Stavro's affairs had turned up no positive evidence against the Double D for encouraging prostitution, nothing that could be proved. All due to Letty, the nominal owner.

Her Uncle Sid had spotted her as a survivor. It was almost the only prediction he ever made which had come true. So far.

In her mid twenties, she had fined down. Her figure, which had always been good, had become trim and sleek and she looked after it. Nothing about her was obvious any more. She dressed well, with rather restrained taste. At the same time, she had given up her blatant make-up and Rita Hayworth hairstyle for something more natural, more suited to her shorter height, the lightest of eyeshadow and lipstick, with a blonde bubble cut. Her new fresh look was a paradox in the twilight world she inhabited. When he met her, Bing Crosby, who had an appreciative eye, called her 'the cutest doll this side of Debbie Reynolds.'

She had ironed out her Suffolk accent, Americanizing the flat vowels. She worked on it, modelling how she spoke on what she remembered of Helen Dereham, low and slightly breathy, often from the back of the throat. It made her very distinctive. 'The greatest turn on since black lace,' Mel Torme said.

Stavro had been infatuated and amused by her, then became dependent on her. She personally selected the escorts for his visiting recording and film stars. Some of the most important demanded Letty, herself, and he made no objection, since it was business, so she got to know Paris, Marbella, and St Tropez, which had become the stars' private playground. For the rest of the time she was understood to be Stavro's girl. He was almost twice her age and made few demands on her, although she was afraid of his occasional fits of jealousy. After two or three men had been severely beaten up for trying to move in on her, she was left strictly alone.

She discovered early on that his true passion was gambling. When she learned more about his business, she warned him. The illegal spielers could only lead to trouble, but he only laughed. They brought him in a great deal of money and satisfied his own fever. He was strong enough to keep out all rivals, even the vicious Maltese. New gangs were forming, however, combinations of previous deadly enemies moving out from the East End, attracted by the more lucrative pickings up West. Yet a series of unsolved gang killings did not end the matter, as Stavro had expected, but only drove the opposition underground.

Letty had seen the cracks starting to appear in the walls of Stavro's empire. He was riding for a fall, but would listen to no one. She thought often about her own future. In theory, he would bring her down with him. She did not intend that to happen. She was unsure about her own feelings for him. At one point she had even imagined herself in love with him, but when he had forced her to choose between him and her baby girl, the illusion had ended. He thought only of himself. She had been in danger of forgetting that number one rule and did not make the mistake again.

The last weeks since his arrest had been traumatic. He had been so sure he could beat the rap that his seven year sentence was a shock. She realized at once that her survival was now solely up to her. And she was alone in a jungle.

Hearing Peter's voice on the telephone had shaken her. It had not been the voice she expected. That came two days later when the caller judged she had been sufficiently softened up.

Her man, Rex, was respectful as he showed Max and Alfie Klyne into Letty's office at the Double D. She had met the brothers once before, at Kempton Park racetrack, and had never forgotten them. No one could. Max slightly hunchbacked with his long, twisted face, and Alfie, the younger, tall and husky, quite goodlooking apart from a cast in his left eye. By cunning and sheer ferocity, they had come to prominence in the rackets spawned by the Black Market. Stavro had guessed that they had set him up, supplying evidence to the police to ensure his conviction. Letty was in no doubt. Whoever came to see her first would be the ones who had shopped him, and here they were.

'I'm quite sure you realize why we've looked in,' Max

said. He was playing it politely, smiling, but the smile on his twisted face was chilling.

'Course, she does. She's a bright girl,' Alfie nodded. 'Pretty as a picture an' all.'

Letty had risen to meet them. He reached out and ran the back of his hand down her cheek, then his fingers trailed down her neck and rested on the swell of her breast under the silk dress. She felt sick. Their specialty was 'protection'. They had come to take over the club, and her with it. There was nothing to stop them. The man's fingers were tightening on her and she winced.

'Naughty, naughty, Alfie,' Max said softly. 'We're here on business.' Reluctantly, Alfie released her. 'You're down as the owner of this place, but the proceeds went to Stavro, right?' Max went on. 'Well, we're not too greedy. We'll take his cut plus an extra five per cent. That suit?'

Letty did not show any reaction, but her mind was racing. The demand was less than she had expected. They could have taken over completely or wrecked the club and put her out of business. Yet the stakes were still worth playing for. 'I don't have much choice, do I?' she answered. 'There's just one thing. The Double D has a reputation. It will still be run my way. I don't want any rough stuff, or any East End gorillas getting drunk and frightening the customers.'

Alfie flushed. 'You need to learn the facts of life, girlie,' he growled. His right hand was clenching and Letty tensed.

'Take it easy now,' Max soothed. 'The little lady has a point. She's on to a goldmine here and we don't want to muck it up, for all our sakes.' His shrewd eyes assessed her. 'You're clever, all right. But just so's you don't get too clever, we'll put in our own barman and doorman. And every week, our accountant will check your books. If he's satisfied, then fine an' dandy. If not . . .' His voice was suddenly flat and deadly. 'You'd better start shoppin' for a new face.'

The Klynes were as good as their word. Letty kept her nose clean and they gave her no trouble. Alfie always frightened her with his hot eyes and itchy fingers, but Max always behaved to her like a gentleman. He had seen that the end of rationing meant the collapse of the Black Market. The old days were over and, on the advice of his accountant, Mr Griffiths, a highly respectable, middle-aged Welshman, he was moving his operations slowly into more legitimate businesses, like scrap metal, second-hand cars and utility furniture, funded by a web of well-regulated protection. Mr Griffiths also showed Letty how to skim a little off the take each week before it reached the Klynes, for a fee of fifty per cent. The rest was her nest egg.

The Double D continued to prosper. It had become one of the few really chic nightclubs which all personalities had heard of and headed for, sure of meeting their own kind. Letty was still available. She was understood to be very choosy and very expensive, so being seen with her was a sign of success. She had no regular lover. When she was not working, it was assumed that she belonged either to Alfie or Max Klyne and was out of bounds. That was how she wanted it.

She had known enough men to last several lifetimes. When she looked back, she saw that she had always been used – even by Harvey, her first lover, Vicky's father. Then by Mario and Patsy and all the other GIs. She had run off to London to her Uncle Sid, who had promised her bright lights and excitement. Very quickly she had realized that all he offered was a life on the streets, with the inevitable sordid end when her looks faded. He had traded her to his chief business rival, Benny, still smalltime, but more powerful. She became Benny's mistress and made certain that he stayed besotted with her and did not discard her. From him she received all the luxuries she could ever want, but no money. He did not want her ever to feel independent.

After two years, Benny had tried to put the bite on a new gambling room which he did not know was run by the

Cypriot mob. Stavro had come to see him the next night, very soft-spoken and courteous, warning him not to repeat the mistake. Nearly all the time his eyes were on Letty and, after he had gone, Benny went crazy, beating her up and swearing to 'take care' of the Greek bighead. 'I'll show him how we used to deal with scum like him in Brighton!' Two days later Benny was found in an alley off Old Compton Street, so badly injured he was in intensive care for a month. During the month, his rackets were quietly taken over and Letty moved into Stavro's penthouse in St John's Wood. Again she made certain she did not move out again. The elegance in which Stavro lived made Benny's flat seem like a doss-house. Through him she discovered how much she still had to learn and she became his prize pupil as well as his mistress. Many of his associates could not work out her hold over him, but any indecent, even suggestive, remark about her brought on one of his rages which could only be appeased by the sight of blood. The subject of Letty became taboo and she was treated with kid gloves. Now that, too, was over and she belonged to the Klynes.

Ten times a day she looked round her office at the photographs on the walls, signed with love and affection, from Bing and Mel and Vic, Frank and Burt and Dana. Beside her desk was a shot of her in a group arriving at a première, including Victor Mature, Richard Burton and Michael Rennie. Beneath it she was arm in arm with Dean Saxon, tanned and curly haired, who had always been one of her favourite singers and now was a good friend. She had her own suite of rooms, wardrobes of clothes, two bank accounts. The fantasies she had had before leaving Market Wetherby had come true, against all the odds. She could not understand why she was not happy.

She was a realist. She knew that the signed hugs and kisses on the photographs meant very little. She had no permanent man in her life, but did not want one. She didn't miss her family, except Peter now and then. As for her daughter, she felt a small tug, but it was mainly curiosity. She only really thought about her when she had drunk too much, and that was seldom as she hated losing control of herself. By all the standards she had set herself, she had it made and could not puzzle out what was wrong with her life. Maybe she needed a change, a new challenge?

When the change came, it was complete and had a brutal suddenness she could never have imagined.

For four and a half years she had not contacted Stavro, nor been to see him. She had heard that he had been moved from Parkhurst because of a developing kidney condition. As with Benny, she did not expect ever to see him again. Then one day her private phone rang and a voice from the past, one of the old Cypriot mob, told her that Stavro was being released at the end of the week with full remission. 'He'll be in touch Saturday,' the voice whispered. 'He has somewhere to stay, but he needs money. He has a few accounts to settle.' When the caller rang off, Letty sat motionless. Her mind was in turmoil and she felt cold. She knew what the accounts were, and with whom. Stavro wanted all the money she could scrape together. She also knew that Max and Alfie were downstairs in the club talking business. If they ever found out that she had been told of Stavro's release and had not warned them . . .

She hurried into evening dress and went down. It was early yet and the Double D only half full. The Klyne brothers were sitting at a corner table and looked up unwelcomingly when she came to them. 'I thought Mr Griffiths was with you,' Letty said.

'We had to talk. We told him to get lost,' Alfie growled. She sat without being invited and they went on looking at her in silence. At last, Alfie said, 'We just had some news.'

'Maybe it's not news to Letty,' Max added, watching her.

'About Stavro?' Letty asked. 'That's why I came down.' Both the brothers relaxed, their suspicions about her lessened. They questioned her and she told them that

Stavro would stay away from the club. All he wanted was some money to live on.

'That's not what 'is boys say!' Alfie snarled. 'The crazy gink thinks he can take over again, thinks he can rub us out.'

'Can't have that,' Max said. 'Nobody wants to start the gang wars all over again. The Hammer Boys have had their day. We can't let old Stavro go spoilin' it for everyone.'

Alfie looked at him. His smile was not pleasant. 'We better arrange a welcome home party for him.'

Max nodded, then turned to Letty and she nearly shivered at the deadness of his eyes. 'It would be better if you hadn't heard that.'

'Heard what?' Letty said. She made herself smile.

She waited all weekend, but Stavro did not contact her. She found out why, when Rex brought her the newspaper on Monday morning and pointed to the Stop Press. 'The body of Vice King, Stavro Paneides, fifty-two, was discovered late last night by a couple walking their dog in Epping Forest. The dead man had been shot twice through the back of the head. Former gang leader Paneides had been released from Maidstone Prison only on Saturday.'

'The Murder Squad'll be on to it by now, nosey bastards,' Rex said. 'They'll want to question everyone who used to know him. Be round here before long.'

Letty disconnected her outside telephones. She had nothing to fear from the police, but she could not forget how the brothers had looked at her. She could tie them in directly with Stavro and before they decided to close her mouth permanently, she had to do something. She shouted down to the doorman to order her a taxi. 'Where to?' he asked, and she nearly panicked. He had never asked before. 'Have my hair done,' she said.

She went through into her apartment. If the doorman was reporting on her to the Klynes, she could not take a suitcase. He might not even let her leave the Double D. She chose her largest handbag and put in a change of underwear, her passport, spare cash, make up and cheque book. As an afterthought, she added a packet of letters. They were from Peter and contained others to him and Rosie from Vi and Hymie and Elmer. Why she took them, she could never explain.

It was only in the cab that she thought of someone who might help her. She had the driver drop her at the corner of Knightsbridge and walked round through the park to the Dorchester, making certain she had not been followed.

Dean Saxon was passing through town on his way to star in a film in Italy. He had been disappointed when she had told him they could not meet over the weekend. When she reached his suite, he had already consumed most of a quart of bourbon and was making a mess of his packing. 'Too late, baby,' he grinned. 'Off I go into the wide blue yonder.'

'You've got to help me, Dean,' she said. 'I'm in trouble.'

He listened gravely while she told him a story about a jealous wife who was trying to cite her in a divorce, then he chuckled. 'Don't talk to me about jealous wives – and husbands. You need to lie low till it's all over, kiddo. And I know just the place. Why don't you come with me to la bella Roma?' Letty pretended to be surprised and doubtful, but he insisted. 'We'll have a ball! All you need's your passport.'

She was afraid to go to her main bank, so went by cab to the smaller branch where she kept her second account. She drew everything out and took another taxi to Heathrow. She travelled second class, having convinced Dean it was better for her to avoid being seen with him, and they did not meet up until they landed at Rome airport, where the film company's representative helped them to avoid the paparazzi by having Dean's limousine brought to a side exit.

The moment they landed, Dean had become almost frenetic. Normally highspirited, he was now virtually floating. 'There's magic in the air. Can't you feel it?' he enthused. Born Dino Saccone in the Italian district of East

244

Side, New York, he had been a skinny kid from a poor family. The struggle to the top had left scars and he still did not feel fully accepted in America. In Rome it was different. The Italians had taken him to their hearts like a prodigal son. He laughed. 'Until I became famous, I never knew I had so many relatives over here.' There was a cocktail cabinet in the back of the limousine and he poured them vermouths laced with vodka. 'There's something I'd better mention. I have a couple or three girlfriends here. So I got to ration myself. Know what I mean?'

'Don't worry, Dean,' she assured him. 'I'm here strictly as a friend.'

He frowned. 'Not too strictly, I hope.' They laughed and he kissed her.

He owned a beautiful apartment off the Piazza Navona and dropped her there, while he was rushed off for costume fittings. Letty took a shower, wrapped herself in one of his bathrobes and waited for him to return.

He did not come back for two days. Luckily the refrigerator was well stocked, for in that time she had not left the flat. 'I'm sorry, baby,' he apologized. 'I met these guys.' She told him not to worry. Being alone, she said, had helped her to straighten some things out in her mind. 'I'd be glad to straighten anything out in mine,' he laughed.

He had three days to spend with her before the shooting on his film started, but they were seldom alone together. Dean kept open house and friends and relatives trooped in and out. They accepted Letty as casually as any other piece of furniture. The production company and the rest of the cast of his film were Italian. They went to restaurants and parties at which Letty laughed a lot and drank more than usual, but understood not one word that was said. She began to get a curious feeling that she was on the outside looking in. It was not merely the language. These people had a common bond, a profession which absorbed them, to which she was a stranger.

Rome itself was a revelation. Letty had never reacted so positively to any place before. It was partly the colour of the old buildings, the palaces and fountains, the sunlight and mysterious glimpses into ancient courtyards where a single tree or statue seemed to hold a special meaning, partly the vivacity, the sheer love of life she felt all around her.

On two nights they sat for hours at one of the cafés on the Via Veneto. As darkness fell, the fashionable street became a parade of the famous, the beautiful and the notorious. With film making so cheap in Italy, at least twenty were being shot in and around Rome, which claimed to be the world's new movie capital. 'Hollywood on the Tiber', they called it, and every star and feature player she had ever seen or read about seemed to walk past their table. Many of them stopped to say hello to Dean. There was much hugging and kissing and shouted greetings. Again, Letty felt strangely detached from it.

She was included in the greetings only in passing. Once she would have accepted that, but she began to resent it. Not least because Dean also frequently forgot about her. He was loving and fun when they were alone, but in public he was a star and she was part of his shadow. She had no identity. Out of her fear of being traced, they had developed a private joke, where every time Dean introduced her to someone he made up a different name for her. It was funny, but it meant that no one really knew her or what to call her.

On the fourth morning, Dean left early for the studios and warned her that he might not be back that night. She had learnt that that probably meant several nights. She had not forgotten the other girlfriends he had told her of and swore quietly for three solid minutes after he had gone. She felt safe in Rome, loved the city and liked being with him, yet the way things were progressing it would not be long before he did not come back at all. She had to prevent that. She had always managed it before, so why not here? She took stock of herself.

Because of the Klynes, she always wore her hair in a headscarf when they went out. The clothes he had helped her choose were like the wardrobe she had left behind in London, discreet, well cut dresses and suits. But what had been alluring in its unexpectedness in the Double D had lost its effect here. By comparison with the gorgeously dressed starlets and pricey hookers of the Via Veneto, she was mousey. And her quietness and carefully adopted good manners completed the impression. No wonder she was passed over.

When Dean finally returned, he had meant to stay only a few hours, but he stopped and stared. Letty had gone out and bought an off-the-shoulder black jersey silk blouse and leopard-skin pants that fitted her so perfectly they seemed almost painted on. With her blonde bubble cut and open-toed shoes she looked sensational. 'Wow!' Dean gasped. 'Get a look at you!'

'Like it?' Letty smiled. 'Where are we going tonight?'

'Let's not go anywhere, baby,' he suggested, moving towards her.

'Down boy,' Letty said. 'You may have been doing the town, but baby has seen nothing but the piazza and these four walls since last week.'

'What could I have been thinking of?' Dean wondered.

That evening on the Via Veneto more than half the people who passed were looking at Letty. She had her photograph taken with Dean at least a dozen times and could tell that he was pleased. 'A new chick with a new look, that's really something in this town,' he told her.

Among the people who passed by them was a tall, worried-looking man who chatted for some minutes with Dean, then asked, 'Well, aren't you going to introduce us?'

'Oh sure. Sorry.' Dean apologized. 'This is Hal Dwyer. He's over here producing *Temptation Summer* with Naomi Race.' As Letty nodded, she saw the devil come into Dean's eyes. 'And this is a friend of mine, an English actress – just starting.' He paused. 'Her name's Laraine Love.'

'That's a good name,' Dwyer said.

'Yes, it is,' Dean agreed solemnly, and Letty and he laughed.

They did not let Dwyer in on the joke, but after a moment he joined in the laughter, a little selfconsciously. It was not hard to laugh, he found, with Dean's light-heartedness and this very striking girl smiling to him. He was beginning to feel better than he had for some time and he held his hand out to Letty. As they shook hands, he said, 'It's been a real pleasure meeting you, Miss Love. A real pleasure.'

When he hurried away, Dean chuckled. 'That's the first time I've seen him crack a smile. I think he fancies you.'

'Bouncing rubber balls,' Letty said, indelicately.

'Even producers have them,' Dean agreed. 'You made a hit there, "Laraine".'

Letty laughed. Raf Vallone was coming out of the Bar Venezia with a crowd of starlets and admirers. Dean waved to him and they were soon surrounded.

Later that night at the Piccolo Mondo, Letty saw the tall man again. He was seated four tables away with a shorter, balding, middle-aged man, who kept nodding as Dwyer spoke. They were both looking at her. 'Who's that?' she whispered.

Dean glanced across. 'The little guy? He's a famous director, at least he used to be. Les Brewer.'

Dean did not need much urging when people begged him to sing and he gave them 'Embraceable You' followed by 'Che Gelida Mannina' from La Bohème, which took everyone by surprise and nearly brought the house down. While she waited for him to come back to their table, Letty looked up to find Dwyer and the other man standing beside her.

'Permit me to introduce myself,' the shorter, balding man said. His speech was American with a trace of a guttural, mid-European accent. 'I am Les Brewer and I'm directing Hal's picture. I believe you met earlier.'

Letty smiled. 'Yes, indeed.'

Dwyer confirmed it. 'Forgive the intrusion, Miss Love,'

he said, 'but Dean did say you were an actress just starting out. We have something to suggest that might interest you.'

Letty nearly told them Dean had only been making a silly joke, but was intrigued and stopped herself.

'It might not be what you're hoping for, but it could give you valuable experience,' Les Brewer told her. 'Miss Race, the star of the film, has been badly affected by the heat. She is far from strong, anyway. And we have had a great deal of difficulty in finding a suitable stand-in and double for her. We think you would fit the bill, Miss Love.'

# TWENTY-FOUR

The evening ended as most of them did, with them going on to another two or three nightspots where Dean was called on to sing and the management saw that their table was never without a supply of vodka and vermouth. It was after three when they got back to the apartment in the Piazza Navona, and Letty was giggling as she tried to stop him giving one more encore to an invisible audience. ' 'Sright, baby. You're so-o right. Mustn't waste my Godgiven talent,' he hiccuped, and bowed to the empty hallway.

She had not had an opportunity to be alone with him, so had not told him of Dwyer's offer. But she had kept thinking about it. Naomi Race was a new young star noted for her delicate, elfin beauty. She had long black hair turning in at the ends and was at least three inches taller than Letty. On the face of it, the whole idea seemed ridiculous to her, although in a way it was tempting.

'My head can't find my neck. That's why it keeps spinning round,' Dean said. 'Come on, baby.' He had stripped off his shirt and was heading for the shower. A long shower, followed by a little gentle love-making, the only infallible method of avoiding a hangover, he claimed.

They showered together. As he was drying her, caressing her slowly with the big fluffy towel, he said, 'Hey, did I see Hal Dwyer trying to chat you? I knew he was gonna make a pass.'

'It wasn't that,' she told him. When she explained about the offer, Dean laughed. 'It's not that funny,' she said.

He shrugged. 'So do you want to accept? Is that what you want to do?'

'I don't know,' she admitted. 'Everybody dreams about it.'

'So you'll never find out if it's for you, until you try it. You'd better ring them.'

The next morning Letty nerved herself up to call the *Temptation Summer* production office and was asked to come over straight away. The salary they proposed was, indeed, generous, and to her surprise, wearing high heels, Naomi Race's costumes fitted her almost exactly. A wig to match the star's style and colour had already been prepared for her double and only needed minor adjustments. It transformed her and she began to feel that she might not be such a strange choice after all.

She was fortunate in being Dean's girlfriend and having been discovered by the producer and the director. Everyone was very kind and she was treated not like an extra, but as one of the cast. Naomi Race, with her almost translucent skin, was just as beautiful off screen, in spite of the dark shadows under her eyes. She was grateful to Letty for saving her from long hours of standing in the sun, which had already nearly prostrated her.

At first, Letty was very tense, her movement stiff, her gestures abrupt and awkward. Brewer was patient and helpful, getting her to relax.

'You must have seen one or two of Naomi's movies,' he said. 'Just imagine you're her. Let your body flow like hers.' When she saw some of the rushes Letty was amazed. She could not believe it was herself and not Naomi on the screen. She also realized another reason why she had been chosen. In the long shots, without her high heels, she made the leading man look taller.

*Temptation Summer* was about a sheltered young heiress whose millionaire father will only let her travel provided she is accompanied by a private-detective. The dashing private detective thinks her a spoilt snob, but saves her from fortune hunters in Florida, Paris and Rome. The final scenes were to be shot in Acapulco, Mexico, where he discovers he is in love with her, himself, and hands in his resignation. Before he leaves, he kisses her and, as he walks away, the heiress realizes she loves him, too. Happy ending. It was flimsy stuff, but Brewer handled it with humour and tenderness. He seemed to like Letty and used her as much as he could, strolling in the ruined Forum, getting in and out of cars, dancing and swimming, whenever the camera did not have to get in too near.

She quickly learned what to do and not do, and the jargon of film making. She understood about tracking and dolly shots, key lights and the importance of the close-up. She was accepted now by Dean's friends as one of themselves, one of the charmed circle. She was cute and she was fun when she let herself go. People began to seek her out for herself. An illustrated magazine ran pictures of her in a daring swimsuit, adding a totally fictitious account of her past life, including a secret romance with an Indian prince. She even got used to being called Laraine.

She loved it all. For the first time in her life she was doing something that wholly absorbed her. Everything about filming fascinated her and she did not notice the tedium of much of the working day. She was a natural, people said. This time she was only doubling, but she had a career ahead of her. Once or twice Brewer shot nearer takes of her when she did not expect it and she thrilled to see herself smiling and natural on the screen. The long dark hair gave her added poise and sophistication. On the screen, the old Letty Mundy had ceased to exist. 'Keep your hair like that,' Brewer advised. 'You can flick it out at the ends, instead of in, so you won't get mixed up with Naomi.'

Best of all, she had most of Dean's attention. She liked him more and more and she knew he would be invaluable in opening doors for her. He was her passport to success.

The leading man in her film, Van, had developed a crush on her. 'That ageing juvenile,' Dean scoffed. When he found that during one of his absences Van had dated her, he flew into a rage and marched out. He came back an hour later with flowers and champagne. He seldom left her alone again. He had fallen just like Benny and Stavro.

There was one major problem, which Letty tried not to

think about. She had been signed only for the Roman sequences. Dean's film was due to finish after hers, but he had not said anything about what happened then. She knew he had to return to the States.

In fact, her film was extended for over two weeks, because of the continued illness of Naomi Race. 'Illness schmillness,' Dean said. 'It's all those pills she keeps popping. She's a hophead.' It was true. The young star was hooked. The pills she took to wake her up and the others she needed to give her energy, then to calm her down and put her to sleep, had become an addiction. The traditional party on the last day of shooting had to be cancelled, because Naomi collapsed after her final take and was rushed to hospital.

'At least, we got finished in Rome,' the cameraman said, while everyone waited to hear the doctors' verdict. The whole future of the film depended on it.

It was not good. Naomi would be unable to work for three, possibly four months. Although it scarcely affected her, Letty was sorry for the others whose jobs were in jeopardy.

She was surprised when she was called to the viewing room, where she found Dwyer and Les Brewer watching footage of the dubbed sequences. 'In Acapulco,' he was saying, 'I can shoot the long shots and over the shoulder stuff. With the right backgrounds, I can cut in close-ups of Naomi anywhere, and she can dub the dialogue later.'

'Will it work?' Dwyer asked.

Les grunted. 'Do we have a choice? We're damned lucky to have Laraine. I can get in fairly close on her and still make it believable.'

Dean was as excited as Letty when she told him she was going to Acapulco with the rest of the crew. There was a gap of two weeks before production recommenced in Mexico. His own film had wrapped that day. 'It's from Heaven, baby,' he laughed. 'Tell you what. Why don't you come with me to LA?'

It was another of Letty's dreams come true. On the

journey, they stopped one night in New York, then flew on next day to Los Angeles. At last, she had got to Hollywood.

Dean had an Italianate villa with an enormous pool, set in its own grounds in Beverly Hills. He was amused by her eagerness to see everything and took her to the Copa and the Brown Derby, to Malibu Beach and to marvel at the stars' hand and footprints in cement outside the Chinese Theatre, his own among them. They went to a studio party at Twentieth Century and had lunch in the commissariat at MGM. His friends threw what they called whingdings for them. She saw several of the people she had met at the Double D, but, because of the black wig Les Brewer had insisted on her wearing all the time in public, only two of them recognized her. For their own reasons, they were happy not to mention it.

The ten days flew past and Letty treasured every minute. Dean showed her off with pride and several important figures took notice of her. She was grateful and loving to him. And discovered something about herself. Her heart was not in deep freeze, after all. Ever since Harvey died, she had never had the need for one man as she did now. She felt vulnerable again, but did not resent it.

On the last day, they lazed about by the pool, reluctant to get on with their packing. In the morning, Letty was flying to Mexico and Dean to Havana for a three weeks singing engagement at the Tropicana. 'I'll never forget these ten days,' she told him. 'This is my magic place, just like Rome is for you.'

'You'll be back soon, never fear,' Dean said. 'Sam Goldwyn wrote your name down three times, and that old goat, Mayer, looked as if he could eat you.'

Letty shrugged. 'I don't have a permit to work here. Only a visitor's visa.'

Dean sipped at his vodka Collins. 'That could be fixed very easily,' he said slowly. 'I could fly down and join you, when I get through in Havana.' He paused. 'We could be married in Acapulco – then you could work here as much as you want.' She was so long in reacting that he was

254

afraid she was going to turn him down. When she smiled, he pulled her to her feet and kissed her. 'Did I ever tell you that I love you?' he said.

Letty kissed him back fiercely. When he saw that she was crying, he laughed and jumped with her into the pool.

The final sequences of *Temptation Summer* passed like a dream. They had agreed to announce their coming marriage when Dean arrived in Acapulco, to ensure the maximum publicity. But Letty had great difficulty in keeping it to herself. She could never remember feeling as happy and Les had to keep reminding her, 'Don't bounce around so much. And do you have to keep smiling? This girl you're playing thinks she's going to be on the shelf forever. She's miserable, although she's trying to hide it. There's no love or happiness in her life any more.'

Letty could remember those feelings very well and even the crew was impressed by her. 'She acts better in long shots than Naomi Race does full face,' the friendly cameraman said. Les was very pleased with her and the relieved producer sent fresh flowers every day to her room.

Letty was afraid she would wake up and only Dean's nightly phone calls from Havana convinced her it was all real. She longed for him to be with her and the waiting to be over.

At the end of the three weeks, she had a day off. It was just as well. She could not have worked, not with Dean arriving any minute. She was stretched out on the sun patio of the hotel, half listening to the radio which was playing soft Latin American music. She was thinking how strange life was and of the past which she preferred to forget. The music cut off all at once for a special newsflash. She missed the beginning, but sat up when she caught something about an aeroplane crash at Mexico City. 'The morning flight from Havana, Cuba,' she heard. 'The cause of the crash is not yet known, but it is feared there are no survivors. Among the dead is the famous American singing star, Dean Saxon.' The music began again.

Letty's mouth had opened in a scream, but she could not make a sound. She was suddenly standing in her father's back garden in Market Wetherby. The rain was falling and she had just heard that Harvey had been killed in a bombing raid on Hamburg. Not again? she pleaded silently. It can't have happened again . . .

She was not aware of Les Brewer who had come up to her, smiling. He had not heard the newscast. 'I've got something to tell you, Laraine,' he said. 'I couldn't wait. We're so pleased with your work, especially these past veeks, that Hal's decided to make a sequel to *Summer*. And this time, you'll play the girl.' He laughed, waiting for her reply.

He was puzzled when she looked up at him with no smile, no excitement. Her mouth was working and her eyes were blank, as if her whole world had crumbled around her.

'I'm not kidding,' he said. 'Maybe you didn't hear. We want you to play the lead in our next movie.'

# TWENTY-FIVE

The year after his election to the Senate, Jack brought a shy, sweetly pretty girl to visit Jim and Helen at Newport and again at Nantucket, Jacqueline Bouvier.

Girls had always flocked around the Kennedy boys, especially around Jack with his winning smile and confident manner. He picked them up and dropped them, almost as if he was trying to set a record, his friends said. Maybe it was all part of his need to impress his father with his manliness, the father who drummed into his sons the necessity of winning at all costs, to fight and brawl, no hold barred, if that was the only way. Jack's indifference to the hearts he broke was not really cruel. He simply seemed unaware that other people's feelings were important. His treatment of Jackie, however, was very different. It was almost touching to see how he hovered around her so protectively, needing the reassurance of her smile, as courtly to her as a high school kid on his first date.

The young couple were obviously very much in love and it was no surprise to Helen when they proudly announced their impending engagement. The marriage took place in a blaze of publicity.

Shortly after, Helen was working with old Doctor Slattery at his Free Clinic, in which she unofficially helped out whenever she could, and happened to mention her pleasure at the happiness of the younger couple. Slattery peered at her over his half-lens glasses and grunted. 'It's made a different man of Jack,' she said. 'I had a few reservations about him, his over-confidence, his brashness with women. But she's given him a new warmth, a stability.'

Slattery grunted again, signing the batch of prescriptions

she had prepared. 'Having a wife like her won't do his future election prospects any harm, either.'

Helen was shocked for a moment, then laughed. 'You're just an old cynic.'

'Maybe. But he's a politician, ain't he? They never do anything just for the love of it. Always calculate the odds.'

'I'm not listening to you,' Helen told him. 'Jim's a politician.'

'So he is,' Slattery conceded. 'Well, maybe he's a little less corruptible than most. So far.'

Shortly after the Kennedys' return from honeymoon, Helen noticed a change in Jackie. It was not something easy to define. If anything, she was prettier and more poised. Happiness and fulfilment had made her beautiful. Yet there was also a new reserve about her. Jack was intensely ambitious and always weighed the odds, as Dr Slattery had divined. It was as if she had taken it from him, absorbed her husband's ambition and attitudes and made them her own. They were an impressive team, if not quite as spontaneous as they had once been.

It did not affect relations between the two couples, which became even closer after Jim's election to the Senate. He was part of the solid group of Stevenson Democrats, who fought the apathy and reactionary attitudes of the Eisenhower administration. He had a strong liking and admiration for Ike, himself, but too many policies were decided by none too scrupulous subordinates, while the President played golf and enjoyed the fruits of success. 'I enjoy a game of golf, myself,' Jim told a cheering audience in New Jersey. 'But I see it as a way of thinking things out, as an aid to concentration, not a means of forgetting everything except a little rubber ball and how many strokes to the next green.'

Jim had quickly overcome the distrust of some of the more progressive Democrats, suspicious of the liberalism of recruits from the wealthy families. 'I don't ask what's in a man's wallet or his bank account,' he told a party conference early on. 'I look at his heart and his actions. I ask you to look at mine.' No one could deny or belittle his outspoken support for Civil Rights, an unfashionable and emotive issue, for welfare and tax relief for those on lower incomes, while his speeches in defence of liberty in Poland and Czechoslovakia won him wide popular support. What he said was endorsed even by many Republicans, notably by their rising star, Richard M. Nixon. 'Not exactly the kind of ally I was aiming for,' Jim said.

It was not long before Helen noticed something odd. Jim and she were very much a part of Washington society. They accepted it for what it was, brittle and ultra sophisticated, a necessary part of political life. Their dinners and parties were eagerly attended, highly success-ful, rivalled by only a few others, which included those given by Jack and Jackie. Helen did not see them in any manner as competition, yet social columnists and com-mentators made capital out of hinting at rivalry between them. Frequently, photographs of the two couples were printed side by side, and fashion editors delighted in describing in minute detail what Jackie and Helen wore at receptions and on official occasions, giving one or the other the prize for effectiveness and looks. They were both amused by it. When Helen appeared with her hair up, suddenly all the ladies went into upswept hairstyles. When Jackie rediscovered elbow-length gloves, all ladies began to wear them. When they were both on the list of the year's best-dressed women, they had a hysterical lunch, remem-bering each other in shapeless shorts and T-shirts, covered in charcoal as they baked potatoes and fried clams on the beach at a driftwood fire. The only thing that Helen envied Jackie for was her ability to give her husband children.

All was not so friendly, however, among John F's supporters. Among them were some who saw Jim as one of his principal rivals for future honours. Jack was mount-ing a deliberate, carefully orchestrated campaign. They could not believe that Jim was not doing the same, encouraged by the increasing respect with which his opinions and speeches were received, and there were some who were not above attempting to sabotage any chances he might have.

One of the main weapons was innuendo. In the artificial world of Washington society, gossip crackled like constant bushfires. Some was true, much of it pure invention, and Jim and Helen made a point of not listening to it. When someone said confidentially, 'Maybe I shouldn't tell you this,' they always agreed and stopped the conversation. There was a cartoon once of the three wise monkeys, which all had Jim's face. The White Knight, the cynics called him, and his spotless Lady.

It was about then that Red and Lorna Jane Burwash came to Washington. Red had the kind of highly responsible job in the Pentagon that Jim had once held, and, meeting him again, Helen was never more surprised. Remembering his daredevil, irreverent attitude in the past, she found it difficult to accept the serious, dedicated man he had become. He had total concentration on the Air Force and his career and, inviting them to parties, running into them elsewhere, she could tell that Lorna Jane was unhappy. A neglected wife, she drank a little too much, became a little too animated and, at parties, attracted round her numbers of men, all of them just waiting until the time was right to take advantage of her loneliness and dissatisfaction.

'Red had better be careful,' Helen told Jim. 'Half the time he seems to forget that Lorna's there. She's too attractive to be left alone for long in this town.'

She tried to arrange regular get togethers with Lorna Jane, but they were not a success. The younger woman had lost her interest in anything except her own problems. She had pushed Red into thinking ahead, channelling his energies into his career. With his experience and combat record, especially the Congressional Medal, there was no reason for him to be stuck halfway up the promotion ladder, but he had to show that he could fit into the Staff mould, that he was not just another daring but unreliable flyboy. He was past that, anyway. Pilots were too old for the new jets in their late twenties. She had turned him into an achiever, and now it was too late, she regretted it.

'One good thing about a Washington posting is that, at least, you're in one place,' Helen said. 'You can have a settled home life.'

'A home life,' Lorna Jane repeated dully. 'That's one thing we've never had.'

When Helen mentioned it to Jim, he agreed that the situation did not sound too healthy. He was sympathetic, yet could not think of anything they could really do to help.

Only a week or so later, Helen was having lunch at Glendons' with some of the people on the ex-servicemen's welfare committee, of which she was secretary. During it, she overheard a piece of gossip. Normally, as usual, she would not have listened, but she caught Jim's name. And then, Lorna Jane's. She tried to put it out of her mind, yet in spite of herself all her former uncertainties about the extent of their relationship returned. It was a subject which they always had avoided. Jim had once said it was an episode of which he was not proud.

'You're being foolish,' she scolded herself. After the lunch, however, coming face to face with the two women in the ladies' room and seeing them fall into a guilty silence when she entered, she asked them point-blank to explain what she had overheard. Reluctantly, they admitted that there was considerable talk about her husband and the beautiful wife of an Air Force colonel, Lorna Jane Burwash. 'I said there couldn't be anything to it,' one of them told Helen soothingly. 'Neither there is,' Helen assured them. 'Nothing could be more natural than them being seen together. We're all very old friends.'

She did not mention it to Jim, waiting for him to say something. He did not. The following week, she decided one afternoon to call on Lorna Jane. She would be able to tell in a few moments from her attitude if she was concealing something, and if, as she expected, she was not, then it would set her mind at rest. She was down town already and took a cab to Thirtieth Street, where the Burwashes had a rather smart apartment. As the cab drew up outside it, she saw Jim's car parked right across the street. There was no mistaking it. She asked the cab driver to take her home and, as soon as she was there, rang Red Burwash at his office. When Red's clerk answered, she heard Red in the background shout, 'No calls! Not at the moment – I'm busy,' and hung up. Red was not at his apartment. But Jim was.

Next day, Jim had a meeting of a Senate committee. She called him in the statutory afternoon break and was told that Senator Kiley had not attended the meeting after lunch. Nor was he in his office.

Helen felt an aching anger at herself for checking up on him in this underhand way, and also a wrenching hurt and disbelief at his obvious betrayal of her. That he was merely picking up where he had left off with Lorna Jane made it no better. Had he gone to comfort her, and then the old attraction and her need for comfort had become too much for them? Perhaps it would be best if she never mentioned it, but let it burn itself out. If it burned itself out.

When he came home in the early evening, he was unusually silent. Normally, he described his day to her, keeping her up with developments in the Senate or in the committee rooms, where often amusing or dramatic things happened. Today he merely asked if she wanted a drink and poured one for himself, when she said no. He nodded and went to his study when she reminded him that they were dining with the Kefauvers. He was still silent later, when they were dressing, and she told him that she had tried to call him both at his office and the committee. He was evasive, unconvincingly evasive. Before she could stop herself, she said, 'You were with Lorna Jane, weren't you?'

He stood motionless for a second or two, then admitted quietly, 'Yes, I was.'

'And it's not the first time.'

'. . . No.'

Helen felt almost sick. After all her doubts and attempts to ignore them, his calm admission seemed almost callous. She tried to find some way to excuse it, to forgive him, but even if he had been no more than sorry for Lorna Jane, to expose them both to scandal was incredibly irresponsible and thoughtless. It was not something she could ever have believed of him, but she was conscious that Lorna Jane at thirty-three had an advantage of twenty years over her. It was not something she had ever been made to feel conscious of before. 'How could you?' she whispered. 'Meeting her in secret, hiding it from me.'

'I take it the Washington grapevine's been at work,' he said.

'If you mean the two of you are being talked about, yes.'

'Has Red heard about it?'

'How would I know?' Helen flashed at him. It was hard to control the anger she felt at his calmness. 'At least you can congratulate yourself on that. You managed to hide it from him, just as you hid it from me.'

'Not very successfully, obviously,' Jim said.

'I'm sorry,' Helen told him, and was angry again at herself for apologizing. 'I tried to ignore the stories. I just couldn't any longer.'

'I should have known I wouldn't be able to keep it from you,' Jim said. 'I'm sorry, too. But you see, it was for Lorna Jane's sake. I promised her I wouldn't say anything.'

Helen was puzzled. 'What do you mean?' She stepped back when Jim reached out to touch her cheek, his way of saying that he loved her, and she could see that he was hurt.

He had brought his drink upstairs from his study. It was still untouched. He picked it up. 'Well, I haven't been having a secret affair with her or anything, though that's clearly what you think.' Helen could not deny it, nor could she quite believe him. 'What else were you to imagine? She got in touch with me a couple of weeks ago,' Jim went on. 'Came round to see me at the office. She'd hardly got in the door, when she started to cry. Lord knows what my secretary would have thought, if she'd looked in. Probably the same as you, I guess.'

'Jim—' Helen began.

'No, no, I owe you an explanation,' he said. He took a drink of his scotch. 'She was just about cracking up, unable to cope. The problem is that her son's dropped out. At thirteen, he's dropped out. He's run away or been expelled from every school they've sent him to. He's just turned his back on everything, everything they've tried to do for him. Red doesn't understand it. He shouts at the boy, telling him he's a failure, throwing away his future, letting them all down. Neither of them would listen to Lorna Jane. She'd been pleading with Red at least to calm down and talk to their son, and with the boy to try to tell them what's wrong. And getting nowhere.'

'She wanted you to talk to Red,' Helen realized.

'That was the idea. But I didn't see how that would help. We'd both be talking in the dark, and, quite rightly, he would resent her for dragging me into it.'

'You went to her apartment,' Helen said.

'A couple of times, to set up a meeting with the boy. It was the best I could think of. And at last we fixed it. I took him for a walk today and bought him an icecream sundae. The kid's so grown up, I had the feeling he'd have preferred a drink. But I'm not one to encourage alcoholism in the young.' Jim smiled. 'It might've loosened him up. It took two hours of me talking and him listening. He's not a bad kid. Even though he seems to hate everyone over the age of twenty. "Why can't I talk to Dad, like I can talk to you?" he asked me, finally. And that's the whole problem.'

'They can't talk to each other?'

Jim finished his scotch. 'It's a growing phenomenon. I don't know what's causing it, maybe the cult of youth in the movies and in advertising, maybe it's the gap left by the war, but more and more people say they can't get through to their kids. Red's no different. Though in his case it's easy to see what's happened. He's got more and more sucked into his career, it's got more and more important to him, and he can hardly think of anything else. His sights are set on success, with a capital S, and he expects his son to be exactly the same. It only took ten minutes to establish that the boy dropped out because he's scared of letting his father down. He'd had the need for top grades, for success, drummed into him so much that he's just running away from it. He's bright, but he's rejecting the effort, even the attempt to do well, because he's too afraid of failure.'

'At that age?' Helen breathed. 'Poor boy. Could you help him?'

'I don't know.' Jim shook his head. 'I had that barrier of distrust to break through. And you see, he thinks his father is really right. To him, Red is perfection, the number one dedicated man, who had never had a failure, never made a slip, never deviated from the strict path of righteousness and fulfilment.' He chuckled. 'I kind of opened his eyes – I told him a few of the things Red had got up to at Market Wetherby during the war. How he got lost in his Fortress, "Ginger Rogers", and landed at a Liberator base, complaining that someone had taken his hardstand. How he took his whole crew up to London, treated them all to girls and so much booze they all got thrown into the slammer and had to miss the next mission. How he was nearly grounded, or worse, half a dozen times for ignoring orders and using his squadron as a personal flying circus, instead of part of a formation. It was all news to the boy. He couldn't believe it.'

'Couldn't you make him believe?'

Jim smiled. 'I rang up old Rufus Krasnowici, and I said, Rufe, what's your candid opinion of Red Burwash? I let Red Junior listen. Rufe said, "That insubordinate son-of-a-bitch? How he ever escaped a court-martial, I'll never know. If he could show off, foul up, disobey orders, he'd do it. I'd have busted him twenty times over – if he hadn't been the best goddamned flyer in the Group. Next to you and me, that is. You answered?" I said, Thanks, Rufe, and hung up.'

Helen was laughing, but she stopped. 'I'm ashamed, Jim,' she said quietly. 'Ashamed and can't forgive myself for what I've been thinking.'

'You've no need,' he told her gently. He took both her hands and pulled her close. 'I shouldn't have agreed to keep it from you in the first place. What else were you to think?' He kissed her and she clung to him, nearly ready to cry, until she realized he was chuckling. She looked at him questioningly. 'I've explained it to you. But I can't go around all the ladies' luncheon clubs scotching rumours.'

'What are you going to do?'

'Why, nothing,' Jim said. 'Rise above it – isn't that what you British always do? It'll die out. We'd better hurry and change.' As she was tying his black tie for him, he smiled. 'You know? If it doesn't die out, I don't think I'll mind too much. I was growing a little tired of that White Knight tag, anyway.'

'A very perfect, gentle knight,' Helen said.

'I really don't mind,' he assured her. 'I even get a kick out of people imagining that a dish like Lorna Jane would go for an old married man like me.'

'Modesty will get you anywhere,' Helen said, and kissed him.

Later, in the car as they drove to the Kefauvers', Helen asked him, 'But what are you going to do about Red and his son?'

'I was afraid you'd ask that,' Jim answered. 'You're the doctor. What do you suggest?'

'I think you'll have to see Red and Lorna Jane together.'

'I was afraid you were going to say that, too.'

The next day, Jim went to Thirtieth Street. When he returned, Helen asked him how it had gone. 'Well, Lorna Jane was scared, and Red didn't want to listen,' Jim said. 'But I made them sit down and told them pretty much what I told you. She understood. I hope Red did. Anyway, I ordered him as his ex-Commanding Officer to put in for a few days leave, and take his son up to Maine for some fishing. Just the two of them. It's something they haven't done for years. And I said it wouldn't be a bad thing, if Red managed to fall out of the boat a couple of times.'

Helen laughed.

A few weeks later, Red Burwash told them that his son had been entered for the Air Force Academy. There was not a prouder man in Washington, and he was very grateful to Jim.

The temporary suspicion that had troubled Helen was over. Neither of them referred to it again, yet it had cast the first faint cloud on their horizon.

# TWENTY-SIX

Chuck bought himself the new model Cadillac, but Vi refused to give up their battered old sedan, in which she still drove the children to school. It looked odd beside the Jaguars and Pontiacs of the other mothers, but just owning two cars seemed enough of an extravagance to Vi.

She had had to be careful for so long that the extravagant life they had begun to lead disturbed her. It was not simply a matter of turning lights off and warming up leftover food, although that still seemed sensible to her to avoid waste. There was the effect on the children. She was trying to bring them up with a sense of values, to take care of their things, their clothes, and toys, and not always to be making demands.

She knew Chuck still had to work very hard for them all and it did not seem fair that their children, like their new school friends, little rich kids, should always be asking for something, their own radios and television sets, ice-skates which they only used twice, new clothes for every party, unlimited sweets, fancy bicycles and gokarts. To her, it was a recipe for unhappiness later in life. But Chuck encouraged them, showering things on them. If they took a single bite of their food and left the table, she would call them back and warn them they would get nothing later on, if they didn't eat now. Chuck would laugh and say, 'Come on, Vi! Rationing's over. If they don't feel hungry, so what? They can help themselves to something after.'

She was shocked one day when her eight-year-old daughter, Helen, told her she was mean. 'Why do you say that?' Vi asked.

Helen pouted. The day before she had had a friend home after school. 'That's what Janie says. That you're mean and cruel and didn't have any of the kinds of icecream she likes and tried to make her eat nasty sausages. And you talk kind of funny. And our pool's too small.'

The contrast with their previous way of life, instead of levelling out, became more marked. Chuck bought more and more expensive clothes and jewellery for her, a mink coat for her birthday. 'I like giving you things. They're presents. Now don't be silly,' he told her. He bought a pony for Helen and Danny, an electric-powered pedal car for little Jack. She had a coloured maid and a gardener to tend the four acres round the villa. He had the pool extended, then completely redesigned.

She rarely had an opportunity to wear the clothes and the jewellery. Occasionally they were invited out by wealthy patients and to the parties which Matt and Rachel gave in their penthouse apartment at Long Beach, but Chuck seemed to be working harder than ever and was often not home till late.

Vi knew it was foolish to resent his success, but sometimes she could not help longing for the old days. She was much alone with all three children at school and she did not see Rachel as much as before. Rachel was developing a new set of friends, while Vi could find little in common with the career wives she met through the school, acquisitive and competitive. Time hung on her hands. Chuck did not like her to help with the housework and there was little cooking or mending to do. The garden was flawlessly tended. She became bored with lying by the pool.

It seemed pointless dressing up just for herself and usually she wore her comfortable old clothes to work in the section of garden she had insisted on keeping for herself. Once when Chuck found her in the cheap cotton flowered dress he had bought for her years before, he became angry and ordered her to change. 'You used to complain because I didn't buy you things. Now you complain because I do!'

It was unfair, but Vi understood what was driving him. She tried to explain. 'Look, you don't have to prove anything. I'm perfectly happy. You don't have to keep buying things for me. I'm proud of you, but I just haven't been able to adjust to all this like you have. I keep remembering how simple our life was. I liked it then.'

'All right, but what's important is the way we are now,' he told her. 'It's called upward mobility. I thought Doc Zimmer was a grasping, self important old shark, but he really opened my eyes to a lot of things. The profession I'm in has enormous potential, earning potential. I'm on the move and, like it or not, you're coming with me.'

Not long after the Korean War broke out, Chuck was asked again to volunteer for service. 'They must be crazy,' he laughed. 'I've done my bit once. Do they think I'm going to throw all this away for World War Two and a half?'

It worried Vi. 'You used to care about things. You used to say that those who could ought to help others who were less fortunate,' she reminded him. 'I believed that. I still do. Now all you seem to think about is making money. Isn't there anything else?'

Chuck was serious. 'Sure, once I thought a lot of things. I even thought of going back to school, studying orthodontics, opening a children's clinic.' He shrugged. 'When you start thinking like that, that's when you get used – when you get walked over. Never again. Life's too short. I think about *my* kids.'

The practice which Chuck and Matt ran had expanded enormously and now they had four main assistants, with hygienists, technicians and their own laboratory. Chuck was elected to the boards of various professional and business associations and told Vi that it would mean more entertaining. They would give regular weekly dinners at home. Vi welcomed it. At least there was something positive for her to do, choosing menus, cooking. 'No, that side of it won't involve you,' Chuck told her. 'You're the hostess. We'll have them catered. No arguments, now. That's how it's done here.'

She felt completely useless. He was still considerate,

loving when he was not too tired, marvellous with the children, but she felt more and more detached from him, less and less a part of the materialistic world they now lived in.

California, here I come . . .

Vi tried to talk about it to Rachel, but Rachel had her own problems. Her friend was losing her optimism. 'You think you've reached the Promised Land,' she said. 'Then you find the wells are drying up and the berries turning sour.' The trouble was that Matt was drinking. The pressures of success were too much for him. He knew how much he owed to Chuck, and how little he might have achieved on his own. It came to a head one night at one of their parties, when he accused Chuck of having an affair with Rachel.

'That's ridiculous,' Chuck told him.

'Is it?' Matt shouted. 'Why is it? You've taken everything else from me. Why not her?'

Afterwards, Chuck was raging. 'How do you like that? That bum! He'd be nothing without me. I do the work. I run the whole show, while all he does is drink and fool around with the nurses. I've a good mind to dump him!'

'You can't dump him,' Vi reminded him quietly. 'It's because of him and his father we're here. The practice is in Matt's name.'

She would almost have preferred it if he had struck her. Instead, he simply gazed at her, shocked, reminded of how fragile was the pinnacle on which he stood. Matt could knock it away whenever he wanted.

Once or twice a year they attended conventions, in places like Denver, Chicago, Salt Lake City. Vi disliked them. She did not fit in. The other wives found her too simple and unaffected and tended to ignore her, while they gossiped and scored over one another. She had a rarity value as a former GI bride, but that had lost the slightly scandalous overtones it once had. Some of the conventioneers were still faintly roguish with her, but not when

271

Chuck was around. Then they were very polite and decorous.

This year it was at Montgomery, Alabama. She told Chuck that she did not want to go. 'You'll have a better time without me.' She did not tell him that she had had enough and could not bear the life they were leading any longer. Even their children were growing up spoilt, making continual demands. She remembered Bette's statistics about war brides who wanted to go home.

'Nonsense! Of course you're coming with me,' Chuck insisted. 'It's in the South. You've always wanted to go there.'

The convention was exactly the same as all the others. As for seeing the true South, in her airconditioned, security conscious hotel, Vi might as well have been in Alaska.

There was one difference, however. Among his colleagues this time, Chuck met an old acquaintance from his Air Force days. Barney Voss was another former Flight Engineer and had served in England in the Eighth, though not at Market Wetherby. He was delighted to meet Vi and the evening they spent with him was a real pleasure.

There were three air bases near Montgomery and, with Barney, they met some of his friends who were still serving. One was now a Captain, married to a Scots girl, Meg. Vi and she took to each other at once. 'Don't you just get fed up with all this sometimes?' Meg said. 'But you're lucky. At least your man's got out of the Air Force and you're not ordered to pull up sticks and move to a new home every two years.'

'Sometimes I wouldn't mind that,' Vi said. Chuck glanced over at her sharply, but did not comment.

'One thing,' the Captain said, 'it's a darn sight warmer over here than it is in Scotland.' Meg dug him in the ribs.

'Overheated, overfed and back over here,' Barney grinned, slapping himself on his comfortable stomach. 'Though I'm not sure I prefer that to how it was — overpaid, oversexed. And over there.' They laughed at the old joke.

'Oversexed is right,' Meg agreed. 'Pete was the first Yank I met who didn't think any British girl was his for the asking.'

'Enough were,' Barney smiled, reminiscently.

'You're a terrible man,' Meg laughed. 'What about you, Vi? What did you think, when you first met Chuck?'

There was a pause. 'He saved my life from a German fighter,' Vi said quietly. 'It was trying to machine gun me on the ground. I thought he was the bravest, kindest, most handsome man I'd ever seen. And the most thoughtful. I still do.'

'Now that's what I call a testimonial, buddy!' Barney exclaimed.

Chuck was embarrassed. 'Yeah. I was just wondering where that guy went to,' he said. They laughed and the Captain fetched another six pack of beers.

On the last night of the convention, to Vi's surprise, Chuck agreed to slip away and join their new friends. That evening he was more like his former self, as if something had reminded him of where they had come from.


There was another visitor in Montgomery that night. Jim Kiley.

His interest in Alabama's capital had been aroused two years before when Mrs Rosa Parks had refused to give up her seat on a bus to a white passenger and had been arrested. That arrest led to a peaceful boycott of the city's transport system, organized by a young local minister, Martin Luther King, which resulted a year later in segregation in the buses being abolished by law. They were the opening moves in what was bound to be a long struggle. Jim had been invited by King to attend a meeting of the committee of his Southern Christian Leadership Conference.

As Jim entered the hall with the secretary sent to escort him, one of the younger committee members said sharply, 'What he doin' here? Get that whitey out of here!' There was a rising murmur of agreement.

Dr King, who was chairman, called for order, apologized to Jim and introduced him. 'This is Senator Jim Kiley. He is here at my invitation. I shouldn't need to explain why. He was a fighter for this country during the war. And he has been a fighter ever since – for freedom, decency and justice. No man has fought more vigorously against prejudice – whether it was McCarthyism or the enemies of civil rights!'

'I didn't come here to make a speech,' Jim said. 'Nor to make political points. I've come here without any announcements, any publicity. I want to learn from you. I just want to sit and listen. The speeches I have made have been from personal belief, not from knowledge. You have much to achieve. I have much to learn. I think we can help each other.' The applause he was given lasted for some time.

After the meeting, he had a long discussion with Dr King who impressed him with his sincerity and complete lack of self interest. When they finally left the hall, he said, 'I'm afraid, Doctor, you have more problems than I had realized. May I speak frankly? I heard three or four different voices in there.'

'That is, indeed, the main problem, Senator,' King agreed. 'My people do not have a united aim. Some want equality. Some want revolution. Some don't want equality, but supremacy. Me, I'd settle for a little dignity, and equal rights for white and black under the constitution. Confirmed by law.'

They walked on down the dark street.

'How long do you think it will take?' Jim asked.

'Oh, ten years, twenty, maybe more. Maybe not even fully in my lifetime. But with help from people like you, come it surely will.'

'I was interested when you mentioned Mahatma Gandhi,' Jim said.

'He is my mentor,' King smiled. 'I've read all his books.'

'I was thinking,' Jim said. 'He faced pretty much the same situation in India as you do here. But he drew the

274

opposing factions together and won independence, peacefully.'

'He was a saint,' King said simply.

'But human and approachable,' Jim pointed out. 'And his disciples could teach valuable, practical lessons which are not in his books.'

King paused. 'Apply to them, you mean? Go to India and study his methods?'

'It would bring your cause to the attention of a lot of people. Somehow, you're going to have to work out how to apply what you've learned here in Montgomery on a larger scale, a national scale. It would not be impossible.'

King seemed to be catching fire at the idea. 'No, it would not. All that was needed was the spur to action. Thank you, Senator.' He smiled, then glanced round, lowering his voice. 'You realize we're being followed?'

'Yes, I've seen them,' Jim said. A battered old limousine had been crawling along a hundred yards behind them. Its number plates sported the Confederate flag. 'It might be for the best if we split up here. Will you be all right?'

'Yes, I'll be fine. By God's grace, I'll come to no harm,' King said. 'Thank you again for your encouragement.'

Jim watched as the younger man turned off into a side street and strode quickly away. As he moved on, Jim heard the limousine start up behind him. For perhaps twenty steps it maintained its distance, then all at once its engine roared, its lights flashed fully on and raced towards him, turning sharply and blocking his way. Four men jumped out quickly, southern rednecks in plaid shirts and jeans. Jim halted, tensing.

'Hold it there, white nigger,' one of the rednecks said.

'Had a nice chat, nigger lover?' another asked.

When Jim made to step round them, the first man brought a baseball bat from behind his back and slashed at him, grunting as Jim leapt quickly out of range. The second man closed in, punching, and the first cursed, unable to get a clear swing at Jim. 'Get in there, Billy! Get him!' he shouted.

Jim had been hit twice. His opponent was strong, but unskilled. When his next wild punch came, Jim blocked it, jabbed the man hard under the heart and, as he fell forward, hit him square on the chin. He did not let him drop, but caught him and hurled him against the man with the baseball bat.

The other two rednecks had been content to watch and egg their friends on, but as Jim tried to break past them, they grabbed him. He shook them off, but tripped and they jumped on him. 'Hold him up! Let me get him!' the man with the bat was shouting.

Vi had insisted on driving, when they returned from the married quarters at the base. It had been a good evening. Chuck was beside her and in the back were Barney and Meg's husband, who had come with them for a last drink. She saw something and slowed down. 'What's that?' she asked.

The street was poorly lit, but a car's lights bounced off the wall and showed someone lying on the sidewalk. Three men appeared to be beating up another.

'Drive on,' Chuck said. 'We don't want to get involved.'

'There's three of them!' Vi protested.

'Chuck's right,' Barney said. 'This is no place to get mixed up in anything.'

The man being attacked had struggled to his feet, blood running down his face. He struck hard with his elbow and one of the men holding him screamed.

The realization came to both Chuck and Vi at the same moment. 'I don't believe it,' Chuck gasped. 'It's General Kiley.'

He was out of the car and running even before it had stopped. Barney and the Air Force Captain jumped out behind him.

The rednecks never knew what hit them. Chuck tore them off Jim one by one and as they spun round, Barney's and the Captain's fists slammed into them. The only one who still tried to fight went down with Chuck's boot in his gut and a piledriver under the ear.

'Better get the General out of here,' the Captain said.

They cleaned as much of the blood off Jim as they could, before smuggling him into the convention hotel and up to Chuck and Vi's room. He had greater powers of recovery than they had feared and, as they lowered him on to the couch, he managed to smile. 'If I haven't said it – thanks. You guys came in like the Seventh Cavalry. I was beginning to think it was Kiley's last stand.' He explained what had happened, thanked them again and asked them not to speak about it. Barney and the Captain saluted and left.

While Vi cleaned him up more thoroughly and took his jacket to mend a rip in the sleeve, he told Chuck and her more about the evening and the circumstances of the attack. One of his teeth had been dislodged and hurt when he touched it.

'You're going to lose that,' Chuck said.

'He'd fix it for you,' Vi said, 'but he doesn't like to get involved.'

'Oh, come on!' Chuck protested.

Jim noticed, but gave no reaction. 'It was a pretty Dickensian coincidence running into you two again,' he said. 'Wait till I tell Helen. How is her namesake, by the way?' He nodded, when they told him how well young Helen was doing, top of her class, at fourteen growing into a very pretty girl. 'Takes after her mother, obviously. My wife will be very pleased to hear it.' He looked at Chuck. 'She's told me a lot about you. You've made a great success.'

'Pretty shabby in comparison to you, General,' Chuck said.

Jim started to say something and stopped. 'I was going to use an old Air Force expression, but I swallowed it in deference to Vi.' She smiled. He looked again at Chuck. 'Don't ever run yourself down. You personify the American dream. Whatever it is, you have made it.' He paused. 'But what now? As they say at Christmas, what next for the man who has everything?'

Chuck glanced at Vi. 'That's the big one, General. A month ago, I'd have answered you straight off – more of the same, onward and upward. But this past week I've been thinking.'

Jim saw that Vi had stopped sewing and had raised her eyes to her husband's. Chuck was speaking to her, no longer to him.

'I'm good at my job,' Chuck went on, 'one of the best, they say. The rewards are high, and I've taken them with both hands. But Vi's right. I didn't start out just to take. Rich people use a dentist instead of a toothbrush. I've got this crazy idea. I don't even know if I can do it. I want to study again, new developments, to use them and improve them. I want to give up the life I've been living, and find a community where I can really be of use, where maybe some of the people can't even afford a toothbrush. I said it was crazy, but I know that with Vi to help me I can do it. Then maybe we'll get back to being ourselves again, us and the kids, Chuck and Vi.'

Vi was smiling. It was the same loving smile that Jim remembered, when young Master Sergeant Ericson brought her to meet him at the Goodwill Dance at Market Wetherby and told him they planned to marry. Jim was happy to admit that he'd been wrong all those years ago. Whatever its ups and downs, this was one marriage that was going to last.

# TWENTY-SEVEN

The pursuit of power can be more fierce than the struggle for survival in the jungle. Helen had her first real taste of the savage infighting of American politics during the presidential election of 'fifty-six. For the second time, it was between Adlai Stevenson and Eisenhower, and Jim was heavily involved.

First there was the Democratic convention to confirm Stevenson as his party's candidate, and everyone waited to hear his choice of running mate as Vice President. Adlai came secretly to dinner with Jim and Helen at Newport and, as they sat afterwards over coffee, startled them by telling them he intended to nominate Jim. 'If I am elected, I shall need someone on whose judgement I can utterly rely,' he said. 'I can't think of anyone I would prefer to have at my side.'

Jim was flattered and took a minute or two before explaining why he hesitated. It was tempting and he was grateful, but, ideally, the choice of running mate should unite the opposite wings of the party. 'Whereas I'm happy to say we're so similar that people can hardly tell the difference between us.' Jim smiled, and went on. 'Might it not be better to throw the nomination open to the convention, to let the party choose between right or left, Kefauver or Humphrey – or one of the young liberals like Jack Kennedy.'

Adlai was doubtful at first, although he agreed it was more democratic to break the custom of the candidate choosing his running mate and to allow the convention to decide.

It was settled when Helen pointed out that by showing his personal preference, he would risk alienating some of the main contenders. Later, she told Jim that she was more proud of him than ever for his decision.

At the convention, it became a fight for the vice-presidential nomination between Kennedy and Estes Kefauver. When Kefauver came out ahead on the first ballot, Jim persuaded Lyndon Johnson of Texas to shift his vote to Kennedy. It was a gamble that nearly worked, but too many of the other states were afraid of the effect on the voters of having a Catholic for the first time standing for the Vice Presidency and they united to ensure a winning majority on the second ballot for Kefauver.

It had all been academic. Stevenson lost the election, which went to Ike for a second term, with the thrusting, young Richard Nixon as his Vice President.

What had been meant as a democratic gesture left a residue of bitterness. Both JFK and Hubert Humphrey had reason to expect Stevenson to have nominated them personally and neither could ever fully forgive him for not doing so. It was at a dinner in the Kennedy compound at Hyannis Port that Helen was shocked to hear Jack speak dismissively in public of Adlai.

'If he'd chosen me to run with him, he'd have had a chance of winning. His only chance,' Jack said. In his disappointment, his ambition showed itself more nakedly than ever.

Helen wanted to tell him about the offer to Jim, but restrained herself. 'You can't be certain of that, Jack,' she said levelly.

He looked at her in surprise, with a hint of annoyance, then shrugged. 'Maybe not.'

'Maybe it's turned out all for the best,' Bobby said soothingly. 'Father never wanted you to stand. He was pretty sure Adlai would lose and, this way, they can't make the excuse that he lost because his running mate was Catholic.' There was a murmur of agreement. 'What do you say, Jim?'

Jim had been sitting quietly. 'With Ike's popularity, I don't think anyone could have beaten him at the moment.

In another four years, it might be a different story.' He looked at Jack. 'I wouldn't take losing the nomination too badly. It brought you to the attention of the whole convention. You won a lot of sympathy and you won a lot of people over, and that can only be in your favour next time round.'

Jack smiled and raised his glass to him. 'Right as usual, Jim. Only, next time I might not be standing as *Vice* President.'

There was laughter round the table, as most of the guests there took it as a joke. Helen had the very distinct impression, however, that Jack was not joking. It became a certainty when she saw the look between him and Jackie, and her answering smile.

It was about this time that the Suez Crisis split Washington society. Helen had to be careful what she said, but she was shocked by America's refusal to back her principal allies, Great Britain and France. The conflict was brought into her own home one evening, during a party she gave for her daughter and son-in-law, Sir Henry and Lady Maylie.

Pat's husband had inherited the title on his father's death. He had had a successful career in Parliament, rising to a junior cabinet post in Eden's government. He was one of the coming men, but had resigned after Suez in support of his chief. He was in Washington as a member of a British trade delegation and Pat had been delighted to accompany him, since it gave her the chance to visit her mother and Jim again. It was a very happy reunion, especially when Pat confided in Helen that she was sure that at long last she was going to have a baby.

The Maylies had brought with them to the party another former Cabinet Minister, Charles Patterson, a tall, distinguished man in his fifties. As she moved round her guests, Helen heard his voice with its slight, appealing Scots accent and paused to listen. He was defending the British decision to invade Egypt along with France and Israel and trying to explain the consternation felt by many people in

Britain at the opposition which had come from Eisenhower, of all people. 'After all,' he said, 'it is in your interests, in the interests of the whole western world, that the Suez canal is kept open to international shipping, and not liable to be arbitrarily closed by a regime which may be unfriendly to us or simply wishes to hold our trade to ransom.' He answered questions succinctly, but fully, not concealing anything, and Helen found herself wishing that her country had more spokesmen like him in America.

Then a florid, middleaged Congressman from the South broke into the conversation with a laugh. 'I guess that's what they call soft soap, Mr Patterson. You'd be dandy at selling patent medicine at a carnival.'

'I'm sorry, I don't follow you, sir,' Patterson smiled.

'And I'm surely glad that Ike didn't follow you,' the Congressman chuckled. 'Can't you admit that all you've been telling these good people is just a smokescreen? Fact is, England can't accept that she's lost her empire. And this was just an excuse to try and snatch back one of her colonies.'

'I'm afraid I can't agree,' Patterson said quietly. 'That's just not the case.'

'You mean you won't admit it,' the Congressman argued. 'But it might pay you to remember you're talking to a bunch of former colonists who had the sense to get out from under.'

Before she could prevent herself, Helen said, 'And it might pay you to learn something about England before you criticize it.' The Congressman and the people around him looked at her in astonishment. Helen was normally so diplomatic and controlled, but she could not stop. 'England did not "lose" her empire. Her parliament and people voluntarily gave the dominions and the colonies the right to self-government. And all of them chose to remain within the Commonwealth. That might tell you something.'

'We were talking about Suez, Mrs Kiley,' the Congressman persisted.

'And congratulating yourselves on having forced your

allies to withdraw,' Helen said. 'Who do you think it will benefit, East or West, to have the canal under the control of a dictatorship which can close it against us at a moment's notice?'

Jim had heard the raised voices and moved in, deftly restoring good humour, steering the conversation to other topics and soothing the Congressman's ruffled feathers.

Later, when their guests had left, he asked Helen what it had all been about. She apologized. 'I just saw red for a minute.'

'You got your dander up, all right,' he chuckled. 'You can't stand to see Egypt twist the tail of the British lion.'

Helen tensed. She had expected him to support her. 'It wasn't Egypt,' she said, 'you know that. It was America that made us withdraw, because Eisenhower thought that would increase US influence in North Africa and the Middle East.'

'We weren't just throwing our weight around. It's important for us to maintain bases and good relations there.'

'Don't you remember what you once told me about Korea? What's happened in Egypt will start to happen in the whole of that middle-eastern area now, and most of it will sooner or later turn to Moscow. The White House may have won a temporary advantage. But what is important is what the situation will be in the Middle East twenty or thirty years from now.'

Jim had grown serious. 'That's as may be,' he said at last. 'Maybe one day your Anthony Eden will be proved to have been right – though I sure as hell hope not.'

Next day, Helen received a small but charming bouquet of flowers with a note from Charles Patterson. 'Thank you for coming so ably and courageously to my defence. I hope I did not spoil your party. To make up for it, may I take you to lunch one day before I leave Washington?'

Helen showed the note to Jim, who had no objection to her being invited. He was even amused. 'You've got to hand it to him. He doesn't give up. You'd better warn him, though, that taking you to lunch will not have any influence on the US Senate.'

In spite of herself, Helen was annoyed. It never occurred to Jim that Patterson, an attractive man, might wish to see her for herself. In fact, apart from one phone call, she did not talk to him again. He rang to say that his half of the delegation was moving on to Detroit and Chicago and that he would, unfortunately, be unable to see her before he left.

Turning into the High Street in Market Wetherby, Helen stepped on the brake so hard that her daughter, Pat, was jolted forward in the passenger seat. 'Sorry, darling,' Helen apologized. 'It was that girl. I thought I'd seen a ghost.'

A young girl had been crossing the street ahead of them, wearing a sweater and jeans, thick dark-blonde hair tumbling to her shoulders. She glanced round at the squeal of brakes, smiled and carried on into the alley at the side of The Plough.

'You mean Vicky?' Pat said. 'Of course, you haven't seen her since she was a baby. That's Vicky Mundy, Letty's daughter.'

No wonder the girl with her wide eyes and heartshaped face had been so familiar, Helen thought. How old must she be now? Seventeen? She was the image of her mother at that age. Helen remembered the wayward Letty so well. She remembered most clearly of all that November night when she had delivered Letty's illegitimate baby at the old cottage hospital, nearly six weeks premature. 'No word of her, I suppose?' Helen asked, as she drove on.

'Not since that one disastrous visit,' Pat said, 'on the day of her brother's wedding. Heaven knows where she is now – if she's still alive.'

'And what about Vicky? How's she turned out?'

Pat smiled. 'A really nice girl, charming. Talented, too. You should have been here last month, when the Wetherby Players put on *A Taste of Honey*.' Pat saw her mother's mouth twitch. 'No, seriously! Henry and I went along

284

because we had to, but Vicky played the girl and made it worthwhile. She was really very good, very touching.'

Helen drove on through the town, across the bridge and up to Dereham House, her old home, where Pat and her husband now lived. She and Jim were on a fleeting visit, two days snatched while Jim was over in Vienna with a party of US Senators for an international conference on aid for the underdeveloped nations.

Two days were all too short after a gap of many years, but while she was relieved to see that outwardly Market Wetherby had altered very little, she was aware of many small and subtle changes. People seemed more prosperous, certainly, yet at the same time more materialistic and more cynical. The Roxy Cinema had closed. There was a rash of television aerials everywhere and the Americanization begun by the GIs during the war was being continued by a daily diet of US police and cowboy and comedy shows. Even at Dereham House, conversation the previous evening had stopped for the nine o'clock news and a British serial which Pat and Henry were following. The hero and heroine appeared to spend most of the episode in bed together. That would never be allowed on American television. Standards in England were certainly different from what they had been. *A Taste of Honey*? It would have been unthinkable for the local amateurs to put on anything as daring as that, even a few years ago. It was a sign of the times.

Henry Maylie, Helen's son-in-law, had never been quite sure what to call Jim Kiley. Strictly speaking, he was not his father-in-law and it seemed too familiar to address the older man as 'Jim'. He had settled happily for the accurate, and inoffensive, 'Senator'. They were in the library and he had just been told something in confidence which relieved him enormously. 'As you know, I'm not a Macmillan man, Senator,' he said. 'But it would be dreadful if the Prime Minister's peace initiative had just gone for nothing.'

'We won't let that happen,' Jim assured him. A year

ago, Harold Macmillan had visited Chairman Khruschev in Moscow to discuss the possibility of ending the nuclear arms race. This year, 1960, a summit conference had been arranged in Paris, but had been abandoned after the shooting down of an American U-2 spy plane over the Soviet Union. Jim had just explained that, as a member of the Foreign Policy Committee of the Democratic Advisory Council, the true purpose of his trip to Vienna had been to contact the Russians unofficially and discover if there was any hope of reopening the discussions, which could lead to a nuclear test ban. 'For all his tough talk, I believe Khruschev would be in favour of it.'

'I wish I shared your belief,' Henry said.

'You must understand,' Jim told him. 'Khruschev is a peasant. He's practical. He's achieved a great deal since Stalin's death and he doesn't want to throw it away. He'd be the last to use the Bomb.' He paused. 'Strangely enough, during this trip, I've begun to wonder if we've not been ignoring an even greater problem, the so-called emerging nations. We have to help them to develop. Because if they're not helped–'

They were interrupted, when Helen came in with Pat. 'Not still talking politics?' Pat sighed. 'Why don't you do something more useful and pour us a drink?'

Jim smiled to Helen as they went through into the drawing room. They saw all too little of each other these days because of his work and he was happy she had decided to come with him. He was impatient to get back to the States, where the run up to the Democratic nomination for the Presidential election was beginning, but he had agreed to this two day stopover for her sake.

Helen was grateful. It was wonderful to spend time with her grandson, little Ronnie, already developing a strong resemblance to his grandfather, after whom he had been named and, it was always good to see Pat, who had matured into a thoroughly capable and charming woman. She loved this old house and was glad that Pat had kept it as the family home. It was strange to be here with Jim again, where it had all begun. So much had happened in this very room. From how he was looking at her, she could tell he was thinking exactly the same thing.

'We were talking about Letty Mundy,' Pat said. 'You remember her, don't you, Jim?'

'I do, indeed,' Jim nodded. One way and another, the tawny-haired Letty had caused quite a bit of trouble at the Base.

'It's just something I'd forgotten, something odd,' Pat went on. 'It was two or three years ago. I was talking to Sally McGraw – Sally Bilton that was. And she told me she'd seen a magazine article about one of the film festivals, Cannes or Venice or somewhere like that, and in one of the photographs, amongst all the stars and producers and what not, was someone she was sure was Letty.'

'Was it really her?' Helen asked, surprised.

'Well, Sally said the hair was different, but otherwise it was her to the life.' Pat laughed. 'Still, I mean, it's hardly likely, is it?'

'Hardly,' Helen agreed. 'Of course, it would be Letty's idea of seventh heaven, but I can't quite imagine her in that sort of setting.'


It was raining when Vicky left The Plough. She hurried across the square and went in through the front door of the shop. Rosie was rearranging one of the shelves and Peter was in the post office section. 'Can I help you, Mum?' Vicky asked.

'No thanks, love,' Rosie smiled. 'I'm nearly done.' Peter and she had long ago given up the attempt to stop their niece from calling them Mum and Dad. It had started when she was a small child, when they had taken over running the shop and looking after her. They had never lied to her about her real mother, although they had not told her everything. As she grew older, she was intelligent enough to work it out for herself and to accept it.

'I've been over at The Plough, having a talk with grandpa,' Vicky said.

There was something in her voice that made Peter curious and he came out from behind the grille. 'What about?' he asked.

Vicky hesitated. 'About what I'm going to do.'

She had finished at school that summer, the earliest she could. She was bright, but not at all academic, and like many young people these days could not wait to do something, if possible to get away from the confines of the little market town. She usually listened to Peter, yet he had been unable to persuade her to stay on at school, especially since she did not really know what she wanted to do. Her grandfather Mundy had been determined she would go to university and was so disappointed he would not speak to her for two weeks after she announced her decision. Jack Blair, Rosie's father, whom she thought of as her other grandfather, had been more understanding. 'It's her life,' he said. 'Neither Vi or Rosie finished school. I thought it was a pity at the time, but they haven't done so badly.'

Rosie had stopped working, too. 'What did Dad have to say?'

'He said I was to tell you I'd made up my mind.' Vicky glanced from one to the other and held her head high, almost defiant. 'I want to go into the theatre, to be an actress.'

Rosie gasped, but it was no surprise to Peter. He had been expecting it, especially after all the praise that had been heaped on her after the last play she did. What did surprise him was her look, the lifted chin, tightened mouth and wide, challenging eyes. It was so exactly how he remembered Letty as a girl on the rare occasions when she had defied their father.

'An actress?' Rosie repeated, with incredulity.

'Don't you think I'm good enough?' Vicky demanded. 'Don't you think I can do it?'

'Of course, you can, love. Others have. There's no reason why you can't,' Peter said, soothingly. 'That's not what we're concerned about. I mean, it can be a hard life, and a disappointing one. But apart from that, and apart from what you want, yourself – there's others to be considered.'

Vicky knew what he meant. In spite of the stroke which had left him semi-paralysed, her grandfather still insisted on being consulted. He could make life very difficult for everyone when things were not done his way. He had taken care of her when she was tiny and, ever afterwards, she had loved him very dearly. He was not an easy man, but had been more indulgent with her than with anyone. This time, however, she realized it would be no simple matter to win him round.

The bell jangled as a customer came in. 'We'll talk about it later,' Peter said quietly.

He brought the subject up himself that evening. The twins were in bed and Albert Mundy's chair had been pushed up to his usual place at the head of the table. Vicky was helping her grandmother, Vera, to serve supper. When she sat down beside Peter, he said casually, 'Vicky's decided to have a go at the theatre, to try to be an actress.'

Albert Mundy was buttering a piece of bread with his good right hand and stopped. 'Actress?' he growled. 'Actress?' He made it sound like a dirty word.

'I just want to try,' Vicky said. 'If I'm no good, I'll find out soon enough.'

'I can tell you now,' Mundy rapped. 'It's not something we're even going to discuss. You can get the whole idea out of your head, my girl.'

'I think we really have to talk about it, Dad,' Peter said. 'It's not something that'll just go away.'

Vicky was encouraged. 'It's the only thing I want to do! I just feel I have to. Grandpa said, if I felt like that, nothing would stop me.'

Mundy was staring at her. 'Jack Blair, you mean? I might have known you'd been talking to him. Well, he's not your grandfather, my girl, and you remember that! He's got no say in what happens to you. None!'

'Now, Albert, you mustn't get excited,' Vera soothed.

'You eat your supper.' She smiled apologetically to Rosie, who was continually upset by the unresolved feud between her father and father-in-law. She sat opposite Vicky. 'What would it mean, love? What's involved?'

'Well, it's getting a start,' Vicky told her, with a glance at her grandfather. 'I've written to all the drama schools I could find.'

'Those letters you've been getting,' Rosie realized. 'What did they say?'

'Nearly all the same thing. I'm not seventeen till November. They all say I'm too young and have to wait at least a year.'

'That's it then,' Mundy said, relieved. 'I'm glad they're responsible enough to point that out. You're far too young to know your own mind.'

'But I do, grandad,' Vicky insisted. 'They also said there were other ways. I could apply to one of the repertory companies for a job as an assistant stage manager. There's only one snag, they pay hardly anything, not enough to live on.'

'You've got it all worked out, have you?'

'She seems to have, Albert,' Vera said, deliberately misunderstanding him. 'What do you think, Peter?'

Peter had sat in silence, listening. Vicky was nervous, suspecting that he also disapproved. She was surprised, when he said, 'I think she should have a go. I know what it's like. There was something I wanted to do that wasn't so very different, you remember. To make a career in music. Well–' He shrugged. 'I'd hate Vicky to feel bitter, because she hadn't at least tried.'

'And what's she to live on?' Mundy asked. 'She's just told us they won't pay her anything. And the shop barely makes enough to support all of us, as it is. So you answer me that.'

'I think she could have a try at Ipswich, or Colchester. They're not too far away,' Peter said slowly. 'And as for money – there's a bit put by in the building society for her. It was to help her, if she went to college or something.

There should be enough by this time to keep her for a year, if she's careful. That should be long enough for her to find if she's cut out to be an actress, if it's the life for her.'

Vicky could not speak. She took his hand and was smiling and crying at the same time. He wanted to tell her that the money had been given to him for her by her mother, her real mother. But it was better that she did not know.

Albert Mundy saw that his wife and daughter-in-law were also smiling, happy for her. It was a total betrayal. All of them were against him. Ever since she was born, he had wanted only the best for his grand-daughter. Now even she was turning against everything he believed in, turning to a life that could drag her down and destroy her. 'If she becomes an actress, she won't use my name. I won't allow it,' he said quietly. They all looked at him. 'And don't blame me. I won't be responsible for her any more. It's in her blood, I suppose, and has to come out. Just don't blame me, if she ends up like her mother.'

He swung his chair away from the table and pushed himself over to the fire, ignoring the protests of Peter and the sobbing of his wife and Vicky. They might have forgotten, but he never would. He had cut Letty out of his heart. Sooner than bear the pain again, he would do the same with his beloved grand-daughter, if she disobeyed him.

At that moment, the phone rang. Peter had had it put in after his father's stroke, in case of an emergency. Vicky could not stop crying and hurried out of the parlour. Rosie answered the telephone. She could hear nothing and passed it to Peter as he came to her. 'Hello?' he said. 'Market Wetherby four three eight.' There was still silence and he hung up. 'Something wrong with it,' he shrugged.

At the other end, in the bedroom of her hotel suite in London, Letty Mundy replaced the receiver.

She came back very infrequently to England, usually only passing through. This time, she had given way to impulse and found out the number of the shop from the operator. She had written it inside the lid of her make-up case, but had changed her mind about using it. This evening, packing to catch the late flight to New York, she had seen it again and could not resist dialling for an outside line and then the number.

She had recognized Rosie's voice, then Peter. In the background, there had been a sound like someone sobbing. Her mother? Had something happened? She nearly spoke, but too much water had flowed under the bridge. There was a whole ocean between her and Market Wetherby. If she had spoken, she had no idea what she would have said. It was a crazy thing to have done.

The impulse had come to her after seeing a photograph of Senator and Mrs Kiley on the front page of the *Evening News*, guests of honour last night at a reception at the US Embassy. The former Mrs Dereham, with her Yankee fancy man, as her father had always called him. How easy and good life was for the likes of Helen Dereham . . . Exactly how hard it could be, Letty had proved.

Leo had come to the door of the bedroom. He was looking impatiently at his watch. She closed the lid of the make-up case. 'All right, I'm coming,' she said.

# TWENTY-EIGHT

The four years following the election of 'fifty-six had been a hectic period for Jim, with his standing in his party and the country constantly rising. He was on several Senate Committees and much in demand as a speaker. The public responded to him and political commentators sought his views. He had made it a rule to leave his office door propped open, so that he would always be available to any of his constituents who wished to see him, to ask his help. It was a gesture adopted, with a fair amount of publicity, by Jack Kennedy, who considered him to be one of his most trusted friends and continually sought his advice, especially when making statements on foreign policy. As a result, Jim had little spare time and much of that was used up in answering letters and drafting speeches.

Helen found herself much on her own. She still had a great deal of entertaining to arrange on their behalf, which she enjoyed, and there were official functions to attend, but Jim and she seemed to have less and less opportunity to be alone, to relax together.

She often thought of Lorna Jane, and how sorry for her she had been, that Red had neglected her. She had been unable to stand the loneliness, particularly when her son went to the Academy, and Red had applied to be relieved of his Staff appointment and to return to more active duty. They were back in Japan. Helen heard from Lorna from time to time, sometimes just a note scribbled on the back of her Christmas card. Red would be unlikely to reach higher than Colonel now, but they seemed very happy.

Certainly, Helen could not call herself neglected. It was merely that she had to take second place to the pressures and demands of Jim's career. And unlike Lorna Jane she had her committee work and many friends. Yet she often had time on her hands. She would escape to the peace of the house on Nantucket, but even there, since old Doctor Slattery had died and his clinic had been taken over by the local authority, she found time weighing on her.

Also, although she would never admit it, she had become less fond of the Kennedys. She still liked Bobby, but her reservations about Jack had become stronger. If only half the stories of his compulsive womanizing were true, she was sorry for his young wife. Yet it was not that. The journalists' habit of inferring rivalry between the Kileys and Kennedys, politically and socially, continued and was still a joke between them. However, Helen was aware, although Jim ignored it, that others among Jack's friends and supporters took it more and more seriously. She was concerned about the effect it might have, because Jack was obviously now preparing himself to be a contender in the next presidential election. Every public and private statement was to that end.

'Why not?' Jim said, when she spoke of it to him. 'It doesn't mean that what he thinks and believes is any less sincere. As a politician, he has every right and need to court popularity.'

'But what if he stands in opposition to Adlai?' Helen asked.

Jim frowned, then shook his head. 'Only a fool would try to displace Adlai. He's the father of the party. And Jack's no fool.'

As the run up to the election began, Jim went to visit Adlai Stevenson to assure him of his backing, as always, and was shaken when Adlai told him in confidence that he would not be standing again. Having been defeated twice, and with a growing distaste for the rough and tumble of politics, he preferred to watch and advise from the sidelines.

'That might sound a bit like sour grapes,' Jim said.

'Then it will have to seem so,' Adlai said. 'My decision is irrevocable. I have thought about it long and deeply and there was none other I could make.'

Jim found it hard to grasp. If it were not for Adlai, he would not himself be a senator. He had sworn to work for this man, until he took his rightful place in the White House. For years he had seen that as essential for the future of America, as had every Democratic party worker. He argued, but it was too late. When Jim finally accepted that his friend would not be dissuaded, he asked him who, then, he would nominate to take his place.

'I couldn't do that,' Adlai told him. 'I couldn't endorse one man. As Helen once pointed out, very correctly, it would be seen as unfair to the others.'

'But if you had to, who would it be?'

Adlai thought. 'John F. Kennedy, I suppose. In spite of his religion, I think people would vote for him, and he would be the best man to unite the separate factions. Without unity of left and right, we have little hope of winning.'

'Then for God's sake, endorse him,' Jim urged, 'otherwise we'll end up helping Richard Nixon to the White House.' Adlai smiled, but Jim was serious. 'That's no possibility. It's a fact. This is no time to sit on the fence.'

Stevenson would not let himself be persuaded. With his legal mind, he saw scrupulous neutrality in the coming contest as the only fair course for him. 'I might endorse you,' he told Jim.

'That's not why I came here,' Jim said.

For the next four or five weeks, Jim travelled the country sounding out local views and voting intentions prior to the convention. Much of what he heard surprised him. Adlai, many people thought, was too cultivated and intellectual to understand and speak for the blue collar workers. They would welcome a change of candidate. Many thought that Jim had come to canvas for himself, and were sceptical when he denied it. One thing seemed clear, however. Attitudes had altered. Kennedy's religion was no longer considered a liability. The Catholic vote might even be valuable.

While Jim was away, Helen was left even more on her

own. She was surprised and pleased one day to receive a call from Charles Patterson, whose career she had followed with interest after his return to England. She had not seen him since then and, when he came to tea, could not observe the slightest change in him.

When she told him so, he smiled. 'I was about to say the same of you – except that you're even more beautiful than I remembered.'

It was true. In her late fifties, Helen had the grace and slim figure of a much younger woman. Her hair had only a faint dusting of grey and her unlined English complexion was widely envied.

She was used to compliments and accepted his lightly. He told her he was to be in the United States for a year. Partly based in Washington, partly in New York, he had been appointed as a kind of semi-official trade ambassador.

It was a long while since Helen found someone to whom she could talk so easily. They had a fairly similar background, and even discovered two mutual friends in England. For the first time in ages, she experienced in talking to him a longing to be back there, to spend more than a short visit, to be with her own people again. Some of what he told her puzzled her and she realized she was getting out of touch with England.

'I suppose I've been Americanized,' she laughed.

'Well, it would be my pleasure to re-indoctrinate you,' he said. 'After all, we don't want to lose you entirely.'

It was so enjoyable that he stayed much longer than he had meant and left with a promise to call her again soon. Two days later, he invited her to the lunch which he had promised her three years before, and, at the weekend, she went with him to a concert at the British Embassy. When he drove her home, she invited him in for a drink. She had expected Jim to be there, but he was still in Philadelphia. The conversation was light and pleasant as always, and he left after an hour, but Helen had reached a decision.

The lateness of the hour and their being alone together

had created a suggestion of intimacy. It was not that it displeased her. On the contrary, she had enjoyed it.

It was pleasing and warming to be with a highly attractive man who concentrated solely on her, whose interests were so similar and who reminded her of so much she had almost forgotten. She was aware that he also found her attractive and had not objected when he kissed her cheek on leaving. 'But it's got to stop there,' she told herself. She liked him and would have to stop seeing him, before she liked him even more. Before he, perhaps, began to think that something might come of it. She had no intention of ever being unfaithful to Jim.

When Jim returned to Washington, he went straight to a long-delayed meeting with Lyndon Johnson. The Senator from Texas was considered by many to be a redneck, simplistic cowboy, but Jim did not underestimate him. He knew Johnson to have one of the most acute political brains in the country, a shrewd manipulator, ruthless in using his connections, with a strong grip on a large section of the Democratic Party. He wanted, and needed, Johnson's support for JFK.

The trouble was that, within a few minutes, it became clear that Johnson had calculated the odds and saw that he had a better than fair chance of capturing the nomination for himself.

'You actually spoke to Adlai?' he queried. 'He's not playing hard to get, not playing hide and seek? You know – let's play hide and seek, and if you catch me, you can make love to me. And if you can't catch me, I'll be in the cupboard.'

Jim smiled. 'No, he's not being coy. Unfortunately, he really means it. So you know what that leaves us with.'

'Well now,' Johnson drawled, 'I admit that Senator Kennedy has gone a long way to reconcile Left and Right to him. He has a fine reputation in Civil Rights. Though so have you. And though I may say my standing on that issue, contrary to what is generally believed, is precisely the same as the both of you. Still, that could collar him a lot of votes.'

'There's no doubt.'

Johnson smiled. 'On the other hand, many folks think he is a young man in a hurry, a sight too ambitious. That could go against him.'

'Ambition is what takes men to the top, Lyndon,' Jim said. 'As for him being young, that's what we need now, to carry us into the 'sixties. I'd like you to back him. That is, unless you are thinking of standing yourself.'

Johnson had expected Jim to be blunt and was not thrown. He moved his heavy shoulders dismissively. 'As to that, I'm not so anxious. However, if there was a need for me, if my people called for me, I couldn't rightly refuse.'

'I appreciate your frankness,' Jim said.

'How about you? You could command a lot of support.'

Jim hesitated. 'I've thought about it. But I gave my word some time ago not to stand against Jack.' Johnson nodded, approving. 'I should tell you, quite a number of people are coming over to him, now that Adlai is definitely out.'

'Mh-hm.' Johnson nodded again, thinking. 'Now I'm not one to suggest that Senator Kennedy's religion would be any impediment.'

'It definitely wouldn't. Might even be an asset,' Jim told him.

'That's just what I reckon. Time all that prejudice was laid to rest. Lot of folks think so. Hell, he's not going to make the Pope Speaker of the Senate, is he?'

Jim smiled. 'So what's your decision?'

Johnson scratched his chin. 'Well, I'll tell you. There's one thing that makes me a might reluctant to come out for Senator Kennedy – and that is his health. I don't mean his back. Some people say he is suffering from Addison's Disease.'

'He explained that rumour,' Jim said. 'Because of fever he got during the war, his adrenal glands don't function properly. It's being treated.'

Johnson paused. 'Well, some people claim it's not just a rumour, and that he's being a touch less than honest about it. If that's so, with a disease like that, he just ought not to run for President.'

Jim smiled. 'Tell me, Lyndon,' he said casually, 'would you confirm to me something that went unreported at the time? That three months ago you had a heart attack?'

Johnson sat in silence, considering him. 'When you flew those B-17s during the war,' he said softly, 'I bet your bombs all hit the target.'

Helen had been at the house in Newport and went to New York in July for the meeting of the Committee on the Welfare of Ex-Servicemen's Dependents, while Jim headed for the convention in Los Angeles. It was left open whether she would join him there, because she knew from past experience that it would be noisy and argumentative and that she would only see him for brief moments.

On her second evening in Manhattan, she joined a group to go to the theatre. Among them, as a guest of one of her friends, was Charles Patterson. Neither had expected to meet the other. The trace of awkwardness between them gradually vanished at the theatre and during dinner, and afterwards he saw her home. 'You've been avoiding me,' he said.

Helen was disconcerted by his directness. 'Hardly that. I've been very busy and travelling.'

'You haven't answered either my phone calls or my letters,' he pointed out. 'And I can't believe it's because you don't really want to see me. Now, what that suggests is that you're afraid to. I don't think that's the best way to handle it. I suggest that we admit we like being together, and that we're both adult enough not to do anything foolish.'

Jim reached Los Angeles to find the convention in confusion. None of the possible candidates, Kennedy, Humphrey or Johnson, could command total support. The call was for Stevenson to change his mind and break the deadlock by putting himself forward. He was certain to be accepted by acclamation.

As a solution, it was heaven sent and Jim hurried to see Stevenson. They had several meetings at which everything seemed settled, then at the last minute he would raise more objections. Even when Jim pleaded with him either to accept nomination or to endorse one of the others, Stevenson could not decide. He was tempted by the crowd's adulation, by the huge cheering whenever he appeared, yet reluctant, nor could he bring himself to write himself completely out by nominating a successor. It was torture for Jim to watch one of his idols crumble, yet he finally realized that nothing was to be hoped for from him. There was no alternative, and he threw himself wholeheartedly into the Kennedy campaign.

Humphrey was fairly quickly disposed of, leaving Johnson, who hoped to split the support for Kennedy by still calling for Stevenson. Other minority candidates were suggested, and rejected. All attention was still on Adlai. There were rounds of feverish wheeling and dealing between Johnson and Kennedy backers, but when Jim finally convinced the Texan that Stevenson was a broken reed, there came the surprise announcement that Lyndon Johnson had agreed to run as Vice President to Kennedy. In the Los Angeles Coliseum, the cheers of the convention, though subdued, welcomed John F. Kennedy, the Democratic candidate in the presidential election, as he called to them to step forward with him to the new frontier.

Then the campaign began in earnest.

Helen had stayed longer in New York than she intended, meeting Charles nearly every day. He had come to visit her again in Washington and she told Jim she had invited him with some other friends to spend a weekend at Newport. 'Good,' Jim said. 'It'll be company for you.'

She felt strangely detached from the election, untouched by the mounting hysteria. Although she was always on hand when Jim needed her, she looked forward most to her time with Charles. They had become very close, and it was fun to see America again through his eyes. As the actual election day approached, she ran up to New York, ostensibly on business, actually to get away from the constant clamour of the Kennedy camp as the contest between Jack and Nixon reached its climax.

She had lunch with Charles and they spent the afternoon at the Metropolitan Museum and walking in Central Park. When he arrived to take her to dinner, she was wearing a new Givenchy evening dress, square cut at the neck, princess line with a slight flare in the skirt. It suited her figure to perfection. 'You look stunning,' he told her. 'I have a suggestion. Let's not go out after all.'

He was smiling, but serious, and Helen knew she was about to be kissed. She felt tense, and excited. She had no thought of stopping him and wondered what her reaction would be, as he came forward and took her in his arms. He kissed her.

It was the first time he had kissed her properly. And suddenly Helen knew that she had been dreadfully unfair to him. She loved being with him, yet she had been pretending to herself and to him. She had not fallen in love with him, and could never do so. She remembered the first time Jim had kissed her, late at night, outside the hospital at Market Wetherby. A kiss as unforeseen as this had been, yet the feeling she had then, the sense of oneness with him, had never left her. Charles's kiss had been pleasant, but meant nothing.

Jim was distracted from the celebrations on election night by Helen's non-return. He tried to reach her at New York, and Newport. He could not get through to Nantucket. He joined in the congratulations and the immediate discussions that followed Jack's narrow victory, all the time expecting Helen to appear.

The next morning, he flew to Hyannis Port, where Jack had asked him to join in the meetings with his closest aides. He found the President-elect surrounded, with Bobby beside him, grinning. 'It's a great day,' Jim said. He could not prevent himself thinking how fit and young Jack looked, a young pioneer, ready to cross that new frontier of his. He had not made the wrong choice.

'A lot of it thanks to you,' Jack pointed out, rising and clasping Jim's hand in both his. 'You know how grateful I am, Jim.' He hesitated. 'I'd like to offer you the post of Secretary of the Air.'

Jim saw that Jack was smiling and, behind him, Bobby's boyish grin was wider, yet there was an uneasiness in them. All at once he understood why.

Secretary of the Air was a leading post, influential and challenging, on the face of it very right for him. Yet throughout the campaign he had been widely tipped to be the next Secretary of State. Jack had even spoken of it as the one job already earmarked for him. That he should have changed his mind could only mean that someone in his entourage had finally convinced him that Jim was a potential rival, someone too powerful to risk giving him a key position through which he could promote himself and endanger Jack's re-election. He was no longer to be among those closest to the throne. Nor, in spite of his use, would he ever be allowed to be so again.

Jim found Helen, as he had expected, at Nantucket. She was not in the house, but walking on the beach, her hair tied back in a scarf, hands deep in the pockets of an old duffel coat. It was intensely cold, but neither of them noticed it as they stood looking at each other. 'I've been very stupid,' she said.

'So have I,' Jim nodded. He told her about the offer of a cabinet post, which Jack had pressed him to accept. 'I turned it down. In future, I don't want anything that takes me away from you,' he said. 'I suddenly realized that, without you, I have nothing.'

She caught her breath. He put his arm round her and she laid her head on his shoulder, crying silently as they walked slowly back to the house.

# TWENTY-NINE

Letty had begun to think of Mexico as a prison. It was as though, every time she was there, she could hear in her mind the metal doors slam shut, the bolts click home. What had once seemed like an exotic haven had become a desert. Although separated from it by electric fences, glass walls and air conditioning, she was only conscious of the heat and dust and dirt and the total indifference of the people to her. There was no one, no friend in whom she could confide or whom she could ask for help, not even for sympathy. Only acquaintances, half strangers, whose interest in her, in spite of their endearments and flattery, was as a possible source of introductions and favours, or money. The drifters and hangers-on, the beach bums of the film world.

The irony was that she knew many of them envied her. And perhaps they were right. Sometimes she told herself, who the hell am I to complain? I've got what I wanted. Nearly everything. As the man said, no use crying for the moon.

After the sudden death of Dean Saxon in the air crash at Mexico City, on the very day they were to announce their coming marriage, Letty had been stunned. It was a full day before she could even cry.

The producer, Hal Dwyer, and the director, Les Brewer, had not known of the planned wedding. Dean had wanted the announcement to be a surprise. They were sorry for her. Les, especially, was very gentle with her, but he had a commitment to finish the picture and Naomi Race, for whom she was doubling, was still hospitalized. He nursed her through the last ten days of shooting, kept at bay reporters who had heard of her involvement with the dead singing star and smuggled her away to an up country villa, when the filming was over.

In the weeks she spent at the villa, she realized how much she had really loved Dean. Les did not fully understand and sympathized with her when they read reports of the sale of Dean's house in Beverly Hills and his relatives squabbling over what was left of his personal fortune. For once, she had not wanted anything from a man, except to be with him.

To console her, Les repeated the offer he had made to give her a leading role in the sequel to the film they had just finished. She thought he was only being kind and was grateful. Short and balding, he was almost twice her age and treated her like a favourite daughter. She had told him her real name and something of her story. In return, he advised her to bury her past and stick to the name Dean had invented for her, Laraine Love. 'It sounds a little like a silent screen star, but so what? And listen, Laraine, I mean it. Hal and I think you have real talent. That's why we want you for the next picture.' When she was doubtful, still depressed, he said, 'You've got the looks. Leave the performance to me. I believe in you, and to prove it I'm prepared to sign you up, myself, personally. A straight seven year contract, no strings.'

Gradually, Letty came to understand that he was serious. She was used to men wanting to possess her, but it was not her body that interested Les. It was something indefinable which he was convinced he could turn into gold on the screen. Dean had said he was a brilliant director, and she had seen that for herself. The contract he offered was standard. He controlled all her appearances for two hundred dollars a week for the first year, rising to three thousand a week by the end. He could lease her services to other producers, but then kept whatever fee he had negotiated for her. His belief in her started Letty's recovery and she signed the contract with relief. For the first time in her life, she would be financially independent, her own mistress. It was welcome. She was thirty, but looked at least five years younger. Les had handed her a whole new life and career.

She tried to thank him in the only way she knew how. Wearing only the diaphanous lace négligée she had kept from her costumes in the film, she went to his room. She had never been in it before. It was littered with scripts and books in Czech and German. There were signed photographs from Conrad Veidt, Louise Brooks and Emil Jannings, ashtrays everywhere, filled with the stubs of his small black cigars. It smelt unaired, of Bourbon and sweat and tobacco smoke.

He was sitting on the floor, his back against the bed, dishevelled, and she saw that he was very drunk. He peered up at her outlined against the light from the door. 'Soft focus,' he slurred. 'Spotlight on the tits.' He shook his head. 'You see before you a fallen angel. Drunk and incapable. Temporarily drunk, permanently incapable. Play the music. End of story.'

It was only after she had signed the contract that she discovered why he had not gone back to Los Angeles, and why he left the dubbing and editing of the film to the producer, Dwyer. She had thought it was for her sake and, when he felt she was ready for it, he would take her there.

She got it out of him bit by bit.

His real name was Leonid Bremer, Leo. He had been a refugee from Czechoslovakia in the 'thirties and, under his real name, had written, then directed, a number of hard hitting, 'realistic' films in the manner of Fritz Lang, which had established his reputation. His more commercial, glossier films of the post war era had not been so critically successful and he was just returning to his earlier style, when the McCarthy witch hunts began. 'Sure, I was a Communist,' Leo confessed. 'I'd escaped from the Nazis and arrived in the States at the tail end of the Depression. And boy, was that depressing! What else was I gonna do? I joined the Party for maybe six months, and then I got the offer to write my first movie. So out went the politics and in came the camera angles. That's all there was to it!'

It was enough to hound him out of Hollywood with a couple of dozen others. And it was enough to keep him out, even though Joe McCarthy was discredited and dying. That was why he only made occasional films now, under pseudonyms like 'Les Brewer'. 'What's in a name?' he said, 'It's the style that counts. That's what sells my kind of movie.'

It was what sold *Temptation Summer*. The film on which Letty had worked became one of the unexpected smash hits of the year. Hal Dwyer obviously agreed that names were unimportant. He left Leo's off and billed himself as both producer and director. Leo was in no position to protest. There was no longer any question of him directing the sequel. 'What the Hell? I got paid,' he said.

Letty could not accept it so philosophically. It had also put an end to her hope of appearing in the film and Leo seemed to have no plans for any others. She felt guilty about accepting her contract salary, which he handed over religiously every month, but he laughed. He was a comparatively wealthy man and assured her he had got her cheap. He made no demands on her and she liked him, except when he got drunk and derided the whole world and her with it.

To pass the time, he worked on her voice and movement, directing her in imaginary scenes with improvised dialogue. He found a good local photographer and posed her for pin-up shots, some of which appeared in US men's magazines. She would not like her family to see some of them, but with her new name, the jet black, flicked up hairstyle he had created for her and her slimmer, more sensual look she was scarcely able to recognize herself. Some of the fan mail she received was sick.

After nearly a year came the breakthrough Leo had been waiting for and he took her to Tijuana to meet an American named Harry G. Rakhin. Rakhin was a thickset man in his fifties with blue jowls and heavy-lidded eyes. He made no secret that his money came from racketeers. With it he packaged films which made him and them considerable legitimate profits. He had seen many of Letty's photographs and wanted her to play the lead in a film he planned to make in Brazil. When he learned that any deal with her also included Leo, he made no objection. Leo would guarantee the project had class. Rakhin agreed to pay his fee, provided he still used a pseudonym.

When Letty read the script she was worried. The story was catchpenny, about a homicidal model who kills her lovers. There were several nude scenes. 'That's what adds the extra something,' Leo told her. 'Trust me. They've never seen anything like it in the States, not since Hedy Lamarr in *Extase*, way back then. It'll cause a sensation.'

Letty could only go along with it. And as always, he was right. The film shot in and around Rio was fun to work on. He directed it with style and wit, handling the nude scenes tastefully so that little was really seen and getting Letty to overact the turgid lines, so that everyone could tell they were not meant to be taken seriously. There was only one jarring moment, when she nearly began an affair with her leading man. Leo marched into her dressing room, furious. 'Not on my time!' he shouted. 'You want a boyfriend? Okay. But not on my time!'

He had learned his lesson and edited the film, *Killer Doll*, himself, adding catchy Latin-American music.

At a sneak preview in Rio it was hugely enjoyed as a comedy thriller and Letty was fêted. She returned to Mexico with Leo, excited, to wait for its impact in the United States.

They were shocked when they read that it was impounded at the border by US Customs as 'offensive to public decency and morality'.

Very soon, pirated copies were circulating. Leo bought one and they watched it together, horrified to discover that Rakhin had re-edited it. Just as Letty had doubled for Naomi Race in *Temptation Summer*, a double had been brought in for her. The nude scenes were made much more explicit and several added which were just short of pornographic. Other key scenes were cut to keep the running time. It altered the whole nature and balance of the picture and Letty's deliberate facial reactions and overemphasis now looked like ludicrously bad acting. Leo tore the film from its reels and set fire to it.

The worst of it was that *Killer Doll* became an underground hit wherever it was banned and brought huge returns for Rakhin from other areas, Latin America, Italy and South-East Asia.

Letty had never achieved her ambition of living in America. She had only been there for a week with Dean and Leo refused to spend more than a night or two when absolutely forced in the country that had rejected his work. She made up for it by watching American television and soon found herself, as Laraine Love, a popular joke. Of any sexy female, 'she's as choosy as Laraine Love' was sure to get a laugh. Once on a talk show she heard her name mentioned and the audience roared at the comedian's follow-up. 'Laraine Love? That's Spanish for Mae West.'

She had other offers for films, many of them, but each was more exploitative and explicit than the last. It hurt her. Its effect on Leo was more destructive. He renounced film-making entirely and his drinking, which had been an occasional over-indulgence, became a problem. That was when Letty learned what it meant to be under exclusive contract. For the monthly payments he owned her body and soul, legally.

He became jealous and suspicious, keeping her near him, spying on her constantly. She could have run away, broken the contract, but she was afraid of being alone. As Laraine Love, there was only one direction in which she could go.

They lived partly in Mexico, partly in his villa on the backwater island of Andros in the Cyclades, an ageing drunk and his beautiful platonic companion. Another joke.

The evening when she had telephoned Market Wetherby, they were leaving for Heathrow. Out of the blue, Leo had been invited to Vancouver to talk to film students about his early Hollywood successes. He had seized the unexpected opportunity, but had realized that to arrive with Letty in tow would damage his status, if she was recognized. She did not object to being left in New York. In fact, she welcomed it. It was a chance she had been hoping for.

One thing she had always kept with her was a packet of letters forwarded to her years before by her brother, Peter. They were to him from Chuck and Elmer and Hymie and he had thought they might interest her. She had kept them as a last link with the dead Lt Harvey Wallis, her first love. She looked up Elmer's address in Yonkers and called him. He was still at the same place, his uncle's cigar store, and was astonished to hear from her. She invited him to her hotel.

Elmer Jones could not get over the voice from the past. The hotel was uptown and very swanky. When he reached her room, he had to confess he would never have known the svelte, sophisticated woman who opened the door to be the Letty Mundy he remembered. Letty was pleased, as it meant he also did not know 'Laraine Love'. He was exactly the same, plump and smooth-faced, perhaps with a few more lines round the eyes, just as friendly and as gentlemanly as ever. 'I can't get over it,' he kept saying. 'Little Letty? It's not possible!'

'Do you still play the mouth organ?' she asked him.

He grinned. 'Fancy you remembering . . . No, I don't have much time any more. I'm kept pretty busy in the store.' She had mixed a very dry Martini, filled his glass and sat him down. 'Tell me, do you ever hear from them – Peter and Rosie?' he asked eagerly. 'I guess I don't have to tell you. I was pretty stuck on Rosie, thought I'd never get over her.'

'Yes, I knew that,' Letty said. 'I can confess it now, it used to upset me. I was very keen on you, myself.'

Elmer blinked. 'Gosh . . . I mean, for real? I didn't know that. I mean – it just never occurred to me.' He looked at the attractive woman sitting opposite him, the dark, silky dress clinging to the sleek lines of her figure and almost blushed.

Letty smiled. It would be even easier than she had thought. She had decided to break with Leo and to remain in America. She had only ever had a temporary visitor's visa, so the only way to achieve what she wanted was to marry an American. Who it was did not matter, as long as he was passable. Elmer would do as well as anyone. She would be good to him. All she wanted was a quiet life, where she could disappear. Another change of hairstyle would manage it.

'My wife'll never believe it, when I tell her,' he said.

Letty was motionless. 'Your wife?'

'Yes, you wouldn't think anyone would have me, but I'm married now,' he chuckled. 'And we have a son, Jamie. Poor kid looks like me, they say.'

Letty poured him another drink, chatted to him about Chuck and Hymie and their wives and families and saw him to the door.

He could never really work out why he had been invited. But he kept the promise she got him to make before he left. He never told anyone he had met her, not his wife, not Peter and Rosie, and not even Hymie.

It was three years before Letty was in London again. She was still with Leo, but it was in very different circumstances. The fascination of the French New Wave critics with the films of the 'thirties included his, which were considered master-pieces of socio-realism. Few serious film societies got through a whole season without representative works of Bremer, Lang or Lubitsch. He was in demand as a speaker and as a judge at Cannes. The American Academy had presented him with a retrospective award for lifetime achievement. It had nearly come too late. He was not drink-ing so much, but the damage had been done. In his sixties, he looked considerably older. 'Appearance doesn't matter so much to me any more,' he had told Letty in the summer. 'The doctors tell me I have less than a year to live.'

It was said so casually that it shocked her. In spite of everything she had grown fond of him and dependent upon him. 'Our contract's nearly up, Laraine,' he said. 'It's a question whether it or I will run out first. Now, I know I haven't been fair to you. I've been selfish and possessive. You've had one or two affairs, of course. Don't bother to deny it. The point is I want to make it up to you.' He paused. 'I'll leave you what's left of my money. Not as much as there was, I'm afraid, but I'd like to leave you something that might be even more useful to you – my name.'

They were married quietly in Mexico and it was as Mrs Bremer that Letty attended with him the opening night of a season of his films at the National Film Theatre. At the party afterwards there were several old friends and much of the showbusiness establishment. It was very enjoyable and Leo was in fine form.

As she looked round the room, Letty saw a girl smiling, talking to two men who clearly admired her, and caught her breath. It was uncanny. She was looking at the image of herself twenty years ago. 'Who's that?' she asked her companion, a young actor. 'Over there?' he queried. 'Oh, that's Vicky Blair. She's all the rage at the moment. She's in a BBC series, about three girlfriends, one's a nurse, one's a law student, and the other's a musician. She plays the nurse. And she's sensational.'

When Letty finally met Vicky Blair, she was introduced as Mrs Bremer, 'formerly Laraine Love'. Vicky had heard of her vaguely as an actress, and complimented her on her husband's films. 'At least, the ones I've been able to catch,' she smiled.

'I must try to catch your series,' Letty said. 'Is it the first thing you've done?'

'The first thing on the box,' Vicky told her. 'But I've had three hard years in rep. Doing everything from painting the scenery to playing the pantomime cat. And that was the week after Ophelia.'

They laughed.

'Is Vicky Blair your real name?' Letty asked.

'Well, half of it is. It's actually Victoria Mundy.' She shrugged. 'But I had to change it.'

Letty felt almost light-headed. She had been unwilling to admit to herself that she might be talking to her own daughter. The physical resemblance had only suggested the possibility. And the girl's voice had no trace of an East Anglian accent, as she had once had. That was ridiculous. If she could change her accent completely, so could her daughter. Her daughter . . .

'Excuse me,' Vicky said, hesitantly. 'Are you all right?'

Letty had not realized she had been silent for so long. She made herself smile. 'I'd hardly any dinner. I'd better go easy on this champagne.' She put down her glass. Vicky was looking round, fascinated by all the celebrities present. 'You'll get used to this sort of thing,' Letty assured her. 'You mentioned you had to change your name. Was that because the new one sounded better or . . . was there opposition?'

Vicky was surprised by the question. 'No, most of my family have been very supportive – except for one. My grandfather.'

'He objected to you going on the stage?'

Vicky laughed. 'Objected is far too mild. He refused to speak to me for the first year. After that, it was only hello, how are you? and goodbye. I think he thought I'd automatically become a fallen woman. He was probably disappointed I didn't.'

'Yes,' Letty said, very quietly.

'Fortunately, my grandmother got him to watch the series, when it started. And it completely brought him round. He couldn't stop raving about it. He hated using the phone, but he kept ringing people up just to tell them to watch.'

'He must be very proud of you,' Letty said.

Vicky frowned. 'He was. But he died a month ago.'

Letty wished she had not put down her drink. Even after so long a break, the news was strangely upsetting. 'I'm sorry to hear that.'

'Oh, he was really quite old.' Vicky shrugged. 'He'd been in a wheelchair for a long time. He'd had a stroke. I try to remember him as he was, when I was a child. I loved him very much.'

'I can see that,' Letty said. She hesitated, but could not resist it. 'The rest of your family must be proud of you, too. Your mother.'

'I don't have a mother,' Vicky said shortly. 'She died when I was very small.'

There was a silence. Letty was saved, as Leo came bustling up, demanding to be introduced. 'You're monopolizing this young lady. I know why. You don't want me to get my old goat's eyes on her.' Vicky laughed, liking him. He examined her critically. 'I can see why my wife's taken a fancy to you. You have quite a resemblance to her, Miss Blair, about the time we made our first movie together.'

Vicky smiled politely to Letty, but turned back to Leo who was more immediately interesting, and might be useful.

Letty watched them as they talked about his films. She was torn by emotions, mainly by sheer surprise at the meeting. Then disbelief that she could have a grown-up daughter. And pride. Vicky had achieved what she had always wanted to do, and had done it on her own. In spite of her grandfather's opposition, and Letty knew how fierce that could be. She wanted to say to her, 'Don't talk to him. Look at me! Don't you know who I am?' But there was no way she could say it. Perhaps Vicky would not even accept the truth, would feel it was too late.

As Letty watched her later, circulating, charming the people she met, she was touched by her youth, and the inexperience she concealed so well with a controlled poise. She desperately wanted to help her, somehow. Perhaps if she did, if she really helped her, she could win her gratitude even friendship. That might be enough.

Perhaps one day she could arrange to meet her with Peter. Or her mother, Vera . . . It was a fantasy. A plot out of one of those old movies they all raved about.

Yet she could do something, she realized. She was talking to Chesney Ekhardt, whom she had known for years. For a short period, quite intimately. He was a producer, noted for his remakes of old favourites. They did not always match the originals, but they were good showcases. He had been speaking about one the other night. 'Ches,' she said, 'I'm going to do you a favour. That remake of *The Constant Nymph* you were on about. I've found just the girl for you. Over there – Vicky Blair.'

Ekhardt looked and nodded. 'Uh-huh. Will I like her?'

'I guarantee it,' Letty promised. 'She's a wonderful actress. A delightful girl – you couldn't find anyone better.'

The next day, Letty was as stunned as everyone else by the news of John F. Kennedy's assassination. As she sat in the evening with Leo, watching the newscasts and tributes, the

313

telephone rang. A voice asked, 'Is that Mrs Bremer? Or Miss Love? I don't know what to call you.'

It was Vicky and Letty, recognizing her, felt the first lifting of the spirits she had had all day. 'It doesn't matter. Either,' she said. 'Did you go to see Ches Ekhardt?'

'Yes I went to his office – as you suggested.'

'Good,' Letty smiled. 'I hope everything worked out all right?'

'Perhaps not from his point of view,' Vicky said. Her voice sounded strained. 'I didn't know people had buttons that could lock the door of their offices by remote control. It took me some time to get out.'

'I don't understand,' Letty said. 'Why did you want to?'

'Perhaps you wouldn't have. But I'm sure what he asked me to do isn't covered by any Equity contract.' Vicky was trying to sound nonchalant. 'He got quite annoyed when I refused. Quite physically annoyed. I have the bruises to remember it by. You must have known what the score was, he said, when Laraine sent you here. She wouldn't recommend a schoolgirl.'

'I – I had no idea,' Letty faltered. 'I'm sorry.'

'No, I'm the one who's sorry,' Vicky said, flatly. 'I didn't recognize you, you see. I didn't realize you were *that* Laraine Love.' She rang off.

Leo had not been listening. He glanced over from the television set and saw that Letty was crying. She was not American. She had never even lived in the States. It was shattering news, but he could not realize why she should cry so much for JFK.

# THIRTY

Nineteen Sixty Three was a watershed year for Hymie Stutz. It was the year he expanded his business and became, in Milwaukee terms, one of those guys whose fortunes were inexorably on the up.

He had a devoted, faithful and talented wife and two great kids. And everything, more than he had ever wanted out of life. Lots of guys like him had never made it home. They'd coughed their guts out in some makeshift, Quonset medical hut, been posted MIA, Missing In Action, or fried to a crisp over Germany. Others had taken years to settle down again. He'd known how he was going to handle civilian life from the start. A hard slog, sure. So what? It had brought nothing but contentment.

But it was a time of sorrow for Elmer Jones. Early that summer, his gentle wife, Shirley, had died, leaving him to raise in New York a twelve-year-old son, Jamie, his absolute image, right down to the fair wavy hair and dimple. Elmer had found total happiness and understanding with Shirley. And now he was lost.

Hymie and Elmer had scarcely seen each other since their days in the 525th at Market Wetherby. Hymie was intent on building up his business and Elmer had somehow kept putting off the phone calls, the letters and the visits to his friend. There had been no lack of invitations. He'd heard Hymie was doing well, how he'd opened a number of hamburger joints after the first prospered, how he'd married that fat friend of Rosie's, and if he questioned himself closely, he realized that it was his own lack of success that had kept them apart. They exchanged cards each Christmas, and they had met briefly once in a bar off Times Square, when Hymie was in the city to meet Jilly Binns, the girl who had sailed the Atlantic to marry him.

But Shirley's sudden death from cancer had altered everything. Elmer had never known her family well. He needed someone to talk to, someone from the old days. His uncle, who owned the cigar store in Yonkers which he managed, had never been a great one for advice, unless it was of the financial kind. Uncle Ben wasn't one for displays of emotion. So Elmer, in desperation, had called Milwaukee long distance, and told Hymie the grim news. Hymie had urged him to visit, and now, in November, he had left his son with his uncle's family for a few days, and was on his way to Milwaukee.

Hymie watched Elmer Jones flat foot across the apron at the city airport. As the portly figure drew near, Hymie could make out the dimple, still dominant, despite the double chins. Elmer, he could see, wasn't smiling.

'See that, Jilly,' he sighed. 'That's how Elmer always looked, back in 'forty-three. Just like he's come off a bad raid.'

'He has in a way,' she replied. 'Now it's up to you to help him get over it. You did it during the war. You can do it again.'

Hymie shrugged. Maybe a trip to Milwaukee would help Elmer get over his troubles, but if he was in that same position, say, if Jilly had died, Heaven forbid, he'd have chosen Miami. But then he wasn't Elmer Jones. No, sir, he'd always seen a way round problems, milked an opportunity, backed a hunch, and that's how he'd got big in burgers.

But Elmer . . . Elmer was a dreamer. The train would have pulled out of Grand Central Station before Elmer would have even considered getting on. When the war ended and the boys had come home, they'd all known they had to start over. Of course, it hadn't been easy. He'd got a disability grant from the government on account of his two lost fingers and he'd invested that money wisely. Yes, sir, hadn't he? His parents had said he was foolish throwing it away on a passage from England for some girl he'd hardly known. And how would girls like her settle in

Milwaukee with its big city sophistication? She probably wouldn't be able even to speak their kind of language. But Hymie knew he was doing right, and now, he was the one who was laughing, the only Stutz in his family who owned not one, not two, but three fast food businesses in the city, and he was a member of the Elks. Boy, had he been right.

Of course, there was some truth in what Hymie's parents had said. Market Wetherby certainly wasn't Milwaukee. And the Americans there did speak a different kind of language. At first Jilly found it difficult making her Suffolk accent understood. In shops, in diners, in stores, even at the movies, she had without fail to repeat her request. But always, at the moment of exasperation, that special smile would emerge and somehow it didn't matter any more. Americans took to her. Hymie's parents were dazzled. She was no beauty, they agreed, but then neither was their son. But the English girl displayed a certain charm, a delightful manner, and above all, common sense. It was odd, Jilly always said, she had made more friends in Milwaukee than ever she had in Market Wetherby.

When the baby came, almost nine months to the day of the marriage, Hymie's mother had to count off the months and tick off the days before she could really allow herself a smile.

As Hymie's business grew, so Jilly's talents as housewife and business partner burgeoned. It was to her that he'd come for advice. If he was worried about overstretching his reserves, then Jilly would supply the solution. The chemistry of British common sense and American drive clicked. And Hymie never forgot it.

As the children grew – when their daughter was born, Hymie's mother didn't bother to count – Jilly took more part in local neighbourhood affairs. She was on the committee of the PTA at the children's junior school, and lately had attended evening classes so she could obtain her cookery diploma. Now the children were almost off her hands, she intended to teach evenings. The subject, cookery, of course.

She'd never been a keen writer of letters, but she and Rosie had kept in touch. She had read of Rosie's wedding in the Market Wetherby rag which her mother had sent over for the first few years she was in the States. She'd been surprised at Letty turning up at the wedding, but Jilly had never been that curious a girl. Her life was in Milwaukee. Not Market Wetherby. Of course, Vi Ericson wrote her once a year with news from home, mainly passed on by Sally and Joe McGraw. But apart from that, her roots were in America. Her children were American, as American as blueberry pie. Her son, she knew, might even be drafted for this Vietnam thing. But she wasn't worried. It would all blow over soon enough.

The others in 'Ginger Rogers" crew had worked to get somewhere, too. Chuck Ericson, of course, had become a dentist. And Ben Kulik, although he'd lost most of an arm, was vice president of some electronics corporation in Grand Rapids.

Red Burwash had stayed in the Air Force, picked up a raft of medals in Korea, and was top brass now. Hymie had read of Burwash's posting to Saigon only that week. Heaven help the Cong, when Red got there!

All the guys were specially proud of their former Air Exec, later CO, Jim Kiley. There'd been the Congressional Medal, of course. Next Hymie had heard of him was in 1954, before he became junior Senator for Massachusetts. When his friend John F. Kennedy was prevented by his back illness from speaking in condemnation of the anti-Communist witch hunts of Joe McCarthy, Kiley made the speech he should have given. Watching the televised scenes of JFK's Presidential Inauguration Ball, Hymie had stood up and cheered when he saw Jim dancing with Jacqueline and the President with Jim's beautiful wife, Helen. 'I didn't used to go for him much. He seemed kinda square,' Hymie admitted. 'But he's a great guy. JFK and him are the tops.'

But Elmer Jones, poor ole Elmer Jones, that guy had problems. Elmer needed a break. His wife had died kind of sudden and there was the boy to look after. Hymie sighed. Poor kid . . .

Elmer dropped his suitcase and shook hands with Hymie, clapping him on the back. For a moment, he was so delighted to see him that he had forgotten his troubles. He smiled to Jilly and impulsively hugged her.

'Gee, you haven't changed, Hymie! Maybe a bit more fur on your lip.'

'And a bit more spread round the waist,' Hymie laughed.

'And Jilly, you look just like you used to, sitting in The Plough.'

Jilly smiled. 'I never thought you noticed me. You were always looking at Rosie.'

Hymie cut her off and led them to the white convertible.

'Boy, you got yourself a class car there, Hymie.'

'Hymie always wanted a sporty one. Now the kids are grown, I told him to go ahead and buy whatever he fancied.'

Hymie laughed. 'I always do as the little lady says, Elmer. Then I don't go wrong.'

It was a fair drive from the airport to the Stutz's house. They chatted to Elmer about their children. The boy had left school and now, at seventeen, he was working in the business. 'Give him five years learning and I might make him a partner,' Hymie said. Their daughter was still at school in the fourth grade. She possessed the brains of the family and, like her mother, that warm smile that instantly put all at ease.

'You got it made, Hymie. A good business, a great home, the car you've always wanted, no trouble with the kids, and what a little cook Jilly has turned out to be.' He helped himself to more buckwheat cakes and sipped the Slitz beer.

'You're a little off beam there, Elmer. Jilly never turned out to be anything. The kid always was hot with food. I guess it was those lousy rations in England that did it. She could feed a king from a garbage can, even in those days.'

'You always said so,' Elmer nodded.

'It was Jilly here who gave me the idea of going into hamburgers. It must have been when you were shot down . . . sometime before VE day anyway. I went round to her place and she served me something she called rissoles, bits of meat and potato. Delicious. Straightaway I knew what I was going to do when I returned to Milwaukee.'

'Never mind him, Elmer. He's always telling that story. If I've heard it once, I've heard it a million times.' She laughed. 'Go on, Elmer, have another beer.'

Elmer helped himself, and looked round the room. It was comfortable and modern. There was a colour TV set, a stereo, and framed photos everywhere. Hymie and Jilly cutting a red tape to open Ginger's Palace, the newest of his establishments. Their son in his high school football strip. Their daughter in the school orchestra, complete with violin. This was a home, lived in and comforting, something he did not possess any longer in New York.

He sipped at his beer, unloosened his tie and thought of Hymie's success and all that he, Elmer Jones, had failed at. His accountancy exams, the qualification he had studied for as the war drew to a close, he'd never got through them. Learning had not come easy and after three years in England, he just hadn't been able to cope with study.

Every year he'd enter the exams. It was a ritual. Every year he'd flunk them. While he was studying his uncle had given him work, on a temporary basis until he'd passed his exams. The job was in his uncle's cigar store, and despite his lack of success in exams, enough accountancy practice had seeped into Elmer for him to manage the books successfully. In fact, he was pretty useful there and his uncle had, as time went on, gradually allowed him more responsibility. When the old man went away on vacation, Elmer minded the store. When the old man was ill with pneumonia in the winter of 'fifty-one, it was Elmer who unravelled all the secrets of his uncle's finances. By the time he'd recovered, chaos had been translated into order.

The shop prospered and so did Elmer's confidence. He began dating. Her name was Shirley, dark haired, trim with shapely legs. She worked in the neighbourhood diner, the one where Elmer regularly took his lunch.

He knew what had attracted him to her. The first day he'd seen her behind the counter of the diner, he'd frozen. There was a girl, smiling to a customer, making a joke, winking at another guy sitting along the bar. He couldn't believe his eyes. Only this wasn't England, wasn't The Plough, and she wasn't Rosie Blair.

They dated through 'forty-eight and 'forty-nine and in the following year they married. Shirley continued to serve at the diner until she was expecting Jamie, and after a particularly distressing labour – the baby was delivered by caesarian section – she stayed at home. He was called after Hymie, but Jamie was the closest Shirley would allow. After all, as she said, Hymie Jones didn't sound quite Kosher.

Now, after thirteen years, Shirley was gone, and Jamie, just starting high school, was being looked after by an old, irascible uncle and a dreamy father . . .

'C'mon, Elmer, we're going out. I'll take you down town. Jilly, don't wait up for us.'

'You don't have to tell me,' she smiled.

The two men climbed into the convertible and followed the road into the city centre. Hymie pulled up outside a bar called Hermann's. They sat at the counter and ordered a couple of cold beers. Elmer felt less tense now he was away from Jilly. She reminded him of the old days. He saw his years in Market Wetherby increasingly as the good times in his life. He'd put to the back of his mind the operations, the tours, the constant anxiety, those days he'd scoured the sky till his eyeballs ached, waiting for the Luftwaffe to intercept. He remembered the good things, the warm beer, watching Bing Crosby at the Roxy with Rosie by his side, Al Jolson giving a concert in the base, leave in London . . . but most of all he remembered Rosie Blair.

If only he'd gone back after the war. Maybe he should have written off the accountancy career before the exams had written him off. Life would have been different in Market Wetherby. Even old Mundy, what was his name? What the hell, it didn't matter, even old Mundy was showing signs of accepting the Yanks. Life would have been lived at a slower pace. Maybe he'd have married Rosie and taken over at The Plough. As a dream, that was a dilly.

'Hymie,' he said, 'you know, my biggest mistake.' Hymie shook his head. 'I should have gone back to England. Back there . . . I kind of fitted that style of life. Nice 'n' easy, nice 'n' slow.'

'Joe McGraw went back there. He's still there. Got a garage. But you, Elmer, back in England? Forget it. It was different then. You wore a uniform. You were a somebody. In civvies, kid, you'd have been a nothing.'

'What's Rosie doing, Hymie?'

'Forget her. It was a long time ago and a lot of nonsense. That poor kid had a rough time, don't you know it?'

He filled up his glass and they talked about Danny Coogan and his nurse, and Rosie's grief at Danny's death.

'So she married young Peter, did she? Well, I guess it's all worked out well for her,' said Elmer.

A crowd of strangers had bustled into the bar, surging up to the counter and surrounding the two friends. As Hymie raised his glass, one of them jostled his arm accidentally and beer slopped from it. 'Watch it, buster,' Hymie warned. 'This is a hundred and fifty buck suit.'

'*Entschuldigen Sie, bitte*,' the man said, and turned away.

Hymie stared at the stranger's back. 'He's a Kraut,' he muttered, and repeated it to Elmer, 'a Kraut.'

'So what?' Elmer shrugged. 'So are you.'

'Thanks to my grandfather,' Hymie admitted. 'Up till Hitler we were German-American. Since then we've been all-American.' He looked back at the German, a middle-aged tourist drinking with American friends. Hymie had been drinking fairly steadily ever since Elmer landed and the accent of the man who had jostled him grated on him. It reminded him of wartime movies, with the Nazis shooting down refugees and torturing Resistance fighters. 'A Kraut – comes here on holiday! Is that what we fought the war for?'

He had spoken loudly enough for the group to hear him. The German stood absolutely still, but his friends turned round angrily. 'Button your lip, shorty,' one of them said.

Hymie's aggressive instincts were aroused. 'What was that?' he demanded. 'Would you care to belch that again?'

Elmer knew the signs and tried to pour oil on stormy waters as he had done a hundred times in the past. 'It's nothing,' he said soothingly. 'Just a misunderstanding.'

'Like Hell!' Hymie insisted. 'I just want to know if now we're supposed to forget what we were fighting for?'

'It's easy for loudmouths like you to talk,' one of the men sneered. 'With a hand like that, you were never in the war.'

'Oh, yeah?' Hymie said, brandishing his hand so they all could see it. 'Where d'you think I got this? Lemme tell you. At thirty thousand feet over Stuttgart.'

The Americans were silent, a little embarrassed, but the German tourist was looking at Hymie with interest. 'You were in the US Air Force?' he asked. 'In Europe?'

'We both were,' Hymie told him, indicating Elmer.

'An honour to meet you,' the man said. 'I was in the Luftwaffe. I learnt my English in a prisoner of war camp in Wales. I was shot down in 1944. I flew Junkers 87s.'

'US Eighth Air Force. 525th Bomb Group. Name's Stutz, Sgt Hymie Stutz, and this here's my mid-section gunner, Sgt Elmer Jones.'

The German saluted humorously. 'It's a long time ago for all of us,' he said, and bought them a drink. He was, he explained, on vacation, staying with relations in Milwaukee. They got to buying more drinks, forgetting the civilians he had come in with, and, of course, the talk returned to the war.

'I never thought I'd actually live to buy one of you guys a drink,' Hymie said, ruefully.

The German smiled. 'We were as determined to get you as you were to get us. We got up to some tricks. We had you Americans fooled. I remember once, I think it was early 'forty-four, we were ordered to dress up our Junkers in American markings. The same camouflage paint, the star, the lot. They even modified our Junkers so it would look at speed and a distance like one of your fighters. We didn't want to go through with it . . . it's not war, but we had to. We cut down the B-17s like cheese wire going through butter. It's not something I'm proud of, *verstehen Sie*.'

'Meet the guys in those Forts. Boy, that was some trick. You sure caught us on the hop. But it only worked on our outfit the once. After that, we had you figured out,' Hymie said, and they laughed, forgetting the pain and blood, and the fear, remembering only the excitement and that they had been young.

It was almost twenty years ago, and in this German-American city, there was no bitterness now. In this bar, Hermann's, they exchanged their memories, beer for beer, until the small hours.

Back home, with Jilly in bed, Hymie and Elmer took a nightcap. Hymie was more than half drunk, but not fuddled, and he had been thinking.

'Elmer, I've got a deal to make . . . now hear me out. I know life's been bum to you and more bum than usual of late. I never met Shirley, but if she was anything like Jilly, I can guess how you're feeling. Look, buddy, my burger joints are doing okay. This year's been my best. I've been able to raise money to open Ginger's Palace, and that place sure is something. Tomorrow we'll go round and look it over.' He hesitated. 'What I'm offering is a partnership for you. Move to Milwaukee. The kid will love it. The schools are good. There's no trouble with minorities – you know what I mean? – and there's the Slitz. What more can you ask?'

Elmer was touched, and tempted. He'd think it over. It could be the break he was looking for. Of course, this would have to be strictly business, he insisted. There was no place for sentiment. 'I couldn't accept if I thought you just felt sorry for me,' he explained.

'Whaddya talking about, Fatso?' Hymie said gruffly. 'This is business.' He punched Elmer on the shoulder, harder than he had meant.

The next morning, Elmer and Hymie and Jilly would never forget, like millions of fellow Americans and many others all over the world. The two friends woke late after a night when each had crammed more beer than he had for years. They ate a late breakfast, reacting with only a grunt to the news on the radio that the Governor of Texas had been gunned down in Dallas. When they realized some time later that the President had been shot in the same cavalcade, they were stunned. 'It can't be true,' Jilly protested. Not JFK . . . He was their generation, the future, the brave new world.

For hours the bulletins were confused, and contradictory. Yet at last it was confirmed. JFK was dead . . . dead of an assassin's bullet in Dallas. They followed the newscasts all through the day and into the night, when Elmer announced he would be leaving for New York. It was time to take stock, to be in one's own home.

'Better get back and see Jamie. Uncle Ben will be worrying, and at his age running the store and looking after a kid is just a bit too much.'

They drove to the airport in silence. Jilly had stayed at home. Hymie's offer was never mentioned. Elmer knew it was still there, but doubted that he would accept. It wouldn't be fair on Hymie's son. Still, it was kind of nice it had been made.

As he dozed in the warmth of the aircraft taking him to La Guardia airport, Elmer knew Hymie had also been right about England. 'I'd never have fitted in there,' he thought. 'OK, so I wore a uniform and felt like a hero because I was aircrew. But take me out of a flying suit, and I was nothing.'

The past had got him fooled. It was last night's beer. He shivered, sitting there in the Boeing, as he suddenly conjured in his mind the inside of a B-17. All at once, he was disoriented, clinging to the armrests. Where was his oxygen mask, his 'chute? Drops of sweat studded his forehead as he heard the explosions of ghostly flak. He made himself peer through the window and saw ahead the Manhattan skyline, lit up and dynamically intact, not the shattered ruins of Cologne or Berlin. Gradually, his panted breathing slowed again.

Maybe he'd be better off forgetting those dreams and sticking to the cigar store in Yonkers.

The plane bumped along the runway. It stopped. The engines shut off. Elmer got up from his seat and breathed out. Another mission was over.

# THIRTY-ONE

It was two years after her first meeting with Vicky before Letty returned to London.

Leo had cheated the doctors. He was still alive, although very frail. They had had to give up the villa on Andros, as medical facilities on the island were so inadequate. If he needed urgent attention, it meant a helicopter coming all the way from mainland Greece to fetch him. They had had one scare and that was enough.

Letty had flown with him in the Sikorsky to Athens, then had been pushed aside to wait, while he was rushed into Intensive Care. After fourteen hours, she had insisted on seeing him and found him alone, except for an Orthodox nun muttering prayers. 'Nothing to be done,' the doctors explained. 'Only we wait.' Leo was in a coma and shook them by coming out of it. The sight of the nun and her obvious amazement at his recovery had nearly been enough to give him a relapse.

'I hate to disappoint you,' he whispered. 'But I think I'm going to live.'

Mexico was little better. He was prostrated by the heat and, again, a helicopter would be needed to carry him to the nearest hospital, if he collapsed. Either that or a three hour drive on jolting dirt roads. They decided not to wait until there was another emergency. 'I'm ready to meet my Maker,' Leo said, 'but not in any great hurry.'

He would not die in America, since they had prevented him for so long from living there. The only sensible alternative was London, although Letty was worried about the effect of its damp and variable climate on him. She had nothing to fear any more from the Klynes. Max had died in a car accident, shortly after Alfie had been knifed to death. No trace of that part of her life remained.

They did not go to a hotel, but took a luxuriously furnished service apartment just off the Brompton Road, complete with maid. Because of delays in waiting for taxis, they hired a chauffeur-driven Daimler. 'On a weekly basis,' Leo insisted. 'I don't want to tempt fate or anything.' He joked about it, but Letty knew he was troubled by how the inflation of recent years had eaten into his savings. It was not that the money would run out, but he was anxious to leave her provided for. She told him it did not matter, that she had banked the salary he had paid her during the seven years of their contract. She had more than enough to cover her needs. 'That's not the point,' he kept muttering. 'Not the point.'

She understood. Although he had never made love to her, he could not bear the thought of her passing to another man after his death. At least, if she were provided for, it would be from choice, not out of necessity. The strange thing was, she did not want anyone, no one permanent. Nothing had changed, since she became his wife, yet she no longer felt trapped. She was fond of him. She had learnt more from him than from anyone else in her life, and, in spite of his increasing weakness, he was fun to be with and still very mentally alert. They both knew he was playing out extra time, and she had begun to dread losing him. He had organized everything, life had revolved around him for so long that she felt almost frightened at the thought of being alone. At one time she had longed for it. Now she was grateful for every day she still had him.

It was a matter of days. Soon after their arrival, he visited a Harley Street specialist who had examined him two years before. The specialist was frankly astounded that he was still alive. He had two suggestions. Medically, there was no explanation of how he had survived. Either he could go into the London Clinic to be cared for and given regular tests, or carry on as he was, living quietly, but liable to collapse at any moment. It could not go on indefinitely, the specialist said. Leo must accept that his life expectancy was no more than a few weeks.

Letty was numbed, when Leo told her. She had been hoping against hope. 'What did he actually say?' she wanted to know.

Leo shrugged it off. 'I can never remember medical dialogue. But I got the gist of it, when he advised me not to buy any long-playing records.'

The weather at least was kind. It was a gentle, warm spring and London was at her prettiest. He liked to be driven to St James's or Regent's Park, to walk for a few minutes on the fresh grass. Twice a week he fed the ducks at each park, alternately. Letty thought it odd. 'I don't know why ducks,' he said. 'Crazy ducks. I just like to watch them. The way their cute little asses wiggle when they dive.'

It was the time of Swinging London, and the Beatles. 'I like these guys,' Leo said. 'If I was ten years younger, I'd sign them up for a movie.' He appreciated the mini skirt and enjoyed being driven slowly down the Kings Road. 'See these little chicks. Their asses wiggle just like the ducks.'

Letty enjoyed the latest styles, too, the fun clothes. She bought many, delighting Leo with minis and hotpants and see-through blouses, which she only wore indoors, and changed her hairstyle again, wearing it much shorter, a dark chestnut colour, to lose entirely the Laraine Love image.

During the two years, she had thought often of Vicky. She had had no contact with her, but through Leo's agent she had kept herself loosely informed of how her daughter's career was progressing. Leo was interested in her, she explained. 'Am I?' he asked. 'Don't remember her.' Not even he knew of the connection. She had left him at home one evening on Andros when she went to the open air cinema and sat twice through a British spy thriller in which Vicky appeared. She was only in two scenes, as an airline stewardess, and had been dubbed into Greek, but Letty again saw herself on the screen, twenty years younger.

329

Her concern about her daughter surprised her and she was unable to analyse her feelings. She had got over the fantasy of a reconciliation scene. She did not want Vicky to acknowledge her or live with her. All her life she had sidestepped responsibility and did not intend to change that now. Yet she still felt hurt by the girl's contempt for her, so obvious in that last telephone call. She had been furious with Ches Ekhardt, but, when she had calmed down, could not really blame him. He had merely been behaving normally for him. Young actresses were fair game for his kind and Letty should have realized it.

Yet she could not forget Vicky's contempt. 'I didn't know you were *that* Laraine Love.' And she resented being rejected because of a false image. Maybe she deserved it, but it had cut deep. Worst was the knowledge that through Ches and his pawing she had lost any hope of staying in touch with her daughter, as she had meant to, as a friend, an older woman who could help her and to whom Vicky might occasionally turn for advice. Fantasy time again.

One day, when Leo's agent dropped in, he said, 'Oh, you know that Blair girl you used to ask about? She's in some play at the South Green Theatre, supposed to be not bad.'

The South Green Theatre was a small theatre club in Hampstead made out of one long room at the rear of the Queen's Head pub. Reasonably equipped, it sat a maximum of eighty people and had a good reputation as a showcase and for try-outs. One of the better theatres of the Fringe, its productions were often reviewed by the critics and this latest, *Friday's Girl*, had received excellent notices. As a result, business was better than average, but Letty was able to get a seat without much difficulty.

In the narrow room, with ordinary chairs for seating, actors and audience were almost on top of each other. In the third row, Letty felt exposed and moved back to avoid any likelihood of Vicky recognizing her. She felt nervous before the lights dimmed, but after the play began was absorbed. It was virtually a threehander, about a girl from

330

the north sharing a flat with two very different men between whom she is expected to choose. It was very funny, yet managed to say a lot about the relationship between the sexes and the roles women were expected to play. From a dominated, submissive plaything to one and a willing, but underestimated helpmate to the other, the girl gradually developed in personality as layers of comedy stereotype were stripped away. When she walked out at the end, having rejected both lovers in favour of independence, the effect was startling.

Letty was impressed by Vicky's performance. It was much more than good. The two men were good. She was outstanding, funny, strong, moving. She deserved her enthusiastic reception at the end.

When the lights came up, Letty had an unpleasant surprise. Still thinking about Vicky's performance, she waited for the crush at the exit to thin out before leaving. The exit was through a side room of the pub, where the club bar was, and the actors who had performed without make-up were already at the bar, talking to some of the audience. Vicky was with another girl and two young men by the far door and Letty paused. She would like to congratulate her, but was not at all certain what the response would be. As she hesitated, Vicky waved to the rest of the cast and went out with her friends.

A young man in a crewneck sweater was standing near Letty. 'Did you enjoy it?' he asked.

She looked at him. He was in his late twenties, with untidy hair and a light fuzz of beard. 'Very much,' she said.

His smile was appealing. 'I'm glad. Thank you.'

'Did you have something to do with it?'

'In a way,' he said. 'I'm Hal Radley. I wrote it and produced it.'

Letty laughed. 'I'm sorry. Do forgive me. But I did like it very much, both the play and the performances. You have a fine cast.'

'Yes, I'm lucky there,' he admitted. He was intrigued by

Letty. He could not guess her age, somewhere in her thirties, he supposed. She had dressed deliberately simply in a little jersey dress with a short coat over it, yet was still easily the most stylish woman here. And the most attractive. She seemed to be alone. 'If you're on your own, may I get you a drink?'

Letty smiled. He was quite sweet. His thought processes had been transparent. After the drink would come the invitation back to his room for coffee. She had no intention of getting into any juvenile entanglement, but she could not resist learning more about Vicky. 'Thank you. A glass of wine would be nice. White, please.'

Radley was self-conscious as he moved with her to the bar, knowing that his friends were watching him, and probably envying him. He caught a wink from one of the two male leads. 'Your play's very clever,' Letty was saying, 'the way it starts just like a standard comedy, and then you begin to wonder why you're laughing. And if you should be laughing at all.'

'That's exactly the effect I was aiming for,' Radley said, pleased.

'Tricky to achieve. You're to be congratulated, and the girl who plays the lead.'

'Vicky's sensational,' Radley agreed. 'I'm the first to admit that she makes it.' He was increasingly fascinated by Letty. She wore her coat draped over her shoulders, revealing her perfect figure. There was a slight drawl in her voice. 'Are you – are you American, by the way?' he asked.

She seemed amused. 'No. I've lived among them for some time, though.'

'Do you have something to do with our business?'

'I was an actress once. Very briefly.'

'I knew it. I just knew it,' he smiled. He had a feeling this one would not be easy to entice back to his bedsit, but if she had been an actress, then at least they spoke the same language. 'You know, you haven't told me your name.'

'I'm Laraine Bremer,' Letty said. As they had been talking, she had had an idea and Radley was the perfect person to carry it out. She reached for her glass, making sure he saw her wedding ring. 'My husband's Leo Bremer.'

The effect was immediate. Radley was making to pick up his glass, but stopped. 'The film director? The one who made *Deadline Tomorrow* and – uh – *Cattletruck*?'

'*Cattlecar*,' Letty said. 'The one.'

Automatically, Radley glanced round. 'Didn't he come with you?'

'Unfortunately, he's not been too well lately.'

'I'm sorry to hear that. I've seen most of his films.' Radley was calculating quickly, all thoughts about getting Letty home with him pushed aside. If Bremer were to see the show, there was more than a chance of a mention in the nationals, good publicity. 'Do you think he might be well enough soon to –? Any night. I'd be honoured to invite him.'

'How long are you on for?' Letty asked.

'We have a three week run,' Radley told her. 'Two to go.'

'And then?'

'In the lap of the gods, I'm afraid,' he said. 'Ideally, we'd like it to transfer to the West End. Some of the big managements have been to see us. They like it, but –' He shrugged. 'The old story. It's splendid, but it's too risky, not commercial. Still, if Mr Bremer would care to come one evening . . .'

'I don't think it's very likely,' Letty said, 'since you're on for such a short time.' She paused. 'He'll be disappointed. He was keen to see Vicky.'

Radley was surprised. 'He knows her?'

'They met in passing, a little while ago,' Letty said. 'He was very taken with her. We both were.'

'She's just this moment gone. Didn't she realize you were here?'

Letty sipped her drink. 'I didn't let her know I was coming.'

'Why ever not?' Radley asked. 'She'll be sorry to have missed you.'

'I shouldn't think so,' Letty said, with a touch of regret. 'I shouldn't have mentioned it.'

Radley was hooked. 'Why not? You can't just leave it there.'

'Well –' Letty began, and hesitated. 'I shouldn't really tell you this, Mr Radley – Hal. The fact is, a couple of years ago we thought we'd like to help her in her career. I set something up and it backfired. Vicky thought it was my fault. It wasn't and I was very upset, but – well, I haven't been in touch with her since.'

A few days later, Letty was doing some shopping in Knightsbridge. Just as she was about to cross Sloane Street, she saw someone coming towards her and stop. It was Vicky. Letty pretended not to notice her and was amused when Vicky passed her, turned and walked back, to pause again in well feigned surprise. 'Excuse me – it's Mrs Bremer, isn't it?'

Letty smiled. 'Hello there, Miss Blair.'

'Funny running into you like this. I heard you were at the play the other night.' Vicky had been on a bus heading for Kensington Church Street. She had got off quickly, when she had spotted Letty.

'Yes, I liked it,' Letty said. 'Very much. You were very good.'

'Thank you,' Vicky smiled, and hesitated. 'I was sorry I didn't have a chance to talk to you.'

Letty could tell that, having engineered the meeting, she now was not sure how to carry it off. 'I'm thinking of having some coffee, Miss Blair,' she said. 'Would you care to join me?'

'Yes, I'd love to,' the girl said, hurriedly. 'But please call me Vicky.'

They found a coffee shop round the corner in Sloane Street. As they sat, Letty asked, 'Do you live around here?'

'No. Church Street. I have a small flat there.' Vicky was

embarrassed. 'I'd like to – to apologize for how I behaved last time we met.'

'No need. It was just a mistake.'

'Yes, I know that now,' Vicky said. 'But you must have thought me very foolish, very naive.'

'Actually, I thought you reacted very well,' Letty said.

Vicky smiled. 'You're very kind, Mrs Bremer. But I realize what a little prude I must have seemed.' She paused. 'I've often thought of that poor man, Mr Ekhardt. If only there had been some way to tell him how badly I felt afterwards about . . . how I behaved.'

'You don't need to worry about him,' Letty said. And what would you tell him? she wondered. That you're so desperate for work now that you'd do anything he wanted? She had noticed Vicky's slightly brittle energy, the quick movements of her hands. Things had not been easy for her. 'I spoke to Hal Radley,' she said. 'He tells me your play may be transferring.'

'If only it was,' Vicky sighed. 'It's about the best part I've ever had, but – well, to go into the West End, it seems we'd need a new set, new wardrobe, everything. And that costs money.'

'How much?' Letty asked.

'Thirty to forty thousand. A few years ago, it wouldn't have been a quarter of that, but costs have gone up so much recently. And of course, no commercial management's going to risk that on something that might only run a week.'

Letty had been toying with the idea of helping, but that kind of money was out of the question on a pure gamble. Even for her daughter. She drew Vicky out about her life and what her ambitions were. Vicky was still very much the dedicated actress. There had been a young actor she thought she was in love with, but it didn't work out. She still had the small flat they had taken together and was finding it expensive to keep up. She was doing reasonably well, compared to many of her friends, but work was still hard to come by. The right work, she said. She had the occasional television part, but the theatre was her real love. She kept hoping for a film, because they paid well, but had little luck there.

'Yes, I saw you in a spy thing,' Letty said. 'You were good, but you were acting.'

Vicky laughed. 'Of course, I was.'

'That was what was wrong.'

Vicky was surprised, then understood. 'Oh, yes. I'm sorry. Film is what you really know about.'

Letty was amused, remembering her years as an usherette at the Roxy. 'When I was young, I spent much of my life in the cinema.' She stubbed out her cigarette. 'Since then, I've learnt a lot more. Enough to tell you that I don't think you're right for it. Some people are very natural on screen. Probably people you despise. The difference is that they are being, you are acting. To succeed in films, you have to believe in what you're doing completely. You learn the technique, then you must forget it. The camera can always spot someone who's only pretending. On the stage you're real. Because that's what you believe in.'

Vicky had been concealing annoyance, when Letty started, but was struck by what she said. She promised to think about it. Letty gave her the phone number of the apartment and told her to keep in touch. 'And if I hear of anything interesting,' she added, 'I'll let you know.'

An extraordinary thing was happening to Leo. Whether it was the rest and the mild air of London or a final surge of vitality, he was looking and feeling fitter than he had for years. There were times when he even seemed to have recovered his old energy, and he shook his agent by agreeing to do a series of television interviews about his career. He rested all day before them and even Letty was surprised by his incisive and vigorous performance.

'Well, I didn't want to be remembered as an old crock,' he told her, and chuckled. 'Did you hear that dumb interviewer? Am I thinking of making another movie? I nearly told him. Where I'm going, I could pick an incredible cast. And a genuine heavenly choir.'

He was more amused, when, the day after the last interview was broadcast, he began to receive film scripts from agents and tentative offers from producers, eager to discuss projects. 'I'm a better actor than I thought,' he said.

'You shouldn't have pretended you were considering something,' Letty told him.

'What else was I gonna answer? I'm all washed up?' He was lying on the settee in the living room of the apartment, exhausted by the strain of the interviews. 'Hey, Laraine,' he said, 'I got a flash. And don't say no. Let's give a party, like we used to.'

'It would be too much for you,' Letty objected.

'So? If I'm going to go out, what better way? Beats hanging around, waiting.'

He would not be talked out of it. The party was arranged at short notice, but everyone who was asked grabbed at the invitation. The trade papers were speculating that Leo Bremer, having recovered from a long illness, was set to make a spectacular comeback to directing. Leo enjoyed it enormously. He spent the week before the party and all day until the first guests arrived resting. The moment the first doorbell sounded, he bounced up and came out like a bantam weight prizefighter, all energy. Few of their many guests had met him when he was younger and it was a revelation. He was amusing, dynamic, flirtatious, moving from group to group and leaving them laughing and stimulated.

Letty had seen Ches Ekhardt come in and suppressed a swell of anger. He was unaware of the two years of heartache he had caused her and she made herself smile and wave to him. He was an essential part of an idea that had occurred to her, an hour after Leo decided on giving the party.

After a time, Ekhardt made his way to her and kissed her cheek. He had put on weight, which did not suit him.

337

His laid-back, cool image was fraying at the edges. 'Laraine, baby, you're looking gorgeous,' he said. 'But what's with Leo? The word was out that he was on his last legs, but look at him.'

'It's having an exciting project at last,' she smiled. 'It's done wonders.'

'So I see. What is the project?'

'It's under wraps yet, but it's really something,' Letty said. 'Light comedy, but very contemporary, controversial. It needs him to make it work and he'll do great things with it.'

'Sounds fantastic. But what is it?' Ekhardt insisted.

Letty smiled teasingly. 'You know I can't tell you, Ches. Not even you. If someone got in before him, it would break him up.'

'You mean he hasn't acquired it yet?'

She could read his mind. 'You're not to go poking around, Ches,' she warned.

'Naturally. You know me,' Ekhardt protested. He turned quickly, listening to Leo who was with an independent producer near them.

'Did you read the treatment I sent you?' the producer asked. 'It's a knockout, isn't it?'

'Yeah, pretty good,' Leo agreed. 'But I got something even better.'

'When are you going to announce it, Leo?' Ekhardt asked.

Leo chuckled. 'Soon. It'll make the front page of every trade paper in the world. I guarantee.'

There was not a moment when he was not surrounded, and he responded to the attention and speculation with great amusement. He had not been so courted for years. Letty saw Ekhardt hovering near him constantly, ingratiating, trying to cut himself in. Once, she heard him say, 'Leo, we've been pals for a long time. Why don't you deal me in? I have funds. If I like it, I can meet all the development expenses. What do you say?'

Leo had never cared for him and chuckled. 'If there's

anyone I'd like to take along with me, Ches, it would be you. But I'll have to go it alone.'

At eleven, Vicky, Hal Radley and the rest of the cast of *Friday's Girl* arrived, straight from the theatre club. And Letty prepared to play out the rest of her comedy.

She led Vicky over to Leo, after reminding him who she was. He kissed Vicky's cheek. 'My wife is impressed with you, Miss Blair,' he said, kindly. 'She tells me I could make you a star. I believe her.'

Vicky was thrilled and flattered, even more when a number of people who had heard began to make much of her. The head of drama at one of the commercial television companies remembered her successful series of two and a half years ago and insisted that she gave him a call.

Letty brought Radley to meet Leo, taking care that they had a few minutes alone. The young writer-producer was very excited to meet one of his heroes and very grateful to have been invited. 'All these agency and company bums, they're only a necessary evil,' Leo told him. 'We're the creative ones. We have to stick together. Laraine tells me I'd like your play. I'm sorry I can't see it.'

'He could send you a copy of the script,' Letty suggested, casually.

Radley was only too willing. 'I can get it to you tomorrow,' he said.

'The sooner, the better.' Leo winked to Letty. 'I hope it's not too long.'

'Long playscripts are difficult to visualize in terms of film,' Letty explained.

Leo chuckled, patted Radley's arm and wished him luck.

'There's other people I want you to meet, Hal,' Letty said and drew him away, out of earshot of Ches Ekhardt who had been closing in. She spoke quietly to Radley, flattering him and kissing him before moving on. Shortly after, she saw Ekhardt join the group to which she had introduced Radley, and there was nothing more she could do. Except make certain that Leo did not overtire himself, and that no one here realized it was his wake.

339

He was showing signs of strain, but the party was at last thinning out and he could relax. She joined him, where he sat on the settee with his agent. 'Has Ava gone?' he asked.

'About five minutes ago,' she told him. 'She said to kiss you goodbye. She didn't want to interrupt.'

'She's looking great. I'm glad she came. And Burt. I didn't know either of them was in town.'

'Passing through,' Letty said. 'They just heard about the party and came along.'

'It's been a night, huh?' he chuckled. 'Like the old times.'

Letty was not surprised when Ekhardt came up to her before he left. He was looking smug, pleased with himself. 'Who's a clever boy, then?' he said.

'I'm sure you are, Ches,' Letty agreed, 'but why in particular?'

'Ever heard of a play called *Friday's Girl*?' he asked, innocently. She tensed, glancing at Leo and back, and Ekhardt laughed.

'All right, Ches,' she said quietly.

He frowned. 'But from what I've been told about it, it doesn't sound suitable for the screen.'

'There are ways,' Letty said. 'You know that. Open it out, make it a little more up-market, sophisticated. The kind of thing Leo's best at.' He nodded. 'And the girl in it is a sensation. Vicky Blair – you may remember her.'

Ekhardt scowled. 'The blonde over there? I thought I knew her from somewhere. She kicked me once, in the most uncomfortable place – and I mean the most uncomfortable. How could I forget?'

'Leo's over the moon about her. He could make her into another Hepburn,' Letty told him, then became very serious and confidential. 'But please, Ches, we haven't talked about this. You know that if that play goes into the West End, whoever owns it could ask a fortune for the film rights. Please, don't mention it to anyone.'

'You needn't ask,' Ekhardt said sincerely. 'My lips are sealed.'

After the party Leo was helped to his bedroom by Letty and his agent. He had just managed to last out and was filled with the joy of it. 'Just like the old times,' he said over and over. 'That little redhead from the Paramount office, she even gave me her phone number.' He chuckled. 'And Zanuck got me pinned in a corner. Did you see that? He hasn't made a movie in years, either. Came all the way over from Paris. He kept asking, so what's it about? Can't you even tell me the title? Sure, I said, it's called *The Last Take*. Great title! he said. Is there a book?' He was too breathless to laugh and they eased him on to the bed.

The party had been on a Friday. The following Monday evening, the telephone rang. Letty was sitting by the bed, where Leo had lain all weekend. There was crackle on the line and a confused murmur of voices in the background, so at first she could not make out what was said.

'Mrs Bremer? It's Vicky,' she made out at last. 'I'm phoning from the pub and it's the interval, so I don't have very long. But there's wonderful news!'

Letty sat up quickly. 'Oh, what's that?'

'We're going in!' Vicky told her excitedly. 'The play's going in – straight in. Two weeks after we close here, we're opening at The Duke's Theatre. Isn't that marvellous?'

'You must be very pleased,' Letty said.

'In a way, it's thanks to you,' Vicky said. 'For inviting us to your party last week. You can't imagine who came to see the play on Saturday – and sent me flowers. Mr Ekhardt . . . I met him afterwards and I was pretty nervous. But he said, no hard feelings, from now on it's strictly business.' She laughed. 'It's him who's bringing it in. He took an option on it that night, and signed the contract today!'

'Well, yes, that is marvellous, Vicky,' Letty said. 'Congratulations.'

'I'll send you tickets for the first night,' Vicky promised. 'Do come. I'm sorry, I must run.'

When she hung up, Letty was smiling. 'Who was that?' Leo asked.

341

'Vicky Blair,' Letty asked. 'She rang to thank us for the party.'

'Nice kid,' Leo grunted, and closed his eyes again.

*Friday's Girl* was the surprise hit of the season and Vicky had rave reviews. 'A star is born!' they proclaimed. 'Beg, borrow or steal, but get a ticket for The Duke's Theatre before they become like gold.'

Letty was not at the first night. Leo went into a coma, three days before the play opened, and this time did not recover consciousness. The film world was shocked by his death, after so much speculation about his return, and he got the front page coverage he had guaranteed. *'The Last Take* was to be his comeback,' *Variety* said. 'Now, he has made his last take.'

Letty did not see Ches Ekhardt in the bar of the theatre. It was a week after the funeral, the first time she had been out of the apartment. She tensed, when he pushed through to her. 'I was very sorry to hear, Laraine,' he said. 'I sent flowers to the crematorium. I hope they were suitable.' Letty had not taken notice of who any of the flowers were from. She had seen nothing that day. 'Look, Laraine,' he went on, 'I've invited a bunch of people to the Savoy after the show. Why don't you join us, if you feel up to it?'

Letty was wary. By now he must have realized he had been set up, but he seemed to be taking it well. It was partly because she wanted to find out why that she went along and, to her surprise, discovered that he had no idea how she had manipulated him. 'I mean, I hope it wasn't my fault,' he said, hesitantly. 'That he didn't take it too badly, my buying the play. All he had to do was call me. I wanted us to be partners.'

Letty decided it was unfair to make him sweat. 'Don't blame yourself, Ches. The end was unexpected.'

'That makes me feel better,' he said with relief. He paused. 'I've been meaning to talk to you. I mean, he was right. That Vicky kid has got something. The script, though. Hal told me he sent a copy to Leo, but he hasn't a clue how he was going to approach it. He didn't tell you,

342

did he?' Letty shook her head. 'No. He always played it close to his chest. I've had a couple of writers look at it, but they can't see how to make it work for the screen. It's all talk. Still . . .' He smiled. 'They tell me it's going to run at The Duke's for a year minimum. I've never been a theatre tycoon before. I stand to make a fortune.'

The next day, he rang Letty up. 'Listen, Laraine, this may come out of left field, but – I trust your judgement and we've always got along pretty well. I'm leaving for the States soon, to see if I can pick up any new plays that might work over here. Frankly, it's all new to me. And I wondered if you might care to come along? No strings.'

Letty nearly hung up on him, but as she thought about it, she controlled herself. She was on her own again. Her mind had adjusted months before to the idea of being without Leo, yet she had not been able to decide finally what to do. Ches was rich, not repulsive, and she would always be several steps ahead of him. And she had watched him last night, doing his best to dazzle Vicky, who was uncertain how to handle him. She had confided to Letty that all her friends thought she was foolish to keep putting him off. He could be invaluable to her career. 'Ches is all right, if you think of him as a stepping stone,' Letty advised her. 'Don't get involved.'

Letty accepted his offer. Again she was granted a visitor's visa, valid for one month. It was the longest she had ever spent in America and she adored every moment of it, although the 'no strings' clause was never mentioned again and Ches booked double rooms wherever they went. He had no idea of the effect she would have on him. For the first time, he was not in control of the situation and it spurred him on. He was crazy about her, could hardly bear to let her out of his sight. After three weeks, when he hurried back to their Boston hotel from a pre-Broadway try-out from which she had begged off due to a headache, he found she had packed her bags and gone. No one knew where. He locked himself in their room and drank himself into a stupor.

343

Letty had only one week left of her month's visitor's permit, not much time to do anything about it. She had made up her mind to go as close to the top as she could and had flown from Boston to Washington, where she booked into the exclusive Hotel Sherman. The next morning she called on Jim Kiley.

The woman in the chic, couture suit, worn with a French cape and classic shoes, bore no resemblance to the dishevelled girl whom Helen and he had found by the roadside outside Market Wetherby and carried to the hospital to have her illegitimate baby. That girl he could never forget. She had been immature and frightened, with tawny blonde hair. This Mrs Bremer was very poised, with short, dark chestnut hair and charming manners, a totally different being. He had always felt that girl had been badly treated, that without the arrival of the 525th she would probably have lived a quiet, uneventful life, untroubled by temptation and scandal. Like so many others, she was a victim of the war. 'I would never have placed you, Letty,' he said. 'I beg your pardon – Mrs Bremer.' Naturally, he had heard of Leo and of his death, yet it still took an effort of will to accept that this was his widow.

'It's rather a long story, I'm afraid,' she said. Her voice was soft and well modulated, not unlike Helen's. 'I don't want to take up too much of your time. I wondered – I'm staying at the Sherman – and I wondered, if it's not too much of an imposition, if you and Mrs Kiley might come to lunch one day. I have always been very grateful to you.'

'It wouldn't be an imposition at all,' Jim assured her. 'Unfortunately, however, Helen is in Newport. How long are you staying?'

'Only a few days.' Letty bit her lip and glanced away. She collected herself and smiled. It was beautifully done.

Jim felt sorry for her and ashamed, without fully knowing why. At the same time, he realized that she needed help. 'If there's anything I can do,' he said.

Letty apologized again for troubling him. She let more anxiety show. She loved America, she told him, always

344

had done and had planned to live here. Her husband, however, despite being a noted American film director, had never taken out citizenship, so she could not claim it as his widow. He had been a victim of McCarthyism and had always intended to return to his adopted land, which he too had loved in spite of everything. Now it was too late and, although she had applied in London for an open ended visa, to allow her to live here, it had not been granted. 'I feel that Leo is still being victimized, through me,' she said. There was a slight break in her voice.

'I understand how you feel,' Jim assured her, sympathetically. 'I'll certainly do what I can. The Immigration people are a law unto themselves, but I think we may be able to get round them.' He smiled at Letty's wordless relief and pleasure. Clearly, she'd had a tough experience. America owed her something. 'I think we might go for a resident's permit,' he said.

'I just don't know how to thank you, Senator,' Letty said. She touched her eyes. 'Please, forgive me. I know there's so much you must want to ask me. I'm sorry Mrs Kiley's not here. However, to show my gratitude, I'd still like to give you that invitation. To lunch, I mean – if it's not against some rule or other.'

'Not at all,' Jim said. He found her touching and appealing, and she had roused his curiosity to hear more of her story. 'I have a light week. When would be convenient?'

'Shall we say tomorrow?' Letty suggested, smiling.

She was still smiling when she returned to her hotel. It had been so much easier than she had expected. Kiley was an attractive man, chivalrous and caring. Late fifties, with an older wife. The thought of the possibilities amused her. Mrs Dereham's Major . . . It was not hard to play the trusting, grateful, wide-eyed game with him. No one was more easily hooked than someone whom you allowed to do you a favour. And, in fact, it was a big favour. He had promised to ring her the next morning, and she looked forward to it.

She decided to change. As she crossed the lounge of her suite, she noticed an envelope which had been pushed under the door and picked it up, wondering what it could be. No one but Kiley knew she was here. It was addressed to 'Mrs L. Bremer' and she opened it.

Inside was a photograph. A photograph of herself taken ten years before, when she had done that pin-up series to publicize the sex comedy, *Killer Doll*. Wearing only a suspender belt, nylons and brassière, the brassière slipping to expose one breast, she was half smiling to the camera with an 'ooh!' of surprise. It was not retouched.

Where had it come from and who had sent it? Why? Her mind was racing. Obviously, someone had recognized her. So what did they want? She had regretted the photographs as soon as she had posed for them. Especially when they were used to publicize the porno version of the film. Laraine Love. She had thought her safely buried for ever.

There was a ring at the doorbell and her head jerked. She put down the photograph and moved to the door. Through the spyhole, she could see a man standing outside, silver haired, rather squat, in a business suit. She opened the door a few inches and the man smiled. 'Good of you to see me, Miss Love,' he said.

It was Harry Rakhin, the crooked producer who had recut *Killer Doll*, ruining Leo and making a killing for himself. She made to close the door, but he brushed past her into the room.

'I can have you thrown out,' Letty said.

'I wouldn't contest it,' Rakhin told her. 'But on the other hand, I can have *you* thrown out – of the country.' He smiled. 'Not that I want to do that.'

'What are you talking about?' Letty demanded.

'I know really quite a lot about you,' he said. 'I've kept track, so to speak, over the years. If Immigration knew, they'd ship you out on a morals charge within twenty-four hours.'

Letty did not doubt it. She also remembered his mob connections, and that he was dangerous. She was shaken, trying to work out what he was after. 'How did you know I was here?'

He chuckled. 'You don't look behind you on airplanes. The hairstyle had me fooled for a while, but there's other things you can't change so easy.' He glanced at the photograph on the table. 'Not when I know them so well.'

'Is this some sort of blackmail?' she asked.

'No. Well, I guess it depends on the point of view.' Rakhin licked the corner of his mouth with his tongue, in a gesture she remembered disliking. 'Now, some of my friends, no doubt, would only be interested in money. But I don't need it – if you recall. And I've always been an admirer of yours. Shall we say, a fervent admirer?'

The next morning, when Jim called the Sherman, he was told that Mrs Bremer had checked out. She had informed the receptionist she was returning to England. Which was odd, because the gentleman she was with had asked the desk to book them air tickets for Las Vegas.

'Are you sure you didn't imagine the whole thing?' Helen asked, when Jim told her later.

'No, I didn't,' he said. 'She had even booked a table for two for lunch.' He thought for a moment. 'To tell the truth, I'm rather glad she went wherever she did. And that I didn't see her again. There's something, I don't know, magnetic about her.'

'Letty?' Helen asked, surprised.

'You'd have to meet her to understand,' Jim said. He smiled. 'Whatever it is she's got – I don't think I could handle it.'

# THIRTY-TWO

Joe McGraw couldn't remember the last time he had set foot inside Mundy's grocery shop. Shopping he had no time for, and that wasn't a successful business man talking. He left that sort of thing to Sally or the children.

Nothing much seemed to have changed. Even though the place had been redecorated, it was still in the same cream and pale green, the old wooden shelves, the grille of the post office section, and that kind of comforting smell of fruit and sweets and spices. The only sign of the times were the wire baskets for customers and a couple of plastic display racks for jams and cookies on one side, toothpaste and detergents on the other. And the back parlour had hardly been touched. Some new chairs, a television set in the corner. It took him back.

He felt rather awkward, kind of out of place, even though he was here on business. He'd already answered the obvious questions Vera Mundy had put so politely. 'I'd like to see Peter, ma'am,' he'd told her. And away up the stairs she'd gone, still sprightly, even though she must now be pushing seventy.

She was a remarkable woman, Joe decided. What a difference Albert's death had made to her. Not that it had come as a shock. Albert had progressively gone downhill ever since he had suffered his stroke after Peter and Rosie's wedding, and that must be over twenty years ago now.

But ever since Albert's stroke, Vera had blossomed, positively blossomed. Mac smiled, remembering her kindness to Sally and him during the war, a kindness she had been forced to conceal from Albert for whom the only worthwhile Yanks were those who dealt in the Black Market. No. That wasn't fair.

Maybe; Joe thought, a woman really comes into her own

348

when there's no man about. Sure, Sally had waited for him after the war. It had taken almost two years to get demobbed and during that time she had developed a sturdy independence that had never really been extinguished.

Joe liked it. A woman who knew her own mind and could take decisions was what he needed during those lean years when he had worked almost every hour of the day to establish his garage business. Now it was thriving, not only the repairs side but car sales, too. He was pleased he'd expanded and that young Joe had wanted to work alongside him. The boy was a good mechanic.

He looked around the small sitting room at the back of the Mundy's shop, moved over to the settee and fingered the electric guitar propped up against the cushions. 'You're not going to join a group, Peter?' he smiled, as Vera brought in her son.

'Not me, Joe. I left that all too late,' Peter said, running his fingers through his thinning hair.

'Anyway,' McGraw said, 'your haircut's miles too short for today's kids.'

'Don't let the twins see you touching that guitar, Joe,' Vera warned. 'They'll be in in a minute.'

'And straight out again,' Peter said, 'off to the church hall to practise. They're in a rock'n'roll group with two other lads in the town.'

'Lucky for you they don't practise at home,' McGraw grinned.

Peter shrugged. 'Actually, they're quite good, even though it's all a bit noisy for Rosie.'

Vera brought Joe a beer and the two men settled into the armchairs.

'Look, Peter, I've got some bad news. Now I really shouldn't be telling you this. You see, it's council business. I've just come from the meeting and I think you ought to know about it before you get the letter.'

'What letter?'

Joe paused and sipped his beer. He looked across at

Peter. 'Some big supermarket chain wants to set up in Market Wetherby, in the Square.'

'Why here?'

'It's the site, I suppose. There's room to expand and, from their point of view, the corner of the main street is ideal.'

'I suppose so,' Peter agreed. 'But why choose a small town like this?'

'They'll be reckoning to pull in everyone for miles around. Foodstuffs and groceries are only part of their stock. They'll have something for everyone – at very competitive prices.'

'Thanks for telling me, Joe, but I don't see that it'll affect me much. People here have always shopped at Mundy's. They will still. I mean, I don't have to sell up or anything, do I? And you know yourself, half those schemes never get off the ground.'

'No, they don't, Peter.'

'Anyway, there's no hurry. They'll have to get planning permission and everything first, won't they?' Peter saw McGraw frown. 'What, Joe? Come on, there's something else.'

'I'm afraid there's a move in the planning committee to give them the go ahead right away. They say it'll bring more business to the town, more people. You know the kind of thing. Save folks going to shop in Ipswich. It's a big chain – Lansburys.'

'I've heard the name,' Peter said.

'Well, you think about it. They could be in operation within six or seven months – and that could put you out of business.'

Peter got up from his seat, walked to the door and called Rosie to come in from the shop.

That night, when he was at home at Bridge Cottage, McGraw told his wife, Sally, about the meeting and going round to the Mundys to break the news.

'And what did Rosie think about it?' she asked.

McGraw grimaced. 'I can never figure out *what* that

girl's thinking, Sal. Never could, and things ain't changed. I imagined she'd be heartbroken. Between them now, they've worked that business for twenty years or more, since old Albert had his first stroke. God knows, if there was a threat to the garage – a real threat it might go bust, I'd have a few problems figuring out what I was going to do.'

'Retire?' Sally suggested.

'You must be kidding,' he said. 'But all Rosie did was smile. Maybe it's what she's always wanted – to leave the shop.'

'What about Peter and Vera?'

'He was kind of . . . noncommittal. You know the way he likes to work things out in his mind. But not upset, definitely not upset. And old Vera kinda smiled. Didn't say anything. Just gave that little smile.'

Sally was puzzled. 'I wonder what she was thinking?'

'Search me.' McGraw shrugged. 'Maybe it was just too big a surprise for them to come to terms with it.'

He was trying to sound casual, but Sally could read the signs, the lowering of his brow and the set jaw. 'Why are you so concerned about it?' she asked.

'I don't rightly know, Sal,' he admitted. 'Just something about that meeting tonight. Nobody even stopped to consider if we really wanted something like a supermarket in the town. The application from Lansburys came with a recommendation from Sir Henry Maylie.'

'Oh, I see,' Sally said. Sir Henry was highly respected. 'Well, if he's in favour of it—'

'He's not God Almighty,' McGraw muttered. As an American, he had a healthy disrespect for the deference with which people round here treated those they considered their betters. He admired Henry Maylie, even liked him, but that didn't mean he thought him a better man than, say, Jack Blair, the landlord of The Plough. 'Okay, so he's in favour. Does that mean we can't even discuss it? Do you want those old houses in the square torn down and a concrete and glass, three storey box to go up? That'll look great, won't it?'

'If you put it like that . . .' Sally said shortly. 'Tell you what – I'll make a pot of tea.'

McGraw smiled and shook his head, as she went through into the kitchen. That was Sally's answer to everything, a pot of tea. His small, black cigar had gone out. As he struck a match and puffed it alight again, he had a vision of Market Wetherby square as it might be in five or ten years' time. The supermarket would only be the start. Then would come other new businesses, clothing stores, chemists, Wimpey bars, rival supermarkets. Let one in and you couldn't keep the others out. He felt sick when he thought of what had happened to so many old country towns already, a quiet beauty that had taken centuries to create destroyed in a few years in the name of progress.

He and his buddies during the war had helped to accelerate it, bringing the craze for everything American, and all the chrome, concrete and plastic that went with it. In some ways, it meant a better, healthier, more interesting life for people, but so much was lost at the same time. Even he could see that. You couldn't hold back the twentieth century, but couldn't you control it? Some places you drove through were beginning to look like miniature versions of Pittsburgh and Cincinnati already. Did it have to happen to Market Wetherby?

With his garage prospering and his stepchildren and his son, little Joe, growing up, McGraw had found time to devote himself to more than just business. He had become a British citizen and, ever since he had been asked to stand for the council and had won his seat three years ago, he had taken an immense interest in the affairs of the town, throwing his energy into local politics. And he had helped to get a lot of things moving. Not that he regarded himself as a wheeler-dealer. No, he was more concerned about how he could help the townspeople who had accepted him as one of themselves. And when it was a case of outsiders, big outsiders, moving in on his territory, he started to bristle. Like he was bristling now.

Of course, there had been changes since he had first come to the town. When the war ended and the Americans had departed as suddenly as they arrived, some towns-people had thought that life would revert to the good old days. But Market Wetherby would never be the same again.

Just as the physical face of the town had altered over the years, so had values and attitudes. Now there was a larger infants school and a library, and talk of a sports centre with a swimming pool and squash court. But change hadn't brought plusses all the time. Market Wetherby was sprouting parking meters. Instead of only one police sergeant, there were an extra four constables to handle a growing crime rate. The cottage hospital had long gone. There was not one GP now, but a group practice, so you never knew which doctor was on call. There was a one-way traffic system which the shopkeepers, notably Peter Mundy and Jack Blair, had resisted, but without success, and the Weaver's Arms had, for a short time admittedly, employed go-go dancers as an attraction on Saturday lunchtimes. Jack Blair had chuckled at the audacity, but it was the Mothers' Union, led by Lady Patricia Maylie, who had stamped on that, using her additional influence as a magistrate.

There were yellow lines painted alongside the kerbs of the main street, and even a set of traffic lights in the square. The regulations about parking and the one-way system everyone agreed were necessary, because of the amount of traffic that rumbled through the town centre. Joe didn't mind that so much. How could he in his line of business?

But this latest incursion was something that had to be resisted. Mundy's shop catered for Market Wetherby. Maybe Sally was right in saying the prices were slightly high, but Joe had yet to meet a woman who didn't complain about what she had to pay out of her housekeeping across a counter. Just like him noticing the price of oil.

No, Mundy's shop was a part of Market Wetherby he felt deeply about. It was part of his history. And of the 525th. To pull it down would be more than a shame. It would be a desecration. No one would dream of knocking down the church and replacing it with an air-conditioned tower block, all glass and plastic, and retailing whatever religion was the flavour of that particular month. No, sir. He was going to mount a campaign to save the Mundy's store. And much else besides.


Peter Mundy was lying in bed, propped up against the pillows watching Rosie comb out her long dark hair. Where the light caught it, it had a sheen of copper. It was a sight he never tired of. She could see him in the mirror and smiled. 'What are you looking so pleased about?' she asked.

'Nothing really, Rosie. A cat can look at a queen.'

'Well, you don't seem too upset about this supermarket. Anyone would think Joe McGraw owned this place, he looked so worried.'

'He's just being McGraw. Looking after our interests. I mean, it's far better coming from him than reading it in a letter. He's an honest man, and I never thought I'd be able to say that about a councillor, Rosie.'

She'd finished brushing her hair and joined him in bed. Her looks, he thought, hadn't changed with the years. She had retained her figure after the birth of the twins and, if anything, was sexier now than she'd been in her twenties.

'Maybe you ought to sell up, Peter. What would we do?'

'I don't really know, but we're both young enough to make a new start. Maybe another business . . .'

Peter was hinting at something. Rosie knew it, and she had more than half an idea what he was thinking about. He would tell her in his own time. Meanwhile, there was nothing to stop her working out plans, herself. And she usually knew how to get what she wanted. She snuggled down and laid her head on his shoulder.

For Vera Mundy, the news might have come as a shock, but secretly she was not displeased. In fact, as she lay in her bed considering McGraw's bombshell, she felt that, after all these years living behind the shop, perhaps a new chapter in her life was about to commence. It's never too late, she thought. Then scolded herself. You ought to be ashamed of yourself, Vera Mundy, at your age . . .

Jack Blair should have retired years ago. That's what everyone, especially Rosie, kept telling him. But he had resisted, laughing off their attempts to make him throw in the cloth he brought out each morning to polish the bar. As long as he could pull a pint, he would stay in The Plough. Other landlords in other pubs had come and gone, but Jack Blair was part of Market Wetherby's folk lore now. He too had seen a lot of changes in the years since the Americans had left the town. He hadn't opposed most. And, he smiled, been proved right more often than not.

When Vi and Chuck had last visited – he scratched his head trying to remember – it didn't come so easy these days, memory was a strange thing – it must have been that good summer in 'sixty nine. They had been both shocked and delighted by the new wallpaper in the lounge bar, thick and red and embossed with flowers, and the furnishings, all old oak and buttoned leather.

'At least it's comfortable here now, Dad,' Vi had told him. The snug had been extended into a games room where children could run around and play the jukebox and bar billiards.

Chuck was most pleased when he downed his first pint. 'Your suggestion before you left for America, remember?' Jack smiled. 'You can have new tables, and chairs, and leather, and serve fancy drinks, Jack, but as long as you keep this beer, I'll always come back.'

And it was true. The one thing Jack would never change

was his beer. He'd had offers from the big breweries to sell their ales, offers accompanied by promises of cash and schemes to gut the bar and install a restaurant. He'd been under a lot of pressure to sell up to the big boys. Rosie had been all for it. 'Go on, Dad, put in a manager, and take it easy in your old age,' she often urged, but Jack knew, somehow, that if he stuck to The Plough and to the beer that he and his father before him had served up from the local brewery for the last fifty years, he'd be all right. And so it had proved. The fad with the new ales had long since disappeared, and if anything now his brew was in greater demand.

He smiled again to himself as he pulled the first half of the morning, sniffing the thick head before he tilted the glass to his lips.

'You're at it early, Jack.' Peter Mundy had walked in, and sat at the bar.

'I was just thinking,' Jack said to his son-in-law, 'about this campaign for real ale. We've been serving it here for donkey's years. Never stocked anything else.'

'Good for business, nowadays, I should think,' Peter said.

'Can't complain. Only, you come in here on a Sunday morning and you'll see them, these real ale folk, sipping half pints of the stuff as if it was rare wine. Don't catch them buying pints. Never mind,' he sighed, pushing over a glass of bitter to Peter, who began to tell him about McGraw's unexpected visit last night.

'I'm tempted,' Peter confided, 'tempted to sell up and move out. This may sound stupid, Jack, but remember what I always wanted to do?'

'Music business, wasn't it?'

'Yes, form my own band. Well, with the money we could get for the shop, what do you think?'

Jack took a pull from his glass to give himself a moment to consider. 'Well, it's what you've always wanted, right enough,' he said, finally. 'But times have altered, so have tastes. I hear that row that comes out of the jukebox of an evening. I can't abide it, yet it's all folks want to hear. Is that the kind of music you want to make?'

'. . . No,' Peter admitted.

'I thought not,' Jack said. 'My advice is, don't go getting your hopes up, or making any plans. Find out first what someone will offer you for the shop. Then think about it again.'

Later that afternoon Jack Blair was sitting in the front passenger seat of Vera Mundy's car. Wednesday was the afternoon they always went out for a drive. It had started when Albert died and Rosie and Peter had persuaded Vera she should learn to drive and then buy a car. Of course, she'd resisted. 'I'm too old to learn about gears and things. And the road signs are getting stranger every day. It's the Common Market that's done it. I mean, Peter, what on earth does that "Give Way" thing mean? I could understand it when it said "Halt" . . .'

But despite her misgivings, out of the money Albert had left, Vera had bought a car. It was a yellow Mini automatic, which Joe McGraw supplied, advising her that this was the best way to get around without having to change gear. And it was Jack Blair who had taught her to drive. Perhaps he was the only person in town who could have achieved it. Peter and Rosie had given up sitting in the Mini with her, so erratic was her steering. She would spot something at the side of the road and be so interested she'd forget she was driving. Twice she ended up in the hedge. Jack Blair had stepped in, ignoring Peter's warnings about Vera's complete lack of road sense.

'I'll say one thing to you, Vera,' he said on the first occasion he had gone out with her in the car. 'Remember, you pay road tax the same as everyone else. So don't be scared. Keep in the middle. You've got as much right to be on the road as the next man.'

Every Wednesday afternoon they drove out together. Six months later, Vera tore up her L plates. She had passed first time, emulating Peter and baffling Rosie, who had taken the test four times, before she too had been able to throw away her plates.

Now, three years on, the Wednesday drive was a regular event. They never went far. To Ipswich or the coast, or sometimes they took tea in a neighbouring village.

'How's Vicky doing?' Jack asked.

'Still very well, it seems,' Vera told him. 'She has a new series starting soon.' Vicky had become well known, alternating with increasing success between stage and television, although never finding the breakthrough into films for which she had hoped. Vera took great pride in her. Jack was aware, however, that another subject was uppermost in her mind today.

'Do you think Rosie and Peter will sell up, or stay?' Vera asked him.

'I don't rightly know, but he came in this morning burbling about going into music. I would have thought by now he'd have forgotten about his army dance band days.'

'His heart's always been set on that. It sounds mad, but I'd like to get out of the shop, too, Jack.'

'And where would you go, my dear?'

Vera looked across at him briefly and then fixed her eyes resolutely back on the road. 'I thought you might be able to answer that, Jack.'

Joe McGraw was furious. He had been unable to talk the rest of the council round into refusing or delaying Lansburys permission to knock down the houses on the corner of the square and construct their branch supermarket. He had tried to rouse local opposition, but the weight of the rest of the council, backed by Sir Henry, was against him. Many people had signed his petition, but others had said, 'What's it got to do with you? You think you know better than Sir Henry? You're an outsider, anyway.' It was the first time anyone had called him that.

Worst of all, most of the shopkeepers, the very ones the petition was designed to protect, had refused to sign. Chief among them was Peter Mundy. McGraw had stared at him in disbelief. 'But, Pete, you've got to sign!' he protested. 'I'm doing all this because of you! And don't you see, it's not only you. We have to preserve what we have here – stop it all being destroyed.'

'I'm sorry, Joe,' Peter said, apologetically. 'Rosie and I just don't want to stay on here. I'll grab at any straw I can to get away. I may as well tell you – I've written to Lansburys, asking them to make me an offer for the shop. I'm selling out.'

McGraw went home that night and drank nearly a whole bottle of scotch. He got so good and drunk that both Sally and young Joe had to help him upstairs to bed and undress him. Sally thought he had passed out, but, half an hour later, when she was easing herself into bed beside him, he said groggily, 'Not so used to the hard stuff as I used to be, I guess.'

'I guess not,' she answered. 'Do you feel sick?'

'Not the way you think,' he told her. 'I'm sick at how people here are throwing their town away. Sick at how they can't see what'll happen. But I'm only an outsider, so what the hell?'

He grunted and really did pass out. Sally lay looking at him, upset by the hurt and disappointment in his voice and sorry that she had not had a chance to tell him how proud she was of him. When Betty was little, her favourite story was one about a gentle giant. That was Joe. She bent over and kissed his forehead. It was the year of their silver wedding and she still loved him as much as the first time he'd taken her in his arms and she'd said, 'I never meant this to happen.' She couldn't help loving him then. And she couldn't now. He was the finest man she had ever known.

# THIRTY-THREE

In the days that followed, people had a tendency to avoid McGraw and that suited him fine. There were not many he would have cared to talk to, anyway. One exception was Jack Blair, who had agreed with him and had signed the petition.

McGraw spent a lot of time at the garage, just tinkering in the workshop, and his mechanics knew better than to bother him. Young Joe would take him in a mug of tea, ask his advice about something, anything, to stop him brooding. And he'd wait to come home with his father for supper, otherwise Mac would have stayed there half the night.

The only place in the town McGraw went to was The Plough. He was sitting alone at a corner of the bar when Jack came up to him. 'Can I have a word, Mac?'

'Any time,' McGraw told him.

Jack lowered his voice. 'I wish you'd go and see Peter.'

'I'd like to oblige you,' McGraw said. 'And maybe in time, I'll bury the hatchet. But just at the moment, that's asking a little too much.'

'Please, Mac,' Jack said, seriously. 'He let you down badly. I won't deny it. However, I think you'll find he's changed his mind. It would be a kindness to him – and to me.'

McGraw finished his beer, not hurrying over it. He had been feeling sorry for himself, he decided. That wasn't healthy. And not too pretty. Okay, so he owed Jack one.

The minute he stepped into the Mundys' parlour, McGraw could see that something was very wrong. Rosie sat in one of the chairs by the fire, silent, hunched up. Peter hurried in from the shop as soon as his mother told him McGraw had arrived. His face was pale and drawn.

'What's the matter?' McGraw asked.

360

'Thanks for coming, Joe,' Peter said. He took a letter from the mantelpiece and handed it over. 'This'll explain it.'

McGraw unfolded the notepaper and saw from the ornate letterhead that it was from Lansburys' head office. He read quickly and looked up. 'This amount they mention, is it realistic?'

Peter had to control himself to answer. 'It's about a third of what the shop was worth a few weeks ago.' He paused, and added bitterly. 'I suppose it's realistic.'

McGraw read the letter from the supermarket chain again. What it said there was no arguing. 'We are under no obligation, nor necessity, to purchase the premises,' it said. 'Our offer is made in the light of that and purely out of goodwill.' Some goodwill . . . 'If it is not acceptable, we see no reason,' it went on, 'why both businesses cannot exist side by side, complementary to each other and fulfilling all the needs of the people of Market Wetherby and outlying areas.'

McGraw refolded the letter and handed it back. 'In other words, if you don't sell to them at their estimate, they'll keep their prices artificially low, with loss leaders and special offers, for as many months as it takes to bankrupt you. You could try to sell the shop elsewhere, but I doubt if you'd do any better.'

Peter's hands were shaking. 'I've no right to ask you to help me, Joe, but . . . what can I do?'

'Frankly, Peter,' McGraw said, 'I haven't the faintest idea. The way things stand, they hold all the cards.'

After McGraw had gone, Peter slumped into one of the chairs at the table. He had been a fool, he knew. Even his thought of taking up music again had been derisory. When he had told the boys, they had laughed at him. He had been angry, yet it had been because their involuntary laughter had forced him to realize that his long-cherished ambition was a pipedream. Having to take over the shop for his father had killed it stone dead – only he had never admitted it. Now he had to. And the family shop had become virtually worthless.

Rosie sat watching him knowing what he was thinking. She would have offered comfort, but she had none to give. She was a fighter and her first instinct was to burn the letter and defy Lansburys, to appeal to their regular customers and carry on. But she was also a realist. Some people might support them for a time, yet customers' loyalty could only stretch as far as their wage packets. The prices in the shop were as competitive as they could be. Even so, they could never be able to match the range of goods or the bulk-buying prices that Lansburys would have on offer.

Since her marriage, Rosie had never been a worrier. She had always remained cool, and been able to cope even when the twins came along. Neither she nor Peter had known they were expecting two babies. Not until the final day when she had been told to have an X-ray at the cottage hospital. The plates had shown what she had secretly suspected all along, and they had proved the doctor wrong. Rosie had always been a slim, slight girl, but as her pregnancy developed, she had become mountainous. Like those push-over toys that always bounce back, Vera liked to describe her.

When the X-rays were developed, Peter had to rush her to Ipswich General, and the twins were born two hours later, John and James Mundy, weighing in at over thirteen pounds between them.

They were almost seventeen now, and had inherited their father's love and instinct for music, and their mother's quiet intelligence. Both intended sitting their A-levels next summer, then planned to go to university.

She knew Peter was thinking that in one year they would be off his hands financially, with both boys eligible for a grant, and she realized that his idea of setting up his own band had much to do with the twins leaving home.

She also saw how ludicrous the whole business was. Everyone harboured fantasies, but most people grew out of them. She could understand the twins dreaming about topping the charts, and appearing on *Top of the Pops* every Thursday night, but Peter in his forties, still playing the organ every third Sunday in church – and trying to prove himself as the son of Joe Loss . . . Her bitterness surprised her, and made her ashamed. Her dream of their moving to Ipswich had been no more down to earth. Peter had worked hard for all of them. He had given up his dream for their sakes all those years ago. He didn't deserve this.

She got up and moved to him. Sensing her standing beside him, he leaned back against her and she held him gently. 'It doesn't matter, love,' she whispered. 'We'll manage. Somehow or other, we'll manage. You'll see.'

They were startled as the door opened and McGraw marched in. 'I'm the biggest, dumbest dummy you ever saw!' he announced. 'Where's that letter?' He went past them to the mantelpiece, took down the Lansburys' letter and read through the impressive list of names and office holders under the letterhead. When he looked up he was grinning. 'D'you know where Sir Henry Maylie is? Is he in London or at home?'

'I think he's at home this weekend,' Rosie said. 'Why?'

'I'd like a word with him,' McGraw told her. 'Nil carborundum, as your father always says. Don't let the bastards grind you down.'

He was gone before they could ask him what he had in mind. Rosie knew it was hopeless, appealing to Sir Henry again. The supermarket had his blessing. He would not change his opinion. She wished she had stopped McGraw. She would not like Lady Pat to think that Peter and she were causing trouble.

McGraw followed the former Pat Dereham into the large, comfortable sitting room in Dereham House. 'Please take a seat, Mr McGraw,' she said. 'I'll let my husband know you're here.'

'Thank you, Lady Patricia,' McGraw nodded. There was a fire blazing, and on the mantelpiece above it he saw a framed photograph of Ronnie, Pat's son, now nineteen and at Cambridge. He was flanked by his grandmother, Helen, and her husband, Senator Kiley. 'He's a grown man now, ma'am,' McGraw said. 'When was he last over there?'

'During the summer vacation. He spent three months in Nantucket. It's so cheap to get there now. The flight only takes a few hours. But your Billy will have flown it many times. He works for one of the airlines, doesn't he?'

'Co-pilot, ma'am,' McGraw told her proudly. 'He's done the New York and Boston runs more times than you could count. The Atlantic's like the village pond these days. And when I think how wide it seemed and how dangerous to cross – even in a Flying Fortress . . .'

Pat smiled. 'Yes, it must seem strange. I'll fetch my husband.'

'McGraw?' Henry Maylie said, when she found him in his study. 'Oh, Lord . . . what on earth does he want?'

'I imagine, one last try at stopping Lansburys from coming here.'

'But surely he realizes it's too late? There's nothing more to be said.'

McGraw was wondering just how he would broach the subject. In their previous discussions, Sir Henry had run rings around him, a master of small talk and argument. A charming man, McGraw admitted, but not one with whom he could ever feel at ease. Though he no longer held a cabinet post, he was still an influential back-bencher. That cut little ice with McGraw, who saw politics, and his work with the town council, in human terms. Party politics just didn't interest him. Nor did its practitioners – except for one. Senator Kiley was his sort of man, not this smooth talking, country gentleman with a safe seat. Senator Kiley talked straight, and acted that way. With politics in the States becoming an increasingly dirty profession, with newspapers over there devoting more and more column inches to exposing bribery and chicanery, Senator Kiley's image had soared. He'd read a lot of sensational garbage about JFK and his peccadilloes with women, and he didn't believe a word of any of it. Even so, no one, but nobody, could throw dirt at Kiley.

He turned as Sir Henry Maylie came in, smiling brightly and clapping him on the shoulder as they shook hands. 'Good to see you again, Mr McGraw. Won't you sit down?'

'I'll get straight to business, Sir Henry,' McGraw said, 'and try not to take up too much of your time. It's about this supermarket. I don't like the idea of it.'

'As you have made abundantly clear.'

'Not enough, apparently,' McGraw went on. 'It'll lead to the ruin of this town.'

Sir Henry cut him short. 'On the contrary. It will provide a service that doesn't exist – that never has existed in Market Wetherby. And jobs. You can't stop progress, McGraw. You can't stop jobs. It's suicide.'

'That's as maybe, but it sure as hell ain't going to help the Mundys.'

'They'll do perfectly well, I'm sure,' Sir Henry said. 'If Peter Mundy is half as able as his father was, then he'll come out of this better off than ever.'

'You've got to be kidding!' McGraw snorted. 'Anyway, he ain't the man old Albert was – not as tough or as cunning. And it's too late for him to start now.'

'There is no need either for toughness or cunning.'

'You don't say?' McGraw doubted. 'Well, there's one thing I'd like to bring up with you, Sir Henry.'

Maylie saw little point in continuing the conversation. 'Mr McGraw, we are wasting each other's time. The matter is all settled. Planning permission has been granted.'

'No, let me finish,' McGraw interrupted. 'I don't mean to be impolite by mentioning it, but there's the small matter of your interest – I think that's the word they use in the newspapers? – yes, your interest in Lansburys.'

Maylie frowned. 'You mean, that I am a director of the company?'

'You got it.'

'I have made no secret of that,' Maylie said.

'You couldn't – since your name's on the company letterhead.'

'For pity's sake, man,' Maylie protested, 'you're surely not implying there's anything illegal in this? I've never denied my connection with Lansburys. It was me who got them to come here. I engineered it. We need anything that will increase opportunities for employment in this area. It will bring extra jobs in the construction and service trades, not to mention the people who will actually be employed there. That's why I want them to open up here.'

It was not an argument which McGraw could counter. He nodded. 'Yeah, I guess from your point of view it's a good deal. And as the man said, you can't make omelettes without breaking eggs. My apologies for taking up your time.' He moved towards the door and paused. 'I guess it'll also mean increased profits for your shareholders.'

'Well, naturally,' Maylie replied curtly.

'And Lady Patricia is a shareholder, isn't she?' McGraw said. It had been a shot in the dark, but he could tell from the sudden lift of Maylie's head that it had struck home. 'I'm not one to moralize,' he went on, 'but I remember her father, Major Dereham. All his life, he did what he could for the people here – just like you're trying to do. But he never took anything. He always gave.'

He left the letter to the Mundys on the table by the door and Maylie read it after he had gone. He showed it to Pat, who frowned as she read it. 'Did you know about this?' she asked.

'No, I didn't,' he told her. 'What do you think McGraw's after?'

'I imagine he's just trying to help them. He's a fixer by nature. I don't know him too well, but my mother thinks very highly of him. Under that blunt exterior, he's very sharp. And bright.'

'A damn sight too bright, if you ask me,' Maylie said. 'Where on earth did he find out about your shares in Lansburys?'

'Don't be naïve, darling,' Pat smiled. 'I'd imagine he was guessing. After all, it wouldn't take an Einstein.'

'Will he go to the Press?'

'It's possible, I suppose,' Pat said, considering. 'I wouldn't think he is a man who enjoys losing. But I'm sure he'd prefer everything to be settled quietly, without fuss and bother. He's that rare and vanishing breed, I'm afraid, who just wants to see fair play.'

Sir Henry looked at his wife, and saw in her a lot of her mother.

He was conscious that, once again, she was steering him in the direction he ought to take. As she had done so often throughout his political life. She had stood by him from his adoption speech, all through the intrigues of the final Churchill years, with the old warrior hanging on and his possible heirs bickering and offering patronage to whoever would support them, righ up to the Suez débâcle and his resignation as a junior Cabinet minister.

Since then, he had left the intrigues to those who enjoyed them and settled instead for a back-bench role. Over the years, his influence had grown. Ironically, today, he was being courted again, not by the present Prime Minister, but by the caucus who were set upon creating a new Tory leader. That the Heath government would fall in the near future he and a number of other MPs were certain. The grammar school boy from Kent had picked a fight he could not win. Instead of making the miners a 'special case', he seemed stubbornly set on a confrontation. The fortunes of the party, Maylie was assured, lay not with Heath but in the hands of the daughter of a grocer from Grantham. Maylie smiled. England in the 'seventies . . . What would Mrs Thatcher do, if her father's business had been threatened by a multinational corporation? He picked up the telephone and called long-distance.

Jack Blair was enjoying the Wednesday outing, as always, but was glad when Vera finally drove into the lay-by outside Lavenham and stopped. Her driving had been nearly as erratic as it used to be in the early days, although it was hardly surprising with so much on her mind. She had told him excitedly about the new offer Lansburys had made to Peter, and very generous it was too. Not only did it take into account the prime site of the Mundys' shop, but also a sum had been added to compensate them for the 'distress situation the establishing of a Lansburys branch would cause'.

'All thanks to Joe McGraw,' Jack said.

'No thanks to him at all,' Vera denied. 'Well, hardly. It's all because Sir Henry Maylie took a stand.'

'Which Mac made him take,' Jack pointed out. 'I'm glad for Peter and Rosie, but the best thing Mac did was get Lansburys to agree to preserve the existing frontage of the buildings they've taken over. Any other new business will have to do the same.'

'No, that wasn't Joe McGraw's doing, either. His petition was the wrong way to go about it,' Vera said. 'No, I was at the meeting, when Sir Henry spoke about how the character of the town ought to be kept. He's saved Market Wetherby.'

'And made his parliamentary seat safe for the next twenty years,' Jack added drily. 'Well, good for him. And what are Peter and Rosie going to do with the money?'

'Rosie's had it all worked out from the beginning. She's found a nice little shop in Ipswich. They can afford it, and they've enough left over to open a records and musical instruments business, guitars and drums and such. Peter's very happy about it.'

'I'll bet the twins are delighted, too,' Jack grinned.

'Oh, their dad's warned them they mustn't touch the stock. He doesn't want them smashing up his guitars like those rock'n roll crooners.'

Jack smiled. 'I don't think they call themselves crooners, love. But what about you – are you going with them?'

Vera hesitated. 'Well, they've asked me to. Though it – it seems unfair on them, always to have me with them. I feel like a liability.'

'You're never that,' Jack said.

'Well, there's nobody else who'd have me, I suppose.' Vera could hardly look at him. She was nervous and slightly flushed. 'Though if – if there was, of course . . . I mean, sometimes I thought there might be.' She glanced at him. 'I was thinking of someone in particular.'

Jack was never a man to shy away from decision, but this was one he had been putting off. She tensed nervously as he took her hand and held it. 'I know what you mean, and I won't deny I've thought about it. Often,' he said gently. 'But it would never work, love.'

'Why not?' she asked.

'We're too set in our ways. You've led your own life, and I've been a widower for more years than I care to recall. Marriage at this age – the whole of Market Wetherby would laugh itself silly. Us, Vera. Imagine it?'

'I have done,' she confessed. 'I've dreamed about it for years. Albert would turn in his grave, I know, but don't you see? We were always cut out for each other.'

'I used to think so, too,' Jack nodded. 'But now, you and I, Vera love, we're too old, too old and decrepit. We're good friends. We go out together for our drives. You come round and help in the pub. I have lunch with you and Peter and Rosie every Sunday. We share grandchildren. What more could we want?'

'I don't want love,' Vera said. 'God knows, I'm past all that. I want companionship. I want someone, you, Jack, to be with, someone to come home to.'

He squeezed her hand more tightly for a moment. 'It sounds tempting . . . but we'd be throwing away an awful lot, if it didn't work. What we need is some time together, just by ourselves. Tell you what Vera, for years I've been putting off a visit to California. Let's go there together, you and me, to see Chuck and Vi.'

'Me go to America!' Vera gasped. 'With you? What would Albert think?' Even as she said it, the incongruity struck her and she could not stop herself laughing.

Jack laughed with her. Only, it was not at the thought

of Vera and him travelling to Santa Barbara. It was at the strangeness of women. He had never been able to fathom them out, not even Vera, who was the simplest and sweetest he had ever known. It must have cost her a tremendous effort to bring this subject into the open, because even now, ten years after he had passed on, all her thoughts, conscious and unconscious, were controlled in part by Albert Mundy. Regretfully, it was not something that Jack could live with.

# THIRTY-FOUR

*December 21, 1976*　　　　　*Floral Avenue*
　　　　　　　　　　　　　　　　*Santa Barbara*
　　　　　　　　　　　　　　　　　*California*
　　　　　　　　　　*Zip Code* 93102 (II)

Dear Sally

It was so nice to hear from you and Mac. Sorry! I never could get used to calling him Joe . . .

Chuck and I still remember the wonderful holiday we spent with you both last year and talk about it often. It was lovely to be home again, even for a little while – although I scarcely recognized Market Wetherby! With all those new houses and the supermarket where Mundy's old store used to be. And I can't bear to think of The Plough. All that plastic and strip lighting. And fruit machines and two jukeboxes. You couldn't tell the difference between it and some of the bars around here. Dad would have had a fit. Still, it was lovely to be in England again. It brought back so many memories.

The children are well, thank you. I can hardly think of them as children any more. Helen had another baby this fall, so that makes me a grandmother three times over. Fancy! I know you've beaten me by two. Does it ever feel odd to you? I mean, when some tiny thing calls you Granny? It does to me.

Oh, and our boy, Jack, has decided to come in with Chuck after all. Which is what I've prayed for. Did I tell you Chuck now has the largest dental practice in Santa B? Which is marvellous, considering he only went to college after the war and had to make his way all on his own. He's never regretted giving up that practice he was in down at Long Beach. It wasn't his and, no matter how hard he worked, it never would be. Poor Matt – I'm sure I told you about him and Rachel, who were such close friends of ours at one time? Anyway, Matt tried to run the practice on his own, after Chuck left, then sold up as soon as his father died. He got quite a lot of money for it, but by that time he was drinking so heavily that Rachel left him. They got back together again and he seemed better for a while. He was trying, anyway. Then he died quite suddenly. Rachel's married again and living in San Francisco. Wouldn't you know it? To another dentist. We see them sometimes at conventions and they seem very happy. He's a nice man, just as serious as Matt used to be, but with more of a sense of humour, so that's better for Rachel. I'm still very fond of her.

Anyway, Chuck's never regretted going into orthodontics. He gets consulted by people from all over the country, and a lot of the time he won't charge any fee. Especially for children. He keeps saying he's going to retire in seven years' time, when he's sixty. I don't believe it, but they do retire so early here. What would you do? Just mooch around the house, getting under my feet? I asked him. Maybe I'll write a book, the history of the 525th Bomb Group, he said. He was only half joking, too. Maybe somebody should write it, before it's all been forgotten.

That reminds me. We had a visit only a month or so ago from guess who? Hymie and Jilly Stutz. I scarcely recognized Hymie, until I saw the two missing fingers. He's round as a barrel now. And so is Jilly. (Jilly Binns that was. Rosie's friend.) But I can't imagine two people who suit each other so well. Their son has just got divorced, by the way. Did you know he lost a hand in Vietnam? 'Like father, like son,' Hymie says. 'Only, he had to go one better!'

Hymie's doing so well. He showed us photographs

of his hamburger parlors. He has eight now, all with names like The Control Tower, The Briefing Hut, The Flak House and so on. The main one, Ginger's Palace, looks really quite something. They were on holiday at Lake Tahoe and drove all this way just to see us. I teased Hymie, reminding him that he might have been my brother-in-law, and Jilly actually blushed! I remember you telling me about Rosie's face the day that Jilly told her Hymie and she were going to be married . . .

He had a few bits of news for us – probably it will be of more interest to Mac. That old General Krasnowici had died and been buried at Arlington Cemetery. Quite a few of the 525th were there. Chuck said he'd have gone if he'd known about it. Senator Kiley gave the address, of course. Apparently, he was nearly in tears. They all were.

Hymie went mainly to meet Elmer Jones again. They hadn't seen each other for over five years. They're always going to visit each other, but never make it. You know how it is. It seems that Elmer has done quite well, too. He never did pass his accountancy exams, but his uncle took him on in some cigar store he owned, somewhere in New York. Anyway, when his uncle died, the store was left to him. He never remarried after his wife died. We never met her, but she sounded very pleasant and nice. I think it was cancer of some sort. Horrid. Elmer's son was with him – Jamie. Hymie says he's the spitting image of Elmer when he was twenty. Double chin and all. He was out in Vietnam, too, but he was luckier than Hymie's boy. I think he's an accountant now. So even if Elmer didn't make it, himself, he must have passed something on . . .

I don't know if you saw over there the tributes to Senator Kiley, when he retired. A really great man, they called him. They told all about the work he had done in Japan during the Occupation, and his stand against Senator McCarthy. I hadn't heard about his missions to the Middle East, though of course everyone knows about his campaigns for Vietnam Veterans and for Civil Rights. A lot of that came from his wife, they said, her encouraging him. She's never once forgotten Helen's birthday, all those years. And after that time we helped him a little, in Montgomery, she wrote me such a nice letter. They've been so kind to us, specially when we were just starting out. I felt quite honoured to have known them.

One of the news programs showed a bit of the old film of Kennedy's Inauguration Ball. I can still remember the thrill of seeing Senator Kiley and Mrs Kiley with the President and Mrs Kennedy. It was hard to say which couple was the more striking. Many people think it was a big mistake that JFK did not give Senator Kiley a post in his cabinet. Chuck says he should have been Vice President. How different a lot of things might have been.

Well, I won't keep going on. I hope that you are all well, as we are, and your children, and *five* grandchildren. I thought that Mac looked splendid when we saw him. He is amazing for his age, isn't he? He hardly seems to have changed a bit. Chuck says if he has any news of the old crowd, he'd be glad to hear it. May come in handy for the book!

We wish you all the season's greetings, a Merry Christmas and, especially, a Happy and Prosperous New Year.

With lots of love,

CHUCK AND VI

*February 12, 1977*                         *Soundings Cottage*
*Westbury*
*Nantucket*

Darling Pat
At last I've found a minute or two to sit down and

write. These last few months since Jim announced his retirement have been really packed. Apart from two days at Newport over the New Year, we've had no time to ourselves.

We were so pleased to hear that young Ronnie had got into Cambridge. His grandfather would have been very proud of him. I know he will do very well. Both his parents were there, so he should! Will he go to Henry's old college?

We had a very charming letter from Vi, just after Christmas. I had sent a little something to Helen's new daughter – another Helen, she's going to be. If things go on like this, it will be confusing . . . Vi says they're all thriving. They're hoping to go out to visit their elder son's grave in Saigon this year, if they can arrange permits and things. Jim might be able to help there. All those young men – it's so sad. Well, at least it's over now. It just seemed endless, and it's done so much damage. And for what?

After all the testimonials and presentations, the speeches and honorary degrees, it's a real relief to get back here for some peace and quiet. The weather is awful, but once a day we walk down to the beach and back – genuine Darby and Joan stuff. It suits us fine. It's nearly thirty years since I spent my first summer in this house and I still love it.

I was embarrassed by the number of times I was mentioned in the tributes to Jim, but he says it was true, he couldn't have done it without me. I'm not so conceited that I believe that entirely, but it was lovely of him to say so. I'm sure he'll miss Washington a great deal, but we both agree he's done enough and it's time to make way for younger men.

You asked what was the 'real' reason for his deciding not to stand for election again. I'm sorry to disappoint you, if you expected anything sensational. Oh, he's been soured from time to time by politics, all that Watergate business and the contract scandals and so on, but it was purely and simply that we decided, while we are still mobile and compos, that we wanted to be together, to enjoy 'our declining years' – if that doesn't sound too morbid. Jim has agreed to write his memoirs, so that should keep him occupied for a while. And this new Carter administration has asked him to serve as a kind of roving ambassador. As we both want to travel, that suits us fine.

The main reason for writing is, in fact, that I expect we'll be seeing you quite soon. I can't give you an exact date, because the details have still to be fixed. But hopefully it will be before the spring is over. I so long to see England in the spring again.

There was the most extraordinary coincidence the other day . . . ! I haven't told anyone about it, and I hope you won't. This is strictly 'off the record'. Jim knows, of course, but he's the only one.

I'm still on one or two committees, charities and so forth. One of them, for the widows and families of ex-servicemen, had its annual dinner in New York, which I went to because Lorna Jane was one of the speakers. She is immensely successful, running her own advertising agency. Her son's an Air Force Major now, by the way, training to take part in the space programme. She sends her love.

Well, at the reception I saw a woman I thought I recognized, very elegant, in her early fifties, I'd say. I didn't get a chance to speak to her, but I saw from the guest list that she was on the West Coast Committee, a Mrs Harry G. Rakhin. It meant nothing. However, during the dinner, I saw her glance at me once or twice and I asked about her. She turned out to be the wife, the widow, actually, of a very wealthy film producer. There had recently been some talk about her, because, just as they were in the process of getting divorced, he had died suddenly, leaving an enormous amount of money and property. The will was contested, but she apparently won the case and inherited nearly everything. She was very aloof and artistocratic, I was told.

Well, afterwards, I'd been talking to Lorna Jane and forgotten about her and, as I turned to leave, I found this Mrs Rakhin standing as if she was waiting for me. 'I see you recognized me,' she said. It was a little embarrassing, since to the best of my knowledge I'd never seen her before. Then she smiled, and it was only then that I knew her. It was Letty Mundy. You remember her. We've talked about her. 'I always wanted to come to America,' Letty said. 'As you can see, I made it.' She was very cool and self-possessed. I didn't know what to say to her.

Jim met her once some time ago and said she had quite an effect on him. I could see what he meant. She had developed a very strong personality. I remembered you telling me her child had become an actress and I asked her if, through her connections, she'd been able to help her career at all. She looked a little strange and said that she had met her daughter two or three times, but that the girl had no idea who she was, and she meant to keep it that way. She had chosen a completely new life for herself, with, I presume, a fictitious background. She admitted that, now she was alone, she would have liked her daughter or someone with her. Yet, as she did not intend to remain alone for long, there was no point. She really is amazing.

She asked me not to let her family know that I had seen her. And I promised. As I must ask you to do, also. One day, she said, she may turn up and surprise them. But somehow I doubt it.

Jim says to tell Henry not to think of following his example. Henry may well have had a better chance of promotion under Ted Heath, but he is not to underestimate Mrs Thatcher. She's a fighter and if

Henry can learn to live with her – I might have put that better! – he might find the next few years stimulating. Henry is young enough, and there is much that a talented and conscientious back-bencher can do – as Jim has proved over and over again.

The rain has stopped and it's nearly time for the daily stroll. Jim's taking a nap, but I have strict orders to wake him up.

I know he'll want to send his love to young Ronnie and you.

As I do, very affectionately, to you all.

Mother and Granny

*July 4, 1977*                              *Bridge Cottage*
                                             *Market Wetherby*

Dear Vi,

I'm sorry it's taken so long to answer your lovely long letter, but I hope you got the Christmas card OK, at least.

To tell the truth, we had a little scare at the beginning of the New Year. Joe had a small heart attack. It could have been more serious, and the doctor says he's to take it as a warning not to do so much at his age. He still goes to the garage every day and, if there's a rush on, he's inside the bonnet or underneath some old banger that needs servicing. And he won't stop smoking. He's rationed himself to four cigars a day, but that's four too many. Anyhow, he's all right now, but I've told young Joe if he sees his father start to roll up his sleeves, he's to read the riot act.

You'll have noticed the date. That's really why I'm writing.

Although he's settled down here like the oldest inhabitant, Joe always celebrates Independence Day and Thanksgiving. They've become sort of special family days. Betty will be over this afternoon with the children, and Billy in the evening, if he's not flying off somewhere. Or if the airline he works for hasn't gone bankrupt. You never know which one's next, these days.

Anyway, thinking about America twinged my conscience, so I took up pen and paper.

I saw Rosie and Peter the other day. I'd gone into Ipswich to get some curtain material for the back bedroom and I called in. Peter's shop is doing really well. Besides musical instruments and records, he's taken over the premises next door and opened a sort of bookshop and coffeeshop combined. That's Rosie's doing, of course. As you say, she won't rest until that one small shop has become a department store! I think they were right to sell out Mundy's old grocery shop here. If they hadn't, the supermarket would just have opened anyway and put them out of business. Old Albert must be turning in his grave. He wanted to leave it to his grand-daughter, Vicky, you know. When she went into the theatre, he swore he'd never forgive her. Of course, he did eventually, after she started doing so well.

I saw her in something on TV, the other day. You could have sworn it was her mother. It was in a play set just after the war, with the clothes and everything. Didn't we look a mess? But it was like seeing a ghost, uncanny. There's a lot of Letty about her, only she's more, what's the word? Soignée. You'd never guess she came from around here, or that as a baby she caused so much upset. Funny to look back on it.

Old Mrs Mundy's still living with Rosie and Peter. She's just the same, but she complains she's getting stiff. Rosie's put on a bit of weight and she still dresses too young. It's the best thing she ever did, though, to marry Peter. He's very quiet, but he keeps her in order, you can see that. Their two boys are a handful. I suppose twins must run in the Mundy family. A little of their grandfather's discipline might have done them a bit of good, when they were younger.

I can't tell you anything about Letty. I know Peter spent a long time trying to find her or get news of her. That was years ago. She just vanished again.

More bad news. Chuck was asking if Joe had ever heard anything of Colonel Burwash, Red. Just by chance, he saw his name in a list of former members of the Eighth Air Force in some veterans' magazine. It seems that Red stayed on in the Air Force for a time and led a strike force, or whatever it's called, at the start of the war in Vietnam. Apparently, he was shot down there by a ground missile and was posted missing, presumed killed. He had married a former WAAC officer, who had actually served here at Market Wetherby. I never met her, but Joe says he remembers her and that she was very pretty. Trust him to remember that.

Oh, yes. You'll think this is quite a coincidence. You were talking about Senator Kiley.

Well, last March after he'd recovered from his bit of illness, Joe took me out for a drive one day. Just around the neighbourhood. And he turned into the lane where the gates of the old Base used to be. From the road you can hardly tell it was ever there now. The Maylies, Lady Pat, you know, Mrs Dereham's daughter, they managed to get most of the land back from the Ministry of Defence after quite a long struggle. They've ploughed up what used to be Dispersal and where all the huts used to be beyond there. There's quite a few of the old Nissen huts still standing – they're used for storing farm equipment, tractors and such now, some for cattle feed. Farther in, you can still make out the old runway and some of the hardstands, thought they're all broken up with grass and weeds. And the Control Tower and briefing rooms scarcely look as if they've been touched. There was an eerie feeling about it.

I hadn't been back for ages and it made me feel strange.

Anyhow, I asked Joe what we were driving in here for and he said it was an anniversary. On that day in March thirty-four years ago, the 525th Bomb Group first arrived at Market Wetherby. Hard to believe it was so long ago.

So we drove round the old taxiway and saw a car parked near the Control Tower. There was a man coming down the steps from the platform, very well dressed, in a grey suit. Joe stopped the car, got out and went over to him. That was when the funny thing happened. I saw Joe stop, draw himself up and salute the man on the steps. It was the oddest thing. Then I saw them shake hands and Joe waved to me to come and join them.

You'll have guessed. It was Major Kiley – Senator Kiley, I should say. I'd have known him anywhere, even with his white hair and fuller moustache. He was still as straight as a ramrod and I couldn't help feeling proud that he remembered Joe so well and was so pleased to see him. He told us he was going to some meeting in Cairo and had stopped off in England for talks with the Foreign Office. He had come here today for the same reason we had.

As we walked over to his car with him, a woman got out. And honestly, Vi, I thought the clock had turned back. It was Mrs Dereham, the Senator's wife as she now is, and it took me minutes to realize that she was any different from what she was all those years ago. She must be in her seventies, but she was even more beautiful than I remembered her. She knew me, too, and asked after Billy and Betty and all of you. I don't mind admitting I was nearly crying, and she kissed me. Joe saluted again when they drove off.

I don't think I've ever seen a couple that life has been kinder to. Or maybe it's just being together that's done it. The way they smiled to each other, how she took his hand when they walked back to their car, it's something I don't think I'll ever forget. I don't believe I've ever seen a couple of any age so happy together, and still so much in love.

Well, there we are. I don't think there's much else. Congratulations on your third grandchild. You don't say if it was a girl or a boy. Young Joe's wife has just had her first, a boy, so that makes it six for me. Four grandsons and two grand-daughters. The way Betty's elder girl carries on, I might be a great grandmother before I know it. (I hope not.)

Give our best regards to Hymie and Jilly, if you see them again. And likewise to Elmer. Maybe we'll see you all, if Joe is spared and we take that holiday in the US we always promised ourselves.

Meanwhile, I hope this finds you all well, as we are. Joe says he can't really believe Chuck will ever retire.

> Much love, all the best.
> SALLY

# POSTSCRIPT

In the summer of 'eighty-one, Chuck Ericson took his youngest grandson as a treat to a travelling Exhibition and Museum of the Air, a fancy name for an old-fashioned flying circus. The exhibition was fun, with stunts and flares and an ex-Navy jet streaming coloured smoke as it skimmed the field. The Museum of the Air was less impressive, the aircraft on display mainly mocked-up models, but the little boy was amused by the Sopwith Camel and excited by the red triplane and the Sabre.

The climax of the show was well staged, a WWI dogfight between the Sopwith and the triplane, followed by a flypast of a Mustang and a Spitfire, trailing the Stars and Stripes and the Union Jack.

After they had circled the field and landed to loud applause, the crowd was preparing to disperse, but paused, hearing something. Chuck's head had risen. 'Listen!' he told his grandson. The sound of the Wright Cyclones was unmistakable.

As the last aircraft came into view, the loudspeaker announced, 'Better late than never – the star of our show, ladies and gentlemen! The most famous aircraft of all time – not a replica – one of the few still operational. A World War Two . . . B-17 Flying Fortress!'

In spite of himself, hearing the cheers and the music of the old Air Corps march as the big-assed bird settled down and landed, Chuck felt his skin prickle. 'Isn't that what you used to fly, Grandpa?' his grandson asked. Chuck nodded. He did not hear the comments, nor fee' *he jostling figures around him as they moved forward wi    .e crowd for a closer look. He was no longer in California. He was on a wet, mist-shrouded airfield in East Anglia.

The crowd surged nearer as the Fortress's engines cut

off. 'Hard to believe they could ever get that thing off the ground,' someone said. There was laughter.

'Could it really fly a long way, Grandpa?' the little boy asked.

'A long, long way,' Chuck told him. 'And what was more important, no matter what they did to it, it could come back – with holes through its tail, half a wing shot off, as long as it had one engine still working, it would come back.'

He moved round it so slowly, most of the crowd had gone by the time he completed the circuit and reached the B-17's nose on the port side. Chuck's breath caught in his throat, and he stared.

After a minute, the little boy looked up at him, puzzled. 'Grandpa,' he asked, 'why are you crying?'

Chuck was gazing at the logo above the rows of small bombs for the number of missions flown and the swastikas for the tally of enemy ships shot down. Faded, the colours dulled, but still decipherable was the star with her radiant smile and long dancer's legs, and the words 'Ginger Rogers II'.